AMERICANS ALL

AMERICANS ALL

STORIES OF AMERICAN
LIFE OF TO-DAY

EDITED BY

BENJAMIN A. HEYDRICK

Short Story Index Reprint Series

BOOKS FOR LIBRARIES PRESS
FREEPORT, NEW YORK

First Published 1920
Reprinted 1971

INTERNATIONAL STANDARD BOOK NUMBER:
0-8369-3913-1

LIBRARY OF CONGRESS CATALOG CARD NUMBER:
74-160934

PRINTED IN THE UNITED STATES OF AMERICA

PREFACE

In the years before the war, when we had more time for light pursuits, a favorite sport of reviewers was to hunt for the Great American Novel. They gave tongue here and there, and pursued the quarry with great excitement in various directions, now north, now south, now west, and the inevitable disappointment at the end of the chase never deterred them from starting off on a fresh scent next day. But in spite of all the frenzied pursuit, the game sought, the Great American Novel, was never captured. Will it ever be captured? The thing they sought was a book that would be so broad, so typical, so true that it would stand as the adequate expression in fiction of American life. Did these tireless hunters ever stop to ask themselves, what is the Great French Novel? what is the Great English Novel? And if neither of these nations has produced a single book which embodies their national life, why should we expect that our life, so much more diverse in its elements, so multifarious in its aspects, could ever be summed up within the covers of a single book?

Yet while the critics continued their hopeless hunt, there was growing up in this country a form of fiction which gave promise of some day achieving the task that this never-to-be written novel should accomplish. This form was the short story. It was the work of many hands, in many places. Each writer studied closely a certain locality, and transcribed faithfully what he saw. Thus the New England village, the western ranch, the southern plantation, all had their chroniclers. Nor was it only various localities that we saw in these one-reel pictures; they dealt with typical occupations, there were stories of travelling salesmen, stories of lumbermen, stories of politicians, stories of the stage, stories of school and college days. If it were possible to bring together in a single volume a group of these, each one reflecting faithfully one facet of our many-sided life, would not such a book be a truer picture of America than any single novel could present?

The present volume is an attempt to do this. That it is only an attempt, that it does not cover the whole field of our national life, no one realizes better than the compiler. The title *Americans All* signifies that the characters in the book are all Americans, not that they are all of the Americans.

This book then differs in its purpose from other collections of short stories. It does not aim to present the world's best short stories, nor to illustrate the development of the form from Roman times to our own day, nor to show how the technique of Poe differs from that of Irving: its purpose is none of these things, but rather to use the short story as a means of interpreting American life. Our country is so vast that few of us know more than a small corner of it, and even in that corner we do not know all our fellow-citizens; differences of color, of race, of creed, of fortune, keep us in separate strata. But through books we may learn to know our fellow-citizens, and the knowledge will make us better Americans.

The story by Dorothy Canfield has a unique interest for the student, in that it is followed by the author's own account of how it was written, from the first glimpse of the theme to the final typing of the story. Teachers who use this book for studying the art of short story construction may prefer to begin with " Flint and Fire " and follow with " The Citizen," tracing in all the others indications of the authors' methods.

BENJAMIN A. HEYDRICK.

NEW YORK CITY,
March, 1920.

CONTENTS

IN SCHOOL DAYS

Are any days more rich in experiences than school days? The day one first enters school, whether it is the little red schoolhouse or the big brick building that holds a thousand pupils,—that day marks the beginning of a new life. One of the best records in fiction of the world of the school room is called EMMY LOU. In this book George Madden Martin has traced the progress of a winsome little maid from the first grade to the end of high school. This is the story of the first days in the strange new world of the school room.

THE RIGHT PROMETHEAN FIRE

BY

GEORGE MADDEN MARTIN

EMMY LOU, laboriously copying digits, looked up. The boy
sitting in line in the next row of desks was making signs to
her.

She had noticed the little boy before. He was a square little
boy, with a sprinkling of freckles over the bridge of the nose
and a cheerful breadth of nostril. His teeth were wide apart,
and his smile was broad and constant. Not that Emmy
Lou could have told all this. She only knew that to her the
knowledge of the little boy concerning the things peculiar to
the Primer World seemed limitless.

And now the little boy was beckoning Emmy Lou. She did
not know him, but neither did she know any of the seventy
other little boys and girls making the Primer Class.

Because of a popular prejudice against whooping-cough,
Emmy Lou had not entered the Primer Class until late. When
she arrived, the seventy little boys and girls were well along
in Alphabetical lore, having long since passed the a, b, c,
of initiation, and become glibly eloquent to a point where the
l, m, n, o, p slipped off their tongues with the liquid ease of
repetition and familiarity.

"But Emmy Lou can catch up," said Emmy Lou's Aunt
Cordelia, a plump and cheery lady, beaming with optimistic
placidity upon the infant populace seated in parallel rows at
desks before her.

Miss Clara, the teacher, lacked Aunt Cordelia's optimism,
also her plumpness. "No doubt she can," agreed Miss Clara,
politely, but without enthusiasm. Miss Clara had stepped

from the graduating rostrum to the schoolroom platform, and she had been there some years. And when one has been there some years, and is already battling with seventy little boys and girls, one cannot greet the advent of a seventy-first with acclaim. Even the fact that one's hair is red is not an always sure indication that one's temperament is sanguine also.

So in answer to Aunt Cordelia, Miss Clara replied politely but without enthusiasm, " No doubt she can."

Then Aunt Cordelia went, and Miss Clara gave Emmy Lou a desk. And Miss Clara then rapping sharply, and calling some small delinquent to order, Emmy Lou's heart sank within her.

Now Miss Clara's tones were tart because she did not know what to do with this late comer. In a class of seventy, spare time is not offering for the bringing up of the backward. The way of the Primer teacher was not made easy in a public school of twenty-five years ago.

So Miss Clara told the new pupil to copy digits.

Now what digits were, Emmy Lou had no idea, but being shown them on the black-board, she copied them diligently. And as the time went on, Emmy Lou went on copying digits. And her one endeavor being to avoid the notice of Miss Clara, it happened the needs of Emmy Lou were frequently lost sight of in the more assertive claims of the seventy.

Emmy Lou was not catching up, and it was January.

But to-day was to be different. The little boy was nodding and beckoning. So far the seventy had left Emmy Lou alone. As a general thing the herd crowds toward the leaders, and the laggard brings up the rear alone.

But to-day the little boy was beckoning. Emmy Lou looked up. Emmy Lou was pink-cheeked and chubby and in her heart there was no guile. There was an ease and swagger about the little boy. And he always knew when to stand up, and what for. Emmy Lou more than once had failed to stand up, and Miss Clara's reminder had been sharp. It was when a bell rang one must stand up. But what for, Emmy Lou never knew, until after the others began to do it.

But the little boy always knew. Emmy Lou had heard him, too, out on the bench glibly tell Miss Clara about the mat, and a bat, and a black rat. To-day he stood forth with confidence and told about a fat hen. Emmy Lou was glad to have the little boy beckon her.

And in her heart there was no guile. That the little boy should be holding out an end of a severed india-rubber band and inviting her to take it, was no stranger than other things happening in the Primer World every day.

The very manner of the infant classification breathed mystery, the sheep from the goats, so to speak, the little girls all one side the central aisle, the little boys all the other—and to over-step the line of demarcation a thing too dreadful to contemplate.

Many things were strange. That one must get up suddenly when a bell rang, was strange.

And to copy digits until one's chubby fingers, tightly gripping the pencil, ached, and then to be expected to take a sponge and wash those digits off, was strange.

And to be told crossly to sit down was bewildering, when in answer to c, a, t, one said " Pussy." And yet there was Pussy washing her face, on the chart, and Miss Clara's pointer pointing to her.

So when the little boy held out the rubber band across the aisle, Emmy Lou took the proffered end.

At this the little boy slid back into his desk holding to his end. At the critical moment of elongation the little boy let go. And the property of elasticity is to rebound.

Emmy Lou's heart stood still. Then it swelled. But in her filling eyes there was no suspicion, only hurt. And even while a tear splashed down, and falling upon the laboriously copied digits, wrought havoc, she smiled bravely across at the little boy. It would have made the little boy feel bad to know how it hurt. So Emmy Lou winked bravely and smiled.

Whereupon the little boy wheeled about suddenly and fell to copying digits furiously. Nor did he look Emmy Lou's way, only drove his pencil into his slate with a fervor that made Miss Clara rap sharply on her desk.

Emmy Lou wondered if the little boy was mad. One would think it had stung the little boy and not her. But since he was not looking, she felt free to let her little fist seek her mouth for comfort.

Nor did Emmy Lou dream, that across the aisle, remorse was eating into a little boy's soul. Or that, along with remorse there went the image of one Emmy Lou, defenceless, pink-cheeked, and smiling bravely.

The next morning Emmy Lou was early. She was always early. Since entering the Primer Class, breakfast had lost its savor to Emmy Lou in the terror of being late.

But this morning the little boy was there before her. Hitherto his tardy and clattering arrival had been a daily happening, provocative of accents sharp and energetic from Miss Clara.

But this morning he was at his desk copying from his Primer on to his slate. The easy, ostentatious way in which he glanced from slate to book was not lost upon Emmy Lou, who lost her place whenever her eyes left·the rows of digits upon the blackboard.

Emmy Lou watched the performance. And the little boy's pencil drove with furious ease and its path was marked with flourishes. Emmy Lou never dreamed that it was because she was watching that the little boy was moved to this brilliant exhibition. Presently reaching the end of his page, he looked up, carelessly, incidentally. It seemed to be borne to him that Emmy Lou was there, whereupon he nodded. Then, as if moved by sudden impulse, he dived into his desk, and after ostentatious search in, on, under it, brought forth a pencil, and held it up for Emmy Lou to see. Nor did she dream that it was for this the little boy had been there since before Uncle Michael had unlocked the Primer door.

Emmy Lou looked across at the pencil. It was a slate-pencil. A fine, long, new slate-pencil grandly encased for half its length in gold paper. One bought them at the drug-store across from the school, and one paid for them the whole of five cents.

Just then a bell rang. Emmy Lou got up suddenly. But it was the bell for school to take up. So she sat down. She was glad Miss Clara was not yet in her place.

After the Primer Class had filed in, with panting and frosty entrance, the bell rang again. This time it was the right bell tapped by Miss Clara, now in her place. So again Emmy Lou got up suddenly and by following the little girl ahead learned that the bell meant, " go out to the bench."

The Primer Class according to the degree of its infant precocity was divided in three sections. Emmy Lou belonged to the third section. It was the last section and she was the last one in it though she had no idea what a section meant nor why she was in it.

Yesterday the third section had said, over and over, in chorus, " One and one are two, two and two are four," etc.— but to-day they said, " Two and one are three, two and two are four."

Emmy Lou wondered, four what? Which put her behind, so that when she began again they were saying, " two and four are six." So now she knew. Four is six. But what is six? Emmy Lou did not know.

When she came back to her desk the pencil was there. The fine, new, long slate-pencil encased in gold paper. And the little boy was gone. He belonged to the first section, and the first section was now on the bench. Emmy Lou leaned across and put the pencil back on the little boy's desk.

Then she prepared herself to copy digits with her stump of

a pencil. Emmy Lou's were always stumps. Her pencil had a way of rolling off her desk while she was gone, and one pencil makes many stumps. The little boy had generally helped her pick them up on her return. But strangely, from this time, her pencils rolled off no more.

But when Emmy Lou took up her slate there was a whole side filled with digits in soldierly rows across, so her heart grew light and free from the weight of digits, and she gave her time to the washing of her desk, a thing in which her soul revelled, and for which, patterning after her little girl neighbors, she kept within that desk a bottle of soapy water and rags of gray and unpleasant nature, that never dried, because of their frequent using. When Emmy Lou first came to school, her cleaning paraphernalia consisted of a sponge secured by a string to her slate, which was the badge of the new and the unsophisticated comer. Emmy Lou had quickly learned that, and no one rejoiced in a fuller assortment of soap, bottle, and rags than she, nor did a sponge longer dangle from the frame of her slate.

On coming in from recess this same day, Emmy Lou found the pencil on her desk again, the beautiful new pencil in the gilded paper. She put it back.

But when she reached home, the pencil, the beautiful pencil that costs all of five cents, was in her companion box along with her stumps and her sponge and her grimy little slate rags. And about the pencil was wrapped a piece of paper. It had the look of the margin of a Primer page. The paper bore marks. They were not digits.

Emmy Lou took the paper to Aunt Cordelia. They were at dinner.

" Can't you read it, Emmy Lou? " asked Aunt Katie, the prettiest aunty.

Emmy Lou shook her head.

" I'll spell the letters," said Aunt Louise, the youngest aunty.

But they did not help Emmy Lou one bit.

Aunt Cordelia looked troubled. " She doesn't seem to be catching up," she said.

" No," said Aunt Katie.

" No," agreed Aunt Louise.

" Nor—on," said Uncle Charlie, the brother of the aunties, lighting up his cigar to go downtown.

Aunt Cordelia spread the paper out. It bore the words: " It is for you."

So Emmy Lou put the pencil away in the companion, and tucked it about with the grimy slate rags that no harm might befall it. And the next day she took it out and used it. But first she looked over at the little boy. The little boy was busy. But when she looked up again, he was looking.

The little boy grew red, and wheeling suddenly, fell to copying digits furiously. And from that moment on the little boy was moved to strange behavior.

Three times before recess did he, boldly ignoring the preface of upraised hand, swagger up to Miss Clara's desk. And going and coming, the little boy's boots with copper toes and run-down heels marked with thumping emphasis upon the echoing boards his processional and recessional. And reaching his desk, the little boy slammed down his slate with clattering reverberations.

Emmy Lou watched him uneasily. She was miserable for him. She did not know that there are times when the emotions are more potent than the subtlest wines. Nor did she know that the male of some species is moved thus to exhibition of prowess, courage, defiance, for the impressing of the chosen female of the species.

Emmy Lou merely knew that she was miserable and that she trembled for the little boy.

Having clattered his slate until Miss Clara rapped sharply, the little boy rose and went swaggering on an excursion around the room to where sat the bucket and dipper. And on his return he came up the center aisle between the sheep and the goats.

Emmy Lou had no idea what happened. It took place behind her. But there was another little girl who did. A little girl who boasted curls, yellow curls in tiered rows about her head. A lachrymosal little girl, who affected great horror of the little boys.

And what Emmy Lou failed to see was this: the little boy, in passing, deftly lifted a cherished curl between finger and thumb and proceeded on his way.

The little girl did not fail the little boy. In the suddenness of the surprise she surprised even him by her outcry. Miss Clara jumped. Emmy Lou jumped. And the sixty-nine jumped. And, following this, the little girl lifted her voice in lachrymal lament.

Miss Clara sat erect. The Primer Class held its breath. It always held its breath when Miss Clara sat erect. Emmy Lou held tightly to her desk besides. She wondered what it was all about.

Then Miss Clara spoke. Her accents cut the silence.

" Billy Traver! "

Billy Traver stood forth. It was the little boy.

" Since you seem pleased to occupy yourself with the little girls, Billy, *go to the pegs!* "

Emmy Lou trembled. " Go to the pegs! " What unknown, inquisitorial terrors lay behind those dread, laconic words, Emmy Lou knew not.

She could only sit and watch the little boy turn and stump back down the aisle and around the room to where along the wall hung rows of feminine apparel.

Here he stopped and scanned the line. Then he paused before a hat. It was a round little hat with silky nap and a curling brim. It had rosettes to keep the ears warm and ribbon that tied beneath the chin. It was Emmy Lou's hat. Aunt Cordelia had cautioned her to care concerning it.

The little boy took it down. There seemed to be no doubt in his mind as to what Miss Clara meant. But then he had been in the Primer Class from the beginning.

Having taken the hat down he proceeded to put it upon his own shock head. His face wore its broad and constant smile. One would have said the little boy was enjoying the affair. As he put the hat on, the sixty-nine laughed. The seventieth did not. It was her hat, and besides, she did not understand.

Miss Clara still erect spoke again: " And now, since you are a little girl, get your book, Billy, and move over with the girls."

Nor did Emmy Lou understand why, when Billy, having gathered his belongings together, moved across the aisle and sat down with her, the sixty-nine laughed again. Emmy Lou did not laugh. She made room for Billy.

Nor did she understand when Billy treated her to a slow and surreptitious wink, his freckled countenance grinning beneath the rosetted hat. It never could have occurred to Emmy Lou that Billy had laid his cunning plans to this very end. Emmy Lou understood nothing of all this. She only pitied Billy. And presently, when public attention had become diverted, she proffered him the hospitality of a grimy little slate rag. When Billy returned the rag there was something in it— something wrapped in a beautiful, glazed, shining bronze paper. It was a candy kiss. One paid five cents for six of them at the drug-store.

On the road home, Emmy Lou ate the candy. The beautiful, shiny paper she put in her Primer. The slip of paper that she found within she carried to Aunt Cordelia. It was sticky and it was smeared. But it had reading on it.

" But this is printing," said Aunt Cordelia; " can't you read it? "

Emmy Lou shook her head.

"Try," said Aunt Katie.

"The easy words," said Aunt Louise.

But Emmy Lou, remembering c-a-t, Pussy, shook her head.

Aunt Cordelia looked troubled. "She certainly isn't catching up," said Aunt Cordelia. Then she read from the slip of paper:

> "Oh, woman, woman, thou wert made
> The peace of Adam to invade."

The aunties laughed, but Emmy Lou put it away with the glazed paper in her Primer. It meant quite as much to her as did the reading in that Primer: Cat, a cat, the cat. The bat, the mat, a rat. It was the jingle to both that appealed to Emmy Lou.

About this time rumors began to reach Emmy Lou. She heard that it was February, and that wonderful things were peculiar to the Fourteenth. At recess the little girls locked arms and talked Valentines. The echoes reached Emmy Lou.

The valentine must come from a little boy, or it wasn't the real thing. And to get no valentine was a dreadful—dreadful thing. And even the timidest of the sheep began to cast eyes across at the goats.

Emmy Lou wondered if she would get a valentine. And if not, how was she to survive the contumely and shame?

You must never, never breathe to a living soul what was on your valentine. To tell even your best and truest little girl friend was to prove faithless to the little boy sending the valentine. These things reached Emmy Lou.

Not for the world would she tell. Emmy Lou was sure of that, so grateful did she feel she would be to anyone sending her a valentine.

And in doubt and wretchedness did she wend her way to school on the Fourteenth Day of February. The drug-store window was full of valentines. But Emmy Lou crossed the street. She did not want to see them. She knew the little girls would ask her if she had gotten a valentine. And she would have to say, No.

She was early. The big, empty room echoed back her footsteps as she went to her desk to lay down book and slate before taking off her wraps. Nor did Emmy Lou dream the eye of the little boy peeped through the crack of the door from Miss Clara's dressing-room.

Emmy Lou's hat and jacket were forgotten. On her desk lay something square and white. It was an envelope. It was a beautiful envelope, all over flowers and scrolls.

Emmy Lou knew it. It was a valentine. Her cheeks grew pink.

She took it out. It was blue. And it was gold. And it had reading on it.

Emmy Lou's heart sank. She could not read the reading. The door opened. Some little girls came in. Emmy Lou hid her valentine in her book, for since you must not—she would never show her valentine—never.

The little girls wanted to know if she had gotten a valentine, and Emmy Lou said, Yes, and her cheeks were pink with the joy of being able to say it.

Through the day, she took peeps between the covers of her Primer, but no one else might see it.

It rested heavy on Emmy Lou's heart, however, that there was reading on it. She studied it surreptitiously. The reading was made up of letters. It was the first time Emmy Lou had thought about that. She knew some of the letters. She would ask someone the letters she did not know by pointing them out on the chart at recess. Emmy Lou was learning. It was the first time since she came to school.

But what did the letters make? She wondered, after recess, studying the valentine again.

Then she went home. She followed Aunt Cordelia about Aunt Cordelia was busy.

"What does it read?" asked Emmy Lou.

Aunt Cordelia listened.

" B," said Emmy Lou, " and e? "

" Be," said Aunt Cordelia.

If B was Be, it was strange that B and e were Be. But many things were strange.

Emmy Lou accepted them all on faith.

After dinner she approached Aunt Katie.

" What does it read? " asked Emmy Lou, " m and y? "

" My," said Aunt Katie.

The rest was harder. She could not remember the letters, and had to copy them off on her slate. Then she sought Tom, the house-boy. Tom was out at the gate talking to another house-boy. She waited until the other boy was gone.

" What does it read? " asked Emmy Lou, and she told the letters off the slate. It took Tom some time, but finally he told her.

Just then a little girl came along. She was a first-section little girl, and at school she never noticed Emmy Lou.

Now she was alone, so she stopped.

" Get any valentines? "

" Yes," said Emmy Lou. Then moved to confidence by the little girl's friendliness, she added, " It has reading on it."

" Pooh," said the little girl, " they all have that. My mamma's been reading the long verses inside to me."

" Can you show them—valentines? " asked Emmy Lou.

" Of course, to grown-up people," said the little girl.

The gas was lit when Emmy Lou came in. Uncle Charlie was there, and the aunties, sitting around, reading.

" I got a valentine," said Emmy Lou.

They all looked up. They had forgotten it was Valentine's Day, and it came to them that if Emmy Lou's mother had not gone away, never to come back, the year before, Valentine's Day would not have been forgotten. Aunt Cordelia smoothed the black dress she was wearing because of the mother who would never come back, and looked troubled.

But Emmy Lou laid the blue and gold valentine on Aunt Cordelia's knee. In the valentine's center were two hands clasping. Emmy Lou's forefinger pointed to the words beneath the clasped hands.

"I can read it," said Emmy Lou.

They listened. Uncle Charlie put down his paper. Aunt Louise looked over Aunt Cordelia's shoulder.

"B," said Emmy Lou, "e—Be."

The aunties nodded.

"M," said Emmy Lou, "y—my."

Emmy Lou did not hesitate. "V," said Emmy Lou, "a, l, e, n, t, i, n, e—Valentine. Be my Valentine."

"There!" said Aunt Cordelia.

"Well!" said Aunt Katie.

"At last!" said Aunt Louise.

"H'm!" said Uncle Charlie.

GEORGE MADDEN MARTIN

In the South it is not unusual to give boys' names to girls, so it happens that George is the real name of the woman who wrote *Emmy Lou*. George Madden was born in Louisville, Kentucky, May 3, 1866. She attended the public schools in Louisville, but on account of ill health did not graduate. She married Atwood R. Martin, and they made their home at Anchorage, a suburb of Louisville. Here in an old house surrounded by great catalpa trees, with cardinals nesting in their branches, she was recovering from an illness, and to pass the time began to write a short story. The title was " How They Missed the Exposition "; when it was sent away, and a check for seventy-five dollars came in payment, she was encouraged to go on. Her next work was the series of stories entitled *Emmy Lou, Her Book and Heart*. This at once took rank as one of the classics of school-room literature. It had a wide popularity in this country, and was translated into French and German. One of the pleasant tributes paid to the book was a review in a Pittsburgh newspaper which took the form of a letter to Emmy Lou. It ran in part as follows:

Dear Little Emmy Lou:

I have read your book, Emmy Lou, and am writing this letter to tell you how much I love you. In my world of books I know a great assembly of lovely ladies, Emmy Lou, crowned with beauty and garlanded with grace, that have inspired poets to song and the hearts of warriors to battle, but, Emmy Lou, I love you better than them all, because you are the dearest little girl I ever met.

I felt very sorry for you when the little boy in the Primer World, who could so glibly tell the teacher all about the mat and the bat and the black rat and the fat hen, hurt your chubby fist by snapping an india-rubber band. I do not think he atoned quite enough when he gave you that fine new long slate pencil, nor when he sent you your first valentine. No, he has not atoned quite enough, Emmy Lou, but now that you are Miss McLaurin, you will doubtless even

16

the score by snapping the india-rubber band of your disdain at his heart. But only to show him how it stings, and then, of course, you'll make up for the hurt and be his valentine—won't you, Emmy Lou? . . .

And when, at twelve years, you find yourself dreaming, Emmy Lou, and watching the clouds through the schoolroom window, still I love you, Emmy Lou, for your conscience, which William told about in his essay. You remember, the two girls who met a cow.

"Look her right in the face and pretend we aren't afraid," said the biggest girl. But the littlest girl—that was you—had a conscience. "Won't it be deceiving the cow?" she wanted to know. Brave, honest Emmy Lou!

Yes, I love you, Emmy Lou, better than all the proud and beauteous heroines in the big grown-up books, because you are so sun-shiny and trustful, so sweet and brave—because you have a heart of gold, Emmy Lou. And I want you to tell George Madden Martin how glad I am that she has told us all about you, the dearest little girl since Alice dropped down into Wonderland.

George Seibel.

The book is more than a delightful piece of fiction. Through its faithful study of the development of a child's mind, and its criticism of the methods employed in many schools, it becomes a valuable contribution to education. As such it is used in the School of Pedagogy of Harvard University.

George Madden Martin told more about Emmy Lou in a second book of stories entitled *Emmy Lou's Road to Grace,* which relates the little girl's experience at home and in Sunday school. Other works from her pen are: *A Warwickshire Lad,* the story of William Shakespeare's early life; *The House of Fulfillment,* a novel; *Abbie Ann,* a story for children; *Letitia; Nursery Corps, U. S. A.,* a story of a child, also showing various aspects of army life; *Selina,* the story of a young girl who has been brought up in luxury, and finds herself confronted with the necessity of earning a living without any equipment for the task. None of these has equalled the success of her first book, but that is one of the few successful portrayals of child life in fiction.

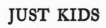

JUST KIDS

That part of New York City known as the East Side, the region south of Fourteenth Street and east of Broadway, is the most densely populated square mile on earth. Its people are of all races; Chinatown, Little Hungary and Little Italy elbow each other; streets where the signs are in Hebrew characters, theatres where plays are given in Yiddish, notices in the parks in four or five languages, make one rub his eyes and wonder if he is not in some foreign land. Into this region Myra Kelly went as a teacher in the public school. Her pupils were largely Russian Jews, and in a series of delightfully humorous stories she has drawn these little citizens to the life.

THE LAND OF HEART'S DESIRE

BY

Myra Kelly

Isaac Borrachsohn, that son of potentates and of Assembly-men, had been taken to Central Park by a proud uncle. For weeks thereafter he was the favorite bard of the First Reader Class and an exceeding great trouble to its sovereign, Miss Bailey, who found him now as garrulous as he had once been silent. There was no subject in the Course of Study to which he could not correlate the wonders of his journey, and Teacher asked herself daily and in vain whether it were more peda-gogically correct to encourage " spontaneous self-expression " or to insist upon " logically essential sequence."

But the other members of the class suffered no such un-certainty. They voted solidly for spontaneity in a self which found expression thus:

" Und in the Central Park stands a water-lake, und in the water-lake stands birds—a big all of birds—und fishes. Und sooner you likes you should come over the water-lake you calls a bird, und you sets on the bird, und the bird makes go his legs, und you comes over the water-lake."

" They could be awful polite birds," Eva Gonorowsky was beginning when Morris interrupted with:

" I had once a auntie und she had a bird, a awful polite bird; on'y sooner somebody calls him he *couldn't* to come the while he sets in a cage."

" Did he have a rubber neck? " Isaac inquired, and Morris reluctantly admitted that he had not been so blessed.

" In the Central Park," Isaac went on, " all the birds is got rubber necks."

"What color from birds be they?" asked Eva.

"All colors. Blue und white und red und yellow."

"Und green," Patrick Brennan interjected determinedly. "The green ones is the best."

"Did you go once?" asked Isaac, slightly disconcerted.

"Naw, but I know. Me big brother told me."

"They could to be stylish birds, too," said Eva wistfully. "Stylish und polite. From red und green birds is awful stylish for hats."

"But these birds is big. Awful big! Mans could ride on 'em und ladies und boys."

"Und little girls, Ikey? Ain't they fer little girls?" asked the only little girl in the group. And a very small girl she was, with a softly gentle voice and darkly gentle eyes fixed pleadingly now upon the bard.

"Yes," answered Isaac grudgingly; "sooner they sets by somebody's side little girls could to go. But sooner nobody holds them by the hand they could to have fraids over the rubber-neck-boat-birds und the water-lake, und the fishes."

"What kind from fishes?" demanded Morris Mogilewsky, monitor of Miss Bailey's gold fish bowl, with professional interest.

"From gold fishes und red fishes und black fishes"—Patrick stirred uneasily and Isaac remembered—"und green fishes; the green ones is the biggest; and blue fishes und *all* kinds from fishes. They lives way down in the water the while they have fraids over the rubber-neck-boat-birds. Say— what you think? Sooner a rubber-neck-boat-bird needs he should eat he longs down his neck und eats a from-gold fish."

"'Out fryin'?" asked Eva, with an incredulous shudder.

"Yes, 'out fryin'. Ain't I told you little girls could to have fraids over 'em? Boys could have fraids too," cried Isaac; and then spurred by the calm of his rival, he added: "The rubber-neck-boat-birds they hollers somethin' fierce."

" I wouldn't be afraid of them. Me pop's a cop," cried Patrick stoutly. " I'd just as lief set on 'em. I'd like to."

" Ah, but you ain't seen 'em, und you ain't heard 'em holler," Isaac retorted.

"Well, I'm goin' to. An' I'm goin' to see the lions an' the tigers an' the el'phants, an' I'm goin' to ride on the water-lake."

" Oh, how I likes I should go too! " Eva broke out. " O-o-oh, *how* I likes I should look on them things! On'y I don't know do I need a ride on somethings what hollers. I don't know be they fer me."

" Well, I'll take ye with me if your mother leaves you go," said Patrick grandly. " An' ye can hold me hand if ye're scared."

" Me too? " implored Morris. " Oh, Patrick, c'n I go too? "

" I guess so," answered the Leader of the Line graciously. But he turned a deaf ear to Isaac Borrachsohn's implorings to be allowed to join the party. Full well did Patrick know of the grandeur of Isaac's holiday attire and the impressionable nature of Eva's soul, and gravely did he fear that his own Sunday finery, albeit fashioned from the blue cloth and brass buttons of his sire, might be outshone.

At Eva's earnest request, Sadie, her cousin, was invited, and Morris suggested that the Monitor of the Window Boxes should not be slighted by his colleagues of the gold fish and the line. So Nathan Spiderwitz was raised to Alpine heights of anticipation by visions of a window box " as big as blocks and streets," where every plant, in contrast to his lanky charges, bore innumerable blossoms. Ignatius Aloysius Diamantstein was unanimously nominated as a member of the expedition; by Patrick, because they were neighbors at St. Mary's Sunday-school; by Morris, because they were classmates under the same rabbi at the synagogue; by Nathan, because Ignatius Aloysius was a member of the " Clinton Street gang "; by Sadie, because he had " long pants sailor suit "; by Eva, because the others wanted him.

Eva reached home that afternoon tingling with anticipation and uncertainty. What if her mother, with one short word, should close forever the gates of joy and boat-birds? But Mrs. Gonorowsky met her small daughter's elaborate plea with the simple question:

" Who pays you the car-fare? "

" Does it need car-fare to go? " faltered Eva.

" Sure does it," answered her mother. " I don't know how much, but some it needs. Who pays it? "

" Patrick ain't said."

" Well, you should better ask him," Mrs. Gonorowsky advised, and, on the next morning, Eva did. She thereby buried the leader under the ruins of his fallen castle of clouds, but he struggled through them with the suggestion that each of his guests should be her, or his, own banker.

" But ain't you got *no* money 't all? " asked the guest of honor.

" Not a cent," responded the host. " But I'll get it. How much have you? "

" A penny. How much do I need? "

" I don't know. Let's ask Miss Bailey."

School had not yet formally begun and Teacher was reading. She was hardly disturbed when the children drove sharp elbows into her shoulder and her lap, and she answered Eva's—" Miss Bailey—oh, Missis Bailey," with an abstracted—" Well, dear? "

" Missis Bailey, how much money takes car-fare to the Central Park? "

Still with divided attention, Teacher replied—" Five cents, honey," and read on, while Patrick called a meeting of his forces and made embarrassing explanations with admirable tact.

There ensued weeks of struggle and economy for the exploring party, to which had been added a chaperon in the large and reassuring person of Becky Zalmonowsky, the class idiot. Sadie Gonorowsky's careful mother had considered Patrick too immature to bear the whole responsibility, and he, with a guile which promised well for his future, had complied with her desires and preserved his own authority unshaken. For Becky, poor child, though twelve years old and of an aspect eminently calculated to inspire trust in those who had never held speech with her, was a member of the First Reader Class only until such time as room could be found for her in some of the institutions where such unfortunates are bestowed.

Slowly and in diverse ways each of the children acquired the essential nickel. Some begged, some stole, some gambled, some bartered, some earned, but their greatest source of income, Miss Bailey, was denied to them. For Patrick knew that she would have insisted upon some really efficient guardian from a higher class, and he announced with much heat that he would not go at all under those circumstances.

At last the leader was called upon to set the day and appointed a Saturday in late May. He was disconcerted to find that only Ignatius Aloysius would travel on that day.

" It's holidays, all Saturdays," Morris explained; " und we dassent to ride on no cars."

" Why not? " asked Patrick.

" It's law, the rabbi says," Nathan supplemented. " I don't know why is it; on'y rides on holidays ain't fer us."

" I guess," Eva sagely surmised; " I guess rubber-neck-boat-birds rides even ain't fer us on holidays. But I don't know do I need rides on birds what hollers."

" You'll be all right," Patrick assured her. " I'm goin' to let ye hold me hand. If ye can't go on Saturday, I'll take ye on Sunday—next Sunday. Yous all must meet me here on the school steps. Bring yer money and bring yer lunch too. It's a long way and ye'll be hungry when ye get there. Ye get a terrible long ride for five cents."

" Does it take all that to get there? " asked the practical Nathan. " Then how are we goin' to get back? "

Poor little poet soul! Celtic and improvident! Patrick's visions had shown him only the triumphant arrival of his host and the beatific joy of Eva as she floated by his side on the most " fancy " of boat-birds. Of the return journey he had taken no thought. And so the saving and planning had to be done all over again. The struggle for the first nickel had been wearing and wearying, but the amassment of the second was beyond description difficult. The children were worn from long strife and many sacrifices, for the temptations to spend six or nine cents are so much more insistent and unusual than are yearnings to squander lesser sums. Almost daily some member of the band would confess a fall from grace and solvency, and almost daily Isaac Borrachsohn was called upon to descant anew upon the glories of the Central Park. Becky, the chaperon, was the most desultory collector of the party. Over and over she reached the proud heights of seven or even eight cents, only to lavish her hoard on the sticky joys of the candy cart of Isidore Belchatosky's papa or on the suddy charms of a strawberry soda.

Then tearfully would she repent of her folly, and bitterly would the others upbraid her, telling again of the joys and wonders she had squandered. Then loudly would she bewail her weakness and plead in extenuation: " I seen the candy. Mouses from choc'late und Foxy Gran'pas from sugar—und I ain't never seen no Central Park."

" But don't you know how Isaac says? " Eva would urge. " Don't you know how all things what is nice fer us stands in the Central Park? Say, Isaac, you should better tell Becky, some more, how the Central Park stands."

And Isaac's tales grew daily more wild and independent of fact until the little girls quivered with yearning terror and the boys burnished up forgotten cap pistols. He told of lions, tigers, elephants, bears, and buffaloes, all of enormous size and strength of lung, so that before many days had passed he had debarred himself, by whole-hearted lying, from the very pos-

sibility of joining the expedition and seeing the disillusionment
of his public. With true artistic spirit he omitted all mention
of confining house or cage and bestowed the gift of speech upon
all the characters, whether brute or human, in his epic. The
merry-go-round he combined with the menagerie into a whole
which was not to be resisted.

" Und all the am'blins," he informed his entranced listeners;
" they goes around, und around, und around, where music plays
und flags is. Und I sets a lion und he runs around, und runs
around, und runs around. Say—what you think? He had
smiling looks und hair on the neck, und sooner he says like
that ' I'm awful thirsty,' I gives him a peanut und I gets
a golden ring."

" Where is it? " asked the jealous and incredulous Patrick.

" To my house." Isaac valiantly lied, for well he remembered the scene in which his scandalized but sympathetic
uncle had discovered his attempt to purloin the brass ring
which, with countless blackened duplicates, is plucked from a
slot by the brandishing swords of the riders upon the merry-go-
round. Truly, its possession had won him another ride—this
time upon an elephant with upturned trunk and wide ears—
but in his mind the return of that ring still ranked as the
only grief in an otherwise perfect day.

Miss Bailey—ably assisted by Æsop, Rudyard Kipling, and
Thompson Seton—had prepared the First Reader Class to
accept garrulous and benevolent lions, cows, panthers, and
elephants, and the exploring party's absolute credulity encouraged Isaac to higher and yet higher flights, until Becky was
strengthened against temptation.

At last, on a Sunday in late June, the cavalcade in splendid
raiment met on the wide steps, boarded a Grand Street car,
and set out for Paradise. Some confusion occurred at the
very beginning of things when Becky Zalmonowsky curtly refused to share her pennies with the conductor. When she
was at last persuaded to yield, an embarrassing five minutes

was consumed in searching for the required amount in the nooks and crannies of her costume where, for safe-keeping, she had cached her fund. One penny was in her shoe, another in her stocking, two in the lining of her hat, and one in the large and dilapidated chatelaine bag which dangled at her knees.

Nathan Spiderwitz, who had preserved absolute silence, now contributed his fare, moist and warm, from his mouth, and Eva turned to him admonishingly.

" Ain't Teacher told you money in the mouth ain't healthy fer you? " she sternly questioned, and Nathan, when he had removed other pennies, was able to answer:

" I washed 'em off—first." And they were indeed most brightly clean. " There's holes in me these here pockets," he explained, and promptly corked himself anew with currency.

" But they don't tastes nice, do they? " Morris remonstrated. Nathan shook a corroborative head. " Und," the Monitor of the Gold Fish further urged, " you could to swallow 'em und then you couldn't never to come by your house no more."

But Nathan was not to be dissuaded, even when the impressional and experimental Becky tried his storage system and suffered keen discomfort before her penny was restored to her by a resourceful fellow traveler who thumped her right lustily on the back until her crowings ceased and the coin was once more in her hand.

At the meeting of Grand Street with the Bowery, wild confusion was made wilder by the addition of seven small persons armed with transfers and clamoring—all except Nathan— for Central Park. Two newsboys and a policeman bestowed them upon a Third Avenue car and all went well until Patrick missed his lunch and charged Ignatius Aloysius with its abstraction. Words ensued which were not easily to be forgotten even when the refreshment was found—flat and horribly distorted—under the portly frame of the chaperon.

Jealousy may have played some part in the misunderstanding, for it was undeniable that there was a sprightliness, a joyant brightness, in the flowing red scarf on Ignatius Aloysius's nautical breast, which was nowhere paralleled in Patrick's more subdued array. And the tenth commandment seemed very arbitrary to Patrick, the star of St. Mary's Sunday-school, when he saw that the red silk was attracting nearly all the attention of his female contingent. If Eva admired flaunting ties it were well that she should say so now. There was yet time to spare himself the agony of riding on rubber-neck-boat-birds with one whose interest wandered from brass buttons. Darkly Patrick scowled upon his unconscious rival, and guilefully he remarked to Eva:

" Red neckties is nice, don't you think? "

" Awful nice," Eva agreed; " but they ain't so stylish like high-stiffs. High-stiffs und derbies is awful stylish."

Gloom and darkness vanished from the heart and countenance of the Knight of Munster, for around his neck he wore, with suppressed agony, the highest and stiffest of " high-stiffs " and his brows—and the back of his neck—were encircled by his big brother's work-a-day derby. Again he saw and described to Eva the vision which had lived in his hopes for now so many weeks: against a background of teeming jungle, mysterious and alive with wild beasts, an amiable boat-bird floated on the water-lake: and upon the boat-bird, trembling but reassured, sat Eva Gonorowsky, hand in hand with her brass-buttoned protector.

As the car sped up the Bowery the children felt that they were indeed adventurers. The clattering Elevated trains overhead, the crowds of brightly decked Sunday strollers, the clanging trolley cars, and the glimpses they caught of shining green as they passed the streets leading to the smaller squares and parks, all contributed to the holiday upliftedness which swelled their unaccustomed hearts. At each vista of green they made ready to disembark and were restrained only by the conductor and by the sage counsel of Eva, who reminded her impulsive companions that the Central Park could be readily identified by " the hollers from all those things what hollers." And so, in happy watching and calm trust of the conductor, they were borne far beyond 59th Street, the first and most popular entrance to the park, before an interested passenger came to their rescue. They tumbled off the car and pressed towards the green only to find themselves shut out by a high stone wall, against which they crouched and listened in vain for identifying hollers. The silence began to frighten them, when suddenly the quiet air was shattered by a shriek which would have done credit to the biggest of boat-birds or of lions, but which was—the children discovered after a moment's panic—only the prelude to an outburst of grief on the chaperon's part. When the inarticulate stage of her sorrow was passed, she demanded instant speech with her mamma. She would seem to have expressed a sentiment common to the majority, for three heads in Spring finery leaned dejectedly against the stone barrier while Nathan removed his car-fare to contribute the remark that he was growing hungry. Patrick was forced to seek aid in the passing crowd on Fifth Avenue, and in response to his pleading eyes and the depression of his party, a lady of gentle aspect and " kind looks " stopped and spoke to them.

" Indeed, yes," she reassured them; " this is Central Park."

" It has looks off the country," Eva commented.

" Because it is a piece of the country," the lady explained.

" Then we dassent to go, the while we ain't none of us got no sickness," cried Eva forlornly. " We're all, all healthy, und the country is for sick childrens."

" I am glad you are well," said the lady kindly; " but you may certainly play in the park. It is meant for all little children. The gate is near. Just walk on near this wall until you come to it."

It was only a few blocks, and they were soon in the land

of their hearts' desire, where were waving trees and flowering shrubs and smoothly sloping lawns, and, framed in all these wonders, a beautiful little water-lake all dotted and brightened by fleets of tiny boats. The pilgrims from the East Side stood for a moment at gaze and then bore down upon the jewel, straight over grass and border, which is a course not lightly to be followed within park precincts and in view of park policemen. The ensuing reprimand dashed their spirits not at all and they were soon assembled close to the margin of the lake, where they got entangled in guiding strings and drew to shore many a craft, to the disgust of many a small owner. Becky Zalmonowsky stood so closely over the lake that she shed the chatelaine bag into its shallow depths and did irreparable damage to her gala costume in her attempts to " dibble " for her property. It was at last recovered, no wetter than the toilette it was intended to adorn, and the cousins Gonorowsky had much difficulty in balking Becky's determination to remove her gown and dry it then and there.

Then Ignatius Aloysius, the exacting, remembered garrulously that he had as yet seen nothing of the rubber-neck-boat-birds and suggested that they were even now graciously " hollering like an'thing " in some remote fastness of the park. So Patrick gave commands and the march was resumed with bliss now beaming on all the faces so lately clouded. Every turn of the endless walks brought new wonders to these little ones who were gazing for the first time upon the great world of growing things of which Miss Bailey had so often told them. The policeman's warning had been explicit and they followed decorously in the paths and picked none of the flowers which as Eva had heard of old, were sticking right up out of the ground. But other flowers there were dangling high or low on tree or shrub, while here and there across the grass a bird came hopping or a squirrel ran. But the pilgrims never swerved. Full well they knew that these delights were not for such as they.

It was, therefore, with surprise and concern that they at last debouched upon a wide green space where a flag waved at the top of a towering pole; for, behold, the grass was covered thick with children, with here and there a beneficent policeman looking serenely on.

" Dast *we* walk on it? " cried Morris. " Oh, Patrick, dast we? "

" Ask the cop," Nathan suggested. It was his first speech for an hour, for Becky's misadventure with the chatelaine bag and the water-lake had made him more than ever sure that his own method of safe-keeping was the best.

" Ask him yerself," retorted Patrick. He had quite intended to accost a large policeman, who would of course recognize and revere the buttons of Mr. Brennan *père,* but a commander cannot well accept the advice of his subordinates. But Nathan was once more beyond the power of speech, and it was Morris Mogilewsky who asked for and obtained permission to walk on God's green earth. With little spurts of running and tentative jumps to test its spring, they crossed Peacock Lawn to the grateful shade of the trees at its further edge and there disposed themselves upon the ground and ate their luncheon. Nathan Spiderwitz waited until Sadie had finished and then entrusted the five gleaming pennies to her care while he wildly bolted an appetizing combination of dark brown bread and un-cooked eel.

Becky reposed flat upon the chatelaine bag and waved her still damp shoes exultantly. Eva lay, face downward beside her, and peered wonderingly deep into the roots of things.

" Don't it smells nice! " she gloated. " Don't it looks nice! My, ain't we havin' the party-time! "

" Don't mention it," said Patrick, in careful imitation of his mother's hostess manner. " I'm pleased to see you, I'm sure."

" The Central Park is awful pretty," Sadie soliloquized as she lay on her back and watched the waving branches and blue sky far above. "Awful pretty! I likes we should live here all the time."

"Well," began Ignatius Aloysius Diamantstein, in slight disparagement of his rival's powers as a cicerone; "well, I ain't seen no lions, nor no rubber-neck-boat-birds. Und we ain't had no rides on nothings. Und I ain't heard no hollers neither."

As if in answer to this criticism there arose, upon the road beyond the trees, a snorting, panting noise, growing momentarily louder and culminating, just as East Side nerves were strained to breaking point, in a long hoarse and terrifying yell. There was a flash of red, a cloud of dust, three other toots of agony, and the thing was gone. Gone, too, were the explorers and gone their peaceful rest. To a distant end of the field they flew, led by the panic-stricken chaperon, and followed by Eva and Patrick, hand in hand, he making show of bravery he was far from feeling, and she frankly terrified. In a secluded corner, near the restaurant, the chaperon was run to earth by her breathless charges:

"I seen the lion," she panted over and over. "I seen the fierce, big red lion, und I don't know where is my mamma."

Patrick saw that one of the attractions had failed to attract, so he tried another.

"Le's go an' see the cows," he proposed. "Don't you know the po'try piece Miss Bailey learned us about cows?"

Again the emotional chaperon interrupted. "I'm loving much mit Miss Bailey, too," she wailed. "Und I don't know where is she neither." But the pride of learning upheld the others and they chanted in sing-song chorus, swaying rhythmically the while from leg to leg:

"The friendly cow all red and white,
    I love with all my heart:
She gives me cream with all her might,
    To eat with apple-tart Robert Louis Stevenson."

Becky's tears ceased. " Be there cows in the Central Park? " she demanded.

" Sure," said Patrick.

" Und what kind from cream will he give us? Ice cream? "

" Sure," said Patrick again.

" Let's go," cried the emotional chaperon. A passing stranger turned the band in the general direction of the menagerie and the reality of the cow brought the whole " memory gem " into strange and undreamed reality.

Gaily they set out through new and always beautiful ways; through tunnels where feet and voices rang with ghostly boomings most pleasant to the ear; over bridges whence they saw—in partial proof of Isaac Borrachsohn's veracity—" mans und ladies ridin'." Of a surety they rode nothing more exciting than horses, but that was, to East Side eyes, an unaccustomed sight, and Eva opined that it was owing, probably, to the shortness of their watch that they saw no lions and tigers similarly amiable. The cows, too, seemed far to seek, but the trees and grass and flowers were everywhere. Through long stretches of " for sure country " they picked their way, until they came, hot but happy, to a green and shady summerhouse on a hill. There they halted to rest, and there Ignatius Aloysius, with questionable delicacy, began to insist once more upon the full measure of his bond.

" We ain't seen the rubber-neck-boat-birds," he complained. " Und we ain't had no rides on nothings."

" You don't know what is polite," cried Eva, greatly shocked at this carping spirit in the presence of a hard-worked host. " You could to think shame over how you says somethings like that on a party."

" This ain't no party," Ignatius Aloysius retorted. " It's a 'scursion. To a party somebody *gives* you what you should eat; to a 'scursion you *brings* it. Und anyway, we ain't had no rides."

" But we heard a holler," the guest of honor reminded him.

"We heard a fierce, big holler from a lion. I don't know do I need a ride on something what hollers. I could to have a fraid maybe."

"Ye wouldn't be afraid on the boats when I hold yer hand, would ye?" Patrick anxiously inquired, and Eva shyly admitted that, thus supported, she might not be dismayed. To work off the pride and joy caused by this avowal, Patrick mounted the broad seat extending all around the summerhouse and began to walk clatteringly upon it. The other pilgrims followed suit and the whole party stamped and danced with infinite enjoyment. Suddenly the leader halted with a loud cry of triumph and pointed grandly out through one of the wistaria-hung openings. Not De Soto on the banks of the Mississippi nor Balboa above the Pacific could have felt more victorious than Patrick did as he announced:

"There's the water-lake!"

His followers closed in upon him so impetuously that he was borne down under their charge and fell ignominiously out on the grass. But he was hardly missed, he had served his purpose. For there, beyond the rocks and lawns and red japonicas, lay the blue and shining water-lake in its confining banks of green. And upon its softly quivering surface floated the rubber-neck-boat-birds, white and sweetly silent instead of red and screaming—and the superlative length and arched beauty of their necks surpassed the wildest of Ikey Borrachsohn's descriptions. And relying upon the strength and politeness of these wondrous birds there were indeed "mans und ladies und boys und little girls" embarking, disembarking, and placidly weaving in and out and round about through scenes of hidden but undoubted beauty.

Over rocks and grass the army charged towards bliss unutterable, strewing their path with overturned and howling babies of prosperity who, clumsy from many nurses and much pampering, failed to make way. Past all barriers, accidental or official, they pressed, nor halted to draw rein or breath until they were established, beatified, upon the waiting swan-boat.

Three minutes later they were standing outside the railings of the landing and regarding, through welling tears, the placid lake, the sunny slopes of grass and tree, the brilliant sky and the gleaming rubber-neck-boat-bird which, as Ikey described, "made go its legs," but only, as he had omitted to mention, for money. So there they stood, seven sorrowful little figures engulfed in the rayless despair of childhood and the bitterness of poverty. For these were the children of the poor, and full well they knew that money was not to be diverted from its mission: that car-fare could not be squandered on bliss.

Becky's woe was so strong and loud that the bitter wailings of the others served merely as its background. But Patrick cared not at all for the general despair. His remorseful eyes never strayed from the bowed figure of Eva Gonorowsky, for whose pleasure and honor he had striven so long and vainly. Slowly she conquered her sobs, slowly she raised her daisy-decked head, deliberately she blew her small pink nose, softly she approached her conquered knight, gently and all untruthfully she faltered, with yearning eyes on the majestic swans:

"Don't you have no sad feelings, Patrick. I ain't got none. Ain't I told you from long, how I don't need no rubber-neck-boat-bird rides? I don't need 'em! I don't need 'em! I"—with a sob of passionate longing—"I'm got all times a awful scare over 'em. Let's go home, Patrick. Becky needs she should see her mamma, und I guess I needs my mamma too."

MYRA KELLY

Is it necessary to say that she was Irish? The humor, the sympathy, the quick understanding, the tenderness, that play through all her stories are the birthright of the children of Erin. Myra Kelly was born in Dublin, Ireland. Her father was Dr. John E. Kelly, a well-known surgeon. When Myra was little more than a baby, the family came to New York City. Here she was educated at the Horace Mann High School, and afterwards at Teachers College, a department of Columbia University, New York. She graduated from Teachers College in 1899. Her first school was in the primary department of Public School 147, on East Broadway, New York, where she taught from 1899 to 1901. Here she met all the " little aliens," the Morris and Isidore, Yetta and Eva of her stories, and won her way into their hearts. To her friends she would sometimes tell of these children, with their odd ideas of life and their dialect. " Why don't you write these stories down? " they asked her, and at last she sat down and wrote her first story, " A Christmas Present for a Lady." She had no knowledge of editorial methods, so she made four copies of the story and sent them to four different magazines. Two of them returned the story, and two of them accepted it, much to her embarrassment. The two acceptances came from *McClure's Magazine* and *The Century.* As *McClure's* replied first she gave the story to them, and most of her other stories were first published in that magazine.

When they appeared in book form, they were welcomed by readers all over the country. Even the President of the United States wrote to express his thanks to her, in the following letter:

Oyster Bay, N. Y.
July, 26, 1905.

My dear Miss Kelly:—

Mrs. Roosevelt and I and most of the children know your very amusing and very pathetic accounts of East Side school children almost by heart, and I really think you must let me write and thank you for them. When I was Police Commissioner I quite often went to the Houston Street public school, and was immensely impressed by what I saw there. I thought there were a good many Miss Baileys there, and the work they were doing among their scholars (who were largely of Russian-Jewish parentage like the children you write of) was very much like what your Miss Bailey has done.

Very sincerely yours,
Theodore Roosevelt.

After two years of school room work, Miss Kelly's health broke down, and she retired from teaching, although she served as critic teacher in the Speyer School, Teachers College, for a year longer. One of the persons who had read her books with delight was Allen Macnaughton. Soon after he met Miss Kelly, and in 1905 they were married. They lived for a time at Oldchester Village, New Jersey, in the Orange mountains, in a colony of literary people which her husband was interested in establishing. After several years of very successful literary work, she developed tuberculosis. She went to Torquay, England, in search of health, and died there March 31, 1910.

Her works include the following titles: *Little Citizens; The Isle of Dreams; Wards of Liberty; Rosnah; the Golden Season; Little Aliens; New Faces*. One of the leading magazines speaks of her as the creator of a new dialect.

HERO WORSHIP

Most of us are hero-worshippers at some time of our lives. The boy finds his hero in the baseball player or athlete, the girl in the matinee idol, or the " movie " star. These objects of worship are not always worthy of the adoration they inspire, but this does not matter greatly, since their worshippers seldom find it out. There is something fine in absolute loyalty to an ideal, even if the ideal is far from reality. " The Tenor " is the story of a famous singer and two of his devoted admirers.

THE TENOR

BY

H. C. BUNNER

It was a dim, quiet room in an old-fashioned New York house, with windows opening upon a garden that was trim and attractive, even in its wintry days—for the rose-bushes were all bundled up in straw ulsters. The room was ample, yet it had a cosy air. Its dark hangings suggested comfort and luxury, with no hint of gloom. A hundred pretty trifles told that it was a young girl's room: in the deep alcove nestled her dainty white bed, draped with creamy lace and ribbons.

" I was *so* afraid that I'd be late! "

The door opened, and two pretty girls came in, one in hat and furs, the other in a modest house dress. The girl in the furs, who had been afraid that she would be late, was fair, with a bright color in her cheeks, and an eager, intent look in her clear brown eyes. The other girl was dark-eyed and dark-haired, dreamy, with a soft, warm dusky color in her face. They were two very pretty girls indeed—or, rather, two girls about to be very pretty, for neither one was eighteen years old.

The dark girl glanced at a little porcelain clock.

" You are in time, dear," she said, and helped her companion to take off her wraps.

Then the two girls crossed the room, and with a caressing and almost a reverent touch, the dark girl opened the doors of a little carven cabinet that hung upon the wall, above a small table covered with a delicate white cloth. In its depths, framed in a mat of odorous double violets, stood the photograph of the face of a handsome man of forty—a face crowned with clustering black locks, from beneath which a pair of large, mournful eyes looked out with something like religious fervor in their rapt gaze. It was the face of a foreigner.

" O Esther! " cried the other girl, " how beautifully you have dressed him to-day! "

" I wanted to get more," Esther said; " but I've spent almost all my allowance—and violets do cost so shockingly. Come, now—" with another glance at the clock—" don't let's lose any more time, Louise dear."

She brought a couple of tiny candles in Sevrès candlesticks, and two little silver saucers, in which she lit fragrant pastilles. As the pale gray smoke arose, floating in faint wreaths and spirals before the enshrined photograph, Louise sat down and gazed intently upon the little altar. Esther went to her piano and watched the clock. It struck two. Her hands fell softly on the keys, and, studying a printed program in front of her, she began to play an overture. After the overture she played one or two pieces of the regular concert stock. Then she paused.

" I can't play the Tschaikowski piece."

" Never mind," said the other. " Let us wait for him in silence."

The hands of the clock pointed to 2:29. Each girl drew a quick breath, and then the one at the piano began to sing softly, almost inaudibly, " les Rameaux " in a transcription for tenor of Faure's great song. When it was ended, she played and sang the *encore*. Then, with her fingers touching the keys so softly that they awakened only an echo-like sound, she ran over the numbers that intervened between the first tenor solo and the second. Then she sang again, as softly as before.

The fair-haired girl sat by the little table, gazing intently on the picture. Her great eyes seemed to devour it, and yet there was something absent-minded, speculative, in her steady look. She did not speak until Esther played the last number on the program.

"He had three encores for that last Saturday," she said, and Esther played the three encores.

Then they closed the piano and the little cabinet, and exchanged an innocent girlish kiss, and Louise went out, and found her father's coupé waiting for her, and was driven away to her great, gloomy, brown-stone home near Central Park.

Louise Laura Latimer and Esther Van Guilder were the only children of two families which, though they were possessed of the three " Rs " which are all and more than are needed to insure admission to New York society—Riches, Respectability and Religion—yet were not in Society; or, at least, in the society that calls itself Society. This was not because Society was not willing to have them. It was because they thought the world too worldly. Perhaps this was one reason—although the social horizon of the two families had expanded somewhat as the girls grew up—why Louise and Esther, who had been playmates from their nursery days, and had grown up to be two uncommonly sentimental, fanciful, enthusiastically morbid girls, were to be found spending a bright Winter afternoon holding a ceremonial service of worship before the photograph of a fashionable French tenor.

It happened to be a French tenor whom they were worshiping. It might as well have been anybody or any thing else. They were both at that period of girlish growth when the young female bosom is torn by a hysterical craving to worship something—any thing. They had been studying music and they had selected the tenor who was the sensation of the hour in New York for their idol. They had heard him only on the concert stage; they were never likely to see him nearer. But it was a mere matter of chance that the idol was not a

Boston Transcendentalist, a Popular Preacher, a Faith-Cure Healer, or a ringleted old maid with advanced ideas of Woman's Mission. The ceremonies might have been different in form: the worship would have been the same.

M. Hyppolite Rémy was certainly the musical hero of the hour. When his advance notices first appeared, the New York critics, who are a singularly unconfiding, incredulous lot, were inclined to discount his European reputation.

When they learned that M. Rémy was not only a great artist, but a man whose character was " wholly free from that deplorable laxity which is so often a blot on the proud escutcheon of his noble profession;" that he had married an American lady; that he had " embraced the Protestant religion "— no sect was specified, possibly to avoid jealousy—and that his health was delicate, they were moved to suspect that he might have to ask that allowances be made for his singing. But when he arrived, his triumph was complete. He was as handsome as his picture, if he *was* a trifle short, a shade too stout.

He was a singer of genius, too; with a splendid voice and a sound method—on the whole. It was before the days of the Wagner autocracy, and perhaps his tremolo passed unchallenged as it could not now; but he was a great artist. He knew his business as well as his advance-agent knew his. The Rémy Concerts were a splendid success. Reserved seats, $5. For the Series of Six, $25.

.   .   .   .

On the following Monday, Esther Van Guilder returned her friend's call, in response to an urgent invitation, despatched by mail. Louise Latimer's great bare room was incapable of transmutation into a cosy nest of a boudoir. There was too much of its heavy raw silk furniture—too much of its vast, sarcophagus-like bed—too much of its upholsterer's elegance, regardless of cost—and taste. An enlargement from an ambrotype of the original Latimer, as he arrived in New York

from New Hampshire, and a photograph of a " child subject "
by Millais, were all her works of art. It was not to be doubted
that they had climbed upstairs from a front parlor of an earlier
stage of social development. The farm-house was six generations behind Esther; two behind Louise.

Esther found her friend in a state of almost feverish excitement. Her eyes shone; the color burned high on her clear
cheeks.

" You never would guess what I've done, dear! " she began,
as soon as they were alone in the big room. " I'm going to
see *him*—to speak to him—*Esther!* " Her voice was solemnly
hushed, " to *serve* him! "

" Oh, Louise! what *do* you mean? "

" To serve him—with my own hands! To—to—help him
on with his coat—I don't know—to do something that a servant does—anything, so that I can say that once, once only,
just for an hour, I have been near him, been of use to him,
served him in one little thing as loyally as he serves OUR
ART."

Music was THEIR art, and no capitals could tell how much
it was theirs or how much of an art it was.

" Louise," demanded Esther, with a frightened look, " are
you crazy? "

" No. Read this! " She handed the other girl a clipping
from the advertising columns of a newspaper.

CHAMBERMAID AND WAITRESS.—WANTED, A NEAT
and willing girl, for light work.   Apply to Mme. Rémy, The
Midlothian,......Broadway.

" I saw it just by accident, Saturday, after I left you. Papa
had left his paper in the coupé. I was going up to my First
Aid to the Injured Class—it's at four o'clock now, you know.
I made up my mind right off—it came to me like an inspiration.
I just waited until it came to the place where they showed
how to tie up arteries, and then I slipped out. Lots of the
girls slip out in the horrid parts, you know. And then, in-

stead of waiting in the ante-room, I put on my wrap, and pulled the hood over my head and ran off to the Midlothian—it's just around the corner, you know. And I saw his wife."

"What was she like?" queried Esther, eagerly.

"Oh, I don't know. Sort of horrid—actressy. She had a pink silk wrapper with swansdown all over it—at four o'clock, think! I was *awfully* frightened when I got there; but it wasn't the least trouble. She hardly looked at me, and she engaged me right off. She just asked me if I was willing to do a whole lot of things—I forgot what they were—and where I'd worked before. I said at Mrs. Barcalow's."

"Mrs. Barcalow's?"

"Why, yes—my Aunt Amanda, don't you know—up in Framingham. I always have to wash the teacups when I go there. Aunty says that everybody has got to do *something* in *her* house."

"Oh, Louise!" cried her friend, in shocked admiration; "how can you think of such things?"

"Well, I did. And she—his wife, you know— just said: 'Oh, I suppose you'll do as well as any one—all you girls are alike.'"

"But did she really take you for a—servant?"

"Why, yes, indeed. It was raining. I had that old ulster on, you know. I'm to go at twelve o'clock next Saturday."

"But, Louise!" cried Esther, aghast, "you don't truly mean to go!"

"I do!" cried Louise, beaming triumphantly.

"*Oh, Louise!*"

"Now, listen, dear," said Miss Latimer, with the decision of an enthusiastic young lady with New England blood in her veins. "Don't say a word till I tell you what my plan is. I've thought it all out, and you've got to help me."

Esther shuddered.

"You foolish child!" cried Louise. Her eyes were sparkling: she was in a state of ecstatic excitement; she could see no obstacles to the carrying out of her plan. " You don't think I mean to *stay* there, do you? I'm just going at twelve o'clock, and at four he comes back from the matinée, and at five o'clock I'm going to slip on my things and run downstairs, and have you waiting for me in the coupé, and off we go. Now do you see? "

It took some time to bring Esther's less venturesome spirit up to the point of assisting in this undertaking; but she began, after a while, to feel the delights of vicarious enterprise, and in the end the two girls, their cheeks flushed, their eyes shining feverishly, their voices tremulous with childish eagerness, re-solved themselves into a committee of ways and means; for they were two well-guarded young women, and to engineer five hours of liberty was difficult to the verge of impossibility. However, there is a financial manœuvre known as " kiting checks," whereby A exchanges a check with B and B swaps with A again, playing an imaginary balance against Time and the Clearing House; and by a similar scheme, which an acute student of social ethics has called " kiting calls," the girls found that they could make Saturday afternoon their own, without one glance from the watchful eyes of Esther's mother or Louise's aunt—Louise had only an aunt to reckon with.

" And, oh, Esther! " cried the bolder of the conspirators, " I've thought of a trunk—of course I've got to have a trunk, or she would ask me where it was, and I couldn't tell her a fib. Don't you remember the French maid who died three days after she came here? Her trunk is up in the store-room still, and I don't believe anybody will ever come for it—it's been there seven years now. Let's go up and look at it."

The girls romped upstairs to the great unused upper story, where heaps of household rubbish obscured the dusty half-windows. In a corner, behind Louise's baby chair and an un-fashionable hat-rack of the old steering-wheel pattern, they found the little brown-painted tin trunk, corded up with clothes-line.

" Louise! " said Esther, hastily, " what did you tell her your name was? "

" I just said ' Louise'."

Esther pointed to the name painted on the trunk,

LOUISE LEVY

" It is the hand of Providence," she said. " Somehow, now, I'm *sure* you're quite right to go."

And neither of these conscientious young ladies reflected for one minute on the discomfort which might be occasioned to Madame Rémy by the defection of her new servant a half-hour before dinner-time on Saturday night.

.   .   .   .

" Oh, child, it's you, is it? " was Mme. Rémy's greeting at twelve o'clock on Saturday. " Well, you're punctual—and you look clean. Now, are you going to break my dishes or are you going to steal my rings? Well, we'll find out soon enough. Your trunk's up in your room. Go up to the servant's quarters—right at the top of those stairs there. Ask for the room that belongs to apartment 11. You are to room with their girl."

Louise was glad of a moment's respite. She had taken the plunge; she was determined to go through to the end. But her heart *would* beat and her hands *would* tremble. She climbed up six flights of winding stairs, and found herself weak and dizzy when she reached the top and gazed around her. She was in a great half-story room, eighty feet square. The most of it was filled with heaps of old furniture and bedding, rolls of carpet, of canvas, of oilcloth, and odds and ends of discard of unused household gear—the dust thick over all. A little space had been left around three sides, to give access to three rows of cell-like rooms, in each of which the ceiling sloped from the very door to a tiny window at the level of the floor. In each room was a bed, a bureau that served for wash-stand, a small looking-glass, and one or two trunks. Women's dresses hung on the whitewashed walls. She found No. 11, threw off, desperately, her hat and jacket, and sunk down on the little brown tin trunk, all trembling from head to foot.

" Hello," called a cheery voice. She looked up and saw a girl in a dirty calico dress.

" Just come? " inquired this person, with agreeable informality. She was a good-looking large girl, with red hair and bright cheeks. She leaned against the door-post and polished her finger-nails with a little brush. Her hands were shapely.

" Ain't got onto the stair-climbing racket yet, eh? You'll get used to it. ' Louise Levy,' " she read the name on the trunk. " You don't look like a sheeny. Can't tell nothin' 'bout names, can you? My name's Slattery. You'd think I was Irish, wouldn't you? Well, I'm straight Ne' York. I'd be dead before I was Irish. Born here. Ninth Ward an' next to an engine house. How's that? There's white Jews, too. I worked for one, pickin' sealskins down in Prince Street. Most took the lungs out of me. But that wasn't why I shook the biz. It queered my hands—see? I'm goin' to be married in the Fall to a German gentleman. He ain't so Dutch when you know him, though. He's a grocer. Drivin' now; but he buys out the boss in the Fall. How's that? He's dead stuck on my hooks, an' I have to keep 'em lookin' good. I come here because the work was light. I don't have to work—only to be doin' somethin', see? Only got five halls and the lamps. You got a fam'ly job, I s'pose? I wouldn't have that. I don't mind the Sooprintendent; but I'd be dead before I'd be bossed by a woman, see? Say, what fam'ly did you say you was with? "

The stream of talk had acted like a nerve-tonic on Louise. She was able to answer:

" M—Mr. Rémy."

" Ramy?—oh, lord! Got the job with His Tonsils? Well, you won't keep it long. They're meaner'n three balls, see?

Rent their room up here and chip in with eleven. Their
girls don't never stay. Well, I got to step, or the Sooprintendent'll be borin' my ear. Well—so long! "

But Louise had fled down the stairs. " His Tonsils " rang
in her ears. What blasphemy! What sacrilege! She could
scarcely pretend to listen to Mme. Rémy's first instructions.

The household *was* parsimonious. Louise washed the caterer's dishes—he made a reduction in his price. Thus she
learned that a late breakfast took the place of luncheon. She
began to feel what this meant. The beds had been made;
but there was work enough. She helped Mme. Rémy to sponge
a heap of faded finery—*her* dresses. If they had been *his*
coats! Louise bent her hot face over the tawdry silks and
satins, and clasped her parboiled little finger-tips over the
wet sponge. At half-past three Mme. Rémy broke the silence.

" We must get ready for Musseer," she said. An ecstatic
joy filled Louise's being. The hour of her reward was at
hand.

Getting ready for " Musseer " proved to be an appalling
process. First they brewed what Mme. Remy called a " teaze
Ann. " After the *tisane,* a host of strange foreign drugs and
cosmetics were marshalled in order. Then water was set to
heat on a gas-stove. Then a little table was neatly set.

" Musseer has his dinner at half-past four," Madame explained. " I don't take mine till he's laid down and I've got
him off to the concert. There, he's coming now. Sometimes
he comes home pretty nervous. If he's nervous, don't you go
and make a fuss, do you hear, child? "

The door opened, and Musseer entered, wrapped in a huge
frogged overcoat. There was no doubt that he was nervous.
He cast his hat upon the floor, as if he were Jove dashing a
thunderbolt. Fire flashed from his eyes. He advanced upon
his wife and thrust a newspaper in her face—a little pinky
sheet, a notorious blackmailing publication.

" Zees," he cried, " is your work! "

"What *is* it now, Hipleet?" demanded Mme. Rémy.

"Vot it ees?" shrieked the tenor. "It ees ze history of how zey have heest me at Nice! It ees all zair—how I have been heest—in zis sacre sheet—in zis handkairchif of infamy! And it ees you zat have told it to zat devil of a Rastignac— *traitresse!*"

"Now, Hipleet," pleaded his wife, "if I can't learn enough French to talk with you, how am I going to tell Rastignac about your being hissed?"

This reasoning silenced Mr. Rémy for an instant—an instant only.

"You *vood* have done it!" he cried, sticking out his chin and thrusting his face forward.

"Well, I didn't," said Madame, "and nobody reads that thing, any way. Now, don't mind it, and let me get your things off, or you'll be catching cold."

Mr. Rémy yielded at last to the necessity of self-preservation, and permitted his wife to remove his frogged overcoat, and to unwind him from a system of silk wraps to which the Gordian knot was a slip-noose. This done, he sat down before the dressing-case, and Mme. Rémy, after tying a bib around his neck, proceeded to dress his hair and put brilliantine on his moustache. Her husband enlivened the operation by reading from the pinky paper.

"It ees not gen-air-al-lee known—zat zees dees-tin-guished tenor vos heest on ze pob-lic staidj at Nice—in ze year—"

Louise leaned against the wall, sick, faint and frightened, with a strange sense of shame and degradation at her heart. At last the tenor's eye fell on her.

"Anozzair eediot?" he inquired.

"She ain't very bright, Hipleet," replied his wife; "but I guess she'll do. Louise, open the door—there's the caterer."

Louise placed the dishes upon the table mechanically. The tenor sat himself at the board, and tucked a napkin in his neck.

" And how did the Benediction Song go this afternoon? " inquired his wife.

" Ze Bénédiction? Ah! One *encore*. One on-lee. Zese pigs of Ameéricains. I t'row my pairls biffo' swine. *Chops once more!* You vant to mordair me? Vat do zis mean, madame? You ar-r-re in lig wiz my enemies. All ze vorlt is against ze ar-r-r-teest! "

The storm that followed made the first seem a zephyr. The tenor exhausted his execratory vocabulary in French and English. At last, by way of a dramatic finale, he seized the plate of chops and flung it from him. He aimed at the wall; but Frenchmen do not pitch well. With a ring and a crash, plate and chops went through the broad window-pane. In the moment of stricken speechlessness that followed, the sound of the final smash came softly up from the sidewalk.

" Ah-a-a-a-a-a-a-a-a-ah! "

The tenor rose to his feet with the howl of an anguished hyena.

" Oh, good gracious! " cried his wife; " he's going to have one of his creezes—his creezes de nare! "

He did have a *crise de nerfs*. " Ten dollair! " he yelled, " for ten dollair of glass! " He tore his pomaded hair; he tore off his bib and his neck-tie, and for three minutes without cessation he shrieked wildly and unintelligibly. It was possible to make out, however, that " arteest " and " ten dollair " were the themes of the improvisation. Finally he sank exhausted into the chair, and his white-faced wife rushed to his side.

" Louise! " she cried, " get the foot-tub out of the closet while I spray his throat, or he can't sing a note. Fill it up with warm water—102 degrees—there's the thermometer—and bathe his feet."

Trembling from head to foot, Louise obeyed her orders, and brought the foot-tub, full of steaming water. Then she knelt down and began to serve the maestro for the first time.

She took off his shoes. Then she looked at his socks. Could she do it?

" Eediot! " gasped the sufferer, " make haste! I die! "

" Hold your mouth open, dear," said Madame, " I haven't half sprayed you."

" Ah! *you!* " cried the tenor. " Cat! Devil! It ees you zat have killed me! " And moved by an access of blind rage, he extended his arm, and thrust his wife violently from him.

Louise rose to her feet, with a hard set, good old New England look on her face. She lifted the tub of water to the level of her breast, and then she inverted it on the tenor's head. For one instant she gazed at the deluge, and at the bath-tub balanced on the maestro's skull like a helmet several sizes too large—then she fled like the wind.

Once in the servant's quarters, she snatched her hat and jacket. From below came mad yells of rage.

" I kill hare! give me my knife—give me my rivvolvare! Au secours! Assassin! "

Miss Slattery appeared in the doorway, still polishing her nails.

" What have you done to His Tonsils? " she inquired. " He's pretty hot, this trip."

" How can I get away from here? " cried Louise.

Miss Slattery pointed to a small door. Louise rushed down a long stairway—another—and yet others—through a great room where there was a smell of cooking and a noise of fires—past white-capped cooks and scullions—through a long stone corridor, and out into the street. She cried aloud as she saw Esther's face at the window of the coupé.

She drove home—cured.

H. C. BUNNER

Henry Cuyler Bunner was his full name, H. C. Bunner was the way he always signed his writings, and " Bunner " was his name to his friends, and even to his wife. He was born in Oswego, New York, August 3, 1855. His parents soon moved to New York City, and Bunner was educated in the public schools there. Then he became a clerk in a business house, but this did not satisfy him, and he began to write for newspapers, finally getting a position on the *Arcadian,* a short-lived journal. In 1877 the publishers of *Puck,* a humorous weekly printed in the German language, decided to issue an edition in English, and made Bunner assistant editor. It was a happy choice. He soon became editor-in-chief, and under his direction the paper became not only the best humorous journal of its time, but a powerful influence in politics as well. Bunner wrote not only editorials, humorous verse, short stories, and titles for pictures, but often suggested the cartoons, which were an important feature of the paper.

Outside the office he was a delightful conversationalist. His friends Brander Matthews, Lawrence Hutton and others speak of his ready wit, his kindness of heart, and his wonderfully varied store of information. He was a constant reader, and a good memory enabled him to retain what he read. It is said that one could hardly name a poem that he had not read, and it was odds but that he could quote its best lines. Next to reading, his chief pleasure was in wandering about odd corners of the city, especially the foreign quarters. He knew all the queer little restaurants and queer little shops in these places.

His first literary work of note was a volume of poems, happily entitled *Airs from Arcady.* It contains verses both grave and gay: one of the cleverest is called " Home, Sweet

54

Home, with Variations." He writes the poem first in the
style of Swinburne, then of Bret Harte, then of Austin Dobson,
then of Oliver Goldsmith and finally of Walt Whitman. The
book also showed his skill in the use of French forms of
verse, as in this dainty triolet:

A PITCHER OF MIGNONETTE

A pitcher of mignonette
  In a tenement's highest casement:
Queer sort of flower-pot—yet
That pitcher of mignonette
Is a garden in heaven set,
  To the little sick child in the basement—
The pitcher of mignonette
  In the tenement's highest casement.

The last poem in the book, called " To Her," was addressed
to Miss Alice Learned, whom he married soon after, and
to whom, as " A. L. B." all his later books were dedicated.
Soon after his marriage he moved to Nutley, New Jersey. Here
he was not only the editor and man of letters but the neighbor
who could always be called on in time of need, and the citizen
who took an active part in the community life, helping to
organize the Village Improvement Society, one of the first
of its kind.

He followed up his first volume by two short novels, *The
Midge* and *The Story of a New York House*. Then he undertook the writing of the short story, his first book being *Zadoc
Pine and other Stories*. The title story of this book contains a
very humorous and faithful delineation of a New Englander who
is transplanted to a New Jersey suburb. Soon after writing
this he began to read the short stories of Guy de Maupassant.
He admired them so much that he half translated, half adapted
a number of them, and published them under the title *Made in
France*. Then he tried writing stories of his own, in the
manner of de Maupassant, and produced in *Short Sixes* a

group of stories which are models of concise narrative, crisply told, artistic in form, and often with a touch of surprise at the end. Other volumes of short stories are *More Short Sixes,* and *Love in Old Cloathes. Jersey Street and Jersey Lane* was a book which grew out of his Nutley life. He also wrote a play, *The Tower of Babel,* which was produced by Marie Wainwright in 1883. He died at Nutley, May 11, 1896. He was one of the first American authors to develop the short story as we know it to-day, and few of his successors have surpassed him in the light, sure style and the firmness of construction which are characteristic of his later work.

SOCIETY IN OUR TOWN

Life in a small town, which means any place of less than a hundred thousand people, is more interesting than life in a big city. Both places have their notables, but in the small town you know these people, in the city you only read about them in the papers. IN OUR TOWN is a series of portraits of the people of a typical small city of the Middle West, seen through the keen eyes of a newspaper editor. This story tells how the question of the social leadership of the town was finally settled.

THE PASSING OF PRISCILLA WINTHROP

BY

WILLIAM ALLEN WHITE

WHAT a dreary waste life in our office must have been before Miss Larrabee came to us to edit a society page for the paper! To be sure we had known in a vague way that there were lines of social cleavage in the town; that there were whist clubs, and dancing clubs and women's clubs, and in a general way that the women who composed these clubs made up our best society, and that those benighted souls beyond the pale of these clubs were out of the caste. We knew that certain persons whose names were always handed in on the lists of guests at parties were what we called "howling swells," but it remained for Miss Larrabee to sort out ten or a dozen of these "howling swells," who belonged to the strictest social caste in town, and call them "howling dervishes." Incidentally it may be said that both Miss Larrabee and her mother were dervishes, but that did not prevent her from making sport of them. From Miss Larrabee we learned that the high priestess of the howling dervishes of our society was Mrs. Mortimer Conklin, known by the sisterhood of the mosque as Priscilla Winthrop. We in our office had never heard her called by that name, but Miss Larrabee explained, rather elaborately, that unless one was permitted to speak of Mrs. Conklin thus, one was quite beyond the hope of a social heaven.

In the first place, Priscilla Winthrop was Mrs. Conklin's maiden name; in the second place, it links her with the Colonial Puritan stock of which she is so justly proud—being scornful of mere Daughters of the Revolution—and finally, though Mrs. Conklin is a grandmother, her maiden name seems to preserve the sweet, vague illusion of girlhood which Mrs. Conklin always carries about her like the shadow of a dream. And Miss Larrabee punctuated this with a wink which we took to be a quotation mark, and she went on with her work. So we knew we had been listening to the language used in the temple.

Our town was organized fifty years ago by Abolitionists from New England, and twenty years ago, when Alphabetical Morrison was getting out one of the numerous boom editions of his real estate circular, he printed an historical article therein in which he said that Priscilla Winthrop was the first white child born on the town site. Her father was territorial judge, afterward member of the State Senate, and after ten years spent in mining in the far West, died in the seventies, the richest man in the State. It was known that he left Priscilla, his only child, half a million dollars in government bonds.

She was the first girl in our town to go away to school. Naturally, she went to Oberlin, famous in those days for admitting colored students. But she finished her education at Vassar, and came back so much of a young lady that the town could hardly contain her. She married Mortimer Conklin, took him to the Centennial on a wedding trip, came home, rebuilt her father's house, covering it with towers and minarets and steeples, and scroll-saw fretwork, and christened it Winthrop Hall. She erected a store building on Main Street, that Mortimer might have a luxurious office on the second floor, and then settled down to the serious business of life, which was building up a titled aristocracy in a Kansas town.

The Conklin children were never sent to the public schools, but had a governess, yet Mortimer Conklin, who was always alert for the call, could not understand why the people never summoned him to any office of honor or trust. He kept his brass signboard polished, went to his office punctually every morning at ten o'clock, and returned home to dinner at five, and made clients wait ten minutes in the outer office before they could see him—at least so both of them say, and there were no others in all the years. He shaved every day, wore a frock-coat and a high hat to church—where for ten years he was the only male member of the Episcopalian flock—and Mrs. Conklin told the women that altogether he was a credit to his sex and his family—a remark which has passed about ribaldly in town for a dozen years, though Mortimer Conklin never knew that he was the subject of a town joke. Once he rebuked a man in the barber shop for speaking of feminine extravagance, and told the shop that he did not stint his wife, that when she asked him for money he always gave it to her without question, and that if she wanted a dress he told her to buy it and send the bill to him. And we are such a polite people that no one in the crowded shop laughed—until Mortimer Conklin went out.

Of course at the office we have known for twenty-five years what the men thought of Mortimer, but not until Miss Larrabee joined the force did we know that among the women Mrs. Conklin was considered an oracle. Miss Larrabee said that her mother has a legend that when Priscilla Winthrop brought home from Boston the first sealskin sacque ever worn in town she gave a party for it, and it lay in its box on the big walnut bureau in the spare room of the Conklin mansion in solemn state, while seventy-five women salaamed to it. After that Priscilla Winthrop was the town authority on sealskins. When any member of the town nobility had a new sealskin, she took it humbly to Priscilla Winthrop to pass judgment upon it. If Priscilla said it was London-dyed, its owner pranced away on clouds of glory; but if she said it was American-dyed, its owner crawled away in shame, and when one admired the disgraced garment, the martyred owner smiled with resigned sweetness and said humbly: " Yes—but it's only American-dyed, you know."

No dervish ever questioned the curse of the priestess. The only time a revolt was imminent was in the autumn of 1884

when the Conklins returned from their season at Duxbury, Massachusetts, and Mrs. Conklin took up the carpets in her house,
heroically sold all of them at the second-hand store, put in
new waxed floors and spread down rugs. The town uprose and
hooted; the outcasts and barbarians in the Methodists and
Baptist Missionary Societies rocked the Conklin home with
their merriment, and ten dervishes with set faces bravely met
the onslaughts of the savages; but among themselves in hushed
whispers, behind locked doors, the faithful wondered if there
was not a mistake some place. However, when Priscilla Winthrop assured them that in all the best homes in Boston rugs
were replacing carpets, their souls were at peace.

All this time we at the office knew nothing of what was
going on. We knew that the Conklins devoted considerable
time to society; but Alphabetical Morrison explained that by
calling attention to the fact that Mrs. Conklin had prematurely gray hair. He said a woman with prematurely gray hair
was as sure to be a social leader as a spotted horse is to join a
circus. But now we know that Colonel Morrison's view was
a superficial one, for he was probably deterred from going
deeper into the subject by his dislike for Mortimer Conklin,
who invested a quarter of a million dollars of the Winthrop
fortune in the Wichita boom, and lost it. Colonel Morrison
naturally thought as long as Conklin was going to lose that
money he could have lost it just as well at home in the
" Queen City of the Prairies," giving the Colonel a chance to
win. And when Conklin, protecting his equities in Wichita, sent
a hundred thousand dollars of good money after the quarter
million of bad money, Colonel Morrison's grief could find no
words; though he did find language for his wrath. When the
Conklins draped their Oriental rugs for airing every Saturday
over the veranda and portico railings of the house front, Colonel Morrison accused the Conklins of hanging out their stamp
collection to let the neighbors see it. This was the only side
of the rug question we ever heard in our office until Miss Larra-

bee came; then she told us that one of the first requirements
of a howling dervish was to be able to quote from Priscilla
Winthrop's Rug book from memory. The Rug book, the
China book and the Old Furniture book were the three sacred
scrolls of the sect.

All this was news to us. However, through Colonel Morrison,
we had received many years ago another sidelight on the social
status of the Conklins. It came out in this way: Time honored custom in our town allows the children of a home where
there is an outbreak of social revelry, whether a church festival
or a meeting of the Cold-Nosed Whist Club, to line up with the
neighbor children on the back stoop or in the kitchen, like
human vultures, waiting to lick the ice-cream freezer and to
devour the bits of cake and chicken salad that are left over.
Colonel Morrison told us that no child was ever known to
adorn the back yard of the Conklin home while a social
cataclysm was going on, but that when Mrs. Morrison entertained the Ladies' Literary League, children from the holy
Conklin family went home from his back porch with their
faces smeared with chicken croquettes and their hands sticky
with jellycake.

This story never gained general circulation in town, but even
if it had been known of all men it would not have shaken
the faith of the devotees. For they did not smile when Priscilla
Winthrop began to refer to old Frank Hagan, who came to milk
the Conklin cow and curry the Conklin horse, as " François,
the man," or to call the girl who did the cooking and general
housework " Cosette, the maid," though every one of the
dozen other women in town whom " Cosette, the maid " had
worked for knew that her name was Fanny Ropes. And
shortly after that the homes of the rich and the great over
on the hill above Main Street began to fill with Lisettes and
Nanons and Fanchons, and Mrs. Julia Neal Worthington called
her girl " Grisette," explaining that they had always had a
Grisette about the house since her mother first went to house-

keeping in Peoria, Illinois, and it sounded so natural to hear the name that they always gave it to a new servant. This story came to the office through the Young Prince, who chuckled over it during the whole hour he consumed in writing Ezra Worthington's obituary.

Miss Larrabee says that the death of Ezra Worthington marks such a distinct epoch in the social life of the town that we must set down here—even if the narrative of the Conklins halts for a moment—how the Worthingtons rose and flourished. Julia Neal, the eldest daughter of Thomas Neal—who lost the "O" before his name somewhere between the docks of Dublin and the west bank of the Missouri River—was for ten years principal of the ward school in that part of our town known as "Arkansaw," where her term of service is still remembered as the "reign of terror." It was said of her then that she could whip any man in the ward—and would do it if he gave her a chance. The same manner which made the neighbors complain that Julia Neal carried her head too high, later in life, when she had money to back it, gave her what the women of the State Federation called a "regal air." In her early thirties she married Ezra Worthington, bachelor, twenty years her senior. Ezra Worthington was at that time, had been for twenty years before, and continued to be until his death, proprietor of the Worthington Poultry and Produce Commission Company. He was owner of the stockyards, president of the Worthington State Bank, vice-president, treasurer and general manager of the Worthington Mercantile Company, and owner of five brick buildings on Main Street. He bought one suit of clothes every five years whether he needed it or not, never let go of a dollar unless the Goddess of Liberty on it was black in the face, and died rated "at $350,000" by all the commercial agencies in the country. And the first thing Mrs. Worthington did after the funeral was to telephone to the bank and ask them to send her a hundred dollars.

The next important thing she did was to put a heavy, im-

movable granite monument over the deceased so that he would
not be restless, and then she built what is known in our town as
the Worthington Palace. It makes the Markley mansion which
cost $25,000 look like a barn. The Worthingtons in the life-
time of Ezra had ventured no further into the social whirl of
the town than to entertain the new Presbyterian preacher at
tea, and to lend their lawn to the King's Daughters for a
social, sending a bill in to the society for the eggs used in the
coffee and the gasoline used in heating it.

To the howling dervishes who surrounded Priscilla Winthrop
the Worthingtons were as mere Christian dogs. It was not
until three years after Ezra Worthington's death that the
glow of the rising Worthington sun began to be seen in the
Winthrop mosque. During those three years Mrs. Worthington
had bought and read four different sets of the best hundred
books, had consumed the Chautauque course, had prepared
and delivered for the Social Science Club, which she organized,
five papers ranging in subject from the home life of Rameses I.,
through a Survey of the Forces Dominating Michael Angelo,
to the Influence of Esoteric Buddhism on Modern Political
Tendencies. More than that, she had been elected president of
the City Federation clubs and being a delegate to the National Federation from the State, was talked of for
the State Federation Presidency. When the State Federation met in our town, Mrs. Worthington gave a reception for
the delegates in the Worthington Palace, a feature of which was
a concert by a Kansas City organist on the new pipe-organ
which she had erected in the music-room of her house, and
despite the fact that the devotees of the Priscilla shrine said
that the crowd was distinctly mixed and not at all representa-
tive of our best social grace and elegance, there is no question
but that Mrs. Worthington's reception made a strong impression upon the best local society. The fact that, as Miss
Larrabee said, " Priscilla Winthrop was so nice about it,"
also may be regarded as ominous. But the women who lent

Mrs. Worthington the spoons and forks for the occasion were delighted, and formed a phalanx about her, which made up in numbers what it might have lacked in distinction. Yet while Mrs. Worthington was in Europe the faithful routed the phalanx, and Mrs. Conklin returned from her summer in Duxbury with half a carload of old furniture from Harrison Sampson's shop and gave a talk to the priestesses of the inner temple on " Heppelwhite in New England."

Miss Larrabee reported the affair for our paper, giving the small list of guests and the long line of refreshments—which included alligator-pear salad, right out of the Smart Set Cook Book. Moreover, when Jefferson appeared in Topeka that fall, Priscilla Winthrop, who had met him through some of her Duxbury friends in Boston, invited him to run down for a luncheon with her and the members of the royal family who surrounded her. It was the proud boast of the defenders of the Winthrop faith in town that week, that though twenty-four people sat down to the table, not only did all the men wear frock coats—not only did Uncle Charlie Haskins of String Town wear the old Winthrop butler's livery without a wrinkle in it, and with only the faint odor of mothballs to mingle with the perfume of the roses—but (and here the voices of the followers of the prophet dropped in awe) not a single knife or fork or spoon or napkin was borrowed! After that, when any of the sisterhood had occasion to speak of the absent Mrs. Worthington, whose house was filled with new mahogany and brass furniture, they referred to her as the Duchess of Grand Rapids, which gave them much comfort.

But joy is short-lived. When Mrs. Worthington came back from Europe and opened her house to the City Federation, and gave a colored lantern-slide lecture on " An evening with the Old Masters," serving punch from her own cut-glass punch bowl instead of renting the hand-painted crockery bowl of the queensware store, the old dull pain came back into the hearts of the dwellers in the inner circle. Then just in the nick

of time Mrs. Conklin went to Kansas City and was operated on
for appendicitis. She came back pale and interesting, and
gave her club a paper called " Hospital Days," fragrant with
iodoform and Henley's poems. Miss Larrabee told us that
it was almost as pleasant as an operation on one's self to
hear Mrs. Conklin tell about hers. And they thought it was
rather brutal—so Miss Larrabee afterward told us—when
Mrs. Worthington went to the hospital one month, and gave
her famous Delsarte lecture course the next month, and explained to the women that if she wasn't as heavy as she used
to be it was because she had had everything cut out of her
below the windpipe. It seemed to the temple priestesses that,
considering what a serious time poor dear Priscilla Winthrop
had gone through, Mrs. Worthington was making light of
serious things.

There is no doubt that the formal rebellion of Mrs. Worthington, Duchess of Grand Rapids, and known of the town's
nobility as the Pretender, began with the hospital contest. The
Pretender planted her siege-guns before the walls of the temple
of the priestess, and prepared for business. The first ma-
neuver made by the beleaguered one was to give a luncheon
in the mosque, at which, though it was midwinter, fresh
tomatoes and fresh strawberries were served, and a real
authoress from Boston talked upon John Fiske's philosophy
and, in the presence of the admiring guests, made a new kind of
salad dressing for the fresh lettuce and tomatoes. Thirty women who watched her forgot what John Fiske's theory of the
cosmos is, and thirty husbands who afterward ate that salad
dressing have learned to suffer and be strong. But that salad
dressing undermined the faith of thirty mere men—raw out-
landers to be sure—in the social omniscience of Priscilla Winthrop. Of course they did not see it made; the spell of the
enchantress was not over them; but in their homes they main-
tained that if Priscilla Winthrop didn't know any more about
cosmic philosophy than to pay a woman forty dollars to make

a salad dressing like that—and the whole town knows that was the price—the vaunted town of Duxbury, Massachusetts, with its old furniture and new culture, which Priscilla spoke of in such repressed ecstasy, is probably no better than Manitou, Colorado, where they get their Indian goods from Buffalo, New York.

Such is the perverse reasoning of man. And Mrs. Worthington, having lived with considerable of a man for fifteen years, hearing echoes of this sedition, attacked the fortification of the faithful on its weakest side. She invited the thirty seditious husbands with their wives to a beefsteak dinner, where she heaped their plates with planked sirloin, garnished the sirloin with big, fat, fresh mushrooms, and topped off the meal with a mince pie of her own concoction, which would make a man leave home to follow it. She passed cigars at the table, and after the guests went into the music-room ten old men with ten old fiddles appeared and contested with old-fashioned tunes for a prize, after which the company danced four quadrilles and a Virginia reel. The men threw down their arms going home and went over in a body to the Pretender. But in a social conflict men are mere non-combatants, and their surrender did not seriously injure the cause that they deserted.

The war went on without abatement. During the spring that followed the winter of the beefsteak dinner many skirmishes, minor engagements, ambushes and midnight raids occurred. But the contest was not decisive. For purposes of military drill, the defenders of the Winthrop faith formed themselves into a Whist Club. *The* Whist Club they called it, just as they spoke of Priscilla Winthrop's gowns as " the black and white one," " the blue brocade," " the white china silk," as if no other black and white or blue brocade or white china silk gowns had been created in the world before and could not be made again by human hands. So, in the language of the inner sanctuary, there was " The Whist Club," to the exclusion of all other possible human Whist Clubs under the stars. When summer came the Whist Club fled as birds to the mountains—save Priscilla Winthrop, who went to Duxbury, and came home with a brass warming-pan and a set of Royal Copenhagen china that were set up as holy objects in the temple.

But Mrs. Worthington went to the National Federation of Women's Clubs, made the acquaintance of the women there who wore clothes from Paris, began tracing her ancestry back to the Maryland Calverts—on her mother's side of the house— brought home a membership in the Daughters of the Revolution, the Colonial Dames and a society which referred to Charles I. as " Charles Martyr," claimed a Stuart as the rightful king of England, affecting to score the impudence of King Edward in sitting on another's throne.   More than this, Mrs. Worthington had secured the promise of Mrs. Ellen Vail Montgomery, Vice-President of the National Federation, to visit Cliff Crest, as Mrs. Worthington called the Worthington mansion, and she turned up her nose at those who worshiped under the towers, turrets and minarets of the Conklin mosque, and played the hose of her ridicule on their outer wall that she might have it spotless for a target when she got ready to raze it with her big gun.

The week that Ellen Vail Montgomery came to town was a busy one for Miss Larrabee.   We turned over the whole fourth page of the paper to her for a daily society page, and charged the Bee Hive and the White Front Dry Goods store people double rates to put their special advertisements on that page while the " National Vice," as the Young Prince called her, was in town.   For the " National Vice " brought the State President and two State Vices down, also four District Presidents and six District Vices, who, as Miss Larrabee said, were monsters " of so frightful mien, that to be hated need but to be seen."   The entire delegation of visiting states- women—Vices and Virtues and Beatitudes as we called them—

were entertained by Mrs. Worthington at Cliff Crest, and there was so much Federation politics going on in our town that the New York *Sun* took five hundred words about it by wire, and Colonel Alphabetical Morrison said that with all those dressed-up women about he felt as though he was living in a Sunday supplement.

The third day of the ghost-dance at Cliff Crest was to be the day of the big event—as the office parlance had it. The ceremonies began at sunrise with a breakfast to which half a dozen of the captains and kings of the besieging host of the Pretender were bidden. It seems to have been a modest orgy, with nothing more astonishing than a new gold-band china set to dishearten the enemy. By ten o'clock Priscilla Winthrop and the Whist Club had recovered from that; but they had been asked to the luncheon—the star feature of the week's round of gayety. It is just as well to be frank, and say that they went with fear and trembling. Panic and terror were in their ranks, for they knew a crisis was at hand. It came when they were " ushered into the dining-hall," as our paper so grandly put it, and saw in the great oak-beamed room a table laid on the polished bare wood—a table laid for forty-eight guests, with a doily for every plate, and every glass, and every salt-cellar, and—here the mosque fell on the heads of the howling dervishes—forty-eight soup-spoons, forty-eight silver-handled knives and forks; forty-eight butter-spreaders, forty-eight spoons, forty-eight salad forks, forty-eight ice-cream spoons, forty-eight coffee spoons. Little did it avail the beleaguered party to peep slyly under the spoon-handles—the word " Sterling " was there, and, more than that, a large, severely plain " W " with a crest glared up at them from every piece of silver. The service had not been rented. They knew their case was hopeless. And so they ate in peace.

When the meal was over it was Mrs. Ellen Vail Montgomery, in her thousand-dollar gown, worshiped by the eyes of forty-eight women, who put her arm about Priscilla Winthrop and led her into the conservatory, where they had " a dear, sweet quarter of an hour," as Mrs. Montgomery afterward told her hostess. In that dear, sweet quarter of an hour Priscilla Winthrop Conklin unbuckled her social sword and handed it to the conqueror, in that she agreed absolutely with Mrs. Montgomery that Mrs. Worthington was " perfectly lovely," that she was " delighted to be of any service " to Mrs. Worthington; that Mrs. Conklin " was sure no one else in our town was so admirably qualified for National Vice " as Mrs. Worthington, and that " it would be such a privilege " for Mrs. Conklin to suggest Mrs. Worthington's name for the office. And then Mrs. Montgomery, " National Vice " and former State Secretary for Vermont of the Colonial Dames, kissed Priscilla Winthrop and they came forth wet-eyed and radiant, holding each other's hands. When the company had been hushed by the magic of a State Vice and two District Virtues, Priscilla Winthrop rose and in the sweetest Kansas Bostonese told the ladies that she thought this an eminently fitting place to let the visiting ladies know how dearly our town esteems its most distinguished townswoman, Mrs. Julia Neal Worthington, and that entirely without her solicitation, indeed quite without her knowledge, the women of our town—and she hoped of our beloved State—were ready now to announce that they were unanimous in their wish that Mrs. Worthington should be National Vice-President of the Federation of Women's Clubs, and that she, the speaker, had entered the contest with her whole soul to bring this end to pass. Then there was hand-clapping and handkerchief waving and some tears, and a little good, honest Irish hugging, and in the twilight two score of women filed down through the formal garden of Cliff Crest and walked by twos and threes in to the town.

There was the usual clatter of home-going wagons; lights winked out of kitchen windows; the tinkle of distant cow-bells was in the air; on Main Street the commerce of the town was gently ebbing, and man and nature seemed utterly oblivious of the great event that had happened. The course of human events was not changed; the great world rolled on, while Priscilla Winthrop went home to a broken shrine to sit among the the potsherds.

WILLIAM ALLEN WHITE

(Written by Mr. White especially for this book.)

I was born in Emporia, Kansas, February 10, 1868, when Emporia was a pioneer village a hundred miles from a railroad. My father came to Emporia in 1859 and my mother in 1855. She was a pioneer school teacher and he a pioneer doctor. She was pure bred Irish, and he of Yankee lineage since 1639. When I was a year old, Emporia became too effete for my parents, and they moved to El Dorado, Kansas. There I grew up. El Dorado was a town of a dozen houses, located on the banks of the Walnut, a sluggish, but a clear and beautiful prairie stream, rock bottom, and spring fed. I grew up in El Dorado, a prairie village boy; went to the large stone school house that " reared its awful form " on the hill above the town before there were any two-story buildings in the place.

In 1884, I was graduated from the town high school, and went to the College of Emporia for a year; worked a year as a printer's devil; learned something of the printer's trade; went to school for another year, working in the afternoons and Saturdays at the printer's case; became a reporter on the *Emporia News;* later went to the State University for three years. After more or less studying and working on the Lawrence papers, I went back to El Dorado as manager of the *El Dorado Republican* for State Senator T. B. Murdock.

From the *El Dorado Republican,* I went to Kansas City to work for the *Kansas City Journal,* and at 24 became an editorial writer on the *Kansas City Star.* For three years I worked on the *Star,* during which time I married Miss Sallie Lindsay, a Kansas City, Kansas, school teacher. In 1895 I bought the *Emporia Gazette* on credit, without a cent in money, and chiefly with the audacity and impudence of youth. It was then a little paper; I paid three thousand dollars for it, and I have lived in Emporia ever since.

In 1896, I published a book of short stories called *The Real Issue;* in 1899, another book of short stories called *The Court of Boyville.* In 1901, I published a third book of short stories called *Stratagems and Spoils;* in 1906, *In Our Town.* In 1909, I published my first novel, *A Certain Rich Man.* In 1910, I published a book of political essays called *The Old Order Changeth;* in 1916, a volume of short stories entitled *God's Puppets.* A volume half novel and half travel sketches called *The Martial Adventures of Henry & Me* filled the gap between my two novels; and the second novel, *In the Heart of a Fool* was published in 1918.

I am a member of the National Institute of Arts and Letters; the Short Ballot Association; the International Peace Society; National Civic Federation; National Academy of Political Science; have honorary degrees from the College of Emporia, Baker University, and Columbia University of the City of New York; was regent of the Kansas State University from 1905 to 1913. Politically I am a Republican and was elected National Republican Committeeman from Kansas in 1912, but resigned to be Progressive National Committeeman from Kansas that year. I am now a member of the Republican National Committee on Platforms and Policies appointed by the National Chairman, Will S. Hays. I am a trustee of the College of Emporia; a member of the Congregational Church, and of the Elks Lodge, and of no other organization.

WILLIAM ALLEN WHITE.

To the above biography a few items about Mr. White's literary work may be added. It was through an editorial that he first became famous. This appeared in the *Emporia Gazette* in 1896, with the title, " What's the matter with

Kansas? " It contained so much good sense, and was written in such vigorous English that it was copied in newspapers all over the country. Perhaps no other editorial ever brought such sudden recognition to its author. In the same year he published his first book, *The Real Issue,* a volume of short stories. Some of them pictured the life of a small town, some centered about politics, and some were stories of small boys. These three subjects were the themes of most of Mr. White's later books.

Stratagems and Spoils, a volume of short stories, dealt chiefly with politics, as seen from the inside. *In Our Town,* from which " The Passing of Priscilla Winthrop " is taken, belongs to the studies of small-town life. His first novel, *A Certain Rich Man,* was published in 1909. Its theme is the development of an American multi-millionaire, from his beginning as a small business man with a reputation for close dealing, his success, his reaching out to greater schemes, growing more and more unscrupulous in his methods, until at last he achieves the great wealth he had sought, but in winning it he loses his soul.

This book was written during a vacation in the Colorado mountains. His family were established in a log cabin, and he set up a tent near by for a workshop. This is his account of his method of writing:

My working day was supposed to begin at nine o'clock in the morning, but the truth is I seldom reached the tent before ten. Then it took me some time to get down to work. From then on until late in the afternoon I would sit at my typewriter, chew my tongue, and pound away. Each night I read to my wife what I had written that day, and Mrs. White would criticise it. While my work was redhot I couldn't get any perspective on it—each day's installment seemed to me the finest literature I had ever read. She didn't always agree with me. When she disapproved of anything I threw it away— after a row—and re-wrote it.

In his next book, *The Old Order Changeth,* Mr. White turned aside from fiction to write a series of papers dealing with various reform movements in our national life. He shows how through these much has been done to regain for the people the control of municipal and state affairs. The material for this book was drawn largely from Mr. White's participation in political affairs.

In 1917 he was sent to France as an observer by the American Red Cross. The lighter side of what he saw there was told in *The Martial Adventures of Henry and Me*. His latest book is a long novel, *In the Heart of a Fool*, another study of American life of to-day.

All in all, he stands as one of the chief interpreters in fiction of the spirit of the Middle West,—a section of our country which some observers say is the most truly American part of America.

A PAIR OF LOVERS

The typical love story begins by telling us how two young people fall in love, allows us to eavesdrop at a proposal, with soft moonlight effects, and then requests our presence at a wedding. Or perhaps an elopement precedes the wedding, which gives us an added thrill. The scene may be laid anywhere, the period may be the present or any time back to the Middle Ages, (apparently people did not fall in love at any earlier periods), but the formula remains the same. O. Henry wrote a love story that does not follow the formula. He called it " The Gift of the Magi."

THE GIFT OF THE MAGI

BY

O. HENRY

ONE dollar and eighty-seven cents. That was all. And sixty cents of it was in pennies. Pennies saved one and two at a time by bulldozing the grocer and the vegetable man and the butcher until one's cheeks burned with the silent imputation of parsimony that such close dealing implied. Three times Della counted it. One dollar and eighty-seven cents. And the next day would be Christmas.

There was clearly nothing to do but flop down on the shabby little couch and howl. So Della did it. Which instigates the moral reflection that life is made up of sobs, sniffles, and smiles, with sniffles predominating.

While the mistress of the house is gradually subsiding from the first stage to the second, take a look at the home. A furnished flat at $8 per week. It did not exactly beggar description, but it certainly had that word on the lookout for the mendicancy squad.

In the vestibule below was a letter-box into which no letter would go, and an electric button from which no mortal finger could coax a ring. Also appertaining thereunto was a card bearing the name " Mr. James Dillingham Young."

The " Dillingham " had been flung to the breeze during a former period of prosperity when its possessor was being paid $30 per week. Now, when the income was shrunk to $20, the letters of " Dillingham " looked blurred, as though they were thinking seriously of contracting to a modest and unassuming D. But whenever Mr. James Dillingham Young came home and reached his flat above he was called " Jim " and greatly hugged by Mrs. James Dillingham Young, already introduced to you as Della. Which is all very good.

Della finished her cry and attended to her cheeks with the powder rag. She stood by the window and looked out dully at a gray cat walking a gray fence in a gray backyard. To-morrow would be Christmas Day, and she had only $1.87 with which to buy Jim a present. She had been saving every penny she could for months, with this result. Twenty dollars a week doesn't go far. Expenses had been greater than she had calculated. They always are. Only $1.87 to buy a present for Jim. Her Jim. Many a happy hour she had spent planning for something nice for him. Something fine and rare and sterling—something just a little bit near to being worthy of the honor of being owned by Jim.

There was a pier-glass between the windows of the room. Perhaps you have seen a pier-glass in an $8 flat. A very thin and very agile person may, by observing his reflection in a rapid sequence of longitudinal strips, obtain a fairly accurate conception of his looks. Della, being slender, had mastered the art.

Suddenly she whirled from the window and stood before the glass. Her eyes were shining brilliantly, but her face had lost its color within twenty seconds. Rapidly she pulled down her hair and let it fall to its full length.

Now, there were two possessions of the James Dillingham Youngs in which they both took a mighty pride. One was Jim's gold watch that had been his father's and his grandfather's. The other was Della's hair. Had the Queen of Sheba lived in the flat across the airshaft, Della would have let her hair hang out the window some day to dry just to depreciate Her Majesty's jewels and gifts. Had King Solomon been the janitor, with all his treasures piled up in the basement, Jim would have pulled out his watch every time he passed, just to see him pluck at his beard from envy.

So now Della's beautiful hair fell about her, rippling and

shining like a cascade of brown waters. It reached below her knee and made itself almost a garment for her. And then she did it up again nervously and quickly. Once she faltered for a minute and stood still while a tear or two splashed on the worn red carpet.

On went her old brown jacket; on went her old brown hat. With a whirl of skirts and with the brilliant sparkle still in her eyes, she fluttered out the door and down the stairs to the street.

Where she stopped the sign read: "Mme. Sofronie. Hair Goods of All Kinds." One flight up Della ran, and collected herself, panting. Madame, large, too white, chilly, hardly looked the "Sofronie."

"Will you buy my hair?" asked Della.

"I buy hair," said Madame. "Take yer hat off and let's have a sight at the looks of it."

Down rippled the brown cascade.

"Twenty dollars," said Madame, lifting the mass with a practised hand.

"Give it to me quick," said Della.

Oh, and the next two hours tripped by on rosy wings. Forget the hashed metaphor. She was ransacking the stores for Jim's present.

She found it at last. It surely had been made for Jim and no one else. There was no other like it in any of the stores, and she had turned all of them inside out. It was a platinum fob chain, simple and chaste in design, properly proclaiming its value by substance and not by meretricious ornamentation —as all good things should do. It was even worthy of The Watch.

As soon as she saw it she knew that it must be Jim's. It was like him. Quietness and value—the description applied to both. Twenty-one dollars they took from her for it, and she hurried home with the 87 cents. With that chain on his watch Jim might be properly anxious about the time in any company. Grand as the watch was, he sometimes looked at it on the sly on account of the old leather strap that he used in place of a chain.

When Della reached home her intoxication gave way a little to prudence and reason. She got out her curling irons and lighted the gas and went to work repairing the ravages made by generosity added to love. Which is always a tremendous task, dear friends—a mammoth task.

Within forty minutes her head was covered with tiny, close-lying curls that made her look wonderfully like a truant schoolboy. She looked at her reflection in the mirror long, carefully, and critically.

"If Jim doesn't kill me," she said to herself, "before he takes a second look at me, he'll say I look like a Coney Island chorus girl. But what could I do—oh! what could I do with a dollar and eighty-seven cents?"

At seven o'clock the coffee was made and the frying-pan was on the back of the stove hot and ready to cook the chops.

Jim was never late. Della doubled the fob chain in her hand and sat on the corner of the table near the door that he always entered. Then she heard his step on the stair away down on the first flight and she turned white for just a moment. She had a habit of saying little silent prayers about the simplest everyday things, and now she whispered:

"Please God, make him think I am still pretty."

The door opened and Jim stepped in and closed it. He looked thin and very serious. Poor fellow, he was only twenty-two—and to be burdened with a family! He needed a new overcoat and he was without gloves.

Jim stopped inside the door, as immovable as a setter at the scent of quail. His eyes were fixed upon Della, and there was an expression in them that she could not read, and it terrified her. It was not anger, nor surprise, nor disapproval, nor horror, nor any of the sentiments that she had been prepared for. He simply stared at her fixedly with that peculiar expression on his face.

Della wriggled off the table and went to him.

" Jim, darling," she cried, " don't look at me that way. I had my hair cut off and sold it because I couldn't have lived through Christmas without giving you a present. It'll grow out again—you won't mind, will you? I just had to do it. My hair grows awfully fast. Say ' Merry Christmas! ' Jim, and let's be happy. You don't know what a nice—what a beautiful, nice gift I've got for you."

" You've cut off your hair? " asked Jim, laboriously, as if he had not arrived at that patent fact yet even after the hardest mental labor.

" Cut it off and sold it," said Della. " Don't you like me just as well, anyhow? I'm me without my hair, ain't I? "

Jim looked about the room curiously.

" You say your hair is gone? " he said, with an air almost of idiocy.

" You needn't look for it," said Della. " It's sold, I tell you—sold and gone, too. It's Christmas Eve, boy. Be good to me, for it went for you. Maybe the hairs of my head were numbered," she went on with a sudden serious sweetness, " but nobody could ever count my love for you. Shall I put the chops on, Jim? "

Out of his trance Jim seemed quickly to awake. He enfolded his Della. For ten seconds let us regard with discreet scrutiny some inconsequential object in the other direction. Eight dollars a week or a million a year—what is the difference? A mathematician or a wit would give you the wrong answer. The magi brought valuable gifts, but that was not among them. This dark assertion will be illuminated later on.

Jim drew a package from his overcoat pocket and threw it upon the table.

" Don't make any mistake, Dell," he said, " about me. I don't think there's anything in the way of a haircut or a shave or a shampoo that could make me like my girl any less. But if you'll unwrap that package you may see why you had me going a while at first."

White fingers and nimble tore at the string and paper. And then an ecstatic scream of joy; and then, alas! a quick feminine change to hysterical tears and wails, necessitating the immediate employment of all the comforting powers of the lord of the flat.

For there lay The combs—the set of combs, side and back, that Della had worshipped for long in a Broadway window. Beautiful combs, pure tortoise shell, with jewelled rims—just the shade to wear in the beautiful vanished hair. They were expensive combs, she knew, and her heart had simply craved and yearned over them without the least hope of possession. And now, they were hers, but the tresses that should have adorned the coveted adornments were gone.

But she hugged them to her bosom, and at length she was able to look up with dim eyes and a smile and say: " My hair grows so fast, Jim! "

And then Della leaped up like a little singed cat and cried, " Oh, oh! "

Jim had not yet seen his beautiful present. She held it out to him eagerly upon her open palm. The dull precious metal seemed to flash with reflection of her bright and ardent spirit.

" Isn't it a dandy, Jim? I hunted all over town to find it. You'll have to look at the time a hundred times a day now. Give me your watch. I want to see how it looks on it."

Instead of obeying, Jim tumbled down on the couch and put his hands under the back of his head and smiled.

" Dell," said he, " let's put our Christmas presents away and keep 'em a while. They're too nice to use just at present. I sold the watch to get the money to buy your combs. And now suppose you put the chops on."

The magi, as you know, were wise men—wonderfully wise men—who brought gifts to the Babe in the manger. They invented the art of giving Christmas presents. Being wise, their gifts were no doubt wise ones, possibly bearing the privilege of exchange in case of duplication. And here I have lamely related to you the uneventful chronicle of two foolish children in a flat who most unwisely sacrificed for each other the greatest treasures of their house. But in a last word to the wise of these days let it be said that of all who give gifts these two were the wisest. Of all who give and receive gifts, such as they are wisest. Everywhere they are wisest. They are the magi.

O. HENRY

He came to New York in 1902 almost unknown. At his death eight years later he was the best known writer of short stories in America. His life was as full of ups and downs, and of strange turns of fortune, as one of his own stories. William Sidney Porter, who always signed his stories as O. Henry, was born in Greenboro, North Carolina, September 11, 1862. His mother died when he was but three years old; and an aunt, Miss Evelina Porter, cared for him and gave him nearly all his education. Books, too, were his teachers. He says that between his thirteenth and nineteenth years he did more reading than in all the years since. His favorite books were *The Arabian Nights,* in Lane's translation, and Burton's *Anatomy of Melancholy,* an old English book in which bits of science, superstition and reflections upon life were strangely mingled. Other books that he enjoyed were the works of Scott, Dickens, Thackeray, Victor Hugo and Alexandre Dumas. He early showed ability as a cartoonist, and was noted among his friends as a good story teller. After school days he became a clerk in his uncle's drug store, and here acquired that knowledge which he used to such good effect in stories like " Makes the Whole World Kin " and " The Love Philtre of Ikey Schoenstein."

His health was not robust, and confinement in a drug store did not improve it. A friend who was going to Texas invited him to go along, and from 1882 to 1884 he lived on a ranch, acting as cowboy, and at odd moments studying French, German and Spanish. Then he went to Austin, where at various times he was clerk, editor, bookkeeper, draftsman, bank teller, actor and cartoonist. In 1887 he married Miss Athol Roach. He began contributing short stories and humorous sketches to newspapers, and finally purchased a paper of his own, which he called *Rolling Stones*, a humorous weekly. After a year the paper failed, and the editor went to Houston to become a reporter on the *Daily Post*. A year later, it was discovered that there were serious irregularities in the bank in which he had worked in Austin. Several arrests were made, and O. Henry was called to stand trial with others. He had not been guilty of wrong doing, but the affairs of the bank had been so loosely managed that he was afraid that he would be convicted, so he fled to Central America. After a year there, he heard that his wife's health was failing, and returned to Austin to give himself up. He was found guilty, and sentenced to five years in the Ohio penitentiary. His wife died before the trial. His time in prison was shortened by good behavior to a little more than three years, ending in 1901. He wrote a number of stories during this time, sending them to friends who in turn mailed them to publishers. The editor of *Ainslie's Magazine* had printed several of them and in 1902 he wrote to O. Henry urging him to come to New York, and offering him a hundred dollars apiece for a dozen stories. He came, and from that time made New York his home, becoming very fond of Little Old-Bagdad-on-the-Subway as he called it.

He had found the work which he wished to do, and he turned out stories very rapidly. These were first published in newspapers and magazines, then collected in book form. The first of these volumes, *Cabbages and Kings*, had Central America as its setting. He said that while there he had knocked around chiefly with refugees and consuls. *The Four Million* was a group of stories of New York; it contained some of his best tales, such as " The Gift of the Magi," and " An Unfinished Story." *The Trimmed Lamp* and *The Voice of the City* also dealt with New York. *The Gentle Grafter* was a collection of stories about confidence men and " crooks." The material for these narratives he had gathered from his companions in his prison days. *Heart of the West* reflects his days on a

Texas ranch. Other books, more or less miscellaneous in their locality, are *Roads of Destiny, Options, Strictly Business, Whirligigs;* and *Sixes and Sevens.* He died in New York, June 5, 1910. After his death a volume containing some of his earliest work was published under the title *Rolling Stones.*

His choice of subjects is thus indicated in the preface to *The Four Million:*

"Not very long ago some one invented the assertion that there were only 'Four Hundred' people in New York who were really worth noticing. But a wiser man has arisen—the census taker—and his larger estimate of human interest has been preferred in marking out the field of these little stories of the 'Four Million.'"

It was the common man,—the clerk, the bartender, the policeman, the waiter, the tramp, that O. Henry chose for his characters. He loved to talk to chance acquaintances on park benches or in cheap lodging houses, to see life from their point of view. His stories are often of the picaresque type; a name given to a kind of story in which the hero is an adventurer, sometimes a rogue. He sees the common humanity, and the redeeming traits even in these. His plots usually have a turn of surprise at the end; sometimes the very last sentence suddenly illuminates the whole story. His style is quick, nervous, often slangy; he is wonderfully dextrous in hitting just the right word or phrase. His descriptions are notable for telling much in a few words. He has almost established a definite type of short story writing, and in many of the stories now written one may clearly see the influence of O. Henry.

IN POLITICS

Politics is democracy in action. If we believe in democracy, we must recognize in politics the instrument, however imperfect, through which democracy works. Brand Whitlock knew politics, first as a political reporter, then as candidate for mayor in four campaigns, in each of which he was successful. Under his administration the city of Toledo became a better place to live in. In THE GOLD BRICK *he describes a municipal campaign, as seen from the point of view of the newspaper office.*

THE GOLD BRICK

BY

BRAND WHITLOCK

TEN thousand dollars a year! Neil Kittrell left the office of the *Morning Telegraph* in a daze. He was insensible of the raw February air, heedless of sloppy pavements, the gray day had suddenly turned gold. He could not realize it all at once; ten thousand a year—for him and Edith! His heart swelled with love of Edith, she had sacrificed so much to become the wife of a man who had tried to make an artist of himself, and of whom fate, or economic determinism, or something, had made a cartoonist. What a surprise for her! He must hurry home.

In this swelling of his heart he felt a love not only of Edith but of the whole world. The people he met seemed dear to him; he felt friendly with every one, and beamed on perfect strangers with broad, cheerful smiles. He stopped to buy some flowers for Edith—daffodils, or tulips, which promised spring, and he took the daffodils, because the girl said:

"I think yellow is such a spirituelle color, don't you?" and inclined her head in a most artistic manner.

But daffodils, after all, which would have been much the day before, seemed insufficient in the light of new prosperity, and Kittrell bought a large azalea, beautiful in its graceful spread of pink blooms.

"Where shall I send it?" asked the girl, whose cheeks were as pink as azaleas themselves.

"I think I'll call a cab and take it to her myself," said Kittrell.

And she sighed over the romance of this rich young gentleman

and the girl of the azalea, who, no doubt, was as beautiful as
the young woman who was playing *Lottie, the Poor Saleslady*
at the Lyceum that very week.

Kittrell and the azalea bowled along Claybourne Avenue; he
leaned back on the cushions, and adopted the expression of
ennui appropriate to that thoroughfare. Would Edith now
prefer Claybourne Avenue? With ten thousand a year they
could, perhaps—and yet, at first it would be best not to put
on airs, but to go right on as they were, in the flat. Then the
thought came to him that now, as the cartoonist on the *Telegraph,* his name would become as well known in Claybourne
Avenue as it had been in the homes of the poor and humble
during his years on the *Post.* And his thoughts flew to those
homes where tired men at evening looked for his cartoons and
children laughed at his funny pictures. It gave him a pang;
he had felt a subtle bond between himself and all those thousands who read the *Post.* It was hard to leave them. The *Post*
might be yellow, but as the girl had said, yellow was a spiritual color, and the *Post* brought something into their lives—
lives that were scorned by the *Telegraph* and by these people on
the avenue. Could he make new friends here where the cartoons
he drew and the *Post* that printed them had been contemned,
if not despised? His mind flew back to the dingy office of
the *Post*; to the boys there, the whole good-natured, happy-
go-lucky gang; and to Hardy—ah, Hardy!— who had been so
good to him, and given him his big chance, had taken such pains
and interest, helping him with ideas and suggestions, criticism
and sympathy. To tell Hardy that he was going to leave him,
here on the eve of the campaign—and Clayton, the mayor, he
would have to tell him, too—oh, the devil! Why must he
think of these things now?

After all, when he had reached home, and had run up-stairs
with the news and the azalea, Edith did not seem delighted.

" But, dearie, business is business," he urged, " and we need
the money! "

" Yes, I know; doubtless you're right. Only please don't say ' business is business;' it isn't like you, and—"

" But think what it will mean—ten thousand a year! "

" Oh, Neil, I've lived on ten thousand a year before, and I never had half the fun that I had when we were getting along on twelve hundred."

" Yes, but then we were always dreaming of the day when I'd make a lot; we lived on that hope, didn't we? "

Edith laughed. " You used to say we lived on love."

" You're not serious." He turned to gaze moodily out of the window. And then she left the azalea, and perched on the flat arm of his chair.

" Dearest," she said, " I am serious. I know all this means to you. We're human, and we don't like to ' chip at crusts like Hindus,' even for the sake of youth and art. I never had illusions about love in a cottage and all that. Only, dear, I have been happy, so very happy, with you, because—well, because I was living in an atmosphere of honest purpose, honest ambition, and honest desire to do some good thing in the world. I had never known such an atmosphere before. At home, you know, father and Uncle James and the boys—well, it was all money, money, money with them, and they couldn't understand why I—"

" Could marry a poor newspaper artist? That's just the point."

She put her hand to his lips.

" Now, dear! If they couldn't understand, so much the worse for them. If they thought it meant sacrifice to me, they were mistaken. I have been happy in this little flat; only—" she leaned back and inclined her head with her eyes asquint— " only the paper in this room is atrocious; it's a typical landlord's selection—McGaw picked it out. You see what it means to be merely rich."

She was so pretty thus that he kissed her, and then she went on:

" And so, dear, if I didn't seem to be as impressed and delighted as you hoped to find me, it is because I was thinking
of Mr. Hardy and the poor, dear common little *Post*, and
then— of Mr. Clayton. Did you think of him? "

" Yes."

" You'll have to—to cartoon him? "

" I suppose so."

The fact he had not allowed himself to face was close to
both of them, and the subject was dropped until, just as he
was going down-town—this time to break the news to Hardy—
he went into the room he sarcastically said he might begin to
call his studio, now that he was getting ten thousand a year,
to look for a sketch he had promised Nolan for the sporting
page. And there on his drawing-board was an unfinished cartoon, a drawing of the strong face of John Clayton. He had
begun it a few days before to use on the occasion of Clayton's
renomination. It had been a labor of love, and Kittrell suddenly realized how good it was. He had put into it all of his
belief in Clayton, all of his devotion to the cause for which
Clayton toiled and sacrificed, and in the simple lines he experienced the artist's ineffable felicity; he had shown how
good, how noble, how true a man Clayton was. All at once
he realized the sensation the cartoon would produce, how it
would delight and hearten Clayton's followers, how it would
please Hardy, and how it would touch Clayton. It would be
a tribute to the man and the friendship, but now a tribute
broken, unfinished. Kittrell gazed a moment longer, and in
that moment Edith came.

" The dear, beautiful soul! " she exclaimed softly. " Neil,
it is wonderful. It is not a cartoon; it is a portrait. It shows
what you might do with a brush."

Kittrell could not speak, and he turned the drawing-board
to the wall.

When he had gone, Edith sat and thought—of Neil, of the
new position, of Clayton. He had loved Neil, and been so proud

of his work; he had shown a frank, naive pleasure in the cartoons Neil had made of him. That last time he was there,
thought Edith, he had said that without Neil the " good old
cause," as he called it, using Whitman's phrase, could never
have triumphed in that town. And now, would he come again?
Would he ever stand in that room and, with his big, hearty
laugh, clasp an arm around Neil's shoulder, or speak of her
in his good friendly way as "the little woman? " Would he
come now, in the terrible days of the approaching campaign,
for rest and sympathy—come as he used to come in other
campaigns, worn and weary from all the brutal opposition,
the vilification and abuse and mud-slinging? She closed her
eyes. She could not think that far.

Kittrell found the task of telling Hardy just as difficult as
he expected it to be, but by some mercy it did not last long.
Explanation had not been necessary; he had only to make the
first hesitating approaches, and Hardy understood. Hardy
was, in a way, hurt; Kittrell saw that, and rushed to his own
defense:

" I hate to go, old man. I don't like it a little bit—but,
you know, business is business, and we need the money."

He even tried to laugh as he advanced this last conclusive
reason, and Hardy, for all he showed in voice or phrase, may
have agreed with him.

" It's all right, Kit," he said. " I'm sorry; I wish we could
pay you more, but—well, good luck."

That was all. Kittrell gathered up the few articles he had
at the office, gave Nolan his sketch, bade the boys good-by—
bade them good-by as if he were going on a long journey,
never to see them more—and then he went.

After he had made the break it did not seem so bad as
he had anticipated. At first things went on smoothly enough.
The campaign had not opened, and he was free to exercise his
talents outside the political field. He drew cartoons dealing
with banal subjects, touching with the gentle satire of his

humorous pencil foibles which all the world agreed about, and let vital questions alone. And he and Edith enjoyed themselves: indulged oftener in things they loved; went more frequently to the theater; appeared at recitals; dined now and then downtown. They began to realize certain luxuries they had not known for a long time—some he himself had never known, some that Edith had not known since she left her father's home to become his bride. In more subtle ways, too, Kittrell felt the change: there was a sense of larger leisure; the future beamed with a broader and brighter light; he formed plans, among which the old dream of going ere long to Paris for serious study took its dignified place. And then there was the sensation his change had created in the newspaper world; that the cartoons signed "Kit," which formerly appeared in the *Post*, should now adorn the broad page of the *Telegraph* was a thing to talk about at the press club; the fact of his large salary got abroad in that little world as well, and, after the way of that world, managed to exaggerate itself, as most facts did. He began to be sensible of attentions from men of prominence—small things, mere nods in the street, perhaps, or smiles in the theater foyer, but enough to show that they recognized him. What those children of the people, those working-men and women who used to be his unknown and admiring friends in the old days on the *Post*, thought of him— whether they missed him, whether they deplored his change as an apostasy or applauded it as a promotion—he did not know. He did not like to think about it.

But March came, and the politicians began to bluster like the season. Late one afternoon he was on his way to the office with a cartoon, the first in which he had seriously to attack Clayton. Benson, the managing editor of the *Telegraph*, had conceived it, and Kittrell had worked on it that day in sickness of heart. Every line of this new presentation of Clayton had cut him like some biting acid; but he had worked on, trying to reassure himself with the argument that he was a mere agent, devoid of personal responsibility. But it had been hard, and when Edith, after her custom, had asked to see it, he had said:

" Oh, you don't want to see it; it's no good."

" Is it of—him? " she had asked.

And when he nodded she had gone away without another word. Now, as he hurried through the crowded streets, he was conscious that it was no good indeed; and he was divided between the artist's regret and the friend's joy in the fact. But it made him tremble. Was his hand to forget its cunning? And then, suddenly, he heard a familiar voice, and there beside him, with his hand on his shoulder, stood the mayor.

" Why, Neil, my boy, how are you? " he said, and he took Kittrell's hand as warmly as ever. For a moment Kittrell was relieved, and then his heart sank; for he had a quick realization that it was the coward within him that felt the relief, and the man the sickness. If Clayton had reproached him, or cut him, it would have made it easier; but Clayton did none of these things, and Kittrell was irresistibly drawn to the subject himself.

" You heard of my—new job? " he asked.

" Yes," said Clayton, " I heard."

" Well—" Kittrell began.

" I'm sorry," Clayton said.

" So was I," Kittrell hastened to say. " But I felt it—well, a duty, some way—to Edith. You know—we—need the money." And he gave the cynical laugh that went with the argument.

" What does *she* think? Does she feel that way about it? "

Kittrell laughed, not cynically now, but uneasily and with embarrassment, for Clayton's blue eyes were on him, those eyes that could look into men and understand them so.

" Of course you know," Kittrell went on nervously, " there is nothing personal in this. We newspaper fellows simply do what we are told; we obey orders like soldiers, you know.

With the policy of the paper we have nothing to do. Just like Dick Jennings, who was a red-hot free-trader and used to write free-trade editorials for the *Times*—he went over to the *Telegraph,* you remember, and writes all those protection arguments."

The mayor did not seem to be interested in Dick Jennings, or in the ethics of his profession.

" Of course, you know I'm for you, Mr. Clayton, just exactly as I've always been. I'm going to vote for you."

This did not seem to interest the mayor, either.

" And, maybe, you know—I thought, perhaps," he snatched at this bright new idea that had come to him just in the nick of time; " that I might help you by my cartoons in the *Telegraph;* that is, I might keep them from being as bad as they might—"

" But that wouldn't be dealing fairly with your new employers, Neil," the mayor said.

Kittrell was making more and more a mess of this whole miserable business, and he was basely glad when they reached the corner.

" Well, good-by, my boy," said the mayor, as they parted. " Remember me to the little woman."

Kittrell watched him as he went on down the avenue, swinging along in his free way, the broad felt hat he wore riding above all the other hats in the throng that filled the sidewalk; and Kittrell sighed in deep depression.

When he turned in his cartoon, Benson scanned it a moment, cocked his head this side and that, puffed his briar pipe, and finally said:

" I'm afraid this is hardly up to you. This figure of Clayton, here—it hasn't got the stuff in it. You want to show him as he *is*. We want the people to know what a four-flushing, hypocritical, demagogical blatherskite he is—with all his rot about the people and their damned rights! "

Benson was all unconscious of the inconsistency of having

concern for a people he so despised, and Kittrell did not observe it, either. He was on the point of defending Clayton, but he restrained himself and listened to Benson's suggestions. He remained at the office for two hours, trying to change the cartoon to Benson's satisfaction, with a growing hatred of the work and a disgust with himself that now and then almost drove him to mad destruction. He felt like splashing the piece with India ink, or ripping it with his knife. But he worked on, and submitted it again. He had failed, of course; failed to express in it that hatred of a class which Benson unconsciously disguised as a hatred of Clayton, a hatred which Kittrell could not express because he did not feel it; and he failed because art deserts her devotees when they are false to truth.

"Well, it'll have to do," said Benson, as he looked it over; "but let's have a little more to the next one. Damn it! I wish I could draw. I'd cartoon the crook!"

In default of which ability, Benson set himself to write one of those savage editorials in which he poured out on Clayton that venom of which he seemed to have such an inexhaustible supply.

But on one point Benson was right: Kittrell was not up to himself. As the campaign opened, as the city was swept with the excitement of it, with meetings at noon-day and at night, office-seekers flying about in automobiles, walls covered with pictures of candidates, hand-bills scattered in the streets to swirl in the wild March winds, and men quarreling over whether Clayton or Ellsworth should be mayor, Kittrell had to draw a political cartoon each day; and as he struggled with his work, less and less the old joy came to cheer and spur him on. To read the ridicule, the abuse, which the *Telegraph* heaped on Clayton, the distortion of facts concerning his candidature, the unfair reports of his meetings, sickened him, and more than all, he was filled with disgust as he tried to match in caricature these libels of the man he so loved and honored. It was bad enough to have to flatter Clayton's opponent, to picture him as a noble, disinterested character, ready to sacrifice himself for the public weal. Into his pictures of this man, attired in the long black coat of conventional respectability, with the smug face of pharisaism, he could get nothing but cant and hypocrisy; but in his caricatures of Clayton there was that which pained him worse—disloyalty, untruth, and now and then, to the discerning few who knew the tragedy of Kittrell's soul, there was pity. And thus his work declined in value; lacking all sincerity, all faith in itself or its purpose, it became false, uncertain, full of jarring notes, and, in short, never once rang true. As for Edith, she never discussed his work now; she spoke of the campaign little, and yet he knew she was deeply concerned, and she grew hot with resentment at the methods of the *Telegraph*. Her only consolation was derived from the *Post*, which of course, supported Clayton; and the final drop of bitterness in Kittrell's cup came one evening when he realized that she was following with sympathetic interest the cartoons in that paper.

For the *Post* had a new cartoonist, Banks, a boy whom Hardy had picked up somewhere and was training to the work Kittrell had laid down. To Kittrell there was a cruel fascination in the progress Banks was making; he watched it with a critical, professional eye, at first with amusement, then with surprise, and now at last, in the discovery of Edith's interest, with a keen jealousy of which he was ashamed. The boy was crude and untrained; his work was not to be compared with Kittrell's, master of line that he was, but Kittrell saw that it had the thing his work now lacked, the vital, primal thing—sincerity, belief, love. The spark was there, and Kittrell knew how Hardy would nurse that spark and fan it, and keep it alive and burning until it should eventually blaze up in a fine white flame. And Kittrell realized, as the days went by, that Banks' work was telling, and that his own was failing. He had, from the first missed the atmosphere of the *Post*, missed the *camaraderie* of the congenial spirits there, animated by a common purpose, inspired and led by Hardy, whom they all loved—loved as he himself once loved him, loved as he loved him still—and dared not look him in the face when they met!

He found the atmosphere of the *Telegraph* alien and distasteful. There all was different; the men had little joy in their work, little interest in it, save perhaps the newspaper man's inborn love of a good story or a beat. They were all cynical, without loyalty or faith; they secretly made fun of the *Telegraph*, of its editors and owners; they had no belief in its cause; and its pretensions to respectability, its parade of virtue, excited only their derision. And slowly it began to dawn on Kittrell that the great moral law worked always and everywhere, even on newspapers, and that there was reflected inevitably and logically in the work of the men on that staff the hatred, the lack of principle, the bigotry and intolerance of its proprietors; and this same lack of principle tainted and made meretricious his own work, and enervated the editorials so that the *Telegraph*, no matter how carefully edited or how dignified in typographical appearance, was, nevertheless, without real influence in the community.

Meanwhile Clayton was gaining ground. It was less than two weeks before election. The campaign waxed more and more bitter, and as the forces opposed to him foresaw defeat, they became ugly in spirit, and desperate. The *Telegraph* took on a tone more menacing and brutal, and Kittrell knew that the crisis had come. The might of the powers massed against Clayton appalled Kittrell; they thundered at him through many brazen mouths, but Clayton held on his high way unperturbed. He was speaking by day and night to thousands. Such meetings he had never had before. Kittrell had visions of him before those immense audiences in halls, in tents, in the raw open air of that rude March weather, making his appeals to the heart of the great mass. A fine, splendid, romantic figure he was, striking to the imagination, this champion of the people's cause, and Kittrell longed for the lost chance. Oh, for one day on the *Post* now!

One morning at breakfast, as Edith read the *Telegraph,* Kittrell saw the tears well slowly in her brown eyes.

" Oh," she said, " it is shameful! " She clenched her little fists. " Oh, if I were only a man I'd—" She could not in her impotent feminine rage say what she would do; she could only grind her teeth. Kittrell bent his head over his plate; his coffee choked him.

" Dearest," she said presently, in another tone, " tell me, how is he? Do you—ever see him? Will he win? "

" No, I never see him. But he'll win; I wouldn't worry."

" He used to come here," she went on, " to rest a moment, to escape from all this hateful confusion and strife. He is killing himself! And they aren't worth it—those ignorant people—they aren't worth such sacrifices."

He got up from the table and turned away, and then realizing quickly, she flew to his side and put her arms about his neck and said:

" Forgive me, dearest, I didn't mean—only—"

" Oh, Edith," he said, " this is killing me. I feel like a dog."

" Don't dear; he is big enough, and good enough; he will understand."

" Yes; that only makes it harder, only makes it hurt the more."

That afternoon, in the car, he heard no talk but of the election; and down-town, in a cigar store where he stopped for cigarettes, he heard some men talking mysteriously, in the hollow voice of rumor, of some sensation, some scandal. It alarmed him, and as he went into the office he met Manning, the *Telegraph's* political man.

" Tell me, Manning," Kittrell said, " how does it look? "

" Damn bad for us."

" For us? "

" Well, for our mob of burglars and second story workers

here—the gang we represent." He took a cigarette from the box Kittrell was opening.

" And will he win? "

" Will he win? " said Manning, exhaling the words on the thin level stream of smoke that came from his lungs. " Will he win? In a walk, I tell you. He's got 'em beat to a standstill right now. That's the dope."

" But what about this story of—"

" Aw, that's all a pipe-dream of Burns'. I'm running it in the morning, but it's nothing; it's a shine. They're big fools to print it at all. But it's their last card; they're desperate. They won't stop at anything, or at any crime, except those requiring courage. Burns is in there with Benson now; so is Salton, and old man Glenn, and the rest of the bunco family. They're framing it up. When I saw old Glenn go in, with his white side-whiskers, I knew the widow and the orphan were in danger again, and that he was going bravely to the front for 'em. Say, that young Banks is comin', isn't he? That's a peach, that cartoon of his to-night."

Kittrell went on down the hall to the art-room to wait until Benson should be free. But it was not long until he was sent for, and as he entered the managing editor's room he was instantly sensible of the somber atmosphere of a grave and solemn council of war. Benson introduced him to Glenn, the banker, to Salton, the party boss, and to Burns, the president of the street-car company; and as Kittrell sat down he looked about him, and could scarcely repress a smile as he recalled Manning's estimate of Glenn. The old man sat there, as solemn and unctuous as ever he had in his pew at church. Benson, red of face, was more plainly perturbed, but Salton was as reserved, as immobile, as inscrutable as ever, his narrow, pointed face, with its vulpine expression, being perhaps paler than usual. Benson had on his desk before him the cartoon Kittrell had finished that day.

" Mr. Kittrell," Benson began, " we've been talking over the political situation, and I was showing these gentlemen this cartoon. It isn't, I fear, in your best style; it lacks the force, the argument, we'd like just at this time. That isn't the *Telegraph* Clayton, Mr. Kittrell." He pointed with the amber stem of his pipe. "Not at all. Clayton is a strong, smart, unscrupulous, dangerous man! We've reached a crisis in this campaign; if we can't turn things in the next three days, we're lost, that's all; we might as well face it. To-morrow we make an important revelation concerning the character of Clayton, and we want to follow it up the morning after by a cartoon that will be a stunner, a clencher. We have discussed it here among ourselves, and this is our idea."

Benson drew a crude, bald outline, indicating the cartoon they wished Kittrell to draw. The idea was so coarse, so brutal, so revolting, that Kittrell stood aghast, and, as he stood, he was aware of Salton's little eyes fixed on him. Benson waited; they all waited.

"Well," said Benson, "what do you think of it?"

Kittrell paused an instant, and then said:

"I won't draw it; that's what I think of it."

Benson flushed angrily and looked up at him.

"We are paying you a very large salary, Mr. Kittrell, and your work, if you will pardon me, has not been up to what we were led to expect."

"You are quite right, Mr. Benson, but I can't draw that cartoon."

"Well, great God!" yelled Burns, "what have we got here— a gold brick?" He rose with a vivid sneer on his red face, plunged his hands in his pockets, and took two or three nervous strides across the room. Kittrell looked at him, and slowly his eyes blazed out of a face that had gone white on the instant.

"What did you say, sir?" he demanded.

Burns thrust his red face, with its prognathic jaw, menacingly toward Kittrell.

"I said that in you we'd got a gold brick."

"You?" said Kittrell. "What have you to do with it? I don't work for you."

"You don't? Well, I guess it's us that puts up—"

"Gentlemen! Gentlemen!" said Glenn, waving a white, pacificatory hand.

"Yes, let me deal with this, if you please," said Benson, looking hard at Burns. The street-car man sneered again, then, in ostentatious contempt, looked out the window. And in the stillness Benson continued:

"Mr. Kittrell, think a minute. Is your decision final?"

"It is final, Mr. Benson," said Kittrell. "And as for you, Burns," he glared angrily at the man, "I wouldn't draw that cartoon for all the dirty money that all the bribing street-car companies in the world could put into Mr. Glenn's bank here. Good evening, gentlemen."

It was not until he stood again in his own home that Kittrell felt the physical effects which the spiritual squalor of such a scene was certain to produce in a nature like his.

"Neil! What is the matter?" Edith fluttered toward him in alarm.

He sank into a chair, and for a moment he looked as if he would faint, but he looked wanly up at her and said:

"Nothing; I'm all right; just a little weak. I've gone through a sickening, horrible scene—"

"Dearest!"

"And I'm off the *Telegraph*—and a man once more!"

He bent over, with his elbows on his knees, his head in his hands, and when Edith put her calm, caressing hand on his brow, she found that it was moist from nervousness. Presently he was able to tell her the whole story.

"It was, after all, Edith, a fitting conclusion to my experience on the *Telegraph*. I suppose, though, that to people who are used to ten thousand a year such scenes are nothing at all." She saw in this trace of his old humor that he was himself again, and she hugged his head to her bosom.

"Oh, dearest," she said, "I'm proud of you—and happy again."

They were, indeed, both happy, happier than they had been in weeks.

The next morning after breakfast, she saw by his manner, by the humorous, almost comical expression about his eyes, that he had an idea. In this mood of satisfaction—this mood that comes too seldom in the artist's life—she knew it was wise to let him alone. And he lighted his pipe and went to work. She heard him now and then, singing or whistling or humming; she scented his pipe, then cigarettes; then, at last, after two hours, he called in a loud, triumphant tone:

"Oh, Edith!"

She was at the door in an instant, and, waving his hand grandly at his drawing-board, he turned to her with that expression which connotes the greatest joy gods or mortals can know—the joy of beholding one's own work and finding it good. He had, as she saw, returned to the cartoon of Clayton he had laid aside when the tempter came; and now it was finished. Its simple lines revealed Clayton's character, as the sufficient answer to all the charges the *Telegraph* might make against him. Edith leaned against the door and looked long and critically.

"It was fine before," she said presently; "it's better now. Before it was a portrait of the man; this shows his soul."

"Well, it's how he looks to me," said Neil, "after a month in which to appreciate him."

"But what," she said, stooping and peering at the edge of the drawing, where, despite much knife-scraping, vague figures appeared, "what's that?"

"Oh, I'm ashamed to tell you," he said. "I'll have to paste over that before it's electrotyped. You see, I had a notion of putting in the gang, and I drew four little figures—Benson,

Burns, Salton and Glenn; they were plotting—oh, it was foolish and unworthy. I decided I didn't want anything of hatred in it—just as he wouldn't want anything of hatred in it; so I rubbed them out."

" Well, I'm glad. It is beautiful; it makes up for everything; it's an appreciation—worthy of the man."

When Kittrell entered the office of the *Post*, the boys greeted him with delight, and his presence made a sensation, for there had been rumors of the break which the absence of a " Kit " cartoon in the *Telegraph* that morning had confirmed. But, if Hardy was surprised, his surprise was swallowed up in his joy, and Kittrell was grateful to him for the delicacy with which he touched the subject that consumed the newspaper and political world with curiosity.

" I'm glad, Kit," was all that he said. " You know that."

Then he forgot everything in the cartoon, and he showed his instant recognition of its significance by snatching out his watch, pushing a button, and saying to Garland, who came to the door in his shirtsleeves:

" Tell Nic to hold the first edition for a five-column first-page cartoon. And send this up right away."

They had a last look at it before it went, and after gazing a moment in silence Hardy said:

" It's the greatest thing you ever did, Kit, and it comes at the psychological moment. It'll elect him."

" Oh, he was elected anyhow."

Hardy shook his head, and in the movement Kittrell saw how the strain of the campaign had told on him. " No, he wasn't; the way they've been hammering him is something fierce; and the *Telegraph*—well, your cartoons and all, you know."

" But my cartoons in the *Telegraph* were rotten. Any work that's not sincere, not intellectually honest——"

Hardy interrupted him:

" Yes; but, Kit, you're so good that your rotten is better

than 'most anybody's best." He smiled, and Kittrell blushed and looked away.

Hardy was right. The " Kit " cartoon, back in the *Post*, created its sensation, and after it appeared the political reporters said it had started a landslide to Clayton; that the betting was 4 to 1 and no takers, and that it was all over but the shouting.

That night, as they were at dinner, the telephone rang, and in a minute Neil knew by Edith's excited and delighted reiteration of " yes," " yes," who had called up. And he then heard her say:

" Indeed I will; I'll come every night and sit in the front seat."

When Kittrell displaced Edith at the telephone, he heard the voice of John Clayton, lower in register and somewhat husky after four weeks' speaking, but more musical than ever in Kittrell's ears when it said:

" I just told the little woman, Neil, that I didn't know how to say it, so I wanted her to thank you for me. It was beautiful in you, and I wish I were worthy of it; it was simply your own good soul expressing itself."

And it was the last delight to Kittrell to hear that voice and to know that all was well.

But one question remained unsettled. Kittrell had been on the *Telegraph* a month, and his contract differed from that ordinarily made by the members of a newspaper staff in that he was paid by the year, though in monthly instalments. Kittrell knew that he had broken his contract on grounds which the sordid law would not see or recognize and the average court think absurd, and that the *Telegraph* might legally refuse to pay him at all. He hoped the *Telegraph* would do this! But it did not; on the contrary, he received the next day a check for his month's work. He held it up for Edith's inspection.

" Of course, I'll have to send it back," he said.

" Certainly."

" Do you think me quixotic? "

" Well, we're poor enough as it is—let's have some luxuries; let's be quixotic until after election, at least."

" Sure," said Neil; " just what I was thinking. I'm going to do a cartoon every day for the *Post* until election day, and I'm not going to take a cent. I don't want to crowd Banks out, you know, and I want to do my part for Clayton and the cause, and do it, just once, for the pure love of the thing."

Those last days of the campaign were, indeed, luxuries to Kittrell and to Edith, days of work and fun and excitement. All day Kittrell worked on his cartoons, and in the evening they went to Clayton's meetings. The experience was a revelation to them both—the crowds, the waiting for the singing of the automobile's siren, the wild cheers that greeted Clayton, and then his speech, his appeals to the best there was in men. He had never made such speeches, and long afterward Edith could hear those cheers and see the faces of those working-men aglow with the hope, the passion, the fervent religion of democracy. And those days came to their glad climax that night when they met at the office of the *Post* to receive the returns, in an atmosphere quivering with excitement, with messenger boys and reporters coming and going, and in the street outside an immense crowd, swaying and rocking between the walls on either side, with screams and shouts and mad huzzas, and the wild blowing of horns—all the hideous, happy noise an American election-night crowd can make.

Late in the evening Clayton had made his way, somehow unnoticed, through the crowd, and entered the office. He was happy in the great triumph he would not accept as personal, claiming it always for the cause; but as he dropped into the chair Hardy pushed toward him, they all saw how weary he was.

Just at that moment the roar in the street below swelled to a mighty crescendo, and Hardy cried:

"Look!"

They ran to the window. The boys up-stairs who were manipulating the stereopticon, had thrown on the screen an enormous picture of Clayton, the portrait Kittrell had drawn for his cartoon.

"Will you say now there isn't the personal note in it?" Edith asked.

Clayton glanced out the window, across the dark, surging street, at the picture.

"Oh, it's not me they're cheering for," he said; "it's for Kit, here."

"Well, perhaps some of it's for him," Edith admitted loyally.

They were silent, seized irresistibly by the emotion that mastered the mighty crowd in the dark streets below. Edith was strangely moved. Presently she could speak:

"Is there anything sweeter in life than to know that you have done a good thing—and done it well?"

"Yes," said Clayton, "just one: to have a few friends who understand."

"You are right," said Edith. "It is so with art, and it must be so with life; it makes an art of life."

It was dark enough there by the window for her to slip her hand into that of Neil, who had been musing silently on the crowd.

"I can never say again," she said softly, "that those people are not worth sacrifice. They are worth all; they are everything; they are the hope of the world; and their longings and their needs, and the possibility of bringing them to pass, are all that give significance to life."

"That's what America is for," said Clayton, "and it's worth while to be allowed to help even in a little way to make, as old Walt says, 'a nation of friends, of equals.'"

BRAND WHITLOCK

Brand Whitlock, lawyer, politician, author and ambassador, was born in Urbana, Ohio, March 4, 1869. His father, Rev. Elias D. Whitlock, was a minister of power and a man of strong convictions. Brand was educated partly in the public schools, partly by private teaching. He never went to college, but this did not mean that his education stopped; he kept on studying, and to such good purpose that in 1916 Brown University gave him the degree of Doctor of Laws. Like many other writers, he received his early training in newspaper work. At eighteen he became a reporter on a Toledo paper, and three years later was reporter and political correspondent for the Chicago *Herald*. While in Chicago he was a member of the old Whitechapel Club, a group of newspaper men which included F. P. Dunne, the creator of *Mr. Dooley;* Alfred Henry Lewis, author of *Wolfville;* and George Ade, whose *Fables in Slang* were widely popular a few years ago.

He was strongly drawn to the law, and in 1893 went to Springfield, Illinois, and entered a law office as a student. He was admitted to the bar, and shortly after went to Toledo, Ohio, to practice. In eight years he had established himself as a successful lawyer, and something more. He was recognized as a man of high executive ability, and as being absolutely " square." Such men are none too common, and Toledo decided that it needed him in the mayor's chair. Without a political machine, without a platform, and without a party, he was elected mayor in 1905, reelected in 1907, again in 1909, again in 1911—and could probably have had the office for life if he had been willing to accept it. In the meantime he had written several successful novels; he wanted more time for writing, and when in 1913 he

was offered the post of United States Minister to Belgium, he
accepted, thinking that he would find in this position an opportunity to observe life from a new angle, and leisure for
literary work. In August 1914 he was on his vacation, and
had begun work on a new novel. In his own words:

> I had the manuscript of my novel before me. . . . It was some-
> how just beginning to take form, beginning to show some signs of
> life; at times some characters in it gave evidence of being human
> and alive; they were beginning to act now and then spontaneously,
> beginning to say and to do things after the manner of human
> beings; the long vista before me, the months of laborious drudging
> toil and pain, the long agony of effort necessary to write any book,
> even a poor one, was beginning to appear less weary, less futile;
> there was the first faint glow of the joy of creative effort.

and then suddenly the telephone bell rang, and announced that
the Archduke of Austria had been assassinated at Sarajevo.

The rest of the story belongs to history. How he went back
to Brussels; how when the city seemed doomed, and all the
government officials left, he stayed on; how when the city was
preparing to resist by force, he went to Burgomaster Max and
convinced him that it was useless, and so saved the city from
the fate of Louvain; how he took charge of the relief work,
how the King of Belgium thanked him for his services to the
country; how the city of Brussels in gratitude gave him a picture by Van Dyck, a priceless thing, which he accepted—not
for himself but for his home city of Toledo; how after the
war, he went back, not as Minister but as Ambassador,—
all these are among the proud memories of America's part in
the World War.

Brand Whitlock is so much more than an author that it
is with an effort that we turn to consider his literary work.
His first book, *The Thirteenth District*, published in 1902, was
a novel of American politics; it contains a capital description
of a convention, and shows the strategy of political leaders as
seen by a keen observer. In *Her Infinite Variety* he dealt with

the suffrage movement as it was in 1904, with determined women seeking the ballot, and equally determined women working just as hard to keep it away from them. *The Happy Average* was a story of an every-day American couple: they were not rich, nor famous, nor divorced,—yet the author thinks their story is typical of most American lives. *The Turn of the Balance* is a novel that grew out of his legal experiences: it deals with the underworld of crime, and often in a depressing way. It reflects the author's belief that the present organization of society, and our methods of administering justice, are the cause of much of the misery in the world. Following these novels came two volumes of short stories, *The Gold Brick* and *The Fall Guy:* both deal with various aspects of American life of to-day. In 1914 he published an autobiography under the title *Forty Years of It*. This is interesting as a picture of political life of the period in Ohio. His latest book, *Memories of Belgium under the German Occupation*, tells the story of four eventful years. In all that trying time, each night, no matter how weary he was, he forced himself to set down the events of the day. From these records he wrote a book that by virtue of its first-hand information and its literary art ranks among the most important of the books called forth by the Great War.

THE TRAVELING SALESMAN

The traveling salesman is a characteristic American type. We laugh at his stories, or we criticise him for his "nerve," but we do not always make allowance for the fact that his life is not an easy one, and that his occupation develops "nerve" just as an athlete's work develops muscle. The best presentation of the traveling salesman in fiction is found in the stories of Edna Ferber. And the fact that her "salesman" is a woman only adds to the interest of the stories. When ex-President Roosevelt read Miss Ferber's book, he wrote her an enthusiastic letter telling her how much he admired Emma McChesney. We meet her in the first words of this story.

HIS MOTHER'S SON

BY

EDNA FERBER

" FULL? " repeated Emma McChesney (and if it weren't for the compositor there'd be an exclamation point after that question mark).

" Sorry, Mrs. McChesney," said the clerk, and he actually looked it, " but there's absolutely nothing stirring. We're full up. The Benevolent Brotherhood of Bisons is holding its regular annual state convention here. We're putting up cots in the hall."

Emma McChesney's keen blue eyes glanced up from their inspection of the little bunch of mail which had just been handed her. " Well, pick out a hall with a southern exposure and set up a cot or so for me," she said, agreeably, " because I've come to stay. After selling Featherloom Petticoats on the road for ten years I don't see myself trailing up and down this town looking for a place to lay my head. I've learned this one large, immovable truth, and that is, that a hotel clerk is a hotel clerk. It makes no difference whether he is stuck back of a marble pillar and hidden by a gold vase full of thirty-six-inch American Beauty roses at the Knickerbocker, or setting the late fall fashions for men in Galesburg, Illinois."

By one small degree was the perfect poise of the peerless personage behind the register jarred. But by only one. He was a hotel night clerk.

" It won't do you any good to get sore, Mrs. McChesney," he began, suavely. " Now a man would——"

" But I'm not a man," interrupted Emma McChesney. " I'm

only doing a man's work and earning a man's salary and demanding to be treated with as much consideration as you'd show a man."

The personage busied himself mightily with a pen, and a blotter, and sundry papers, as is the manner of personages when annoyed. " I'd like to accommodate you; I'd like to do it."

" Cheer up," said Emma McChesney, " you're going to. I don't mind a little discomfort. Though I want to mention in passing that if there are any lady Bisons present you needn't bank on doubling me up with them. I've had one experience of that kind. It was in Albia, Iowa. I'd sleep in the kitchen range before I'd go through another."

Up went the erstwhile falling poise. " You're badly mistaken, madam. I'm a member of this order myself, and a finer lot of fellows it has never been my pleasure to know."

" Yes, I know," drawled Emma McChesney. " Do you know, the thing that gets me is the inconsistency of it. Along come a lot of boobs who never use a hotel the year around except to loaf in the lobby, and wear out the leather chairs, and use up the matches and toothpicks and get the baseball returns, and immediately you turn away a traveling man who uses a three-dollar-a-day room, with a sample room downstairs for his stuff, who tips every porter and bell-boy in the place, asks for no favors, and who, if you give him a halfway decent cup of coffee for breakfast, will fall in love with the place and boom it all over the country. Half of your Benevolent Bisons are here on the European plan, with a view to patronizing the free-lunch counters or being asked to take dinner at the home of some local Bison whose wife has been cooking up on pies, and chicken salad and veal roast for the last week."

Emma McChesney leaned over the desk a little, and lowered her voice to the tone of confidence. " Now, I'm not in the habit of making a nuisance of myself like this. I don't get so chatty as a rule, and I know that I could jump over to Monmouth and get first-class accommodations there. But just this once I've a good reason for wanting to make you and myself a little miserable. Y'see, my son is traveling with me this trip."

" Son! " echoed the clerk, staring.

" Thanks. That's what they all do. After a while I'll begin to believe that there must be something hauntingly beautiful and girlish about me or every one wouldn't petrify when I announce that I've a six-foot son attached to my apron-strings. He looks twenty-one, but he's seventeen. He thinks the world's rotten because he can't grow one of those fuzzy little mustaches that the men are cultivating to match their hats. He's down at the depot now, straightening out our baggage. Now I want to say this before he gets here. He's been out with me just four days. Those four days have been a revelation, an eye-opener, and a series of rude jolts. He used to think that his mother's job consisted of traveling in Pullmans, eating delicate viands turned out by the hotel chefs, and strewing Featherloom Petticoats along the path. I gave him plenty of money, and he got into the habit of looking lightly upon anything more trifling than a five-dollar bill. He's changing his mind by great leaps. I'm prepared to spend the night in the coal cellar if you'll just fix him up—not too comfortably. It'll be a great lesson for him. There he is now. Just coming in. Fuzzy coat and hat and English stick. Hist! As they say on the stage."

The boy crossed the crowded lobby. There was a little worried, annoyed frown between his eyes. He laid a protecting hand on his mother's arm. Emma McChesney was conscious of a little thrill of pride as she realized that he did not have to look up to meet her gaze.

" Look here, Mother, they tell me there's some sort of a convention here, and the town's packed. That's what all those banners and things were for. I hope they've got something decent for us here. I came up with a man who said he didn't think there was a hole left to sleep in."

" You don't say! " exclaimed Emma McChesney, and turned to the clerk. " This is my son, Jock McChesney—Mr. Sims. Is this true? "

" Glad to know you, sir," said Mr. Sims. " Why, yes, I'm afraid we are pretty well filled up, but seeing it's you maybe we can do something for you."

He ruminated, tapping his teeth with a penholder, and eying the pair before him with a maddening blankness of gaze. Finally:

" I'll do my best, but you can't expect much. I guess I can squeeze another cot into eight-seven for the young man. There's—let's see now—who's in eighty-seven? Well, there's two Bisons in the double bed, and one in the single, and Fat Ed Meyers in the cot and——"

Emma McChesney stiffened into acute attention. " Meyers? " she interrupted. " Do you mean Ed Meyers of the Strauss Sans-silk Skirt Company? "

" That's so. You two are in the same line, aren't you? He's a great little piano player, Ed is. Ever hear him play? "

" When did he get in? "

" Oh, he just came in fifteen minutes ago on the Ashland division. He's in at supper."

" Oh," said Emma McChesney. The two letters breathed relief.

But relief had no place in the voice, or on the countenance of Jock McChesney. He bristled with belligerence. " This cattle-car style of sleeping don't make a hit. I haven't had a decent night's rest for three nights. I never could sleep on a sleeper. Can't you fix us up better than that? "

" Best I can do."

" But where's mother going? I see you advertise ' three

large and commodious steam-heated sample rooms in connection.' I suppose mother's due to sleep on one of the tables there."

" Jock," Emma McChesney reproved him, " Mr. Sims is doing us a great favor. There isn't another hotel in town that would——"

" You're right, there isn't," agreed Mr. Sims. " I guess the young man is new to this traveling game. As I said, I'd like to accommodate you, but—— Let's see now. Tell you what I'll do. If I can get the housekeeper to go over and sleep in the maids' quarters just for to-night, you can use her room. There you are! Of course, it's over the kitchen, and there may be some little noise early in the morning——"

Emma McChesney raised a protesting hand. " Don't mention it. Just lead me thither. I'm so tired I could sleep in an excursion special that was switching at Pittsburgh. Jock, me child, we're in luck. That's twice in the same place. The first time was when we were inspired to eat our supper on the diner instead of waiting until we reached here to take the left-overs from the Bisons' grazing. I hope that housekeeper hasn't a picture of her departed husband dangling life-size on the wall at the foot of the bed. But they always have. Good-night, son. Don't let the Bisons bite you. I'll be up at seven."

But it was just 6.30 A.M. when Emma McChesney turned the little bend in the stairway that led to the office. The scrub-woman was still in possession. The cigar-counter girl had not yet made her appearance. There was about the place a general air of the night before. All but the night clerk. He was as spruce and trim, and alert and smooth-shaven as only a night clerk can be after a night's vigil.

" 'Morning! " Emma McChesney called to him. She wore blue serge, and a smart fall hat. The late autumn morning was not crisper and sunnier than she.

"Good-morning, Mrs. McChesney," returned Mr. Sims, sonorously. "Have a good night's sleep? I hope the kitchen noises didn't wake you."

Emma McChesney paused with her hand on the door. "Kitchen? Oh, no. I could sleep through a vaudeville china-juggling act. But—what an extraordinarily unpleasant-looking man that housekeeper's husband must have been."

That November morning boasted all those qualities which November-morning writers are so prone to bestow upon the month. But the words wine, and sparkle, and sting, and glow, and snap do not seem to cover it. Emma McChesney stood on the bottom step, looking up and down Main Street and breathing in great draughts of that unadjectivable air. Her complexion stood the test of the merciless, astringent morning and came up triumphantly and healthily firm and pink and smooth. The town was still asleep. She started to walk briskly down the bare and ugly Main Street of the little town. In her big, generous heart, and her keen, alert mind, there were many sensations and myriad thoughts, but varied and diverse as they were they all led back to the boy up there in the stuffy, over-crowded hotel room—the boy who was learning his lesson.

Half an hour later she reentered the hotel, her cheeks glowing. Jock was not yet down. So she ordered and ate her wise and cautious breakfast of fruit and cereal and toast and coffee, skimming over her morning paper as she ate. At 7:30 she was back in the lobby, newspaper in hand. The Bisons were already astir. She seated herself in a deep chair in a quiet corner, her eyes glancing up over the top of her paper toward the stairway. At eight o'clock Jock McChesney came down.

There was nothing of jauntiness about him. His eyelids were red. His face had the doughy look of one whose sleep has been brief and feverish. As he came toward his mother you noticed a stain on his coat, and a sunburst of wrinkles across one leg of his modish brown trousers.

" Good-morning, son! " said Emma McChesney. " Was it as bad as that? "

Jock McChesney's long fingers curled into a fist.

" Say," he began, his tone venomous, " do you know what those—those—those——"

" Say it! " commanded Emma McChesney. " I'm only your mother. If you keep that in your system your breakfast will curdle in your stomach."

Jock McChesney said it. I know no phrase better fitted to describe his tone than that old favorite of the erotic novelists. It was vibrant with passion. It breathed bitterness. It sizzled with savagery. It—Oh, alliteration is useless.

" Well," said Emma McChesney, encouragingly, " go on."

" Well! " gulped Jock McChesney, and glared; " those two double-bedded, bloomin', blasted Bisons came in at twelve, and the single one about fifteen minutes later. They didn't surprise me. There was a herd of about ninety-three of 'em in the hall, all saying good-night to each other, and planning where they'd meet in the morning, and the time, and place and probable weather conditions. For that matter, there were droves of 'em pounding up and down the halls all night. I never saw such restless cattle. If you'll tell me what makes more noise in the middle of the night than the metal disk of a hotel key banging and clanging up against a door, I'd like to know what it is. My three Bisons were all dolled up with fool ribbons and badges and striped paper canes. When they switched on the light I gave a crack imitation of a tired working man trying to get a little sleep. I breathed regularly and heavily, with an occasional moaning snore. But if those two hippopotamus Bisons had been alone on their native plains they couldn't have cared less. They bellowed, and pawed the earth, and threw their shoes around, and yawned, and stretched and discussed their plans for the next day, and reviewed all their doings of that day. Then one of them said something about turning in, and I was so happy I forgot to snore. Just then another key clanged at the door, in walked a fat man in a brown suit and a brown derby, and stuff was off."

" That," said Emma McChesney, " would be Ed Meyers, of the Strauss Sans-silk Skirt Company."

" None other than our hero." Jock's tone had an added acidity. " It took those four about two minutes to get acquainted. In three minutes they had told their real names, and it turned out that Meyers belonged to an organization that was a second cousin of the Bisons. In five minutes they had got together a deck and a pile of chips and were shirt-sleeving it around a game of pinochle. I would doze off to the slap of cards, and the click of chips, and wake up when the bell-boy came in with another round, which he did every six minutes. When I got up this morning I found that Fat Ed Meyers had been sitting on the chair over which I trustingly had draped my trousers. This sunburst of wrinkles is where he mostly sat. This spot on my coat is where a Bison drank his beer."

Emma McChesney folded her paper and rose, smiling. " It Is sort of trying, I suppose, if you're not used to it."

" Used to it! " shouted the outraged Jock. " Used to it! Do you mean to tell me there's nothing unusual about——"

" Not a thing. Oh, of course you don't strike a bunch of Bisons every day. But it happens a good many times. The world is full of Ancient Orders and they're everlastingly getting together and drawing up resolutions and electing officers. Don't you think you'd better go in to breakfast before the Bisons begin to forage? I've had mine."

The gloom which had overspread Jock McChesney's face lifted a little. The hungry boy in him was uppermost. " That's so. I'm going to have some wheat cakes, and steak, and eggs, and coffee, and fruit, and toast, and rolls."

" Why slight the fish? " inquired his mother. Then, as he turned toward the dining-room, " I've two letters to get out. Then I'm going down the street to see a customer. I'll be up at the Sulzberg-Stein department store at nine sharp.

There's no use trying to see old Sulzberg before ten, but I'll be there, anyway, and so will Ed Meyers, or I'm no skirt salesman. I want you to meet me there. It will do you good to watch how the overripe orders just drop, ker-plunk, into my lap."

Maybe you know Sulzberg & Stein's big store? No? That's because you've always lived in the city. Old Sulzberg sends his buyers to the New York market twice a year, and they need two floor managers on the main floor now. The money those people spend for red and green decorations at Christmas time, apple-blossoms and pink crêpe paper shades in the spring, must be something awful. Young Stein goes to Chicago to have his clothes made, and old Sulzberg likes to keep the traveling men waiting in the little ante-room outside his private office.

Jock McChesney finished his huge breakfast, strolled over to Sulzberg & Stein's, and inquired his way to the office only to find that his mother was not yet there. There were three men in the little waiting-room. One of them was Fat Ed Meyers. His huge bulk overflowed the spindle-legged chair on which he sat. His brown derby was in his hands. His eyes were on the closed door at the other side of the room. So were the eyes of the other two travelers. Jock took a vacant seat next to Fat Ed Meyers so that he might, in his mind's eye, pick out a particularly choice spot upon which his hard young fist might land—if only he had the chance. Breaking up a man's sleep like that, the great big overgrown mutt!

"What's your line?" said Ed Meyers, suddenly turning toward Jock.

Prompted by some imp—"Skirts," answered Jock. "Ladies' petticoats." ("As if men ever wore 'em!" he giggled inwardly.)

Ed Meyers shifted around in his chair so that he might better stare at this new foe in the field. His little red mouth was open ludicrously.

"Who're you out for?" he demanded next.

There was a look of Emma McChesney on Jock's face. "Why—er—the Union Underskirt and Hosiery Company of Chicago. New concern."

"Must be," ruminated Ed Meyers. "I never heard of 'em, and I know 'em all. You're starting in young, ain't you, kid! Well, it'll never hurt you. You'll learn something new every day. Now me, I——"

In breezed Emma McChesney. Her quick glance rested immediately upon Meyers and the boy. And in that moment some instinct prompted Jock McChesney to shake his head, ever so slightly, and assume a blankness of expression. And Emma McChesney, with that shrewdness which had made her one of the best salesmen on the road, saw, and miraculously understood.

"How do, Mrs. McChesney," grinned Fat Ed Meyers. "You see I beat you to it."

"So I see," smiled Emma, cheerfully. "I was delayed. Just sold a nice little bill to Watkins down the street." She seated herself across the way, and kept her eyes on that closed door.

"Say, kid," Meyers began, in the husky whisper of the fat man, "I'm going to put you wise to something, seeing you're new to this game. See that lady over there?" He nodded discreetly in Emma McChesney's direction.

"Pretty, isn't she?" said Jock, appreciatively.

"Know who she is?"

"Well—I—she does look familiar, but——"

"Oh, come now, quit your bluffing. If you'd ever met that dame you'd remember it. Her name's McChesney—Emma McChesney, and she sells T. A. Buck's Featherloom Petticoats. I'll give her her dues; she's the best little salesman on the road. I'll bet that girl could sell a ruffled, accordion-plaited underskirt to a fat woman who was trying to reduce. She's got the darndest way with her. And at that she's straight, too."

If Ed Meyers had not been gazing so intently into his hat,

trying at the same time to look cherubically benign he might have seen a quick and painful scarlet sweep the face of the boy, coupled with a certain tense look of the muscles around the jaw.

"Well, now, look here," he went on, still in a whisper. "We're both skirt men, you and me. Everything's fair in this game. Maybe you don't know it, but when there's a bunch of the boys waiting around to see the head of the store like this, and there happens to be a lady traveler in the crowd, why, it's considered kind of a professional courtesy to let the lady have the first look-in. See? It ain't so often that three people in the same line get together like this. She knows it, and she's sitting on the edge of her chair, waiting to bolt when that door opens, even if she does act like she was hanging on the words of that lady clerk there. The minute it does open a crack she'll jump up and give me a fleeting, grateful smile, and sail in and cop a fat order away from the old man and his skirt buyer. I'm wise. Say, he may be an oyster, but he knows a pretty woman when he sees one. By the time she's through with him he'll have enough petticoats on hand to last him from now until Turkey goes suffrage. Get me? "

"I get you," answered Jock.

"I say, this is business, and good manners be hanged. When a woman breaks into a man's game like this, let her take her chances like a man. Ain't that straight? "

"You've said something," agreed Jock.

"Now, look here, kid. When that door opens I get up. See? And shoot straight for the old man's office. See? Like a duck. See? Say, I may be fat, kid, but I'm what they call light on my feet, and when I see an order getting away from me I can be so fleet that I have Diana looking like old Weston doing a stretch of muddy country road in a coast-to-coast hike. See? Now you help me out on this and I'll see that you don't suffer for it. I'll stick in a good word for you, believe me. You take the word of an old stager like me and you won't go far—"

The door opened. Simultaneously three figures sprang into action. Jock had the seat nearest the door. With marvelous clumsiness he managed to place himself in Ed Meyers' path, then reddened, began an apology, stepped on both of Ed's feet, jabbed his elbow into his stomach, and dropped his hat. A second later the door of old Sulzberg's private office closed upon Emma McChesney's smart, erect, confident figure.

Now, Ed Meyers' hands were peculiar hands for a fat man. They were tapering, slender, delicate, blue-veined, temperamental hands. At this moment, despite his purpling face, and his staring eyes, they were the most noticeable thing about him. His fingers clawed the empty air, quivering, vibrant, as though poised to clutch at Jock's throat.

Then words came. They spluttered from his lips. They popped like corn kernels in the heat of his wrath; they tripped over each other; they exploded.

" You darned kid, you! " he began, with fascinating fluency. " You thousand-legged, double-jointed, ox-footed truck horse! Come on out of here and I'll lick the shine off your shoes, you blue-eyed babe, you! What did you get up for, huh? What did you think this was going to be—a flag drill? "

With a whoop of pure joy Jock McChesney turned and fled.

They dined together at one o'clock, Emma McChesney and her son Jock. Suddenly Jock stopped eating. His eyes were on the door. " There's that fathead now," he said, excitedly. " The nerve of him! He's coming over here."

Ed Meyers was waddling toward them with the quick light step of the fat man. His pink, full-jowled face was glowing. His eyes were bright as a boy's. He stopped at their table and paused for one dramatic moment.

" So, me beauty, you two were in cahoots, huh? That's the second low-down deal you've handed me. I haven't forgotten that trick you turned with Nussbaum at DeKalb. Never mind, little girl. I'll get back at you yet."

He nodded a contemptous head in Jock's direction. " Carrying a packer? "

Emma McChesney wiped her fingers daintily on her napkin, crushed it on the table, and leaned back in her chair. " Men," she observed, wonderingly, " are the cussedest creatures. This chap occupied the same room with you last night and you don't even know his name. Funny! If two strange women had found themselves occupying the same room for a night they wouldn't have got to the kimono and back hair stage before they would not only have known each other's names, but they'd have tried on each other's hats, swapped corset cover patterns, found mutual friends living in Dayton, Ohio, taught each other a new Irish crochet stitch, showed their family photographs, told how their married sister's little girl nearly died with swollen glands, and divided off the mirror into two sections to paste their newly-washed handkerchiefs on. Don't tell *me* men have a genius for friendship."

" Well, who is he? " insisted Ed Meyers. " He told me everything but his name this morning. I wish I had throttled him with a bunch of Bisons' badges last night."

" His name," smiled Emma McChesney, " is Jock McChesney. He's my one and only son, and he's put through his first little business deal this morning just to show his mother that he can be a help to his folks if he wants to. Now, Ed Meyers, if you're going to have apoplexy, don't you go and have it around this table. My boy is only on his second piece of pie, and I won't have his appetite spoiled."

EDNA FERBER

A professor of literature once began a lecture on Lowell by saying: "It makes a great deal of difference to an author whether he is born in Cambridge or Kalamazoo." Miss Ferber was born in Kalamazoo, but it hasn't made much difference to her. The date was August 15, 1887. She attended high school at Appleton, Wisconsin, and at seventeen secured a position as reporter on the Appleton *Daily Crescent*. That she was successful in newspaper work is shown by the fact that she soon had a similar position on the *Milwaukee Journal*, and went from there to the staff of the *Chicago Tribune*, one of the leading newspapers in the United States.

But journalism, engrossing as it is, did not take all of her time. She began a novel, working on it in spare moments, but when it was finished she was so dissatisfied with it that she threw the manuscript into the waste basket. Here her mother found it, and sent it to a publisher, who accepted it at once. The book was *Dawn O' Hara*. It was dedicated "To my dear mother who frequently interrupts, and to my sister Fannie who says Sh-sh-sh outside my door." With this book Miss Ferber, at twenty-four, found herself the author of one of the successful novels of the year.

Her next work was in the field of the short story, and here too she quickly gained recognition. The field that she has made particularly her own is the delineation of the American business woman, a type familiar in our daily life, but never adequately presented in fiction until Emma McChesney appeared. The fidelity with which these stories describe the life of a traveling salesman show that Miss Ferber knew her subject through and through before she began to write. Her knowledge of other things is shown in an amusing letter which she wrote to the editor of the *Bookman* in 1912. He had criticized her for writing a story about baseball, saying that no woman really knew baseball. This was her reply, in part:

You, buried up there in your office, or your apartment, with your books, books, books, and your pipe, and your everlasting manuscripts, and makers of manuscripts, don't you know that your woman secretary knows more about baseball than you do? Don't you know that every American girl knows baseball, and that most of us read the sporting page, not as a pose, but because we're interested in things that happen on the field, and track, and links, and gridiron? Bless your heart, that baseball story was the worst story in the book, but it was written after a solid summer of watching our bush league team play ball in the little Wisconsin town that I used to call home.

Humanity? Which of us really knows it? But take a fairly intelligent girl of seventeen, put her on a country daily newspaper, and then keep her on one paper or another, country and city, for six years, and—well, she just naturally can't help learning some things about some folks, now can she? . . .

You say that two or three more such books may entitle me to serious consideration. If I can get the editors to take more stories, why I suppose there'll be more books. But please don't perform any more serious consideration stuff over 'em. Because me'n Georgie Cohan, we jest aims to amuse.

Her first book of short stories was called *Buttered Side Down* (her titles are always unusual). This was followed by *Roast Beef, Medium,* in which Mrs. McChesney appears as the successful distributor of Featherloom skirts. *Personality Plus* tells of the adventures of her son Jock as an advertising man. *Cheerful—by Request* introduces Mrs. McChesney and some other people. By this time her favorite character had become so well known that the stage called for her, so Miss Ferber collaborated with George V. Hobart in a play called *Our Mrs. McChesney,* which was produced with Ethel Barrymore in the title role. Her latest book, *Fanny Herself,* is a novel, and in its pages Mrs. McChesney appears again.

Her stories show the effect of her newspaper training. The style is crisp; the descriptions show close observation. Humor lights up every page, and underlying all her stories is a belief in people, a faith that life is worth while, a courage in the face of obstacles, that we like to think is characteristically American. In the structure and the style of her stories, Miss Ferber shows the influence of O. Henry, or as a newspaper wit put it,

> O. Henry's fame, unless mistaken I'm
> Goes ednaferberating down through time.

AFTER THE BIG STORE CLOSES

We all go to the Big Store to buy its bargains, and sometimes we wonder idly what the clerks are like when they are not behind the counter. This story deals with the lives of two people who punched the time-clock. When the store closes, it is like the striking of the clock in the fairy tales: the clerks are transformed into human beings, and become so much like ourselves that it is hard to tell the difference.

BITTER-SWEET

BY

FANNIE HURST

MUCH of the tragical lore of the infant mortality, the mal-
nutrition, and the five-in-a-room morality of the city's poor
is written in statistics, and the statistical path to the heart
is more figurative than literal.

It is difficult to write stylistically a per-annum report of
1,327 curvatures of the spine, whereas the poor specific little
vertebra of Mamie O'Grady, daughter to Lou, your laundress,
whose alcoholic husband once invaded your very own basement
and attempted to strangle her in the coal-bin, can instantly
create an apron bazaar in the church vestry-rooms.

That is why it is possible to drink your morning coffee without nausea for it, over the head-lines of forty thousand casual-
ties at Ypres, but to push back abruptly at a three-line notice
of little Tony's, your corner bootblack's, fatal dive before a
street-car.

Gertie Slayback was statistically down as a woman wage-
earner; a typhoid case among the thousands of the Borough of
Manhattan for 1901; and her twice-a-day share in the Subway fares collected in the present year of our Lord.

She was a very atomic one of the city's four millions. But
after all, what are the kings and peasants, poets and dray-
men, but great, greater, or greatest, less, lesser, or least atoms
of us? If not of the least, Gertie Slayback was of the very
lesser. When she unlocked the front door to her rooming-
house of evenings, there was no one to expect her, except on
Tuesdays, which evening it so happened her week was up. And

when she left of mornings with her breakfast crumblessly cleared up and the box of biscuit and condensed-milk can tucked unsuspectedly behind her camisole in the top drawer there was no one to regret her.

There are some of us who call this freedom. Again there are those for whom one spark of home fire burning would light the world.

Gertie Slayback was one of these. Half a life-time of opening her door upon this or that desert-aisle of hall bedroom had not taught her heart how not to sink or the feel of daily rising in one such room to seem less like a damp bathing-suit, donned at dawn.

The only picture—or call it atavism if you will—which adorned Miss Slayback's dun-colored walls was a passe-partout snowscape, night closing in, and pink cottage windows peering out from under eaves. She could visualize that interior as if she had only to turn the frame for the smell of wood fire and the snap of pine logs and for the scene of two high-back chairs and the wooden crib between.

What a fragile, gracile thing is the mind that can leap thus from nine bargain basement hours of hairpins and darning-balls to the downy business of lining a crib in Never-Never Land and warming No Man's slippers before the fire of imagination.

There was that picture so acidly etched into Miss Slayback's brain that she had only to close her eyes in the slit-like sanctity of her room and in the brief moment of courting sleep feel the pink penumbra of her vision begin to glow.

Of late years, or, more specifically, for two years and eight months, another picture had invaded, even superseded the old. A stamp-photograph likeness of Mr. James P. Batch in the corner of Miss Slayback's mirror, and thereafter No Man's slippers became number eight-and-a-half C, and the hearth a gilded radiator in a dining-living-room somewhere between the Fourteenth Street Subway and the land of the Bronx.

How Miss Slayback, by habit not gregarious, met Mr. Batch is of no consequence, except to those snug ones of us to whom an introduction is the only means to such an end.

At a six o'clock that invaded even Union Square with heliotrope dusk, Mr. James Batch mistook, who shall say otherwise, Miss Gertie Slayback, as she stepped down into the wintry shade of a Subway kiosk, for Miss Whodoesitmatter. At seven o'clock, over a dish of lamb stew *à la* White Kitchen, he confessed, and if Miss Slayback affected too great surprise and too little indignation, try to conceive six nine-hour week-in-and week-out days of hairpins and darning-balls, and then, at a heliotrope dusk, James P. Batch, in invitational mood, stepping in between it and the papered walls of a dun-colored evening. To further enlist your tolerance, Gertie Slayback's eyes were as blue as the noon of June, and James P. Batch, in a belted-in coat and five kid finger-points protruding ever so slightly and rightly from a breast pocket, was hewn and honed in the image of youth. His the smile of one for whom life's cup holds a heady wine, a wrinkle or two at the eye only serving to enhance that smile; a one-inch feather stuck upright in his derby hatband.

It was a forelock once stamped a Corsican with the look of emperor. It was this hat feather, a cock's feather at that and worn without sense of humor, to which Miss Slayback was fond of attributing the consequences of that heliotrope dusk.

" It was the feather in your cap did it, Jimmie. I can see you yet, stepping up with that innocent grin of yours. You think I didn't know you were flirting? Cousin from Long Island City! ' Say,' I says to myself, I says, ' I look as much like his cousin from Long Island City, if he's got one, as my cousin from Hoboken (and I haven't got any) would look like my sister if I had one.' It was that sassy little feather in your hat! "

They would laugh over this ever-green reminiscence on Sunday park benches and at intermission at moving pictures when they remained through it to see the show twice. Be the land-lady's front parlor ever so permanently rented out, the motion-picture theater has brought to thousands of young city starve-lings, if not the quietude of the home, then at least the warmth and a juxtaposition and a deep darkness that can lave the sub-basement throb of temples and is filled with music with a hum in it.

For two years and eight months of Saturday nights, each one of them a semaphore dropping out across the gray road of the week, Gertie Slayback and Jimmie Batch dined for one hour and sixty cents at the White Kitchen. Then arm and arm up the million-candle-power flare of Broadway, content, these two who had never seen a lake reflect a moon, or a slim fir pointing to a star, that life could be so manifold. And always, too, on Saturday, the tenth from the last row of the De Luxe Cinematograph, Broadway's Best, Orchestra Chairs, fifty cents; Last Ten Rows, thirty-five. The give of velvet-upholstered chairs, perfumed darkness, and any old love story moving across it to the ecstatic ache of Gertie Slayback's high young heart.

On a Saturday evening that was already pointed with stars at the six-o'clock closing of Hoffheimer's Fourteenth Street Emporium, Miss Slayback, whose blondness under fatigue could become ashy, emerged from the Bargain Basement al-most the first of its frantic exodus, taking the place of her weekly appointment in the entrance of the Popular Drug Store adjoining, her gaze, something even frantic in it, sifting the passing crowd.

At six o'clock Fourteenth Street pours up from its base-ments, down from its lofts, and out from its five-and-ten-cent stores, shows, and arcades, in a great homeward torrent—a sweeping torrent that flows full flush to the Subway, the Ele-vated, and the surface car, and then spreads thinly into the least pretentious of the city's homes—the five flights up, the two rooms rear, and the third floor back.

Standing there, this eager tide of the Fourteenth Street Emporium, thus released by the six-o'clock flood-gates, flowed past Miss Slayback. White-nosed, low-chested girls in short-vamp shoes and no-carat gold vanity-cases. Older men resigned that ambition could be flayed by a yard-stick; young men still impatient of their clerkship.

It was into the trickle of these last that Miss Slayback bored her glance, the darting, eager glance of hot eyeballs and inner trembling. She was not so pathetically young as she was pathetically blond, a treacherous, ready-to-fade kind of blondness that one day, now that she had found that very morning her first gray hair, would leave her ashy.

Suddenly, with a small catch of breath that was audible in her throat, Miss Slayback stepped out of that doorway, squirming her way across the tight congestion of the sidewalk to its curb, then in and out, brushing this elbow and that shoulder, worming her way in an absolutely supreme anxiety to keep in view a brown derby hat bobbing right briskly along with the crowd, a greenish-black bit of feather upright in its band.

At Broadway, Fourteenth Street cuts quite a caper, deploying out into Union Square, an island of park, beginning to be succulent at the first false feint of spring, rising as it were from a sea of asphalt. Across this park Miss Slayback worked her rather frenzied way, breaking into a run when the derby threatened to sink into the confusion of a hundred others, and finally learning to keep its course by the faint but distinguishing fact of a slight dent in the crown. At Broadway, some blocks before that highway bursts into its famous flare, Mr. Batch, than whom it was no other, turned off suddenly at right angles down into a dim pocket of side-street and into the illuminated entrance of Ceiner's Café Hungarian. Meals at all hours. Lunch, thirty cents. Dinner, fifty cents. Our Goulash is Famous.

New York, which expresses itself in more languages to the square block than any other area in the world, Babylon included, loves thus to dine linguistically, so to speak. To the

Crescent Turkish Restaurant for its Business Men's Lunch comes Fourth Avenue, whose antique-shop patois reads across the page from right to left. Sight-seeing automobiles on mission and commission bent allow Altoona, Iowa City, and Quincy, Illinois, fifteen minutes' stop-in at Ching Ling-Foo's Chinatown Delmonico's. Spaghetti and red wine have set New York racing to reserve its table d'hôtes. All except the Latin race.

Jimmie Batch, who had first seen light, and that gaslight, in a block in lower Manhattan which has since been given over to a milk-station for a highly congested district, had the palate, if not the purse, of the cosmopolite. His digestive range included *borsch* and *chow main; risotta* and " ham and."

To-night, as he turned into Café Hungarian, Miss Slayback slowed and drew back into the overshadowing protection of an adjoining office-building. She was breathing hard, and her little face, somehow smaller from chill, was nevertheless a high pink at the cheek-bones.

The wind swept around the corner, jerking her hat, and her hand flew up to it. There was a fair stream of passers-by even here, and occasionally one turned for a backward glance at her standing there so frankly indeterminate.

Suddenly Miss Slayback adjusted her tam-o'-shanter to its flop over her right ear, and, drawing off a pair of dark-blue silk gloves from over immaculately new white ones, entered Ceiner's Café Hungarian. In its light she was not so obviously blonder than young, the pink spots in her cheeks had a deepening value to the blue of her eyes, and a black velvet tam-o'-shanter revealing just the right fringe of yellow curls is no mean aid.

First of all, Ceiner's is an eating-place. There is no music except at five cents in the slot, and its tables for four are perpetually set each with a dish of sliced radishes, a bouquet of celery, and a mound of bread, half the stack rye. Its menus are well thumbed and badly mimeographed. Who enters

Ceiner's is prepared to dine from barley soup to apple strudel. At something after six begins the rising sound of cutlery, and already the new-comer fears to find no table.

Off at the side, Mr. Jimmie Batch had already disposed of his hat and gray overcoat, and tilting the chair opposite him to indicate its reservation, shook open his evening paper, the waiter withholding the menu at this sign of rendezvous.

Straight toward that table Miss Slayback worked quick, swift way, through this and that aisle, jerking back and seating herself on the chair opposite almost before Mr. Batch could raise his eyes from off the sporting page.

There was an instant of silence between them—the kind of silence that can shape itself into a commentary upon the inefficacy of mere speech—a widening silence which, as they sat there facing, deepened until, when she finally spoke, it was as if her words were pebbles dropping down into a well.

" Don't look so surprised, Jimmie," she said, propping her face calmly, even boldly, into the white-kid palms. " You might fall off the Christmas tree."

Above the snug, four-inch collar and bow tie Mr. Batch's face was taking on a dull ox-blood tinge that spread back, even reddening his ears. Mr. Batch had the frontal bone of a clerk, the horn-rimmed glasses of the literarily astigmatic, and the sartorial perfection that only the rich can afford not to attain.

He was staring now quite frankly, and his mouth had fallen open. " Gert! " he said.

" Yes," said Miss Slayback, her insouciance gaining with his discomposure, her eyes widening and then a dolly kind of glassiness seeming to set in. " You wasn't expecting me, Jimmie? "

He jerked up his hand, not meeting her glance. " What's the idea of the comedy? "

" You don't look glad to see me, Jimmie."

" If you—think you're funny."

She was working out of and then back into the freshly white gloves in a betraying kind of nervousness that belied the toss of her voice. "Well, of all things! Mad-cat! Mad, just because you didn't seem to be expecting me."

"I—There's some things that are just the limit, that's what they are. Some things that are just the limit, that no fellow would stand from any girl, and this—this is one of them."

Her lips were trembling now. "You—you bet your life there's some things that are just the limit."

He slid out his watch, pushing back. "Well, I guess this place is too small for a fellow and a girl that can follow him around the town like a—like——"

She sat forward, grasping the table-sides, her chair tilting with her. "Don't you dare to get up and leave me sitting here! Jimmie Batch, don't you dare! "

The waiter intervened, card extended.

"We—we're waiting for another party," said Miss Slayback, her hands still rigidly over the table-sides and her glance like a steady drill into Mr. Batch's own.

There was a second of this silence while the waiter withdrew, and then Mr. Batch whipped out his watch again, a gun-metal one with an open face.

"Now look here. I got a date here in ten minutes, and one or the other of us has got to clear. You—you're one too many, if you got to know it."

"Oh, I do know it, Jimmie! I been one too many for the last four Saturday nights. I been one too many ever since May Scully came into five hundred dollars' inheritance and quit the Ladies' Neckwear. I been one too many ever since May Scully became a lady."

"If I was a girl and didn't have more shame! "

"Shame! Now you're shouting, Jimmie Batch. I haven't got shame, and I don't care who knows it. A girl don't stop to have shame when she's fighting for her rights."

He was leaning on his elbow, profile to her. "That movie talk can't scare me. You can't tell me what to do and what not to do. I've given you a square deal all right. There's not a word ever passed between us that ties me to your apron-strings. I don't say I'm not without my obligations to you, but that's not one of them. No, siree—no apron-strings."

"I know it isn't, Jimmie. You're the kind of a fellow wouldn't even talk to himself for fear of committing himself."

"I got a date here now any minute, Gert, and the sooner you——"

"You're the guy who passed up the Sixty-first for the Safety First regiment."

"I'll show you my regiment some day."

"I—I know you're not tied to my apron-strings, Jimmie. I—I wouldn't have you there for anything. Don't you think I know you too well for that? That's just it. Nobody on God's earth knows you the way I do. I know you better than you know yourself."

"You better beat it, Gertie. I tell you I'm getting sore."

Her face flashed from him to the door and back again, her anxiety almost edged with hysteria. "Come on, Jimmie—out the side entrance before she gets here. May Scully ain't the company for you. You think if she was, honey, I'd—I'd see myself come butting in between you this way, like—like a— common girl? She's not the girl to keep you straight. Honest to God she's not, honey."

"My business is my business, let me tell you that."

"She's speedy, Jimmie. She was the speediest girl on the main floor, and now that she's come into those five hundred, instead of planting it for a rainy day, she's quit work and gone plumb crazy with it."

"When I want advice about my friends I ask for it."

"It's not the good name that worries me, Jimmie, because she ain't got any. It's you. She's got you crazy with that five hundred, too—that's what's got me scared."

"Gee! you ought to let the Salvation Army tie a bonnet under your chin."

"She's always had her eyes on you, Jimmie. Ain't you men got no sense for seein' things? Since the day they moved the Gents' Furnishings across from the Ladies' Neckwear she's had you spotted. Her goings-on used to leak down to the basement, alrighty. She's not a good girl, May ain't, Jimmie. She ain't, and you know it. Is she? Is she?"

"Aw!" said Jimmie Batch.

"You see! See! Ain't got the nerve to answer, have you?"

"Aw—maybe I know, too that she's not the kind of a girl that would turn up where she's not——"

"If you wasn't a classy-looking kind of boy, Jimmie, that a fly girl like May likes to be seen out with, she couldn't find you with magnifying glasses, not if you was born with the golden rule in your mouth and had swallowed it. She's not the kind of girl, Jimmie, a fellow like you needs behind him. If—if you was ever to marry her and get your hands on them five hundred dollars——"

"It would be my business."

"It'll be your ruination. You're not strong enough to stand up under nothing like that. With a few hundred unearned dollars in your pocket you—you'd go up in spontaneous combustion, you would."

"It would be my own spontaneous combustion."

"You got to be drove, Jimmie, like a kid. With them few dollars you wouldn't start up a little cigar-store like you think you would. You and her would blow yourselves to the dogs in two months. Cigar-stores ain't the place for you, Jimmie. You seen how only clerking in them was nearly your ruination—the little gambling-room-in-the-back kind that you pick out. They ain't cigar-stores; they're only false faces for gambling."

"You know it all, don't you?"

" Oh, I'm dealing it to you straight! There's too many sporty crowds loafing around those joints for a fellow like you to stand up under. I found you in one, and as yellow-fingered and as loafing as they come, a new job a week, a——"

" Yeh, and there was some pep to variety, too."

" Don't throw over, Jimmie, what my getting you out of it to a decent job in a department store has begun to do for you. And you're making good, too. Higgins told me to-day, if you don't let your head swell, there won't be a fellow in the department can stack up his sales-book any higher."

" Aw! "

" Don't throw it all over, Jimmie—and me—for a crop of dyed red hair and a few dollars to ruin yourself with."

He shot her a look of constantly growing nervousness, his mouth pulled to an oblique, his glance constantly toward the door.

" Don't keep no date with her to-night, Jimmie. You haven't got the constitution to stand her pace. It's telling on you. Look at those fingers yellowing again—looka——"

" They're my fingers, ain't they? "

" You see, Jimmie, I—I'm the only person in the world that likes you just for what—you ain't—and hasn't got any pipe dreams about you. That's what counts, Jimmie, the folks that like you in spite, and not because of."

" We will now sing psalm number two hundred and twenty-three."

" I know there's not a better fellow in the world if he's kept nailed to the right job, and I know, too, there's not another fellow can go to the dogs any easier."

" To hear you talk, you'd think I was about six."

" I'm the only girl that'll ever be willing to make a whip out of herself that'll keep you going and won't sting, honey. I know you're soft and lazy and selfish and——"

" Don't forget any."

" And I know you're my good-looking good-for-nothing, and

I know, too, that you—you don't care as much—as much for me from head to toe as I do for your little finger. But I— like you just the same, Jimmie. That—that's what I mean about having no shame. I—do like you so—so terribly, Jimmie."

" Aw now—Gert! "

" I know it, Jimmie—that I ought to be ashamed. Don't think I haven't cried myself to sleep with it whole nights in succession."

" Aw now—Gert! "

" Don't think I don't know it, that I'm laying myself before you pretty common. I know it's common for a girl to—to come to a fellow like this, but—but I haven't got any shame about it—I haven't got anything, Jimmie, except fight for—for what's eating me. And the way things are between us now is eating me."

" I—— Why, I got a mighty high regard for you, Gert."

" There's a time in a girl's life, Jimmie, when she's been starved like I have for something of her own all her days; there's times, no matter how she's held in, that all of a sudden comes a minute when she busts out."

" I understand, Gert, but——"

" For two years and eight months, Jimmie, life has got to be worth while living to me because I could see the day, even if we—you—never talked about it, when you would be made over from a flip kid to—to the kind of a fellow would want to settle down to making a little two-by-four home for us. A little two-by-four all our own, with you steady on the job and advanced maybe to forty or fifty a week and——"

" For God's sake, Gertie, this ain't the time or the place to——"

" Oh yes, it is! It's got to be, because it's the first time in four weeks that you didn't see me coming first."

" But not now, Gert. I——"

" I'm not ashamed to tell you, Jimmie Batch, that I've been

the making of you since that night you threw the wink at me. And—and it hurts, this does. God! how it hurts! "

He was pleating the table-cloth, swallowing as if his throat had constricted, and still rearing his head this way and that in the tight collar.

" I—never claimed not to be a bad egg. This ain't the time and the place for rehashing, that's all. Sure you been a friend to me. I don't say you haven't. Only I can't be bossed by a girl like you. I don't say May Scully's any better than she ought to be. Only that's my business. You hear? my business. I got to have life and see a darn sight more future for myself than selling shirts in a Fourteenth Street department store."

" May Scully can't give it to you—her and her fast crowd."

" Maybe she can and maybe she can't."

" Them few dollars won't make you; they'll break you."

" That's for her to decide, not you."

" I'll tell her myself. I'll face her right here and——"

" Now, look here, if you think I'm going to be let in for a holy show between you two girls, you got another think coming. One of us has got to clear out of here, and quick, too. You been talking about the side door; there it is. In five minutes I got a date in this place that I thought I could keep like any law-abiding citizen. One of us has got to clear, and quick, too. Gad! you wimmin make me sick, the whole lot of you! "

" If anything makes you sick, I know what it is. It's dodging me to fly around all hours of the night with May Scully, the girl who put the tang in tango. It's eating around in swell sixty-cent restaurants like this and——"

" Gad! your middle name ought to be Nagalene."

" Aw, now, Jimmie, maybe it does sound like nagging, but it ain't, honey. It—it's only my—my fear that I'm losing you, and—and my hate for the every-day grind of things, and——"

" I can't help that, can I? "

" Why, there—there's nothing on God's earth I hate, Jimmie, like I hate that Bargain-Basement. When I think it's down there in that manhole I've spent the best years of my life, I—I wanna die. The day I get out of it, the day I don't have to punch that old time-clock down there next to the Complaints and Adjustment Desk, I—I'll never put my foot below sidewalk level again to the hour I die. Not even if it was to take a walk in my own gold-mine."

" It ain't exactly a garden of roses down there."

" Why, I hate it so terrible, Jimmie, that sometimes I wake up nights gritting my teeth with the smell of steam-pipes and the tramp of feet on the glass sidewalk up over me. Oh, God! you dunno—you dunno! "

" When it comes to that, the main floor ain't exactly a maiden's dream, or a fellow's, for that matter."

" With a man it's different. It's his job in life, earning, and—and the woman making the two ends of it meet. That's why, Jimmie, these last two years and eight months, if not for what I was hoping for us, why—why—I—why, on your twenty a week, Jimmie, there's nobody could run a flat like I could. Why, the days wouldn't be long enough to putter in. I— Don't throw away what I been building up for us, Jimmie, step by step! Don't, Jimmie! '

" Good Lord, girl! You deserve better'n me."

" I know I got a big job, Jimmie, but I want to make a man out of you, temper, laziness, gambling, and all. You got it in you to be something more than a tango lizard or a cigar-store bum, honey. It's only you ain't got the stuff in you to stand up under a five-hundred-dollar windfall and—a—and a sporty girl. If—if two glasses of beer make you as silly as they do, Jimmie, why, five hundred dollars would land you under the table for life."

" Aw—there you go again! "

" I can't help it, Jimmie. It's because I never knew a fellow had what's he's cut out for written all over him so. You're a born clerk, Jimmie."

" Sure, I'm a slick clerk, but——"

" You're born to be a clerk, a good clerk, even a two-hundred-a-month clerk, the way you can win the trade, but never your own boss. I know what I'm talking about. I know your measure better than any human on earth can ever know your measure. I know things about you that you don't even know yourself."

" I never set myself up to nobody for anything I wasn't."

" Maybe not, Jimmie, but I know about you and—and that Central Street gang that time, and——"

" You! "

" Yes, honey, and there's not another human living but me knows how little it was your fault. Just bad company, that was all. That's how much I—I love you, Jimmie, enough to understand that. Why, if I thought May Scully and a set-up in business was the thing for you, Jimmie, I'd say to her, I'd say, if it was like taking my own heart out in my hand and squashing it, I'd say to her, I'd say, ' Take him, May.' That's how I—I love you, Jimmie. Oh, ain't it nothing, honey, a girl can come here and lay herself this low to you——"

" Well, haven't I just said you—you deserve better."

" I don't want better, Jimmie. I want you. I want to take hold of your life and finish the job of making it the kind we can both be proud of. Us two, Jimmie, in—in our own decent two-by-four. Shopping on Saturday nights. Frying in our own frying-pan in our own kitchen. Listening to our own phonograph in our own parlor. Geraniums and—and kids—and—and things. Gas-logs. Stationary washtubs. Jimmie! Jimmie! "

Mr. James P. Batch reached up for his hat and overcoat, cramming the newspaper into a rear pocket.

" Come on," he said, stalking toward the side door and not waiting to see her to her feet.

Outside, a banner of stars was over the narrow street. For a chain of five blocks he walked, with a silence and speed that Miss Slayback could only match with a running quickstep. But she was not out of breath. Her head was up, and her hand where it hooked into Mr. Batch's elbow, was in a vise that tightened with each block.

You who will mete out no other approval than that vouched for by the stamp of time and whose contempt for the contemporary is from behind the easy refuge of the classics, suffer you the shuddering analogy that between Aspasia who inspired Pericles, Theodora who suggested the Justinian code, and Gertie Slayback who commandeered Jimmie Batch, is a sistership which rounds them, like a lasso thrown back into time, into one and the same petticoat dynasty behind the throne.

True, Gertie Slayback's *mise en scène* was a two-room kitchenette apartment situated in the Bronx at a surveyor's farthest point between two Subway stations, and her present state one of frequent red-faced forays down into a packing-case. But there was that in her eyes which witchingly bespoke the conquered, but not the conqueror. Hers was actually the titillating wonder of a bird which, captured, closes its wings, that surrender can be so sweet.

Once she sat on the edge of the packing-case, dallying with a hammer, then laid it aside suddenly, to cross the littered room and place the side of her head to the immaculate waistcoat of Mr. Jimmie Batch, red-faced, too, over wrenching up with hatchet-edge a barrel-top.

" Jimmie darling, I—I just never will get over your finding this place for us."

Mr. Batch wiped his forearm across his brow, his voice jerking between the squeak of nails extracted from wood.

"It was you, honey. You give me the to-let ad. and I came to look, that's all."

" Just the samey, it was my boy found it. If you hadn't

come to look we might have been forced into taking that old
dark coop over on Simpson Street."

" What's all this junk in this barrel? "

" Them's kitchen utensils, honey."

" Kitchen what? "

" Kitchen things that you don't know nothing about except
to eat good things out of."

" What's this? "

" Don't bend it!   That's a celery-brush.   Ain't it cute? "

" A celery-brush!   Why didn't you get it a comb, too? "

" Ah, now, honey-bee, don't go trying to be funny and
picking through these things you don't know nothing about!
They're just cute things I'm going to cook something grand
suppers in, for my something awful bad boy."

He leaned down to kiss her at that.   " Gee! "

She was standing, her shoulder to him and head thrown back
against his chest.   She looked up to stroke his cheek, her face
foreshortened.

" I'm all black and blue pinching myself, Jimmie."

" Me too."

" Every night when I get home from working here in the flat
I say to myself in the looking-glass, I say, ' Gertie Slayback, what if you're only dreamin' ? "

" Me too."

" I say to myself, ' Are you sure that darling flat up there,
with the new pink-and-white wall-paper and the furniture
arriving every day, is going to be yours in a few days when
you're Mrs. Jimmie Batch? ' "

" Mrs. Jimmie Batch—say, that's immense."

" I keep saying it to myself every night, ' One day less.'
Last night it was two days.   To-night it'll be—one day, Jimmie, till I'm—her."

She closed her eyes and let her hand linger up to his cheek,
head still back against him, so that, inclining his head, he
could rest his lips in the ash-blond fluff of her hair.

"Talk about can't wait! If to-morrow was any farther off they'd have to sweep out a padded cell for me."

She turned to rumple the smooth light thatch of his hair. "Bad boy! Can't wait! And here we are getting married all of a sudden, just like that. Up to the time of this draft business, Jimmie Batch, 'pretty soon' was the only date I could ever get out of you, and now here you are crying over one day's wait. Bad honey boy!"

He reached back for the pink newspaper so habitually protruding from his hip-pocket. "You ought to see the way they're neck-breaking for the marriage-license bureaus since the draft. First thing we know the whole shebang of the boys will be claiming exemption of sole support of wife."

"It's a good thing we made up our minds quick, Jimmie. They'll be getting wise. If too many get exemption from the army by marrying right away, it'll be a give-away."

"I'd like to know who can lay his hands on the exemption of a little wife to support."

"Oh, Jimmie, it—it sounds so funny. Being supported! Me that always did the supporting, not only to me, but to my mother and great-grandmother up to the day they died."

"I'm the greatest little supporter you ever seen."

"Me getting up mornings to stay at home in my own darling little flat, and no basement or time-clock. Nothing but a busy little hubby to eat him nice, smelly, bacon breakfast and grab him nice morning newspaper, kiss him wifie, and run downtown to support her. Jimmie, every morning for your breakfast I'm going to fry——"

"You bet your life he's going to support her, and he's going to pay back that forty dollars of his girl's that went into his wedding duds, that hundred and ninety of his girl's savings that went into furniture——"

"We got to meet our instalments every month first, Jimmie. That's what we want—no debts and every little darling piece of furniture paid up."

" We—I'm going to pay it, too."

" And my Jimmie is going to work to get himself promoted and quit being a sorehead at his steady hours and all."

" I know more about selling, honey, than the whole bunch of dubs in that store put together if they'd give me a chance to prove it."

She laid her palm to his lips.

" 'Shh-h-h! You don't nothing of the kind. It's not conceit, it's work is going to get my boy his raise."

" If they'd listen to me, that department would——"

" Sh-h-h! J. G. Hoffheimer don't have to get pointers from Jimmie Batch how to run his department store."

" There you go again. What's J. G. Hoffheimer got that I ain't? Luck and a few dollars in his pocket that, if I had in mine, would——"

" It was his own grit put those dollars there, Jimmie. Just put it out of your head that it's luck makes a self-made man."

" Self-made! You mean things just broke right for him. That's two-thirds of this self-made business."

" You mean he buckled right down to brass tacks, and that's what my boy is going to do."

" The trouble with this world is it takes money to make money. Get your first few dollars, I always say, no matter how, and then when you're on your feet scratch your conscience if it itches. That's why I said in the beginning, if we had took that hundred and ninety furniture money and staked it on——"

" Jimmie, please—please! You wouldn't want to take a girl's savings of years and years to gamble on a sporty cigar proposition with a card-room in the rear. You wouldn't, Jimmie. You ain't that kind of fellow. Tell me you wouldn't, Jimmie."

He turned away to dive into the barrel. " Naw," he said. " I wouldn't."

The sun had receded, leaving a sudden sullen gray; the little square room, littered with an upheaval of excelsior, sheet-shrouded furniture, and the paper-hanger's paraphernalia and inimitable smells, darkening and seeming to chill.

"We got to quit now, Jimmie. It's getting dark and the gas ain't turned on in the meter yet."

He rose up out of the barrel, holding out at arm's-length what might have been a tinsmith's version of a porcupine.

"What in— What's this thing that scratched me?"

She danced to take it. "It's a grater, a darling grater for horseradish and nutmeg and cocoanut. I'm going to fix you a cocoanut cake for our honeymoon supper to-morrow night, honey-bee. Essie Wohlgemuth over in the cake-demonstrating department is going to bring me the recipe. Cocoanut cake! And I'm going to fry us a little steak in this darling little skillet. Ain't it the cutest!"

"Cute she calls a tin skillet."

"Look what's pasted on it. 'Little Housewife's Skillet. The Kitchen Fairy.' That's what I'm going to be, Jimmie, the kitchen fairy. Give me that. It's a rolling-pin. All my life I've wanted a rolling-pin. Look honey, a little string to hang it up by. I'm going to hang everything up in rows. It's going to look like Tiffany's kitchen, all shiny. Give me, honey; that's an egg-beater. Look at it whiz. And this—this is a pan for war bread. I'm going to make us war bread to help the soldiers."

"You're a little soldier yourself," he said.

"That's what I would be if I was a man, a soldier all in brass buttons."

"There's a bunch of the fellows going," said Mr. Batch, standing at the window, looking out over roofs, dilly-dallying up and down on his heels and breaking into a low, contemplative whistle.

She was at his shoulder, peering over it. "You wouldn't be afraid, would you, Jimmie?"

"You bet your life I wouldn't."

She was tiptoes now, her arms creeping up to him. "Only

my boy's got a wife—a brand-new wifie to support, ain't he? "

" That's what he has," said Mr. Batch, stroking her forearm, but still gazing through and beyond whatever roofs he was seeing.

" Jimmie! "

" Huh? "

" Look! We got a view of the Hudson River from our flat, just like we lived on Riverside Drive."

" All the Hudson River I can see is fifteen smokestacks and somebody's wash-line out."

" It ain't so. We got a grand view. Look! Stand on tip-toe, Jimmie, like me. There, between that water-tank on that black roof over there and them two chimneys. See? Watch my finger. A little stream of something over there that moves."

" No, I don't see."

" Look, honey-bee, close! See that little streak? "

" All right, then, if you see it I see it."

" To think we got a river view from our flat! It's like liv-ing in the country. I'll peek out at it all day long. God! honey, I just never will be over the happiness of being done with basements."

" It was swell of old Higgins to give us this half-Saturday. It shows where you stood with the management, Gert—this and a five-dollar gold piece. Lord knows they wouldn't pony up that way if it was me getting married by myself."

" It's because my boy ain't shown them down there yet the best that's in him. You just watch his little safety-first wife see to it that from now on he keeps up her record of never in seven years pushing the time-clock even one minute late, and that he keeps his stock shelves O. K. and shows his depart-ment he's a comer-on."

" With that bunch of boobs a fellow's got a swell chance to get anywheres."

" It's getting late, Jimmie. It don't look nice for us to

stay here so late alone, not till—to-morrow. Ruby and Essie and Charley are going to meet us in the minister's back parlor at ten sharp in the morning. We can be back here by noon and get the place cleared up enough to give 'em a little lunch, just a fun lunch without fixings."

"I hope the old guy don't waste no time splicing us. It's one of the things a fellow likes to have over with."

"Jimmie! Why, it's the most beautiful thing in the world, like a garden of lilies or—or something, a marriage ceremony is! You got the ring safe, honey-bee, and the license?"

"Pinned in my pocket where you put 'em, Flirty Gertie."

"Flirty Gertie! Now you'll begin teasing me with that all our life—the way I didn't slap your face that night when I should have. I just couldn't have, honey. Goes to show we were just cut and dried for each other, don't it? Me, a girl that never in her life let a fellow even bat his eyes at her without an introduction. But that night when you winked, honey—something inside of me just winked back."

"My girl!"

"You mean it, boy? You ain't sorry about nothing, Jimmie?"

"Sorry? Well, I guess not!"

"You seen the way—she—May—you seen for yourself what she was, when we seen her walking, that next night after Ceiner's, nearly staggering, up Sixth Avenue with Budge Evans."

"I never took no stock in her, honey. I was just letting her like me."

She sat back on the box edge, regarding him, her face so soft and wont to smile that she could not keep its composure.

"Get me my hat and coat, honey. We'll walk down. Got the key?"

They skirmished in the gloom, moving through slit-like aisles of furniture and packing-box.

"Ouch!"

"Oh, the running water is hot, Jimmie, just like the ad. said! We got red-hot running water in our flat. Close the front windows, honey. We don't want it to rain in on our new green sofa. Not till it's paid for, anyways."

"Hurry."

"I'm ready."

They met at the door, kissing on the inside and the outside of it; at the head of the fourth and the third and the second balustrade down.

"We'll always make 'em little love landings, Jimmie, so we can't ever get tired climbing them."

"Yep."

Outside there was still a pink glow in a clean sky. The first flush of spring in the air had died, leaving chill. They walked briskly, arm in arm, down the asphalt incline of sidewalk leading from their apartment-house, a new street of canned homes built on a hillside—the sepulchral abode of the city's trapped whose only escape is down the fire-escape, and then only when the alternative is death. At the base of the hill there flows, in constant hubbub, a great up-and-down artery of street, repeating itself, mile after mile, in terms of the butcher, the baker, and the every-other-corner drug-store of a million dollar corporation. Housewives with perambulators and oilcloth shopping bags. Children on roller-skates. The din of small tradesmen and the humdrum of every city block where the homes remain unboarded all summer, and every wife is on haggling terms with the purveyor of her evening roundsteak and mess of rutabaga.

Then there is the soap-box provender, too, sure of a crowd, offering creed, propaganda, patent medicine, and politics. It is the pulpit of the reformer and the housetop of the fanatic, this soap-box. From it the voice to the city is often a pious one, an impious one, and almost always a raucous one. Luther and Sophocles and even a Citizen of Nazareth made of the four winds of the street corner the walls of a temple of wisdom. What more fitting acropolis for freedom of speech than the great out-of-doors!

Turning from the incline of cross-street into this petty Bagdad of the petty wise, the voice of the street corner lifted itself above the inarticulate din of the thoroughfare. A youth, thewed like an ox, surmounted on a stack of three self-provided canned-goods boxes, his in-at-the-waist silhouette thrown out against a sky that was almost ready to break out in stars; a crowd tightening about him.

" It's a soldier-boy talkin', Gert."

" If it ain't! " They tiptoed at the fringe of the circle, heads back.

" Look, Gert, he's a lieutenant; he's got a shoulder-bar. And those four down there holding the flag are just privates. You can always tell a lieutenant by the bar."

" Uh-huh."

" Say, them boys do stack up some for Uncle Sam."

" 'Shh-h-h, Jimmie! "

" I'm here to tell you that them boys stack up some."

A banner stiffened out in the breeze, Mr. Batch reading: " Enlist before you are drafted. Last chance to beat the draft. Prove your patriotism. Enlist now! Your country calls! "

" Come on," said Mr. Batch.

" Wait. I want to hear what he's saying."

" . . . there's not a man here before me can afford to shirk his duty to his country. The slacker can't get along without his country, but his country can very easily get along without him."

Cheers.

" The poor exemption boobs are already running for doctors' certificates and marriage licenses, but even if they get by with it—and it is ninety-nine to one they won't—they can't run away from their own degradation and shame."

" Come on, Jimmie."

" Wait."

" Men of America, for every one of you who tries to dodge his duty to his country there is a yellow streak somewhere underneath the hide of you. Women of America, every one of you that helps to foster the spirit of cowardice in your particular man or men is helping to make a coward. It's the cowards and the quitters and the slackers and dodgers that need this war more than the patriotic ones who are willing to buckle on and go!

" Don't be a buttonhole patriot! A government that is good enough to live under is good enough to fight under! "

Cheers.

" If there is any reason on earth that has manifested itself for this devastating and terrible war it is that it has been a maker of men.

" Ladies and gentlemen, I am back from four months in the trenches with the French army, and I've come home, now that my own country is at war, to give her every ounce of energy I've got to offer. As soon as a hole in my side is healed up I'm going back to those trenches, and I want to say to you that them four months of mine face to face with life and with death have done more for me than all my twenty-four civilian years put together."

Cheers.

" I'll be a different man, if I live to come back home after this war and take up my work again as a draftsman. Why, I've seen weaklings and self-confessed failures and even ninnies go into them trenches and come out—oh yes, plenty of them do come out—men. Men that have got close enough down to the facts of things to feel new realizations of what life means come over them. Men that have gotten back their pep, their ambitions, their unselfishness. That's what war can do for your men, you women who are helping them to foster the spirit of holding back, of cheating their government. That's what war can do for your men. Make of them the kind of men who some day can face their children without having to hang their heads. Men who can answer for their part in making the world a safe place for democracy."

An hour they stood there, the air quieting but chilling, and lavishly sown stars cropping out. Street lights had come out, too, throwing up in ever darker relief the figure above the heads of the crowd. His voice had coarsened and taken on a raw edge, but every gesture was flung from the socket, and from where they had forced themselves into the tight circle Gertie Slayback, her mouth fallen open and her head still back, could see the sinews of him ripple under khaki and the diaphragm lift for voice.

There was a shift of speakers then, this time a private, still too rangy, but his looseness of frame seeming already to conform to the exigency of uniform.

"Come on, Jimmie. I—I'm cold."

They worked out into the freedom of the sidewalk, and for ten minutes, down blocks of petty shops already lighted, walked in a silence that grew apace.

He was suddenly conscious that she was crying, quietly, her handkerchief wadded against her mouth. He strode on with a scowl and his head bent.

"Let's sit down in this little park, Jimmie. I'm tired."

They rested on a bench on one of those small triangles of breathing-space which the city ekes out now and then; mill ends of land parcels.

He took immediately to roving the toe of his shoe in and out among the gravel. She stole out her hand to his arm.

"Well, Jimmie?" Her voice was in the gauze of a whisper that hardly left her throat.

"Well, what?" he said, still toeing.

"There—there's a lot of things we never thought about, Jimmie."

"Aw!"

"Eh, Jimmie?"

"You mean *you* never thought about."

" What do you mean? "

" I know what I mean alrighty."

" I—I was the one that suggested it, Jimmie, but—but you fell in. I—I just couldn't bear to think of it, Jimmie—your going and all. I suggested it, but—you fell in."

" Say, when a fellow's shoved he falls. I never gave a thought to sneaking an exemption until it was put in my head. I'd smash the fellow in the face that calls me coward, I will."

" You could have knocked me down with a feather, Jimmie, looking at it his way, all of a sudden."

" You couldn't me. Don't think I was ever strong for the whole business. I mean the exemption part. I wasn't going to say nothing. What's the use, seeing the way you had your heart set on—on things? But the whole business, if you want to know it, went against my grain. I'll smash the fellow in the face that calls me a coward."

" I know, Jimmie; you—you're right. It was me suggested hurrying things like this. Sneakin'! Oh, God! ain't I the messer-up! "

" Lay easy, girl. I'm going to see it through. I guess there's been fellows before me and will be after me who have done worse. I'm going to see it through. All I got to say is I'll smash up the fellow calls me coward. Come on, forget it. Let's go."

She was close to him, her cheek crinkled against his with the frank kind of social unconsciousness the park bench seems to engender.

" Come on, Gert. I got a hunger on."

" 'Shh-h-h, Jimmie! Let me think. I'm thinking."

" Too much thinking killed a cat. Come on."

" Jimmie! "

" Huh? "

" Jimmie—would you—had you ever thought about being a soldier? "

"Sure. I came in an ace of going into the army that time after—after that little Central Street trouble of mine. I've got a book in my trunk this minute on military tactics. Wouldn't surprise me a bit to see me land in the army some day."

"It's a fine thing, Jimmie, for a fellow—the army."

"Yeh, good for what ails him."

She drew him back, pulling at his shoulder so that finally he faced her. "Jimmie!"

"Huh?"

"I got an idea."

"Shoot."

"You remember once, honey-bee, how I put it to you that night at Ceiner's how, if it was for your good, no sacrifice was too much to make."

"Forget it."

"You didn't believe it."

"Aw, say now, what's the use digging up ancient history?"

"You'd be right, Jimmie, not to believe it. I haven't lived up to what I said."

"Oh Lord, honey! What's eating you now? Come to the point."

She would not meet his eyes, turning her head from him to hide lips that would quiver. "Honey, it—it ain't coming off—that's all. Not now—anyways."

"What ain't?"

"Us."

"Who?"

"You know what I mean, Jimmie. It's like everything the soldier boy on the corner just said. I—I saw you getting red clear behind your ears over it. I—I was, too, Jimmie. It's like that soldier boy was put there on that corner just to show me, before it was too late, how wrong I been in every one of my ways. Us women who are helping to foster slackers.

That's what we're making of them—slackers for life. And here I been thinking it was your good I had in mind, when all along it's been mine. That's what it's been, mine! "

" Aw, now, Gert——"

" You got to go, Jimmie. You got to go, because you want to go and—because I want you to go."

" Where? "

" To war."

He took hold of her two arms because they were trembling. " Aw, now, Gert, I didn't say anything complaining. I——"

" You did, Jimmie, you did, and—and I never was so glad over you that you did complain. I just never was so glad. I want you to go, Jimmie. I want you to go and get a man made out of you. They'll make a better job out of you than ever I can. I want you to get the yellow streak washed out. I want you to get to be all the things he said you would. For every line he was talking up there, I could see my boy coming home to me some day better than anything I could make out of him, babying him the way I can't help doing. I could see you, honey-bee, coming back to me with the kind of lift to your head a fellow has when he's been fighting to make the world a safe place for dem—for whatever it was he said. I want you to go, Jimmie. I want you to beat the draft, too. Nothing on earth can make me not want you to go."

" Why, Gert—you're kiddin'! "

" Honey, you want to go, don't you? You want to square up those shoulders and put on khaki, don't you? Tell me you want to go! "

" Why—why, yes, Gert, if——"

" Oh, you're going, Jimmie! You're going! "

" Why, girl—you're crazy! Our flat! Our furniture—our——"

" What's a flat? What's furniture? What's anything? There's not a firm in business wouldn't take back a boy's furni-

ture—a boy's everything—that's going out to fight for—for
dem-o-cracy! What's a flat? What's anything? "

He let drop his head to hide his eyes.

Do you know it is said that on the Desert of Sahara, the
slope of Sorrento, and the marble of Fifth Avenue the sun can
shine whitest?   There is an iridescence to its glittering on
bleached sand, blue bay, and Carrara façade that is sheer light
distilled to its utmost.

On one such day when, standing on the high slope of Fifth
Avenue where it rises toward the Park, and looking down on
it, surging to and fro, it was as if, so manifest the brilliancy,
every head wore a tin helmet, parrying sunlight at a thousand
angles of refraction.

Parade-day, all this glittering midstream is swept to the
clean sheen of a strip of moiré, this splendid desolation blocked
on each side by crowds half the density of the sidewalk.

On one of these sun-drenched Saturdays dedicated by a growing tradition to this or that national expression, the Ninety-
ninth Regiment, to a flare of music that made the heart leap
out against its walls, turned into a scene thus swept clean for
it, a wave of olive drab, impeccable row after impeccable row
of scissors-like legs advancing.   Recruits, raw if you will, but
already caparisoned, sniffing and scenting, as it were, for the
great primordial mire of war.

There is no state of being so finely sensitized as national consciousness. A gauntlet down, and it surges up. One ripple of a
flag defended can goose-flesh a nation. How bitter and how
sweet it is to give a soldier!

To the seething kinetic chemistry of such mingling emotions
there were women who stood in the frontal crowds of the sidewalks stifling hysteria, or ran after in terror at sight of one so
personally hers, receding in that great impersonal wave of olive
drab.

And yet the air was martial with banner and with shout.

And the ecstasy of such moments is like a dam against reality, pressing it back. It is in the pompless watches of the night or of too long days that such dams break, excoriating.

For the thirty blocks of its course Gertie Slayback followed that wave of men, half run and half walk. Down from the curb, and at the beck and call of this or that policeman up again, only to find opportunity for still another dive out from the invisible roping off of the sidewalk crowds.

From the middle of his line, she could see, sometimes, the tail of Jimmie Batch's glance roving for her, but to all purports his eye was solely for his own replica in front of him, and at such times, when he marched, his back had a little additional straightness that was almost swayback.

Nor was Gertie Slayback crying. On the contrary, she was inclined to laughter. A little too inclined to a high and brittle sort of dissonance over which she seemed to have no control.

" 'By, Jimmie. So long! Jimmie! You-hoo! "

Tramp. Tramp. Tramp-tramp-tramp.

" You-hoo! Jimmie! So long, Jimmie! "

At Fourteenth Street, and to the solemn stroke of one from a tower, she broke off suddenly without even a second look back, dodging under the very arms of the crowd as she ran out from it.

She was one and three-quarter minutes late when she punched the time-clock beside the Complaints and Adjustment Desk in the Bargain-Basement.

FANNIE HURST

" I find myself at twenty-nine exactly where at fourteen I had planned I would be." So Miss Hurst, in a sketch written for the *American Magazine* (March, 1919), sums up the story of a remarkable literary career.

Fannie Hurst was born in St. Louis, October 19, 1889. She attended the public schools, and began to write—with the firm intention of becoming an author—before she was out of grammar school. " At fourteen," she tells us in the article just referred to, " the one pigeon-hole of my little girl's desk was already stuffed with packets of rejected verse which had been furtively written, furtively mailed, and still more furtively received back again by heading off the postman a block before he reached our door." To this dream of authorship—the secret of which was carefully guarded from her family—she sacrificed her play and even her study hours. The first shock to her family came on St. Valentine's Day. There was to be a party that night, her first real party. A new dress was ready for the occasion, and a boy escort was to call for her in a cab. It happened that Valentine's day fell on Saturday, and Saturday was her time for writing. That day she turned from poetry to fiction, and was just in the middle of her first story when it came time to get ready for the party. She did not get ready. The escort arrived, cab and all; the family protested, but all to no purpose. She finished the story, mailed it, three weeks later received it back, and began her second story. All through her high school days she mailed a manuscript every Saturday, and they always came back.

After high school she entered Washington University, St. Louis, graduating in 1909. And still she kept writing. To one journal alone she sent during those four years, thirty-four short stories. And they all came back—all but one. Just before graduation she sold her first article, a little sketch first written as a daily theme, which was published in a local weekly, and brought her three dollars. This was the total result of eight years' literary effort. So quite naturally she determined to go on.

She announced to her family that she was going to New York City to become a writer. There was a stormy discussion in the Hurst family, but it ended in her going away, with a bundle of manuscripts in her trunk, to brave the big city alone. She found a tiny furnished room and set forth to besiege the editors' offices. One evening she returned, to find the house being raided, a patrol wagon at the curb, and the lodgers being hustled into it. She crossed the street and walked on, and never saw her bag or baggage again. By the help of the Young Women's Christian Association she found another room, in different surroundings, and set out again to make the round of the editorial offices.

Then followed months and months of " writing, rewriting, rejections, and re-rejections." From home came letters now beseeching, now commanding her to return, and at length cutting off her allowance. So she returned her rented typewriter and applied at a theatrical agency. She secured a small part in a Broadway company, and then came her first acceptance of a story, with an actual check for thirty dollars. She left the stage and rented another typewriter,—but it was six months before she sold another story.

In all this time she dipped deeply into the great stream of the city's life. To quote her own account:

For a month I lived with an Armenian family on West Broadway, in a room over a tobacconist's shop. I apprenticed myself as a sales-girl in New York's most gigantic department store. Four and one-quarter yards of ribbon at seven and a half cents a yard proved my Waterloo, and my resignation at the end of one week was not entirely voluntary. I served as waitress in one of New York's most gigantic chain of white-tiled lunch rooms. I stitched boys' pants in a Polish sweatshop, and lived for two days in New York's most rococo hotel. I took a graduate course in Anglo Saxon at Columbia University, and one in lamp-shade making at Wanamaker's: wormed into a Broadway musical show as wardrobe girl, and went out on a self-appointed newspaper assignment to interview the mother of the richest baby in the world.

All these experiences yielded rich material for stories, but no one would print them. Her money was gone; so was a diamond ring that had been a Commencement present; it seemed as if there was nothing left but to give up the struggle and go back home. Then, just as she had struck bottom, an editor actually told her she could write, and followed up his remark by buying three stories. Since that time she has never had a story rejected, and her checks have gone up from two figures into four. And so, at the end of a long fight, as she says, " I find myself at twenty-nine exactly where at fourteen I had planned I would be. And best of all, what popular success I am enjoying has come not from pandering to popular demand or editorial policy, but from pandering to my own inner convictions, which are like little soul-tapers, lighting the way."

All her work has been in the form of the short story. Her first book, *Just Around the Corner,* published in 1914, is a collection of stories dealing with the life of working girls in a city. *Every Soul Hath Its Song* is a similar collection; the title suggests the author's outlook upon life. Some one has said that in looking at a puddle of water, you may see either the mud at the bottom or the sky reflected on its surface. Miss Hurst sees the reflection of the sky. The *Boston Transcript* said of this book: " Here at last is a story writer who is bent on listening to the voices of America and interpreting them." *Gaslight Sonatas,* from which " Bitter-Sweet " is taken, showed an advance over her earlier work. Two of the stories from this volume were selected by Mr. O'Brien for his volume, *Best*

Short Stories, for 1916 and 1917. *Humoresque,* her latest work, continues her studies of city types, drawn from New York and St. Louis. The stories show her insight into character and her graphic descriptive power. Miss Hurst is also the author of two plays, *The Land of the Free* and *The Good Provider.*

IN THE LUMBER COUNTRY.

The men of the woods are not as the men of the cities. The great open spaces where men battle with the primeval forest set their mark upon their inhabitants, not only in physique but in character. The lumberman,—rough, frank, independent, humorous, equally ready for a fight or a frolic, has been portrayed at full length by Stewart Edward White in THE BLAZED TRAIL *and* THE RIVERMAN. *In the following sketch, taken from his* BLAZED TRAIL STORIES, *he shows the lumberman at work and at play.*

THE RIVERMAN

BY

STEWART EDWARD WHITE

I FIRST met him one Fourth of July afternoon in the middle eighties. The sawdust streets and high board sidewalks of the lumber town were filled to the brim with people. The permanent population, dressed in the stiffness of its Sunday best, escorted gingham wives or sweethearts; a dozen outsiders like myself tried not to be too conspicuous in a city smartness; but the great multitude was composed of the men of the woods. I sat, chair-tilted by the hotel, watching them pass. Their heavy woollen shirts crossed by the broad suspenders, the red of their sashes or leather shine of their belts, their short kersey trousers " stagged " off to leave a gap between the knee and the heavily spiked " cork boots "—all these were distinctive enough of their class, but most interesting to me were the eyes that peered from beneath their little round hats tilted rakishly askew. They were all subtly alike, those eyes. Some were black, some were brown, or gray, or blue, but all were steady and unabashed, all looked straight at you with a strange humorous blending of aggression and respect for your own business, and all without exception wrinkled at the corners with a suggestion of dry humor. In my half-conscious scrutiny I probably stared harder than I knew, for all at once a laughing pair of blue eyes suddenly met mine full, and an ironical voice drawled,

" Say, bub, you look as interested as a man killing snakes. Am I your long-lost friend? "

The tone of the voice matched accurately the attitude of the man, and that was quite non-committal. He stood cheerfully ready to meet the emergency. If I sought trouble, it was here to my hand; or if I needed help he was willing to offer it.

" I guess you are," I replied, " if you can tell me what all this outfit's headed for."

He thrust back his hat and ran his hand through a mop of closely cropped light curls.

" Birling match," he explained briefly. " Come on."

I joined him, and together we followed the crowd to the river, where we roosted like cormorants on adjacent piles overlooking a patch of clear water among filled booms.

" Drive just over," my new friend informed me. " Rear come down last night. Fourther July celebration. This little town will scratch fer th' tall timber along about midnight when the boys goes in to take her apart."

A half-dozen men with peavies rolled a white-pine log of about a foot and a half in diameter into the clear water, where it lay rocking back and forth, three or four feet from the boom piles. Suddenly a man ran the length of the boom, leaped easily into the air, and landed with both feet square on one end of the floating log. That end disappeared in an ankle-deep swirl of white foam, the other rose suddenly, the whole timber, projected forward by the shock, drove headlong to the middle of the little pond. And the man, his arms folded, his knees just bent in the graceful nervous attitude of the circus-rider, stood upright like a statue of bronze.

A roar approved this feat.

" That's Dickey Darrell," said my informant, " Roaring Dick. He's hell *and* repeat. Watch him."

The man on the log was small, with clean beautiful haunches and shoulders, but with hanging baboon arms. Perhaps his most striking feature was a mop of reddish-brown hair that overshadowed a little triangular white face accented by two reddish-brown quadrilaterals that served as eyebrows and a pair of inscrutable chipmunk eyes.

For a moment he poised erect in the great calm of the public performer. Then slowly he began to revolve the log under his feet. The lofty gaze, the folded arms, the straight supple waist budged not by a hair's breadth; only the feet stepped forward, at first deliberately, then faster and faster, until the rolling log threw a blue spray a foot into the air. Then suddenly *slap! slap!* the heavy caulks stamped a reversal. The log came instantaneously to rest, quivering exactly like some animal that had been spurred through its paces.

" Magnificent! " I cried.

" Hell, that's nothing! " my companion repressed me, " anybody can birl a log. Watch this."

Roaring Dick for the first time unfolded his arms. With some appearance of caution he balanced his unstable footing into absolute immobility. Then he turned a somersault.

This was the real thing. My friend uttered a wild yell of applause which was lost in a general roar.

A long pike-pole shot out, bit the end of the timber, and towed it to the boom pile. Another man stepped on the log with Darrell. They stood facing each other, bent-kneed, alert. Suddenly with one accord they commenced to birl the log from left to right. The pace grew hot. Like squirrels treading a cage their feet twinkled. Then it became apparent that Darrell's opponent was gradually being forced from the top of the log. He could not keep up. Little by little, still moving desperately, he dropped back to the slant, then at last to the edge, and so off into the river with a mighty splash.

" Clean birled! " commented my friend.

One after another a half-dozen rivermen tackled the imperturbable Dick, but none of them possessed the agility to stay on top in the pace he set them. One boy of eighteen seemed for a moment to hold his own, and managed at least to keep out of the water even when Darrell had apparently reached his maximum speed. But that expert merely threw his entire weight into two reversing stamps of his feet, and the young fellow dove forward as abruptly as though he had been shied over a horse's head.

The crowd was by now getting uproarious and impatient of volunteer effort to humble Darrell's challenge. It wanted the best, and at once. It began, with increasing insistence, to shout a name.

" Jimmy Powers! " it vociferated, " Jimmy Powers! "

And then by shamefaced bashfulness, by profane protest, by muttered and comprehensive curses I knew that my companion on the other pile was indicated.

A dozen men near at hand began to shout. " Here he is! " they cried. " Come on, Jimmy." " Don't be a high banker." " Hang his hide on the fence."

Jimmy, still red and swearing, suffered himself to be pulled from his elevation and disappeared in the throng. A moment later I caught his head and shoulders pushing toward the boom piles, and so in a moment he stepped warily aboard to face his antagonist.

This was evidently no question to be determined by the simplicity of force or the simplicity of a child's trick. The two men stood half-crouched, face to face, watching each other narrowly, but making no move. To me they seemed like two wrestlers sparring for an opening. Slowly the log revolved one way; then slowly the other. It was a mere courtesy of salute. All at once Dick birled three rapid strokes from left to right as though about to roll the log, leaped into the air and landed square with both feet on the other slant of the timber. Jimmy Powers felt the jar, and acknowledged it by a spasmodic jerk with which he counterbalanced Darrell's weight. But he was not thrown.

As though this daring and hazardous manœuvre had opened the combat, both men sprang to life. Sometimes the log rolled one way, sometimes the other, sometimes it jerked from side to side like a crazy thing, but always with the rapidity of light, always in a smother of spray and foam. The decided *spat, spat, spat* of the reversing blows from the caulked boots sounded like picket firing. I could not make out the different leads, feints, parries, and counters of this strange method of boxing, nor could I distinguish to whose initiative the various evolutions of that log could be ascribed. But I retain still a vivid mental picture of two men nearly motionless above the waist, nearly vibrant below it, dominating the insane gyrations of a stick of pine.

The crowd was appreciative and partisan—for Jimmy Powers. It howled wildly, and rose thereby to even higher excitement. Then it forgot its manners utterly and groaned when it made out that a sudden splash represented its favorite, while the indomitable Darrell still trod the quarter-deck as champion birler for the year.

I must confess I was as sorry as anybody. I climbed down from my cormorant roost, and picked my way between the alleys of aromatic piled lumber in order to avoid the press, and cursed the little gods heartily for undue partiality in the wrong direction. In this manner I happened on Jimmy Powers himself seated dripping on a board and examining his bare foot.

"I'm sorry," said I behind him. "How did he do it?"

He whirled, and I could see that his laughing boyish face had become suddenly grim and stern, and that his eyes were shot with blood.

"Oh, it's you, is it?" he growled disparagingly. "Well, that's how he did it."

He held out his foot. Across the instep and at the base of the toes ran two rows of tiny round punctures from which the blood was oozing. I looked very inquiring.

"He corked me!" Jimmy Powers explained. "Jammed his spikes into me! Stepped on my foot and tripped me, the——"
Jimmy Powers certainly could swear.

"Why didn't you make a kick?" I cried.

"That ain't how I do it," he muttered, pulling on his heavy woollen sock.

"But no," I insisted, my indignation mounting. "It's an outrage! That crowd was with you. All you had to do was to *say* something——"

He cut me short. "And give myself away as a damn fool—sure Mike. I ought to know Dickey Darrell by this time, and I ought to be big enough to take care of myself." He stamped his foot into his driver's shoe and took me by the arm, his good humor apparently restored. "No, don't lose any hair, bub; I'll get even with Roaring Dick."

That night, having by the advice of the proprietor moved my bureau and trunk against the bedroom door, I lay wide awake listening to the taking of the town apart. At each especially vicious crash I wondered if that might be Jimmy Powers getting even with Roaring Dick.

The following year, but earlier in the season, I again visited my little lumber town. In striking contrast to the life of that other midsummer day were the deserted streets. The landlord knew me, and after I had washed and eaten approached me with a suggestion.

"You got all day in front of you," said he; "why don't you take a horse and buggy and make a visit to the big jam? Everybody's up there more or less."

In response to my inquiry, he replied:

"They've jammed at the upper bend, jammed bad. The crew's been picking at her for near a week now, and last night Darrell was down to see about some more dynamite. It's worth seein'. The breast of her is near thirty feet high, and lots of water in the river."

"Darrell?" said I, catching at the name.

"Yes. He's rear boss this year. Do you think you'd like to take a look at her?"

"I think I should," I assented.

The horse and I jogged slowly along a deep sand road,

through wastes of pine stumps and belts of hardwood beautiful with the early spring, until finally we arrived at a clearing in which stood two huge tents, a mammoth kettle slung over a fire of logs, and drying racks about the timbers of another fire. A fat cook in the inevitable battered derby hat, two bare-armed cookees, and a chore " boy " of seventy-odd summers were the only human beings in sight. One of the cookees agreed to keep an eye on my horse. I picked my way down a well-worn trail toward the regular *clank, clank, click* of the peavies.

I emerged finally to a plateau elevated some fifty or sixty feet above the river. A half-dozen spectators were already gathered. Among them I could not but notice a tall, spare, broad-shouldered young fellow dressed in a quiet business suit, somewhat wrinkled, whose square, strong, clean-cut face and muscular hands were tanned by the weather to a dark umber-brown. In another moment I looked down on the jam.

The breast, as my landlord had told me, rose sheer from the water to the height of at least twenty-five feet, bristling and formidable. Back of it pressed the volume of logs packed closely in an apparently inextricable tangle as far as the eye could reach. A man near informed me that the tail was a good three miles up stream. From beneath this wonderful *chevaux de frise* foamed the current of the river, irresistible to any force less mighty than the statics of such a mass.

A crew of forty or fifty men were at work. They clamped their peavies to the reluctant timbers, heaved, pushed, slid, and rolled them one by one into the current, where they were caught and borne away. They had been doing this for a week. As yet their efforts had made but slight impression on the bulk of the jam, but some time, with patience, they would reach the key-logs. Then the tangle would melt like sugar in the freshet, and these imperturbable workers would have to escape suddenly over the plunging logs to shore.

My eye ranged over the men, and finally rested on Dickey

Darrell. He was standing on the slanting end of an up-heaved log dominating the scene. His little triangular face with the accents of the quadrilateral eyebrows was pale with the blaze of his energy, and his chipmunk eyes seemed to flame with a dynamic vehemence that caused those on whom they fell to jump as though they had been touched with a hot poker. I had heard more of Dickey Darrell since my last visit, and was glad of the chance to observe Morrison & Daly's best " driver " at work.

The jam seemed on the very edge of breaking. After half an hour's strained expectation it seemed still on the very ᵉdge of breaking. So I sat down on a stump. Then for the first time I noticed another acquaintance, handling his peavie near the very person of the rear boss.

" Hullo," said I to myself, " that's funny. I wonder if Jimmy Powers got even; and if so, why he is working so amicably and so near Roaring Dick."

At noon the men came ashore for dinner. I paid a quarter into the cook's private exchequer and so was fed. After the meal I approached my acquaintance of the year before.

" Hello, Powers," I greeted him, " I suppose you don't re-member me? "

" Sure," he responded heartily. " Ain't you a little early this year? "

" No," I disclaimed, " this is a better sight than a birling match."

I offered him a cigar, which he immediately substituted for his corn-cob pipe. We sat at the root of a tree.

" It'll be a great sight when that jam pulls," said I.

" You bet," he replied, " but she's a teaser. Even old Tim Shearer would have a picnic to make out just where the key-logs are. We've started her three times, but she's plugged tight every trip. Likely to pull almost any time."

We discussed various topics. Finally I ventured:

" I see your old friend Darrell is rear boss."

" Yes," said Jimmy Powers, dryly.

" By the way, did you fellows ever square up on that birling match? "

" No," said Jimmy Powers; then after an instant, " Not yet."

I glanced at him to recognize the square set to the jaw that had impressed me so formidably the year before. And again his face relaxed almost quizzically as he caught sight of mine.

" Bub," said he, getting to his feet, " those little marks are on my foot yet. And just you tie into one idea: Dickey Darrell's got it coming." His face darkened with a swift anger. " God damn his soul! " he said, deliberately. It was no mere profanity. It was an imprecation, and in its very deliberation I glimpsed the flare of an undying hate.

About three o'clock that afternoon Jimmy's prediction was fulfilled. Without the slightest warning the jam "pulled." Usually certain premonitory *cracks,* certain sinkings down, groanings forward, grumblings, shruggings, and sullen, reluctant shiftings of the logs give opportunity for the men to assure their safety. This jam, after inexplicably hanging fire for a week, as inexplicably started like a sprinter almost into its full gait. The first few tiers toppled smash into the current, raising a waterspout like that made by a dynamite explosion; the mass behind plunged forward blindly, rising and falling as the integral logs were up-ended, turned over, thrust one side, or forced bodily into the air by the mighty power playing jack-straws with them.

The rivermen, though caught unaware, reached either bank. They held their peavies across their bodies as balancing-poles, and zig-zagged ashore with a calmness and lack of haste that were in reality only an indication of the keenness with which they fore-estimated each chance. Long experience with the ways of saw-logs brought them out. They knew the correlation of these many forces just as the expert billiard-player knows instinctively the various angles of incident and reflection between his cue-ball and its mark. Consequently they avoided the centers of eruption, paused on the spots steadied for the moment, dodged moving logs, trod those not yet under way, and so arrived on solid ground. The jam itself started with every indication of meaning business, gained momentum for a hundred feet, and then plugged to a standstill. The "break" was abortive.

Now we all had leisure to notice two things. First, the movement had not been of the whole jam, as we had at first supposed, but only of a block or section of it twenty rods or so in extent. Thus between the part that had moved and the greater bulk that had not stirred lay a hundred feet of open water in which floated a number of loose logs. The second fact was, that Dickey Darrell had fallen into that open stretch of water and was in the act of swimming toward one of the floating logs. That much we were given time to appreciate thoroughly. Then the other section of the jam rumbled and began to break. Roaring Dick was caught between two gigantic millstones moving to crush him out of sight.

An active figure darted down the tail of the first section, out over the floating logs, seized Darrell by the coat-collar, and so burdened began desperately to scale the very face of the breaking jam.

Never was a more magnificent rescue. The logs were rolling, falling, diving against the laden man. He climbed as over a treadmill, a treadmill whose speed was constantly increasing. And when he finally gained the top, it was as the gap closed splintering beneath him and the man he had saved.

It is not in the woodsman to be demonstrative at any time, but here was work demanding attention. Without a pause for breath or congratulation they turned to the necessity of the moment. The jam, the whole jam, was moving at last. Jimmy Powers ran ashore for his peavie. Roaring Dick, like a demon incarnate, threw himself into the work. Forty men attacked the jam in a dozen places, encouraging the movement, twisting aside the timbers that threatened to lock anew, directing pigmy-like the titanic forces into the channel of their effi- ciency. Roaring like wild cattle the logs swept by, at first slowly, then with the railroad rush of the curbed freshet. Men were everywhere, taking chances, like cowboys before the stampeded herd. And so, out of sight around the lower bend swept the front of the jam in a swirl of glory, the rivermen riding the great boom back of the creature they subdued, until at last, with the slackening current, the logs floated by free, can- noning with hollow sound one against the other. A half-dozen watchers, leaning statuesquely on the shafts of their peavies, watched the ordered ranks pass by.

One by one the spectators departed. At last only myself and the brown-faced young man remained. He sat on a stump, staring with sightless eyes into vacancy. I did not disturb his thoughts.

The sun dipped. A cool breeze of evening sucked up the river. Over near the cook-camp a big fire commenced to crackle by the drying frames. At dusk the rivermen straggled in from the down-river trail.

The brown-faced young man arose and went to meet them. I saw him return in close conversation with Jimmy Powers. Before they reached us he had turned away with a gesture of farewell.

Jimmy Powers stood looking after him long after his form had disappeared, and indeed even after the sound of his wheels had died toward town. As I approached, the riverman turned to me a face from which the reckless, contained self-reliance of the woods-worker had faded. It was wide-eyed with an al- most awe-stricken wonder and adoration.

" Do you know who that is? " he asked me in a hushed voice " That's Thorpe, Harry Thorpe. And do you know what he said to me just now, *me?* He told me he wanted me to work in Camp One next winter, Thorpe's One. And he told me I was the first man he ever hired straight into One."

His breath caught with something like a sob.

I had heard of the man and of his methods. I knew he had made it a practice of recruiting for his prize camp only from the employees of his other camps, that, as Jimmy said, he never " hired straight into One." I had heard, too, of his reputation among his own and other woodsmen. But this was the first time I had ever come into personal contact with his influence. It impressed me the more in that I had come to know Jimmy Powers and his kind.

" You deserve it, every bit," said I. " I'm not going to call you a hero, because that would make you tired. What you did this afternoon showed nerve. It was a brave act. But it was a better act because your rescued your enemy, because you forgot everything but your common humanity when danger——"

I broke off. Jimmy was again looking at me with his ironically quizzical grin.

" Bub," said he, " if you're going to hang any stars of Bethlehem on my Christmas tree, just call a halt right here. I didn't rescue that scalawag because I had any Christian senti-ments, nary bit. I was just naturally savin' him for the birling match next Fourther July."

STEWART EDWARD WHITE

There are some authors whom we think of as bookmen; there are others whom we think of as men first, and as writers secondarily. Lowell, for example was a bookman; Roosevelt was a man of action who wrote books. Stewart Edward White, far more of a literary artist than Roosevelt, gives like him the impression of a man who has done things, of one who lives a full life, and produces books as a sort of by-product: very valuable, but not the chief end of existence.

Mr. White was born in a small town near Grand Rapids, Michigan, March 12, 1873. His parents had their own ideas about bringing up children. Instead of sending him to school they sent for a teacher to instruct him, they encouraged him to read, they took him traveling, not only to cities but to the silent places, the great forests, and to the lumber camps. He spent four years in California, and became a good horseman, making many trips in the saddle to the picturesque old ranches. When finally, he entered high school, at sixteen, he went in with boys of his own age, and graduated at eighteen, president of his class. And what he was most proud of was that he won and still holds, the five-mile running record of his school. He was intensely interested in birds at this time, and spent all his spare hours in the woods, studying bird-life. The result was a series of articles on birds, published in various scientific journals,— papers whose columns are not usually open to high school contributors.

Then came a college course at the University of Michigan, with vacations spent in cruising about the Great Lakes in a twenty-eight-foot cutter sloop. After graduation he worked for a time in a packing house, then hearing of the discovery of gold in the Black Hills, he set off with the other gold-diggers. He did not find a mine, but the experience gave him a background for two later novels, *The Claim Jumpers,* and *The Westerners.*

He went east for a year of graduate study at Columbia University. Like many other students, he found a friend in Professor Brander Matthews, who encouraged him to write of some of his western experiences. He sold a few short stories to magazines, and his first novel, *The Claim Jumpers* was accepted by Appleton's. *The Westerners,* his next book, brought him $500 for the serial rights, and with its publication he definitely determined upon making authorship his calling. But it was not authorship in a study. *The Blazed Trail* was written in a lumber camp in midwinter. He got up at four o'clock, wrote until eight, then put on his snowshoes and went out for a day's work. When the story was finished he gave it to the foreman of the camp to read. The man began it after supper, and when White got up next morning at four, he found him still reading, so he felt that the book would succeed.

Another year he made a trip to the Hudson Bay country, and on his return wrote *Conjurer's House.* This was dramatized by George Broadhurst, and was very successful on the stage. With Thomas Fogarty, the artist, he made a long canoe trip, and the resulting book, *The Forest,* was illustrated by Mr. Fogarty. A camping trip in the Sierra Mountains of California was followed by the writing of *The Mountains.* His next book, *The Mystery,* was written jointly by Mr. White and Samuel Hopkins Adams. When it was finished they not only divided the proceeds but divided the characters for future stories, White taking Handy Solomon, whom he used again in *Arizona Nights,* and Darrow, who appeared in *The Sign at Six.*

Then without warning, Mr. White went to Africa. His explanation was simple:

I went because I wanted to. About once in so often the wheels get rusty and I have to get up and do something real or else blow up. Africa seemed to me a pretty real thing. Let me add that I did not go for material. I never go anywhere for material; if I did I should not get it. That attitude of mine would give me merely externals, which are not worth writing about. I go places merely because for one reason or another they attract me. Then if it happens that I get close enough to the life, I may later find that I have something to write about. A man rarely writes anything convincing unless he has lived the life; not with his critical faculty alert, but whole-heartedly and because, for the time being, it is his life.

Naturally he found that he had something to write about on his return. *The Land of Footprints, African Camp Fires, Simba,* and *The Leopard Woman* were books that grew out of his African trip. Mr. White next planned to write a series of three novels dealing with the romantic history of the state of California. The first of these books, *Gold,* describes the mad rush of the Forty-Niners on the first discovery of gold in California. *The Gray Dawn,* the second of the series, tells of the days of the Vigilantes, when the wild life of the mining camps slowly settled down to law and order. The coming of the World War was a fresh challenge to his adventurous spirit, and he saw service in France as a major in the U. S. Field Artillery.

From this sketch it is apparent that Mr. White's books have all grown out of his experience, in the sense that the background is one that he has known. This explains the strong feeling of reality that we experience as we read his stories.

NEW ENGLAND GRANITE

From the day the Pilgrims landed on a rockbound coast, the name New Englander has suggested certain traits of character. It connotes a restraint of feeling which more impulsive persons may mistake for absence of feeling; a reserve carried almost to the point of coldness; a quiet dignity which to a breezy Westerner seems like " stand-offishness." But those who come to know New England people well, find that beneath the flint is fire. Dorothy Canfield suggests the theme of her story in the title—" Flint and Fire."

FLINT AND FIRE

BY

Dorothy Canfield

My husband's cousin had come up from the city, slightly more fagged and sardonic than usual, and as he stretched himself out in the big porch-chair he was even more caustic than was his wont about the bareness and emotional sterility of the lives of our country people.

"Perhaps they had, a couple of centuries ago, when the Puritan hallucination was still strong, a certain fierce savor of religious intolerance; but now that that has died out, and no material prosperity has come to let them share in the larger life of their century, there is a flatness, a mean absence of warmth or color, a deadness to all emotions but the pettiest sorts——"

I pushed the pitcher nearer him, clinking the ice invitingly, and directed his attention to our iris-bed as a more cheerful object of contemplation than the degeneracy of the inhabitants of Vermont. The flowers burned on their tall stalks like yellow tongues of flame. The strong, sword-like green leaves thrust themselves boldly up into the spring air like a challenge. The plants vibrated with vigorous life.

In the field beyond them, as vigorous as they, strode Adoniram Purdon behind his team, the reins tied together behind his muscular neck, his hands grasping the plow with the masterful sureness of the successful practitioner of an art. The hot, sweet spring sunshine shone down on 'Niram's head with its thick crest of brown hair, the ineffable odor of newly turned earth steamed up about him like incense, the mountain stream beyond him leaped and shouted. His powerful body answered every call made on it with the precision of a splen-

did machine. But there was no elation in the grimly set face as
'Niram wrenched the plow around a big stone, or as, in a
more favorable furrow, the gleaming share sped steadily along
before the plowman, turning over a long, unbroken brown ribbon of earth.

My cousin-in-law waved a nervous hand toward the sternly
silent figure as it stepped doggedly behind the straining team,
the head bent forward, the eyes fixed on the horses' heels.

"There!" he said. "There is an example of what I mean.
Is there another race on earth which could produce a man
in such a situation who would not on such a day sing, or
whistle, or at least hold up his head and look at all the earthly
glories about him?"

I was silent, but not for lack of material for speech.
'Niram's reasons for austere self-control were not such as I
cared to discuss with a man of my cousin's mental attitude.
As we sat looking at him the noon whistle from the village
blew and the wise old horses stopped in the middle of a furrow.
'Niram unharnessed them, led them to the shade of a tree,
and put on their nose-bags. Then he turned and came toward the house.

"Don't I seem to remember," murmured my cousin under
his breath, "that, even though he is a New-Englander, he
has been known to make up errands to your kitchen to see
your pretty Ev'leen Ann?"

I looked at him hard; but he was only gazing down, rather
cross-eyed, on his grizzled mustache, with an obvious petu-
lant interest in the increase of white hairs in it. Evidently
his had been but a chance shot. 'Niram stepped up on the
grass at the edge of the porch. He was so tall that he
overtopped the railing easily, and, reaching a long arm over
to where I sat, he handed me a small package done up in
yellowish tissue-paper. Without hat-raisings, or good-morn-
ings or any other of the greetings usual in a more effusive
civilization, he explained briefly:

" My stepmother wanted I should give you this. She said to thank you for the grape-juice." As he spoke he looked at me gravely out of deep-set blue eyes, and when he had delivered his message he held his peace.

I expressed myself with the babbling volubility of one whose manners have been corrupted by occasional sojourns in the city. " Oh, 'Niram! " I cried protestingly, as I opened the package and took out an exquisitely wrought old-fashioned collar. " Oh, 'Niram! How *could* your stepmother give such a thing away? Why, it must be one of her precious old relics. I don't *want* her to give me something every time I do some little thing for her. Can't a neighbor send her in a few bottles of grape-juice without her thinking she must pay it back somehow? It's not kind of her. She has never yet let me do the least thing for her without repaying me with something that is worth ever so much more than my trifling services."

When I had finished my prattling, 'Niram repeated, with an accent of finality, " She wanted I should give it to you."

The older man stirred in his chair. Without looking at him I knew that his gaze on the young rustic was quizzical and that he was recording on the tablets of his merciless memory the ungraceful abruptness of the other's action and manner.

" How is your stepmother feeling to-day, 'Niram? " I asked.

" Worse."

'Niram came to a full stop with the word. My cousin covered his satirical mouth with his hand.

" Can't the doctor do anything to relieve her? " I asked.

'Niram moved at last from his Indian-like immobility. He looked up under the brim of his felt hat at the sky-line of the mountain, shimmering iridescent above us. " He says maybe 'lectricity would help her some. I'm goin' to git her the batteries and things soon's I git the rubber bandages paid for."

There was a long silence. My cousin stood up, yawning, and sauntered away toward the door. " Shall I send Ev'leen

Ann out to get the pitcher and glasses? " he asked in an accent which he evidently thought very humorously significant.

The strong face under the felt hat turned white, the jaw muscles set hard, but for all this show of strength there was an instant when the man's eyes looked out with the sick, helpless revelation of pain they might have had when 'Niram was a little boy of ten, a third of his present age, and less than half his present stature. Occasionally it is horrifying to see how a chance shot rings the bell.

" No, no! Never mind! " I said hastily. " I'll take the tray in when I go."

Without salutation or farewell 'Niram Purdon turned and went back to his work.

The porch was an enchanted place, walled around with star-lit darkness, visited by wisps of breezes shaking down from their wings the breath of lilac and syringa, flowering wild grapes, and plowed fields. Down at the foot of our sloping lawn the little river, still swollen by the melted snow from the mountains, plunged between its stony banks and shouted its brave song to the stars.

We three middle-aged people—Paul, his cousin, and I— had disposed our uncomely, useful, middle-aged bodies in the big wicker chairs and left them there while our young souls wandered abroad in the sweet, dark glory of the night. At least Paul and I were doing this, as we sat, hand in hand, thinking of a May night twenty years before. One never knows what Horace is thinking of, but apparently he was not in his usual captious vein, for after a long pause he remarked, " It is a night almost indecorously inviting to the making of love."

My answer seemed grotesquely out of key with this, but its sequence was clear in my mind. I got up, saying: " Oh, that reminds me—I must go and see Ev'leen Ann. I'd forgotten to plan to-morrow's dinner."

" Oh, everlastingly Ev'leen Ann! " mocked Horace from his

corner. " Can't you think of anything but Ev'leen Ann and her affairs? "

I felt my way through the darkness of the house, toward the kitchen, both doors of which were tightly closed. When I stepped into the hot, close room, smelling of food and fire, I saw Ev'leen Ann sitting on the straight kitchen chair, the yellow light of the bracket-lamp bearing down on her heavy braids and bringing out the exquisitely subtle modeling of her smooth young face. Her hands were folded in her lap. She was staring at the blank wall, and the expression of her eyes so startled and shocked me that I stopped short and would have retreated if it had not been too late. She had seen me, roused herself, and said quietly, as though continuing a conversation interrupted the moment before:

" I had been thinking that there was enough left of the roast to make hash-balls for dinner "—" hash-balls " is Ev'leen Ann's decent Anglo-Saxon name for croquettes—" and maybe you'd like a rhubarb pie."

I knew well enough she had been thinking of no such thing, but I could as easily have slapped a reigning sovereign on the back as broken in on the regal reserve of Ev'leen Ann in her clean gingham.

" Well, yes, Ev'leen Ann," I answered in her own tone of reasonable consideration of the matter; " that would be nice, and your pie-crust is so flaky that even Mr. Horace will have to be pleased."

" Mr. Horace " is our title for the sardonic cousin whose carping ways are half a joke, and half a menace in our family.

Ev'leen Ann could not manage the smile which should have greeted this sally. She looked down soberly at the white-pine top of the kitchen table and said, " I guess there is enough sparrow-grass up in the garden for a mess, too, if you'd like that."

" That would taste very good," I agreed, my heart aching for her.

"And creamed potatoes," she finished bravely, thrusting my unspoken pity from her.

"You know I like creamed potatoes better than any other kind," I concurred.

There was a silence. It seemed inhuman to go and leave the stricken young thing to fight her trouble alone in the ugly prison, her work-place, though I thought I could guess why Ev'leen Ann had shut the doors so tightly. I hung near her, searching my head for something to say, but she helped me by no casual remark. 'Niram is not the only one of our people who possesses to the full the supreme gift of silence. Finally I mentioned the report of a case of measles in the village, and Ev'leen Ann responded in kind with the news that her Aunt Emma had bought a potato-planter. Ev'leen Ann is an orphan, brought up by a well-to-do spinster aunt, who is strong-minded and runs her own farm. After a time we glided by way of similar transitions to the mention of his name.

"'Niram Purdon tells me his stepmother is no better," I said. "Isn't it too bad?" I thought it well for Ev'leen Ann to be dragged out of her black cave of silence once in a while, even if it could be done only by force. As she made no answer, I went on. "Everybody who knows 'Niram thinks it splendid of him to do so much for his stepmother."

Ev'leen Ann responded with a detached air, as though speaking of a matter in China: "Well, it ain't any more than what he should. She was awful good to him when he was little and his father got so sick. I guess 'Niram wouldn't ha' had much to eat if she hadn't ha' gone out sewing to earn it for him and Mr. Purdon." She added firmly, after a moment's pause, "No, ma'am, I don't guess it's any more than what 'Niram had ought to do."

"But it's very hard on a young man to feel that he's not able to marry," I continued. Once in a great while we came so near the matter as this. Ev'leen Ann made no answer. Her face took on a pinched look of sickness. She set her lips as though she would never speak again. But I knew that a criticism of 'Niram would always rouse her, and said: " And really, I think 'Niram makes a great mistake to act as he does. A wife would be a help to him. She could take care of Mrs. Purdon and keep the house."

Ev'leen Ann rose to the bait, speaking quickly with some heat: " I guess 'Niram knows what's right for him to do! He can't afford to marry when he can't even keep up with the doctor's bills and all. He keeps the house himself, nights and mornings, and Mrs. Purdon is awful handy about taking care of herself, for all she's bedridden. That's her way, you know. She can't bear to have folks do for her. She'd die before she'd let anybody do anything for her that she could anyways do for herself! "

I sighed acquiescingly. Mrs. Purdon's fierce independence was a rock on which every attempt at sympathy or help shattered itself to atoms. There seemed to be no other emotion left in her poor old work-worn shell of a body. As I looked at Ev'leen Ann it seemed rather a hateful characteristic, and I remarked, " It seems to me it's asking a good deal of 'Niram to spoil his life in order that his stepmother can go on pretending she's independent."

Ev'leen Ann explained hastily: " Oh, 'Niram doesn't tell her anything about—She doesn't know he would like to—he don't want she should be worried—and, anyhow, as 'tis, he can't earn enough to keep ahead of all the doctors cost."

" But the right kind of a wife—a good, competent girl— could help out by earning something, too."

Ev'leen Ann looked at me forlornly, with no surprise. The idea was evidently not new to her. " Yes, ma'am, she could. But 'Niram says he ain't the kind of man to let his wife go out working." Even while she dropped under the killing verdict of his pride she was loyal to his standards and uttered no complaint. She went on, " 'Niram wants Aunt Em'line to have things the way she wants 'em, as near as he can give 'em to her—and it's right she should."

" Aunt Emeline? " I repeated, surprised at her absence of mind. " You mean Mrs. Purdon, don't you? "

Ev'leen Ann looked vexed at her slip, but she scorned to attempt any concealment. She explained dryly, with the shy, stiff embarrassment our country people have in speaking of private affairs: " Well, she *is* my Aunt Em'line, Mrs. Purdon is, though I don't hardly ever call her that. You see, Aunt Emma brought me up, and she and Aunt Em'line don't have anything to do with each other. They were twins, and when they were girls they got edgeways over 'Niram's father, when 'Niram was a baby and his father was a young widower and come courting. Then Aunt Em'line married him, and Aunt Emma never spoke to her afterward."

Occasionally, in walking unsuspectingly along one of our leafy lanes, some such fiery geyser of ancient heat uprears itself in a boiling column. I never get used to it, and started back now.

" Why, I never heard of that before, and I've known your Aunt Emma and Mrs. Purdon for years! "

" Well, they're pretty old now," said Ev'leen Ann listlessly, with the natural indifference of self-centered youth to the bygone tragedies of the preceding generation. " It happened quite some time ago. And both of them were so touchy, if anybody seemed to speak about it, that folks got in the way of letting it alone. First Aunt Emma wouldn't speak to her sister because she'd married the man she'd wanted, and then when Aunt Emma made out so well farmin' and got so well off, why, then Mrs. Purdon wouldn't try to make up because she was so poor. That was after Mr. Purdon had had his stroke of paralysis and they'd lost their farm and she'd taken to goin' out sewin'—not but what she was always perfectly satisfied with her bargain. She always acted as though she'd rather have her husband's old shirt stuffed with straw than any other man's whole body. He was a real nice man, I guess, Mr. Purdon was."

There I had it—the curt, unexpanded chronicle of two passionate lives. And there I had also the key to Mrs. Purdon's fury of independence. It was the only way in which she could defend her husband against the charge, so damning to her world, of not having provided for his wife. It was the only monument she could rear to her husband's memory. And her husband had been all there was in life for her!

I stood looking at her young kinswoman's face, noting the granite under the velvet softness of its youth, and divining the flame underlying the granite. I longed to break through her wall and to put my arms about her, and on the impulse of the moment I cast aside the pretense of causualness in our talk.

" Oh, my dear! " I said. " Are you and 'Niram always to go on like this? Can't anybody help you? "

Ev'leen Ann looked at me, her face suddenly old and gray. " No, ma'am; we ain't going to go on this way. We've decided, 'Niram and I have, that it ain't no use. We've decided that we'd better not go places together any more or see each other. It's too—If 'Niram thinks we can't "—she flamed so that I knew she was burning from head to foot—" it's better for us not——" She ended in a muffled voice, hiding her face in the crook of her arm.

Ah, yes; now I knew why Ev'leen Ann had shut out the passionate breath of the spring night!

I stood near her, a lump in my throat, but I divined the anguish of her shame at her involuntary self-revelation, and respected it. I dared do no more than to touch her shoulder gently.

The door behind us rattled. Ev'leen Ann sprang up and turned her face toward the wall. Paul's cousin came in, shuffling a little, blinking his eyes in the light of the unshaded lamp, and looking very cross and tired. He glanced at us without comment as he went over to the sink. "Nobody offered me anything good to drink," he complained, "so I came in to get some water from the faucet for my nightcap."

When he had drunk with ostentation from the tin dipper he went to the outside door and flung it open. "Don't you people know how hot and smelly it is in here?" he said, with his usual unceremonious abruptness.

The night wind burst in, eddying, and puffed out the lamp with a breath. In an instant the room was filled with coolness and perfumes and the rushing sound of the river. Out of the darkness came Ev'leen Ann's young voice. "It seems to me," she said, as though speaking to herself, "that I never heard the Mill Brook sound so loud as it has this spring."

I woke up that night with the start one has at a sudden call. But there had been no call. A profound silence spread itself through the sleeping house. Outdoors the wind had died down. Only the loud brawl of the river broke the stillness under the stars. But all through this silence and this vibrant song there rang a soundless menace which brought me out of bed and to my feet before I was awake. I heard Paul say, "What's the matter?" in a sleepy voice, and "Nothing," I answered, reaching for my dressing gown and slippers. I listened for a moment, my head ringing with all the frightened tales of the morbid vein of violence which runs through the character of our reticent people. There was still no sound. I went along the hall and up the stairs to Ev'leen Ann's room, and I opened the door without knocking. The room was empty.

Then how I ran! Calling loudly for Paul to join me, I ran down the two flights of stairs, out of the open door, and along the hedged path which leads down to the little river. The starlight was clear. I could see everything as plainly as though in early dawn. I saw the river, and I saw—Ev'leen Ann.

There was a dreadful moment of horror, which I shall never

remember very clearly, and then Ev'leen Ann and I—both very wet—stood on the bank, shuddering in each other's arms.

Into our hysteria there dropped, like a pungent caustic, the arid voice of Horace, remarking, "Well, are you two people crazy, or are you walking in your sleep?"

I could feel Ev'leen Ann stiffen in my arms, and I fairly stepped back from her in astonished admiration as I heard her snatch at the straw thus offered, and still shuddering horribly from head to foot, force herself to say quite connectedly: "Why—yes—of course—I've always heard about my grandfather Parkman's walking in his sleep. Folks *said* 'twould come out in the family some time."

Paul was close behind Horace—I wondered a little at his not being first—and with many astonished and inane ejaculations, such as people always make on startling occasions, we made our way back into the house to hot blankets and toddies. But I slept no more that night.

Some time after dawn, however, I did fall into a troubled unconsciousness full of bad dreams, and only woke when the sun was quite high. I opened my eyes to see Ev'leen Ann about to close the door.

"Oh, did I wake you up?" she said. "I didn't mean to. That little Harris boy is here with a letter for you."

She spoke with a slightly defiant tone of self-possession. I tried to play up to her interpretation of her rôle.

"The little Harris boy?" I said, sitting up in bed. "What in the world is he bringing me a letter for?"

Ev'leen Ann, with her usual clear perception of the superfluous in conversation, vouchsafed no opinion on a matter where she had no information, but went downstairs and brought back the note. It was of four lines, and—surprisingly enough—from old Mrs. Purdon, who asked me abruptly if I would have my husband take me to see her. She specified, and underlined the specification, that I was to come "right off, and in the automobile." Wondering extremely at this mysterious bidding,

I sought out Paul, who obediently cranked up our small car and carried me off. There was no sign of Horace about the house, but some distance on the other side of the village we saw his tall, stooping figure swinging along the road. He carried a cane and was characteristically occupied in violently switching off the heads from the wayside weeds as he walked. He refused our offer to take him in, alleging that he was out for exercise and to reduce his flesh—an ancient jibe at his bony frame which made him for an instant show a leathery smile.

There was, of course, no one at Mrs. Purdon's to let us into the tiny, three-roomed house, since the bedridden invalid spent her days there alone while 'Niram worked his team on other people's fields. Not knowing what we might find, Paul stayed outside in the car, while I stepped inside in answer to Mrs. Purdon's " Come *in*, why don't you! " which sounded quite as dry as usual. But when I saw her I knew that things were not as usual.

She lay flat on her back, the little emaciated wisp of humanity, hardly raising the piecework quilt enough to make the bed seem occupied, and to account for the thin, worn old face on the pillow. But as I entered the room her eyes seized on mine, and I was aware of nothing but them and some fury of determination behind them. With a fierce heat of impatience at my first natural but quickly repressed exclamation of surprise she explained briefly that she wanted Paul to lift her into the automobile and take her into the next township to the Hulett farm. " I'm so shrunk away to nuthin', I know I can lay on the back seat if I crook myself up," she said, with a cool accent but a rather shaky voice. Seeming to realize that even her intense desire to strike the matter-of-fact note could not take the place of any and all explanation of her extraordinary request, she added, holding my eyes steady with her own: " Emma Hulett's my twin sister. I guess it ain't so queer, my wanting to see her."

I thought, of course, we were to be used as the medium for some strange, sudden family reconciliation, and went out to ask Paul if he thought he could carry the old invalid to the car. He replied that, so far as that went, he could carry so thin an old body ten times around the town, but that he refused absolutely to take such a risk without authorization from her doctor. I remembered the burning eyes of resolution I had left inside, and sent him to present his objections to Mrs. Purdon herself.

In a few moments I saw him emerge from the house with the old woman in his arms. He had evidently taken her up just as she lay. The piecework quilt hung down in long folds, flashing its brilliant reds and greens in the sunshine, which shone so strangely upon the pallid old countenance, facing the open sky for the first time in years.

We drove in silence through the green and gold lyric of the spring day, an elderly company sadly out of key with the triumphant note of eternal youth which rang through all the visible world. Mrs. Purdon looked at nothing, said nothing, seemed to be aware of nothing but the purpose in her heart, whatever that might be. Paul and I, taking a leaf from our neighbors' book, held, with a courage like theirs, to their excellent habit of saying nothing when there is nothing to say. We arrived at the fine old Hulett place without the exchange of a single word.

"Now carry me in," said Mrs. Purdon briefly, evidently hoarding her strength.

"Wouldn't I better go and see if Miss Hulett is at home?" I asked.

Mrs. Purdon shook her head impatiently and turned her compelling eyes on my husband. I went up the path before them to knock at the door, wondering what the people in the house would possibly be thinking of us. There was no answer to my knock. "Open the door and go in," commanded Mrs. Purdon from out her quilt.

There was no one in the spacious, white-paneled hall, and no sound in all the big, many-roomed house.

" Emma's out feeding the hens," conjectured Mrs. Purdon, not, I fancied, without a faint hint of relief in her voice. " Now carry me up-stairs to the first room on the right."

Half hidden by his burden, Paul rolled wildly inquiring eyes at me; but he obediently staggered up the broad old staircase, and waiting till I had opened the first door to the right, stepped into the big bedroom.

" Put me down on the bed, and open them shutters," Mrs. Purdon commanded.

She still marshaled her forces with no lack of decision, but with a fainting voice which made me run over to her quickly as Paul laid her down on the four-poster. Her eyes were still indomitable, but her mouth hung open slackly and her color was startling. " Oh, Paul, quick! quick! Haven't you your flask with you? "

Mrs. Purdon informed me in a barely audible whisper, " In the corner cupboard at the head of the stairs," and I flew down the hallway. I returned with a bottle, evidently of great age. There was only a little brandy in the bottom, but it whipped up a faint color into the sick woman's lips.

As I was bending over her and Paul was thrusting open the shutters, letting in a flood of sunshine and flecky leaf-shadows, a firm, rapid step came down the hall, and a vigorous woman, with a tanned face and a clean, faded gingham dress, stopped short in the doorway with an expression of stupefaction.

Mrs. Purdon put me on one side, and although she was physically incapable of moving her body by a hair's breadth, she gave the effect of having risen to meet the newcomer. " Well, Emma, here I am," she said in a queer voice, with involuntary quavers in it. As she went on she had it more under control, although in the course of her extraordinarily succinct speech it broke and failed her occasionally. When it did, she drew in her breath with an audible, painful effort, struggling

forward steadily in what she had to say. " You see, Emma,
it's this way: My 'Niram and your Ev'leen Ann have been keeping company—ever since they went to school together—you
know that 's well as I do, for all we let on we didn't, only I
didn't know till just now how hard they took it. They can't
get married because 'Niram can't keep even, let alone get
ahead any, because I cost so much bein' sick, and the doctor
says I may live for years this way, same's Aunt Hettie did.
An' 'Niram is thirty-one, an' Ev'leen Ann is twenty-eight, an'
they've had 'bout's much waitin' as is good for folks that set
such store by each other. I've thought of every way out of it—
and there ain't any. The Lord knows I don't enjoy livin' any,
not. so's to notice the enjoyment, and I'd thought of cutting
my throat like Uncle Lish, but that'd make 'Niram and Ev'-
leen Ann feel so—to think why I'd done it; they'd never take
the comfort they'd ought in bein' married; so that won't do.
There's only one thing to do. I guess you'll have to take care
of me till the Lord calls me. Maybe I won't last so long as the
doctor thinks."

When she finished, I felt my ears ringing in the silence. She
had walked to the sacrificial altar with so steady a step, and
laid upon it her precious all with so gallant a front of quiet
resolution, that for an instant I failed to take in the sublimity
of her self-immolation. Mrs. Purdon asking for charity! And
asking the one woman who had most reason to refuse it to her.

Paul looked at me miserably, the craven desire to escape
a scene written all over him. " Wouldn't we better be going,
Mrs. Purdon? " I said uneasily. I had not ventured to look
at the woman in the doorway.

Mrs. Purdon motioned me to remain, with an imperious
gesture whose fierceness showed the tumult underlying her
brave front. " No; I want you should stay. I want you should
hear what I say, so's you can tell folks, if you have to. Now,
look here, Emma," she went on to the other, still obstinately
silent; " you must look at it the way 'tis. We're neither of us

any good to anybody, the way we are—and I'm dreadfully in the way of the only two folks we care a pin about—either of us. You've got plenty to do with, and nothing to spend it on. I can't get myself out of their way by dying without going against what's Scripture and proper, but——" Her steely calm broke. She burst out in a screaming, hysterical voice: " You've just *got* to, Emma Hulett! You've just *got* to! If you don't I won't never go back to 'Niram's house! I'll lie in the ditch by the roadside till the poor-master comes to get me—and I'll tell everybody that it's because my own twin sister, with a house and a farm and money in the bank, turned me out to starve—" A fearful spasm cut her short. She lay twisted and limp, the whites of her eyes showing between the lids.

" Good God, she's gone! " cried Paul, running to the bed.

I was aware that the woman in the doorway had relaxed her frozen immobility and was between Paul and me as we rubbed the thin, icy hands and forced brandy between the placid lips. We all three thought her dead or dying, and labored over her with the frightened thankfulness for one another's living presence which always marks that dreadful moment. But even as we fanned and rubbed, and cried out to one another to open the windows and to bring water, the blue lips moved to a ghostly whisper: " Em, listen——" The old woman went back to the nickname of their common youth. " Em—your Ev'leen Ann—tried to drown herself—in the Mill Brook last night . . . That's what decided me—to——" And then we were plunged into another desperate struggle with Death for the possession of the battered old habitation of the dauntless soul before us.

" Isn't there any hot water in the house? " cried Paul, and " Yes, yes; a tea-kettle on the stove! " answered the woman who labored with us. Paul, divining that she meant the kitchen, fled down-stairs. I stole a look at Emma Hulett's face as she bent over the sister she had not seen in thirty years, and I knew that Mrs. Purdon's battle was won. It even seemed that she had won another skirmish in her never-ending war with death, for a little warmth began to come back into her hands.

When Paul returned with the tea-kettle, and a hot-water bottle had been filled, the owner of the house straightened herself, assumed her rightful position as mistress of the situation, and began to issue commands. "You git right in the automobile, and go git the doctor," she told Paul. "That'll be the quickest. She's better now, and your wife and I can keep her goin' till the doctor gits here."

As Paul left the room she snatched something white from a bureau-drawer, stripped the worn, patched old cotton nightgown from the skeleton-like body, and, handling the invalid with a strong, sure touch, slipped on a soft, woolly outing-flannel wrapper with a curious trimming of zigzag braid down the front. Mrs. Purdon opened her eyes very slightly, but shut them again at her sister's quick command, "You lay still, Em'line, and drink some of this brandy." She obeyed without comment, but after a pause she opened her eyes again and looked down at the new garment which clad her. She had that moment turned back from the door of death, but her first breath was used to set the scene for a return to a decent decorum.

"You're still a great hand for rick-rack work, Em, I see," she murmured in a faint whisper. "Do you remember how surprised Aunt Su was when you made up a pattern?"

"Well, I hadn't thought of it for quite some time," returned Miss Hulett, in exactly the same tone of everyday remark. As she spoke she slipped her arm under the other's head and poked the pillow to a more comfortable shape. "Now you lay perfectly still," she commanded in the hectoring tone of the born nurse; "I'm goin' to run down and make you up a good hot cup of sassafras tea."

I followed her down into the kitchen and was met by the same refusal to be melodramatic which I had encountered in Ev'leen Ann. I was most anxious to know what version of my extraordinary morning I was to give out to the world, but hung silent, positively abashed by the cool casualness of the other woman as she mixed her brew. Finally, " Shall I tell 'Niram— What shall I say to Ev'leen Ann? If anybody asks me——" I brought out with clumsy hesitation.

At the realization that her reserve and family pride were wholly at the mercy of any report I might choose to give, even my iron hostess faltered. She stopped short in the middle of the floor, looked at me silently, piteously, and found no word.

I hastened to assure her that I would attempt no hateful picturesquness of narration. " Suppose I just say that you were rather lonely here, now that Ev'leen Ann has left you, and that you thought it would be nice to have your sister come to stay with you, so that 'Niram and Ev'leen Ann can be married? "

Emma Hulett breathed again. She walked toward the stairs with the steaming cup in her hand. Over her shoulder she remarked, " Well, yes, ma'am; that would be as good a way to put it as any, I guess."

'Niram and Ev'leen Ann were standing up to be married. They looked very stiff and self-conscious, and Ev'leen Ann was very pale. 'Niram's big hands, bent in the crook of a man who handles tools, hung down by his new black trousers. Ev'-leen Ann's strong fingers stood out stiffly from one another. They looked hard at the minister and repeated after him in low and meaningless tones the solemn and touching words of the marriage service. Back of them stood the wedding company, in freshly washed and ironed white dresses, new straw hats, and black suits smelling of camphor. In the background among the other elders, stood Paul and Horace and I— my husband and I hand in hand; Horace twiddling the black ribbon which holds his watch, and looking bored. Through the open windows into the stuffiness of the best room came an echo of the deep organ note of midsummer.

" Whom God hath joined together——" said the minister, and the epitome of humanity which filled the room held its breath—the old with a wonder upon their life-scarred faces, the young half frightened to feel the stir of the great wings soaring so near them.

Then it was all over. 'Niram and Ev'leen Ann were married, and the rest of us were bustling about to serve the hot biscuit and coffee and chicken salad, and to dish up the ice-cream. Afterward there were no citified refinements of cramming rice down the necks of the departing pair or tying placards to the carriage in which they went away. Some of the men went out to the barn and hitched up for 'Niram, and we all went down to the gate to see them drive off. They might have been going for one of their Sunday afternoon " buggy-rides " except for the wet eyes of the foolish women and girls who stood waving their hands in answer to the flutter of Ev'leen Ann's handkerchief as the carriage went down the hill.

We had nothing to say to one another after they left, and began soberly to disperse to our respective vehicles. But as I was getting into our car a new thought suddenly struck me.

" Why," I cried, " I never thought of it before! However in the world did old Mrs. Purdon know about Ev'leen Ann—that night? "

Horace was pulling at the door, which was badly adjusted and shut hard. He closed it with a vicious slam " *I* told her," he said crossly.

(Reprinted from *Americans All*)

HOW "FLINT AND FIRE" STARTED AND GREW

BY

Dorothy Canfield

I feel very dubious about the wisdom or usefulness of publishing the following statement of how one of my stories came into existence. This is not on account of the obvious danger of seeming to have illusions about the value of my work, as though I imagined one of my stories was inherently worth in itself a careful public analysis of its growth; the chance, remote as it might be, of usefulness to students, would outweigh this personal consideration. What is more important is the danger that some student may take the explanation as a recipe or rule for the construction of other stories, and I totally disbelieve in such rules or recipes.

As a rule, when a story is finished, and certainly always by the time it is published, I have no recollection of the various phases of its development. In the case of " Flint and Fire ", an old friend chanced to ask me, shortly after the tale was completed, to write out for his English classes, the stages of the construction of a short story. I set them down, hastily, formlessly, but just as they happened, and this gives me a record which I could not reproduce for any other story I ever wrote. These notes are here published on the chance that such a truthful record of the growth of one short story, may have some general suggestiveness for students.

No two of my stories are ever constructed in the same way, but broadly viewed they all have exactly the same genesis, and I confess I cannot conceive of any creative fiction written from any other beginning . . . that of a generally intensified emotional sensibility, such as every human being experiences with more or less frequency. Everybody knows such occasional hours or days of freshened emotional responses when events that usually pass almost unnoticed, suddenly move you deeply, when a sunset lifts you to exaltation, when a squeaking door throws you into a fit of exasperation, when a clear look of trust in a child's eyes moves you to tears, or an injustice reported in the newspapers to flaming indignation, a good action to a sunny warm love of human nature, a discovered meanness in yourself or another, to despair.

I have no idea whence this tide comes, or where it goes, but when it begins to rise in my heart, I know that a story is hovering in the offing. It does not always come safely to port. The daily routine of ordinary life kills off many a vagrant emotion. Or if daily humdrum occupation does not stifle it, perhaps this saturated solution of feeling does not happen to crystallize about any concrete fact, episode, word or phrase. In my own case, it is far more likely to seize on some slight trifle, the shade of expression on somebody's face, or the tone of somebody's voice, than to accept a more complete, ready-made episode. Especially this emotion refuses to crystallize about, or to have anything to do with those narrations of our actual life, offered by friends who are sure that such-and-such a happening is so strange or interesting that " it ought to go in a story."

The beginning of a story is then for me in more than usual sensitiveness to emotion. If this encounters the right focus (and heaven only knows why it is the " right " one) I get simultaneously a strong thrill of intense feeling, and an intense desire to pass it on to other people. This emotion may be any one of the infinitely varied ones which life affords, laughter, sorrow, indignation, gayety, admiration, scorn, pleasure. I recognize it for the " right " one when it brings with it an irresistible impulse to try to make other people feel it.

And I know that when it comes, the story is begun. At this point, the story begins to be more or less under my conscious control, and it is here that the work of construction begins.

" Flint and Fire " thus hovered vaguely in a shimmer of general emotional tensity, and thus abruptly crystallized itself about a chance phrase and the cadence of the voice which pronounced it. For several days I had been almost painfully alive to the beauty of an especially lovely spring, always so lovely after the long winter in the mountains. One evening, going on a very prosaic errand to a farm-house of our region, I walked along a narrow path through dark pines, beside a brook swollen with melting snow, and found the old man I came to see, sitting silent and alone before his blackened small old house. I did my errand, and then not to offend against our country standards of sociability, sat for half an hour beside him.

The old man had been for some years desperately unhappy about a tragic and permanent element in his life. I had known this, every one knew it. But that evening, played upon as I had been by the stars, the darkness of the pines and the shouting voice of the brook, I suddenly stopped merely knowing it, and felt it. It seemed to me that his misery emanated from him like a soundless wail of anguish. We talked very little, odds and ends of neighborhood gossip, until the old man, shifting his position, drew a long breath and said, " Seems to me I never heard the brook sound so loud as it has this spring." There came instantly to my mind the recollection that his grandfather had drowned himself in that brook, and I sat silent, shaken by that thought and by the sound of his voice. I have no words to attempt to reproduce his voice, or to try to make you feel as I did, hot and cold with the awe of that glimpse into a naked human heart. I felt my own heart contract dreadfully with helpless sympathy . . . and, I hope this is not as ugly as it sounds, I knew at the same instant that I would try to get that pang of emotion into a story and make other people feel it.

That is all. That particular phase of the construction of the story came and went between two heart-beats.

I came home by the same path through the same pines along the same brook, sinfully blind and deaf to the beauty that had so moved me an hour ago. I was too busy now to notice anything outside the rapid activity going on inside my head. My mind was working with a swiftness and a coolness which I am somewhat ashamed to mention, and my emotions were calmed, relaxed, let down from the tension of the last few days and the last few moments. They had found their way out to an attempt at self-expression and were at rest. I realize that this is not at all estimable. The old man was just as unhappy as he had been when I had felt my heart breaking with sympathy for him, but now he seemed very far away.

I was snatching up one possibility after another, considering it for a moment, casting it away and pouncing on another. First of all, the story must be made as remote as possible from resembling the old man or his trouble, lest he or any one in the world might think he was intended, and be wounded.

What is the opposite pole from an old man's tragedy? A lover's tragedy, of course. Yes, it must be separated lovers, young and passionate and beautiful, because they would fit in with the back-ground of spring, and swollen shouting starlit brooks, and the yearly resurrection which was so closely connected with that ache of emotion that they were a part of it.

Should the separation come from the weakness or faithlessness of one of the lovers? No, ah no, I wanted it without ugliness, pure beautiful sorrow, to fit that dark shadow of the pines . . . the lovers must be separated by outside forces.

What outside forces? Lack of money? Family opposition? Both, perhaps. I knew plenty of cases of both in the life of our valley.

By this time I had come again to our own house and was swallowed in the usual thousand home-activities. But underneath all that, quite steadily my mind continued to work on the story as a wasp in a barn keeps on silently plastering up the cells of his nest in the midst of the noisy activities of farm-life. I said to one of the children, " Yes, dear, wasn't it fun! " and to myself, " To be typical of our tradition-ridden valley-people, the opposition ought to come from the dead hand of the past." I asked a caller, " One lump or two? " and thought as I poured the tea, " And if the character of that opposition could be made to indicate a fierce capacity for passionate feel-ing in the older generation, that would make it doubly useful in the story, not only as part of the machinery of the plot, but as indicating an inheritance of passionate feeling in the younger generation, with whom the story is concerned." I dozed off at night, and woke to find myself saying, " It could come from the jealousy of two sisters, now old women."

But that meant that under ordinary circumstances the lovers would have been first cousins, and this might cause a subcon-scious wavering of attention on the part of some readers . . . . just as well to get that stone out of the path! I darned a sock and thought out the relationship in the story, and was rewarded with a revelation of the character of the sick old woman, 'Niram's step-mother.

Upon this, came one of those veering lists of the ballast aboard which are so disconcerting to the author. The story got out of hand. The old woman silent, indomitable, fed and deeply satisfied for all of her hard and grinding life by her love for the husband whom she had taken from her sister, she stepped to the front of my stage, and from that moment on, dominated the action. I did not expect this, nor desire it, and I was very much afraid that the result would be a perilously di-vided interest which would spoil the unity of impression of the story. It now occurs to me that this unexpected shifting of values may have been the emergence of the element of tragic old age which had been the start of the story and which I had conscientiously tried to smother out of sight. At any rate, there she was, more touching, pathetic, striking, to my eyes with her life-time proof of the reality of her passion, than my untried young lovers who up to that time had seemed to me, in the full fatuous flush of invention as I was, as ill-starred, innocent and touching lovers as anybody had ever seen.

Alarmed about this double interest I went on with the weaving back and forth of the elements of the plot which now involved the attempt to arouse in the reader's heart as in mine a sympathy for the bed-ridden old Mrs. Purdon and a comprehension of her sacrifice.

My daily routine continued as usual, gardening, telling stories, music, sewing, dusting, motoring, callers . . . one of them, a self-consciously sophisticated Europeanized American, not having of course any idea of what was filling my inner life, rubbed me frightfully the wrong way by making a slighting condescending allusion to what he called the mean, emotional poverty of our inarticulate mountain people. I flew into a silent rage at him, though scorning to discuss with him a matter I felt him incapable of understanding, and the character of Cousin Horace went into the story. He was for the first day or two, a very poor cheap element, quite unreal, unrealized, a mere man of straw to be knocked over by the personages of the tale. Then I took myself to task, told myself that I was spoiling a story merely to revenge myself on a man I cared nothing about, and that I must either take Cousin Horace out or make him human. One day, working in the garden, I laughed out suddenly, delighted with the whimsical idea of making him, almost in spite of himself, the *deus ex machina* of my little drama, quite soft and sympathetic under his shell of would-be worldly disillusion, as occasionally happens to elderly bachelors.

At this point the character of 'Niram's long-dead father came to life and tried to push his way into the story, a delightful, gentle, upright man, with charm and a sense of humor, such as none of the rest of my stark characters possessed. I felt that he was necessary to explain the fierceness of the sisters' rivalry for him. I planned one or two ways to get him in, in retrospect—and liked one of the scenes better than anything that finally was left in the story. Finally, very heavy-hearted, I put him out of the story, for the merely material reason that there was no room for him. As usual with my story-making, this plot was sprouting out in a dozen places, expanding, opening up, till I perceived that I had enough material for a novel. For a day or so I hung undecided. Would it perhaps be better to make it a novel and really tell about those characters all I knew and guessed? But again a consideration that has nothing to do with artistic form, settled the matter. I saw no earthly possibility of getting time enough to write a novel. So I left Mr. Purdon out, and began to think of ways to compress my material, to make one detail do double work so that space might be saved.

One detail of the mechanism remained to be arranged, and this ended by deciding the whole form of the story, and the first-person character of the recital. This was the question of just how it would have been materially possible for the bed-ridden old woman to break down the life-long barrier between her and her sister, and how she could have reached her effectively and forced her hand. I could see no way to manage this except by somehow transporting her bodily to the sister's house, so that she could not be put out on the road without public scandal. This transportation must be managed by some character not in the main action, as none of the persons involved would have been willing to help her to this. It looked like putting in another character, just for that purpose, and of course he could not be put in without taking the time to make him plausible, human, understandable . . . and I had just left out that charming widower for sheer lack of space. Well, why not make it a first person story, and have the narrator be the one who takes Mrs. Purdon to her sister's? The narrator of the story never needs to be explained, always seems sufficiently living and real by virtue of the supremely human act of so often saying " I ".

Now the materials were ready, the characters fully alive in my mind and entirely visualized, even to the smoothly braided hair of Ev'leen Ann, the patch-work quilt of the old woman out-of-doors, and the rustic wedding at the end, all details which had recently chanced to draw my attention; I heard everything through the song of the swollen brook, one of the main characters in the story, (although by this time in actual fact, June and lower water had come and the brook slid quiet and gleaming, between placid green banks) and I often found myself smiling foolishly in pleasure over the buggy going down the hill, freighted so richly with hearty human joy.

The story was now ready to write.

I drew a long breath of mingled anticipation and apprehension, somewhat as you do when you stand, breathing quickly, balanced on your skis, at the top of a long white slope you are not sure you are clever enough to manage. Sitting down at my desk one morning, I " pushed off and with a tingle of not altogether pleasurable exciement and alarm, felt myself " going." I " went " almost as precipitately as skis go down a long white slope, scribbling as rapidly as my pencil could go, indicating whole words with a dash and a jiggle, filling page after page with scrawls . . . it seemed to me that I had been at work perhaps half an hour, when someone was calling me impatiently to lunch. I had been writing four hours without stopping. My cheeks were flaming, my feet were cold, my lips parched. It was high time someone called me to lunch.

The next morning, back at the desk, I looked over what I had written, conquered the usual sick qualms of discouragement at finding it so infinitely flat and insipid compared to what I had wished to make it, and with a very clear idea of what remained to be done, plodded ahead doggedly, and finished the first draught before noon. It was almost twice too long.

After this came a period of steady desk work, every morning, of re-writing, compression, more compression, and the more or less mechanical work of technical revision, what a member of my family calls " cutting out the 'whiches' ". The first thing to do each morning was to read a part of it over aloud, sentence by sentence, to try to catch clumsy, ungraceful phrases, overweights at one end or the other, " ringing " them as you ring a dubious coin, clipping off too-trailing relative clauses, " listening " hard. This work depends on what is known in music as " ear ", and in my case it cannot be kept up long at a time, because I find my attention flagging. When I begin to suspect that my ear is dulling, I turn to other varieties of revision, of which there are plenty to keep anybody busy; for instance revision to explain facts; in this category is the sentence just after the narrator suspects Ev'leen Ann has gone down to the brook, " my ears ringing with all the frightening tales of the morbid vein of violence which runs through the characters of our reticent people." It seemed too on re-reading the story for the tenth or eleventh time, that for readers who do not know our valley people, the girl's attempt at suicide might seem improbable. Some reference ought to be brought in, giving the facts that their sorrow and despair is terrible in proportion to the nervous strain of their tradition of repression, and that suicide is by no means unknown. I tried bringing that fact in, as part of the conversation with Cousin Horace, but it never fused with the rest there, " stayed on top of the page " as bad sentences will do, never sank in, and always made the disagreeable impression on me that a false intonation in an actor's voice does. So it came out from there. I tried putting it in Ev'leen Ann's mouth, in a carefully arranged form, but it was so shockingly out of character there, that it was snatched out at once. There I hung over the manuscript with that necessary fact in my hand and no place to lay it down. Finally I perceived a possible opening for it, where it now is in the

story, and squeezing it in there discontentedly left it, for I
still think it only inoffensively and not well placed.

Then there is the traditional, obvious revision for suggestiveness, such as the recurrent mention of the mountain brook
at the beginning of each of the first scenes; revision for ordinary sense, in the first draught I had honeysuckle among the
scents on the darkened porch, whereas honeysuckle does not
bloom in Vermont till late June; revision for movement to get
the narrator rapidly from her bed to the brook; for sound, sense
proportion, even grammar . . . and always interwoven with
these mechanical revisions recurrent intense visualizations of
the scenes. This is the mental trick which can be learned, I
think, by practice and effort. Personally, although I never
used as material any events in my own intimate life, I can write
nothing if I cannot achieve these very definite, very complete
visualizations of the scenes; which means that I can write nothing at all about places, people or phases of life which I do not
intimately know, down to the last detail. If my life depended
on it, it does not seem to me I could possibly write a story
about Siberian hunters or East-side factory hands without having lived long among them. Now the story was what one
calls " finished," and I made a clear copy, picking my way with
difficulty among the alterations, the scratched-out passages,
and the cued-in paragraphs, the inserted pages, the re-arranged
phrases. As I typed, the interest and pleasure in the story
lasted just through that process. It still seemed pretty good
to me, the wedding still touched me, the whimsical ending still
amused me.

But on taking up the legible typed copy and beginning to
glance rapidly over it, I felt fall over me the black shadow
of that intolerable reaction which is enough to make any author
abjure his calling for ever. By the time I had reached the end,
the full misery was there, the heart-sick, helpless consciousness
of failure. What! I had had the presumption to try to trans-

late into words, and make others feel a thrill of sacred living human feeling, that should not be touched save by worthy hands. And what had I produced? A trivial, paltry, complicated tale, with certain cheaply ingenious devices in it. I heard again the incommunicable note of profound emotion in the old man's voice, suffered again with his sufferings; and those little black marks on white paper lay dead, dead in my hands. What horrible people second-rate authors were! They ought to be prohibited by law from sending out their caricatures of life. I would never write again. All that effort, enough to have achieved a master-piece it seemed at the time . . . and this, *this*, for result!

From the subconscious depths of long experience came up the cynical, slightly contemptuous consolation, " You know this never lasts. You always throw this same fit, and get over it."

So, suffering from really acute humiliation and unhappiness, I went out hastily to weed a flower-bed.

And sure enough, the next morning, after a long night's sleep, I felt quite rested, calm, and blessedly matter-of-fact. " Flint and Fire " seemed already very far away and vague, and the question of whether it was good or bad, not very important or interesting, like the chart of your temperature in a fever now gone by.

DOROTHY CANFIELD

Dorothy Canfield grew up in an atmosphere of books and learning. Her father, James H. Canfield, was president of Kansas University, at Lawrence, and there Dorothy was born, Feb. 17, 1879. She attended the high school at Lawrence, and became friends with a young army officer who was teaching at the near-by Army post, and who taught her to ride horseback. In 1917 when the first American troops entered Paris, Dorothy Canfield, who had gone to Paris to help in war work, again met this army officer, General John J. Pershing.

But this is getting ahead of the story. Dr. Canfield was called from Kansas to become president of Ohio State University, and later to be librarian at Columbia University, and so it happened that Dorothy took her college course at Ohio State and her graduate work at Columbia. She specialized in Romance languages, and took her degree as Doctor of Philosophy in 1904. In connection with Professor Carpenter of Columbia she wrote a text book on rhetoric. But books did not absorb quite all of her time, for the next item in her biography is her marriage to John R. Fisher, who had been the captain of the Columbia football team. They made their home at Arlington, Vermont, with frequent visits to Europe. In 1911-1912 they spent the winter in Rome. Here they came to know Madame Montessori, famous for developing a new system of training children. Dorothy Canfield spent many days at the " House of Childhood," studying the methods of this gifted teacher. The result of this was a book, *A Montessori Mother*, in which the system was adapted to the needs of American children.

The Squirrel Cage, published in 1912, was a study of an unhappy marriage. The book was favorably received by the critics, but found only a moderately wide public. A second novel, *The Bent Twig,* had college life as its setting; the chief character was the daughter of a professor in a Middle Western university. Meantime she had been publishing in magazines a number of short stories dealing with various types of New England country people, and in 1916 these were gathered into a volume with the title *Hillsboro People.* This book met with a wide acceptance, not only in this country but in France, where, like her other books, it was quickly translated and published. " Flint and Fire " is taken from this book. *The Real Motive,* another book of short stories, and *Understood Betsy,* a book for younger readers, were her next publications.

Meantime the Great War had come, and its summons was heard in their quiet mountain home. Mr. Fisher went to France with the Ambulance Corps; his wife as a war-relief worker. A letter from a friend thus described her work:

She has gone on doing a prodigious amount of work. First running, almost entirely alone, the work for soldiers blinded in battle, editing a magazine for them, running the presses, often with her own hands, getting books written for them; all the time looking out for refugees and personal cases that came under her attention: caring for children from the evacuated portions of France, organizing work for them, and establishing a Red Cross hospital for them.

Out of the fullness of these experiences she wrote her next book, *Home Fires in France,* which at once took rank as one of the most notable pieces of literature inspired by the war. It is in the form of short stories, but only the form is fiction: it is a perfectly truthful portrayal of the French women and of some Americans who, far back of the trenches, kept up the life of a nation when all its people were gone. It reveals the soul of the French people. *The Day of Glory,* her latest book, is a series of further impressions of the war in France.

It is not often that an author takes us into his workshop and lets us see just how his stories are written. The preceding account of Dorothy Canfield's literary methods was written especially for this book.

DUSKY AMERICANS

Most stories of Negro life fall into one of two groups. There is the story of the Civil War period, which pictures the " darky " on the old plantation, devoted to " young Massa " or " old Miss,"—the Negro of slavery. Then there are stories of recent times in which the Negro is used purely for comic effect, a sort of minstrel-show character. Neither of these is the Negro of to-day. A truer picture is found in the stories of Paul Laurence Dunbar. The following story is from his FOLKS FROM DIXIE.

THE ORDEAL AT MT. HOPE

BY

PAUL LAURENCE DUNBAR

"AND this is Mt. Hope," said the Rev. Howard Dokesbury to himself as he descended, bag in hand, from the smoky, dingy coach, or part of a coach, which was assigned to his people, and stepped upon the rotten planks of the station platform. The car he had just left was not a palace, nor had his reception by his fellow-passengers or his intercourse with them been of such cordial nature as to endear them to him. But he watched the choky little engine with its three black cars wind out of sight with a look as regretful as if he were witnessing the departure of his dearest friend. Then he turned his attention again to his surroundings, and a sigh welled up from his heart. "And this is Mt. Hope," he repeated. A note in his voice indicated that he fully appreciated the spirit of keen irony in which the place had been named.

The color scheme of the picture that met his eyes was in dingy blacks and grays. The building that held the ticket, telegraph, and train despatchers' offices was a miserably old ramshackle affair, standing well in the foreground of this scene of gloom and desolation. Its windows were so coated with smoke and grime that they seemed to have been painted over in order to secure secrecy within. Here and there a lazy cur lay drowsily snapping at the flies, and at the end of the station, perched on boxes or leaning against the wall, making a living picture of equal laziness, stood a group of idle Negroes exchanging rude badinage with their white counterparts across the street.

After a while this bantering interchange would grow more

keen and personal, a free-for-all friendly fight would follow, and the newspaper correspondent in that section would write it up as a "race war." But this had not happened yet that day.

"This is Mt. Hope," repeated the new-comer; "this is the field of my labors."

Rev. Howard Dokesbury, as may already have been inferred, was a Negro,—there could be no mistake about that. The deep dark brown of his skin, the rich over-fullness of his lips, and the close curl of his short black hair were evidences that admitted of no argument. He was a finely proportioned, stal-wart-looking man, with a general air of self-possession and self-sufficiency in his manner. There was firmness in the set of his lips. A reader of character would have said of him, "Here is a man of solid judgement, careful in deliberation, prompt in execution. and decisive."

It was the perception in him of these very qualities which had prompted the authorities of the little college where he had taken his degree and received his theological training, to urge him to go among his people at the South, and there to exert his powers for good where the field was broad and the laborers few.

Born of Southern parents from whom he had learned many of the superstitions and traditions of the South, Howard Dokes-bury himself had never before been below Mason and Dixon's line. But with a confidence born of youth and a consciousness of personal power, he had started South with the idea that he knew the people with whom he had to deal, and was equipped with the proper weapons to cope with their shortcomings.

But as he looked around upon the scene which now met his eye, a doubt arose in his mind. He picked up his bag with a sigh, and approached a man who had been standing apart from the rest of the loungers and regarding him with indolent in-tentness.

"Could you direct me to the house of Stephen Gray?" asked the minister.

The interrogated took time to change his position from left foot to right and shift his quid, before he drawled forth, " I reckon you's de new Mefdis preachah, huh? "

" Yes," replied Howard, in the most conciliatory tone he could command, " and I hope I find in you one of my flock."

" No, suh, I's a Babtist myse'f. I wa'n't raised up no place erroun' Mt. Hope; I'm nachelly f'om way up in Adams County. Dey jes' sont me down hyeah to fin' you an' tek you up to Steve's. Steve, he's workin' to-day an' couldn't come down."

He laid particular stress upon the " to-day," as if Steve's spell of activity were not an every-day occurrence.

" Is it far from here? " asked Dokesbury.

" 'T ain't mo' 'n a mile an' a ha'f by de shawt cut."

" Well, then, let's take the short cut, by all means," said the preacher.

They trudged along for a while in silence, and then the young man asked, " What do you men about here do mostly for a living? "

" Oh, well, we does odd jobs, we saws an' splits wood an' totes bundles, an' some of 'em raises gyahden, but mos' of us, we fishes. De fish bites an' we ketches 'em. Sometimes we eats 'em an' sometimes we sells 'em; a string o' fish'll bring a peck o' co'n any time."

" And is that all you do? "

" 'Bout."

" Why, I don't see how you live that way."

" Oh, we lives all right," answered the man; " we has plenty to eat an' drink, an' clothes to wear, an' some place to stay. I reckon folks ain't got much use fu' nuffin' mo'."

Dokesbury sighed. Here indeed was virgin soil for his ministerial labors. His spirits were not materially raised when, some time later, he came in sight of the house which was to be his abode. To be sure, it was better than most of the houses which he had seen in the Negro part of Mt. Hope; but even at that it was far from being good or comfortable-looking. It was small and mean in appearance. The weather boarding was broken, and in some places entirely fallen away, showing the great unhewn logs beneath; while off the boards that remained the whitewash had peeled in scrofulous spots.

The minister's guide went up to the closed door, and rapped loudly with a heavy stick.

" G' 'way f'om dah, an' quit you' foolin'," came in a large voice from within.

The guide grinned, and rapped again. There was a sound of shuffling feet and the pushing back of a chair, and then the same voice asking: " I bet I'll mek you git away f'om dat do'."

" Dat's A'nt Ca'line," the guide said, and laughed.

The door was flung back as quickly as its worn hinges and sagging bottom would allow, and a large body surmounted by a face like a big round full moon presented itself in the opening. A broomstick showed itself aggressively in one fat shiny hand.

" It's you, Tom Scott, is it—you trif'nin'——" and then, catching sight of the stranger, her whole manner changed, and she dropped the broomstick with an embarrassed " 'Scuse me, suh."

Tom chuckled all over as he said, " A'nt Ca'line, dis is yo' new preachah."

The big black face lighted up with a broad smile as the old woman extended her hand and enveloped that of the young minister's.

" Come in," she said. " I's mighty glad to see you—that no-'count Tom come put' nigh mekin' me 'spose myse'f." Then turning to Tom, she exclaimed with good-natured severity, " An' you go 'long, you scoun'll you! "

The preacher entered the cabin—it was hardly more—and seated himself in the rush-bottomed chair which A'nt Ca'line had been industriously polishing with her apron.

" An' now, Brothah——"

" Dokesbury," supplemented the young man.

" Brothah Dokesbury, I jes' want you to mek yo'se'f at home right erway. I know you ain't use to ouah ways down hyeah; but you jes' got to set in an' git ust to 'em. You mus'n' feel bad ef things don't go yo' way f'om de ve'y fust. Have you got a mammy? "

The question was very abrupt, and a lump suddenly jumped up in Dokesbury's throat and pushed the water into his eyes. He did have a mother away back there at home. She was all alone, and he was her heart and the hope of her life.

" Yes," he said, " I've got a little mother up there in Ohio."

" Well, I's gwine to be yo' mothah down hyeah; dat is, ef I ain't too rough an' common fu' you."

" Hush! " exclaimed the preacher, and he got up and took the old lady's hand in both of his own. " You shall be my mother down here; you shall help me, as you have done to-day. I feel better already."

" I knowed you would," and the old face beamed on the young one. " An' now jes' go out de do' dah an' wash yo' face. Dey's a pan an' soap an' watah right dah, an' hyeah's a towel; den you kin go right into yo' room, fu' I knows you want to be erlone fu' a while. I'll fix yo' suppah while you rests."

He did as he was bidden. On a rough bench outside the door, he found a basin and a bucket of water with a tin dipper in it. To one side, in a broken saucer, lay a piece of coarse soap. The facilities for copious ablutions were not abundant, but one thing the minister noted with pleasure: the towel, which was rough and hurt his skin, was, nevertheless, scrupulously clean. He went to his room feeling fresher and better, and although he found the place little and dark and warm, it too was clean, and a sense of its homeness began to take possession of him.

The room was off the main living-room into which he had been first ushered. It had one small window that opened out on a fairly neat yard. A table with a chair before it stood beside the window, and across the room—if the three feet of space which intervened could be called " across "—stood the little bed with its dark calico quilt and white pillows. There was no carpet on the floor, and the absence of a washstand indicated very plainly that the occupant was expected to wash outside. The young minister knelt for a few minutes beside the bed, and then rising cast himself into the chair to rest.

It was possibly half an hour later when his partial nap was broken in upon by the sound of a gruff voice from without saying, " He's hyeah, is he—oomph! Well, what's he ac' lak? Want us to git down on ouah knees an' crawl to him? If he do, I reckon he'll fin' dat Mt. Hope ain't de place fo' him."

The minister did not hear the answer, which was in a low voice and came, he conjectured, from Aunt " Ca'line "; but the gruff voice subsided, and there was the sound of footsteps going out of the room. A tap came on the preacher's door, and he opened it to the old woman. She smiled reassuringly.

" Dat' uz my ol' man," she said. " I sont him out to git some wood, so's I'd have time to post you. Don't you mind him; he's lots mo' ba'k dan bite. He's one o' dese little yaller men, an' you know dey kin be powahful contra'y when dey sets dey hai'd to it. But jes' you treat him nice an' don't let on, an' I'll be boun' you'll bring him erroun' in little er no time."

The Rev. Mr. Dokesbury received this advice with some misgiving. Albeit he had assumed his pleasantest manner when, after his return to the living-room, the little " yaller " man came through the door with his bundle of wood.

He responded cordially to Aunt Caroline's, " Dis is my husband, Brothah Dokesbury," and heartily shook his host's reluctant hand.

" I hope I find you well, Brother Gray," he said.

" Moder't, jes' moder't," was the answer.

"Come to suppah now, bofe o' you," said the old lady, and they all sat down to the evening meal of crisp bacon, well-fried potatoes, egg-pone, and coffee.

The young man did his best to be agreeable, but it was rather discouraging to receive only gruff monosyllabic rejoinders to his most interesting observations. But the cheery old wife came bravely to the rescue, and the minister was continually floated into safety on the flow of her conversation. Now and then, as he talked, he could catch a stealthy upflashing of Stephen Gray's eye, as suddenly lowered again, that told him that the old man was listening. But as an indication that they would get on together, the supper, taken as a whole, was not a success. The evening that followed proved hardly more fortunate. About the only remarks that could be elicited from the "little yaller man" were a reluctant "oomph" or "oomph-uh."

It was just before going to bed that, after a period of reflection, Aunt Caroline began slowly: "We got a son"—her husband immediately bristled up and his eyes flashed, but the old woman went on; "he named 'Lias, an' we thinks a heap o' 'Lias, we does; but—" the old man had subsided, but he bristled up again at the word—"he ain't jes' whut we want him to be." Her husband opened his mouth as if to speak in defense of his son, but was silent in satisfaction at his wife's explanation: "'Lias ain't bad; he jes' ca'less. Sometimes he stays at home, but right sma't o' de time he stays down at "—she looked at her husband and hesitated—"at de colo'ed s'loon. We don't lak dat. It ain't no fitten place fu' him. But 'Lias ain't bad, he jes' ca'less, an' me an' de ol' man we 'membahs him in ouah pra'ahs, an' I jes' t'ought I'd ax you to 'membah him too, Brothah Dokesbury."

The minister felt the old woman's pleading look and the husband's intense gaze upon his face, and suddenly there came to him an intimate sympathy in their trouble and with it an unexpected strength.

"There is no better time than now," he said, "to take his case to the Almighty Power; let us pray."

Perhaps it was the same prayer he had prayed many times before; perhaps the words of supplication and the plea for light and guidance were the same; but somehow to the young man kneeling there amid those humble surroundings, with the sorrow of these poor ignorant people weighing upon his heart, it seemed very different. It came more fervently from his lips, and the words had a deeper meaning. When he arose, there was a warmth at his heart just the like of which he had never before experienced.

Aunt Caroline blundered up from her knees, saying, as she wiped her eyes, "Blessed is dey dat mou'n, fu' dey shall be comfo'ted." The old man, as he turned to go to bed, shook the young man's hand warmly and in silence; but there was a moisture in the old eyes that told the minister that his plummet of prayer had sounded the depths.

Alone in his own room Howard Dokesbury sat down to study the situation in which he had been placed. Had his thorough college training anticipated specifically any such circumstance as this? After all, did he know his own people? Was it possible that they could be so different from what he had seen and known? He had always been such a loyal Negro, so proud of his honest brown; but had he been mistaken? Was he, after all, different from the majority of the people with whom he was supposed to have all thoughts, feelings, and emotions in common?

These and other questions he asked himself without being able to arrive at any satisfactory conclusion. He did not go to sleep soon after retiring, and the night brought many thoughts. The next day would be Saturday. The ordeal had already begun,—now there were twenty-four hours between him and the supreme trial. What would be its outcome? There were moments when he felt, as every man, howsoever brave, must feel at times, that he would like to shift all his responsibilities and go away from the place that seemed destined to tax his powers beyond their capability of endurance. What could he do for the inhabitants of Mt. Hope? What was required of him to do? Ever through his mind ran that world-old question: "Am I my brother's keeper?" He had never asked, "Are these people my brothers?"

He was up early the next morning, and as soon as breakfast was done, he sat down to add a few touches to the sermon he had prepared as his introduction. It was not the first time that he had retouched it and polished it up here and there. Indeed, he had taken some pride in it. But as he read it over that day, it did not sound to him as it had sounded before. It appeared flat and without substance. After a while he laid it aside, telling himself that he was nervous and it was on this account that he could not see matters as he did in his calmer moments. He told himself, too, that he must not again take up the offending discourse until time to use it, lest the discovery of more imaginary flaws should so weaken his confidence that he would not be able to deliver it with effect.

In order better to keep his resolve, he put on his hat and went out for a walk through the streets of Mt. Hope. He did not find an encouraging prospect as he went along. The Negroes whom he met viewed him with ill-favor, and the whites who passed looked on him with unconcealed distrust and contempt. He began to feel lost, alone, and helpless. The squalor and shiftlessness which were plainly in evidence about the houses which he saw filled him with disgust and a dreary hopelessness.

He passed vacant lots which lay open and inviting children to healthful play; but instead of marbles or leap-frog or ball, he found little boys in ragged knickerbockers huddled together on the ground, "shooting craps" with precocious avidity and quarreling over the pennies that made the pitiful wagers. He heard glib profanity rolling from the lips of children who should have been stumbling through baby catechisms; and his heart ached for them.

He would have turned and gone back to his room, but the sound of shouts, laughter, and the tum-tum of a musical instrument drew him on down the street. At the turn of a corner, the place from which the noise emanated met his eyes. It was a rude frame building, low and unpainted. The panes in its windows whose places had not been supplied by sheets of tin were daubed a dingy red. Numerous kegs and bottles on the outside attested the nature of the place. The front door was open, but the interior was concealed by a gaudy curtain stretched across the entrance within. Over the door was the inscription, in straggling characters, " Sander's Place; " and when he saw half-a-dozen Negroes enter, the minister knew instantly that he now beheld the colored saloon which was the frequenting-place of his hostess's son 'Lias; and he wondered, if, as the mother said, her boy was not bad, how anything good could be preserved in such a place of evil.

The cries of boisterous laughter mingled with the strumming of the banjo and the shuffling of feet told him that they were engaged in one of their rude hoe-down dances. He had not passed a dozen paces beyond the door when the music was suddenly stopped, the sound of a quick blow followed, then ensued a scuffle, and a young fellow half ran, half fell through the open door. He was closely followed by a heavily built ruffian who was striking him as he ran. The young fellow was very much the weaker and slighter of the two, and was suffering great punishment. In an instant all the preacher's sense of justice was stung into sudden life. Just as the brute was about to give his victim a blow that would have sent him into the gutter, he felt his arm grasped in a detaining hold and heard a commanding voice,—" Stop! "

He turned with increased fury upon this meddler, but his other wrist was caught and held in a vise-like grip. For a moment the two men looked into each other's eyes. Hot words rose to the young man's lips, but he choked them back. Until this moment he had deplored the possession of a spirit so easily fired that it had been a test of his manhood to keep from "slugging" on the football field; now he was glad of it. He did not attempt to strike the man, but stood holding his arms and meeting the brute glare with manly flashing eyes. Either the natural cowardice of the bully or something in his new opponent's face had quelled the big fellow's spirit, and he said doggedly, " Lemme go. I wasn't a-go'n to kill him no-how, but ef I ketch him dancin' with my gal any mo', I——" He cast a glance full of malice at his victim, who stood on the pavement a few feet away, as much amazed as the dum-founded crowd which thronged the door of " Sander's Place." Loosing his hold, the preacher turned, and, putting his hand on the young fellow's shoulder, led him away.

For a time they walked on in silence. Dokesbury had to calm the tempest in his breast before he could trust his voice. After a while he said: " That fellow was making it pretty hot for you, my young friend. What had you done to him? "

" Nothin'," replied the other. " I was jes' dancin' 'long an' not thinkin' 'bout him, when all of a sudden he hollered dat I had his gal an' commenced hittin' me."

" He's a bully and a coward, or he would not have made use of his superior strength in that way. What's your name, friend? "

" 'Lias Gray," was the answer, which startled the minister into exclaiming,—

" What! are you Aunt Caroline's son? "

" Yes, suh, I sho is; does you know my mothah? "

" Why, I'm stopping with her, and we were talking about you last night. My name is Dokesbury, and I am to take charge of the church here."

" I thought mebbe you was a preachah, but I couldn't scarcely believe it after I seen de way you held Sam an' looked at him."

Dokesbury laughed, and his merriment seemed to make his companion feel better, for the sullen, abashed look left his face, and he laughed a little himself as he said: " I wasn't a-pesterin' Sam, but I tell you he pestered me mighty."

Dokesbury looked into the boy's face,—he was hardly more than a boy,—lit up as it was by a smile, and concluded that Aunt Caroline was right. 'Lias might be " ca'less," but he wasn't a bad boy. The face was too open and the eyes too honest for that. 'Lias wasn't bad; but environment does so much, and he would be if something were not done for him. Here, then, was work for a pastor's hands.

" You'll walk on home with me, 'Lias, won't you? "

" I reckon I mout ez well," replied the boy. " I don't stay erroun' home ez much ez I oughter."

" You'll be around more, of course, now that I am there. It will be so much less lonesome for two young people than for one. Then, you can be a great help to me, too."

The preacher did not look down to see how wide his listener's eyes grew as he answered: " Oh, I ain't fittin' to be no he'p to you, suh. Fust thing, I ain't nevah got religion, an' then I ain't well larned enough."

" Oh, there are a thousand other ways in which you can help, and I feel sure that you will."

" Of co'se, I'll do de ve'y bes' I kin."

" There is one thing I want you to do soon, as a favor to me."

" I can't go to de mou'nah's bench," cried the boy, in consternation.

" And I don't want you to," was the calm reply.

Another look of wide-eyed astonishment took in the preacher's face. These were strange words from one of his guild. But without noticing the surprise he had created, Dokesbury went on: " What I want is that you will take me fishing as soon as you can. I never get tired of fishing and I am anxious to go here. Tom Scott says you fish a great deal about here."

" Why, we kin go dis ve'y afternoon," exclaimed 'Lias, in relief and delight; " I's mighty fond o' fishin', myse'f."

" All right; I'm in your hands from now on."

'Lias drew his shoulders up, with an unconscious motion. The preacher saw it, and mentally rejoiced. He felt that the first thing the boy beside him needed was a consciousness of responsibility, and the lifted shoulders meant progress in that direction, a sort of physical straightening up to correspond with the moral one.

On seeing her son walk in with the minister, Aunt " Ca'-line's " delight was boundless. " La! Brothah Dokesbury," she exclaimed, " wha'd you fin' dat scamp? "

" Oh, down the street here," the young man replied lightly. " I got hold of his name and made myself acquainted, so he came home to go fishing with me."

" 'Lias is pow'ful fon' o' fishin', hisse'f. I 'low he kin show you some mighty good places. Cain't you, 'Lias? "

" I reckon."

'Lias was thinking. He was distinctly grateful that the circumstances of his meeting with the minister had been so deftly passed over. But with a half idea of the superior moral responsibility under which a man in Dokesbury's position labored, he wondered vaguely—to put it in his own thought-words— " ef de preachah hadn't put' nigh lied." However, he was willing to forgive this little lapse of veracity, if such it was, out of consideration for the anxiety it spared his mother.

When Stephen Gray came in to dinner, he was no less pleased than his wife to note the terms of friendship on which the minister received his son. On his face was the first smile that Dokesbury had seen there, and he awakened from his taciturnity and proffered much information as to the fishing-places thereabout. The young minister accounted this a distinct gain. Anything more than a frowning silence from the " little yaller man " was gain.

The fishing that afternoon was particularly good. Catfish,

chubs, and suckers were landed in numbers sufficient to please the heart of any amateur angler.

'Lias was happy, and the minister was in the best of spirits, for his charge seemed promising. He looked on at the boy's jovial face, and laughed within himself; for, mused he, " it is so much harder for the devil to get into a cheerful heart than into a sullen, gloomy one." By the time they were ready to go home Harold Dokesbury had received a promise from 'Lias to attend service the next morning and hear the sermon.

There was a great jollification over the fish supper that night, and 'Lias and the minister were the heroes of the occasion. The old man again broke his silence, and recounted, with infinite dryness, ancient tales of his prowess with rod and line; while Aunt " Ca'line " told of famous fish suppers that in the bygone days she had cooked for " de white folks." In the midst of it all, however, 'Lias disappeared. No one had noticed when he slipped out, but all seemed to become conscious of his absence about the same time. The talk shifted, and finally simmered into silence.

When the Rev. Mr. Dokesbury went to bed that night, his charge had not yet returned.

The young minister woke early on the Sabbath morning, and he may be forgiven that the prospect of the ordeal through which he had to pass drove his care for 'Lias out of mind for the first few hours. But as he walked to church, flanked on one side by Aunt Caroline in the stiffest of ginghams and on the other by her husband stately in the magnificence of an antiquated " Jim-swinger," his mind went back to the boy with sorrow. Where was he? What was he doing? Had the fear of a dull church service frightened him back to his old habits and haunts? There was a new sadness at the preacher's heart as he threaded his way down the crowded church and ascended the rude pulpit.

The church was stiflingly hot, and the morning sun still beat relentlessly in through the plain windows. The seats were rude wooden benches, in some instances without backs. To the right, filling the inner corner, sat the pillars of the church, stern, grim, and critical. Opposite them, and, like them, in seats at right angles to the main body, sat the older sisters, some of them dressed with good old-fashioned simplicity, while others yielding to newer tendencies were gotten up in gaudy attempts at finery. In the rear seats a dozen or so much beribboned mulatto girls tittered and giggled, and cast bold glances at the minister.

The young man sighed as he placed the manuscript of his sermon between the leaves of the tattered Bible. " And this is Mt. Hope," he was again saying to himself.

It was after the prayer and in the midst of the second hymn that a more pronounced titter from the back seats drew his attention. He raised his head to cast a reproving glance at the irreverent, but the sight that met his eyes turned that look into one of horror. 'Lias had just entered the church, and with every mark of beastly intoxication was staggering up the aisle to a seat, into which he tumbled in a drunken heap. The preacher's soul turned sick within him, and his eyes sought the face of the mother and father. The old woman was wiping her eyes, and the old man sat with his gaze bent upon the floor, lines of sorrow drawn about his wrinkled mouth.

All of a sudden a great revulsion of feeling came over Dokesbury. Trembling he rose and opened the Bible. There lay his sermon, polished and perfected. The opening lines seemed to him like glints from a bright cold crystal. What had he to say to these people, when the full realization of human sorrow and care and of human degradation had just come to him? What had they to do with firstlies and secondlies, with premises and conclusions? What they wanted was a strong hand to help them over the hard places of life and a loud voice to cheer them through the dark. He closed the book again upon his precious sermon. A something new had been born in his heart. He let his glance rest for another instant on the mother's

pained face and the father's bowed form, and then turning to
the congregation began, " Come unto me, all ye that labor and
are heavy laden, and I will give you rest. Take my yoke upon
you, and learn of me: for I am meek and lowly in heart: and
ye shall find rest unto your souls." Out of the fullness of
his heart he spoke unto them. Their great need informed his
utterance. He forgot his carefully turned sentences and perfectly rounded periods. He forgot all save that here was the
well-being of a community put into his hands whose real condition he had not even suspected until now. The situation
wrought him up. His words went forth like winged fire, and
the emotional people were moved beyond control. They
shouted, and clapped their hands, and praised the Lord loudly.

When the service was over, there was much gathering about
the young preacher, and handshaking. Through all 'Lias had
slept. His mother started toward him; but the minister
managed to whisper to her, " Leave him to me." When the
congregation had passed out, Dokesbury shook 'Lias. The boy
woke. partially sobered, and his face fell before the preacher's
eyes.

" Come, my boy, let's go home." Arm in arm they went
out into the street, where a number of scoffers had gathered
to have a laugh at the abashed boy; but Harold Dokesbury's
strong arm steadied his steps, and something in his face checked
the crowd's hilarity. Silently they cleared the way, and the
two passed among them and went home.

The minister saw clearly the things which he had to combat in his community, and through this one victim he determined to fight the general evil. The people with whom he
had to deal were children who must be led by the hand. The
boy lying in drunken sleep upon his bed was no worse than
the rest of them. He was an epitome of the evil, as his
parents were of the sorrows, of the place.

He could not talk to Elias. He could not lecture him. He
would only be dashing his words against the accumulated evil

of years of bondage as the ripples of a summer sea beat against a stone wall. It was not the wickedness of this boy he was fighting or even the wrong-doing of Mt. Hope. It was the aggregation of the evils of the fathers, the grandfathers, the masters and mistresses of these people. Against this what could talk avail?

The boy slept on, and the afternoon passed heavily away. Aunt Caroline was finding solace in her pipe, and Stephen Gray sulked in moody silence beside the hearth. Neither of them joined their guest at evening service.

He went, however. It was hard to face those people again after the events of the morning. He could feel them covertly nudging each other and grinning as he went up to the pulpit. He chided himself for the momentary annoyance it caused him. Were they not like so many naughty, irresponsible children?

The service passed without unpleasantness, save that he went home with an annoyingly vivid impression of a yellow girl with red ribbons on her hat, who pretended to be impressed by his sermon and made eyes at him from behind her handkerchief.

On the way to his room that night, as he passed Stephen Gray, the old man whispered huskily, " It's de fus' time 'Lias evah done dat."

It was the only word he had spoken since morning.

A sound sleep refreshed Dokesbury, and restored the tone to his overtaxed nerves. When he came out in the morning, Elias was already in the kitchen. He too had slept off his indisposition, but it had. been succeeded by a painful embarrassment that proved an effectual barrier to all intercourse with him. The minister talked lightly and amusingly, but the boy never raised his eyes from his plate, and only spoke when he was compelled to answer some direct questions.

Harold Dokesbury knew that unless he could overcome this reserve, his power over the youth was gone. He bent every effort to do it.

" What do you say to a turn down the street with me? " he asked as he rose from breakfast.

'Lias shook his head.

" What! You haven't deserted me already? "

The older people had gone out, but young Gray looked furtively about before he replied: " You know I ain't fittin' to go out with you—aftah—aftah—yestiddy."

A dozen appropriate texts rose in the preacher's mind, but he knew that it was not a preaching time, so he contented himself with saying,—

" Oh, get out! Come along! "

" No, I cain't. I cain't. I wisht I could! You needn't think I's ashamed, 'cause I ain't. Plenty of 'em git drunk, an' I don't keer nothin' 'bout dat "—this in a defiant tone.

" Well, why not come along then? "

" I tell you I cain't. Don't ax me no mo'. It ain't on my account I won't go. It's you."

" Me! Why, I want you to go."

" I know you does, but I mustn't. Cain't you see that dey'd be glad to say dat—dat you was in cahoots wif me an' you tuk yo' dram on de sly? "

" I don't care what they say so long as it isn't true. Are you coming? "

" No, I ain't."

He was perfectly determined, and Dokesbury saw that there was no use arguing with him. So with a resigned " All right! " he strode out the gate and up the street, thinking of the problem he had to solve.

There was good in Elias Gray, he knew. It was a shame that it should be lost. It would be lost unless he were drawn strongly away from the paths he was treading. But how could it be done? Was there no point in his mind that could be reached by what was other than evil? That was the thing to be found out. Then he paused to ask himself if, after all, he were not trying to do too much,—trying, in fact, to play Providence to Elias. He found himself involuntarily wanting to shift the responsibility of planning for the youth. He wished that something entirely independent of his intentions would happen.

Just then something did happen. A piece of soft mud hurled from some unknown source caught the minister square in the chest, and spattered over his clothes. He raised his eyes and glanced about quickly, but no one was in sight. Whoever the foe was, he was securely ambushed.

"Thrown by the hand of a man," mused Dokesbury, "prompted by the malice of a child."

He went on his way, finished his business, and returned to the house.

"La, Brothah Dokesbury!" exclaimed Aunt Caroline, "what's de mattah 'f you' shu't bosom?"

"Oh, that's where one of our good citizens left his card."

"You don' mean to say none o' dem low-life scoun'els——"

"I don't know who did it. He took particular pains to keep out of sight."

"'Lias!" the old woman cried, turning on her son, "wha' 'd you let Brothah Dokesbury go off by hisse'f fu? Why n't you go 'long an' tek keer o' him?"

The old lady stopped even in the midst of her tirade, as her eyes took in the expression on her son's face.

"I'll kill some o' dem damn——"

"'Lias!"

"'Scuse me, Mistah Dokesbury, but I feel lak I'll bus' ef I don't 'spress myse'f. It makes me so mad. Don't you go out o' hyeah no mo' 'dout me. I'll go 'long an' I'll brek somebody's haid wif a stone."

"'Lias! how you talkin' fo' de ministah?"

"Well, dat's whut I'll do, 'cause I kin outth'ow any of 'em an' I know dey hidin'-places."

"I'll be glad to accept your protection," said Dokesbury.

He saw his advantage, and was thankful for the mud,—the

one thing that without an effort restored the easy relations between himself and his protégé.

Ostensibly these relations were reversed, and Elias went out with the preacher as a guardian and protector. But the minister was laying his nets. It was on one of these rambles that he broached to 'Lias a subject which he had been considering for some time."

" Look here, 'Lias," he said, " what are you going to do with that big back yard of yours? "

" Oh, nothin'. 'Tain't no 'count to raise nothin' in."

" It may not be fit for vegetables, but it will raise something."

" What? "

" Chickens. That's what."

Elias laughed sympathetically.

" I'd lak to eat de chickens I raise. I wouldn't want to be feedin' de neighborhood."

" Plenty of boards, slats, wire, and a good lock and key would fix that all right."

" Yes, but whah 'm I gwine to git all dem things? "

" Why, I'll go in with you and furnish the money, and help you build the coops. Then you can sell chickens and eggs, and we'll go halves on the profits."

" Hush man! " cried 'Lias, in delight.

So the matter was settled, and, as Aunt Caroline expressed it, " Fu' a week er sich a mattah, you nevah did see sich ta'in' down an' buildin' up in all yo' bo'n days."

'Lias went at the work with zest and Dokesbury noticed his skill with tools. He let fall the remark: " Say, 'Lias, there's a school near here where they teach carpentry; why don't you go and learn? "

" What I gwine to do with bein' a cyahpenter? "

" Repair some of these houses around Mt. Hope, if nothing more," Dokesbury responded, laughing; and there the matter rested.

The work prospered, and as the weeks went on, 'Lias's enterprise became the town's talk. One of Aunt Caroline's patrons who had come with some orders about work regarded the changed condition of affairs, and said, "Why, Aunt Caroline, this doesn't look like the same place. I'll have to buy some eggs from you; you keep your yard and hen-house so nice, it's an advertisement for the eggs."

"Don't talk to me nothin' 'bout dat ya'd, Miss Lucy," Aunt Caroline had retorted. "Dat 'long to 'Lias an' de preachah. Hit dey doin's. Dey done mos' nigh drove me out wif dey cleanness. I ain't nevah seed no sich ca'in' on in my life befo'. Why, my 'Lias done got right brigity an' talk about bein' somep'n."

Dokesbury had retired from his partnership with the boy save in so far as he acted as a general supervisor. His share had been sold to a friend of 'Lias, Jim Hughes. The two seemed to have no other thought save of raising, tending, and selling chickens.

Mt. Hope looked on and ceased to scoff. Money is a great dignifier, and Jim and 'Lias were making money. There had been some sniffs when the latter had hinged the front gate and whitewashed his mother's cabin, but even that had been accepted now as a matter of course.

Dokesbury had done his work. He, too, looked on, and in some satisfaction.

"Let the leaven work," he said, "and all Mt. Hope must rise."

It was one day, nearly a year later, that "old lady Hughes" dropped in on Aunt Caroline for a chat.

"Well, I do say, Sis' Ca'line, dem two boys o' ourn done sot dis town on fiah."

"What now, Sis' Lizy?"

"Why, evah sence 'Lias tuk it into his haid to be a cyahpenter an' Jim 'cided to go 'long an' lu'n to be a blacksmiff, some o' dese hyeah othah young people's been trying to do some-p'n'."

" All dey wanted was a staht."

" Well, now will you b'lieve me, dat no-'count Tom John-son done opened a fish sto', an' he has de boys an' men bring him dey fish all de time. He gives 'em a little somep'n fu' dey ketch, den he go sell 'em to de white folks."

" Lawd, how long! "

" An' what you think he say? "

" I do' know, sis'."

" He say ez soon 'z he git money enough, he gwine to dat school whah 'Lias and Jim gone an' lu'n to fahm scientific."

" Bless de Lawd! Well, 'um, I don' put nothin' pas' de young folks now."

Mt. Hope had at last awakened. Something had come to her to which she might aspire,—something that she could understand and reach. She was not soaring, but she was ris-ing above the degradation in which Harold Dokesbury had found her. And for her and him the ordeal had passed.

PAUL LAURENCE DUNBAR

The Negro race in America has produced musicians, composers and painters, but it was left for Paul Laurence Dunbar to give it fame in literature. He was of pure African stock; his father and mother were born in slavery, and neither had any schooling, although the father had taught himself to read. Paul was born in Dayton, Ohio, June 27, 1872. He was christened Paul, because his father said that he was to be a great man. He was a diligent pupil at school, and began to make verses when he was still a child. His ability was recognized by his class mates; he was made editor of the high school paper, and wrote the class song for his commencement.

The death of his father made it necessary for him to support his mother. He sought for some employment where his education might be put to some use, but finding such places closed to him, he became an elevator boy. He continued to write, however, and in 1892 his first volume was published, a book of poems called *Oak and Ivy*. The publishers were so doubtful of its success that they would not bring it out until a friend advanced the cost of publication. Paul now sold books to the passengers in his elevator, and realized enough to repay his friend. He was occasionally asked to give readings from his poetry. Gifted as he was with a deep, melodious voice, and a fine power of mimicry, he was very successful. In 1893 he was sought out by a man who was organizing a concert company and who engaged Paul to go along as reader. Full of enthusiasm, he set to work committing his poems to memory, and writing new ones. Ten days before the company was to start, word came that it had been disbanded. Paul found himself at the approach of winter without money and without work, and with his mother in real need. In his discouragement he even thought of suicide, but by the help of a friend he found work, and with it courage. In a letter written about this time he tells of his ambitions: " I did once want to be a lawyer, but that ambition has long since died out before the all-absorbing desire to be a worthy singer of the songs of God and nature. To be able to interpret my own people through song and story, and to prove to the many that we are more human than African."

A second volume of poems, *Majors and Minors*, appeared in 1895. Like his first book it was printed by a local publisher, and had but a small sale. The actor James A. Herne happened to be playing *Shore Acres* in Toledo; Paul saw him, admired his acting, and timidly presented him with a copy of his book. Mr. Herne read it with great pleasure, and sent it on to his friend William Dean Howells, who was then editor of *Harper's Weekly*. In June, 1896, there appeared in that journal a full-page review of the work of Paul Laurence Dunbar, quoting freely from his poems, and praising them highly. This recognition by America's greatest critic was the beginning of Paul's national reputation. Orders came for his books from all over the country; a manager engaged him for a series of readings from his poems, and a New York firm, Dodd Mead & Co., arranged to bring out his next book, *Lyrics of Lowly Life*.

In 1897 he went to England to give a series of readings. Here he was a guest at the Savage Club, one of the best-known clubs of London. His readings were very successful, but a dishonest manager cheated him out of the proceeds, and he was obliged to cable to his friends for money to come home.

Through the efforts of Col. Robert G. Ingersoll, the young poet obtained a position in the Congressional Library at Washington. It was thought that this would give him just the opportunity he needed for study, but the work proved too confining for his health. The year 1898 was marked by two events: the publication of his first book of short stories, *Folks From Dixie,* and his marriage to Miss Alice R. Moore. In 1899 at the request of Booker T. Washington he went to Tuskeegee and gave several readings and lectures before the students, also writing a school song for them. He made a tour through the South, giving readings with much success, but the strain of public appearances was beginning to tell upon his health. He continued to write, and in 1899 published *Lyrics of the Hearthside,* dedicated to his wife. He was invited to go to Albany to read before a distinguished audience, where Theodore Roosevelt, then governor, was to introduce him. He started, but was unable to get farther than New York. Here he lay sick for weeks, and when he grew stronger, the doctors said that his lungs were affected and he must have a change of climate. He went to Colorado in the fall of 1899, and wrote back to a friend: " Well, it is something to sit under the shadow of the Rocky Mountains, even if one only goes there to die." From this time on his life was one long fight for health, and usually a losing battle, but he faced it as courageously as Robert Louis Stevenson had done. In Colorado he wrote a novel, *The Love of Landry,* whose scene was laid in his new surroundings. He returned to Washington in 1900, and gave occasional readings, but it was evident that his strength was failing. He published two more volumes, *The Strength of Gideon,* a book of short stories, and *Poems of Cabin and Field,* which showed that his genius had lost none of its power. His last years were spent in Dayton, his old home, with his mother. He died February 10, 1906.

One of the finest tributes to him was paid by his friend Brand Whitlock, then Mayor of Toledo, who has since become famous as United States Minister to Belgium during the Great War. This is from a letter written when he heard that the young poet was dead:

Paul was a poet: and I find that when I have said that I have said the greatest and most splendid thing that can be said about a man. . . . Nature, who knows so much better than man about everything, cares nothing at all for the little distinctions, and when she elects one of her children for her most important work, bestows on him the rich gift of poesy, and assigns him a post in the greatest of the arts, she invariably seizes the opportunity to show her contempt of rank and title and race and land and creed. She took Burns from a plough and Paul from an elevator, and Paul has done for his own people what Burns did for the peasants of Scotland—he has expressed them in their own way and in their own words.

WITH THE POLICE

Not all Americans are good Americans. For the law-breakers, American born or otherwise, we need men to enforce the law. Of these guardians of public safety, one body, the Pennsylvania State Police, has become famous for its achievements. Katherine Mayo studied their work at first hand, met the men of the force, visited the scenes of their activity, and in THE STANDARD BEARERS, *tells of their daring exploits. This story is taken from that book.*

ISRAEL DRAKE

BY

KATHERINE MAYO

ISRAEL DRAKE was a bandit for simple love of the thing. To hunt for another reason would be a waste of time. The blood in his veins was pure English, unmixed since long ago. His environment was that of his neighbors. His habitat was the noble hills. But Israel Drake was a bandit, just as his neighbors were farmers—just as a hawk is a hawk while its neighbors are barnyard fowls.

Israel Drake was swarthy-visaged, high of cheek bone, with large, dark, deep-set eyes, and a thin-lipped mouth covered by a long and drooping black mustache. Barefooted, he stood six feet two inches tall. Lean as a panther, and as supple, he could clear a five-foot rail fence without the aid of his hand. He ran like a deer. As a woodsman the very deer could have taught him little. With rifle and revolver he was an expert shot, and the weapons he used were the truest and best.

All the hill-people of Cumberland County dreaded him. All the scattered valley-folk spoke softly at his name. And the jest and joy of Israel's care-free life was to make them skip and shiver and dance to the tune of their trepidations.

As a matter of fact, he was leader of a gang, outlaws every one. But his own strong aura eclipsed the rest, and he glared alone, in the thought of his world, endued with terrors of diverse origin.

His genius kept him fully aware of the value of this pre-eminence, and it lay in his wisdom and pleasure to fan the flame of his own repute. In this it amused him to seek the picturesque—the unexpected. With an imagination fed by primeval humor and checked by no outward circumstances of law, he achieved a ready facility. Once, for example, while trundling through his town of Shippensburg on the rear platform of a freight train, he chanced to spy a Borough Constable crossing a bridge near the track.

" Happy thought! Let's touch the good soul up. He's getting stodgy."

Israel drew a revolver and fired, neatly nicking the Contable's hat. Then with a mountaineer's hoot, he gayly proclaimed his identity.

Again, and many times, he would send into this or that town or settlement a message addressed to the Constable or Chief of Police:—

" I am coming down this afternoon. Get away out of town. Don't let me find you there."

Obediently they went away. And Israel, strolling the streets that afternoon just as he had promised to do, would enter shop after shop, look over the stock at his leisure, and, with perfect good-humor, pick out whatever pleased him, regardless of cost.

" I think I'll take this here article," he would say to the trembling store-keeper, affably pocketing his choice.

" Help yourself, Mr. Drake! Help yourself, sir! Glad we are able to please you to-day."

Which was indeed the truth. And many of them there were who would have hastened to curry favor with their persecutor by whispering in his ear a word of warning had they known of any impending attempt against him by the agents of peace.

Such was their estimate of the relative strength of Israel Drake and of the law forces of the Sovereign State of Pennsylvania.

In the earlier times they had tried to arrest him. Once the attempt succeeded and Israel went to the Penitentiary for a term. But he emerged a better and wilier bandit than before, to embark upon a career that made his former life seem tame. Sheriffs and constables now proved powerless against him, whatever they essayed.

Then came a grand, determined effort when the Sheriff, supported by fifteen deputies, all heavily armed, actually surrounded Drake's house. But the master-outlaw, alone and at ease at an upper window, his Winchester repeating-rifle in his hand and a smile of still content on his face, coolly stood the whole army off until, weary of empty danger, it gave up the siege and went home.

This disastrous expedition ended the attempts of the local authorities to capture Israel Drake. Thenceforth he pursued his natural course without pretense of let or hindrance. At the time when this story begins, no fewer than fourteen warrants were out for his apprehension, issued on charges ranging from burglary and highway robbery through a long list of felonies. But the warrants, slowly accumulating, lay in the bottom of official drawers, apprehending nothing but dust. No one undertook to serve them. Life was too sweet—too short.

Then came a turn of fate. Israel chanced to bethink himself of a certain aged farmer living with his old wife near a spot called Lee's Cross-Road. The two dwelt by themselves, without companions on their farm, and without neighbors. And they were reputed to have money.

The money might not be much—might be exceedingly little. But, even so, Israel could use it, and in any event there would be the fun of the trick. So Israel summoned one Carey Morrison, a gifted mate and subordinate, with whom he proceeded to act.

At dead of night the two broke into the farmhouse—crept into the chamber of the old pair—crept softly, softly, lest the farmer might keep a shotgun by his side. Sneaking to the foot of the bed, Israel suddenly flashed his lantern full upon the pillows—upon the two pale, deep-seamed faces crowned with silver hair.

The woman sat up with a piercing scream. The farmer clutched at his gun. But Israel, bringing the glinting barrel of his revolver into the lantern's shaft of light, ordered both to lie down. Carey, slouching at hand, awaited orders.

"Where is your money?" demanded Israel, indicating the farmer by the point of his gun.

"I have no money, you coward!"

"It's no use your lying to me. *Where's the money?*"

"I have no money, I tell you."

"Carey," observed Israel, "hunt a candle."

While Carey looked for the candle, Israel surveyed his victims with a cheerful, anticipatory grin.

The candle came; was lighted.

"Carey," Israel spoke again, "you pin the old woman down. Pull the quilt off. Clamp her feet together. So!"

Then he thrust the candle-flame against the soles of those gnarled old feet—thrust it close, while the flame bent upward, and the melting tallow poured upon the bed.

The woman screamed again, this time in pain. The farmer half rose, with a quivering cry of rage, but Israel's gun stared him between the eyes. The woman screamed without interval. There was a smell of burning flesh.

"Now we'll change about," remarked Israel, beaming. "I'll hold the old feller. You take the candle, Carey. You don't reely need your gun—now, do ye, boy?"

And so they began afresh.

It was not a game to last long. Before dawn the two were back in their own place, bearing the little all of value that the rifled house had contained.

When the news of the matter spread abroad, it seemed, somehow, just a straw too much. The District Attorney of the County of Cumberland blazed into white heat. But he was powerless, he found. Not an officer within his entire jurisdiction expressed any willingness even to attempt an arrest.

"Then we shall see," said District Attorney Rhey, "what the State will do for us, since we cannot help ourselves!" And he rushed off a telegram, confirmed by post, to the Superintendent of the Department of State Police.

The Superintendent of the Department of State Police promptly referred the matter to the Captain of "C" Troop, with orders to act. For Cumberland County, being within the southeastern quarter of the Commonwealth, lies under "C" Troop's special care.

It was Adams, in those days, who held that command— Lynn G. Adams, now Captain of "A" Troop, although for the duration of the war serving in the regular army, even as his fathers before him have served in our every war, including that which put the country on the map. Truer soldier, finer officer, braver or straighter or surer dealer with men and things need not be sought. His victories leave no needless scar behind, and his command would die by inches rather than fail him anywhere.

The Captain of "C" Troop, then, choosing with judgment, picked his man—picked Trooper Edward Hallisey, a Boston Irishman, square of jaw, shrewd of eye, quick of wit, strong of wind and limb. And he ordered Private Hallisey to proceed at once to Carlisle, county seat of Cumberland, and report to the District Attorney for service toward effecting the apprehension of Israel Drake.

Three days later—it was the 28th of September, to be exact —Private Edward Hallisey sent in his report to his Troop Commander. He had made all necessary observations, he said, and was ready to arrest the criminal. In this he would like to have the assistance of two Troopers, who should join him at Carlisle.

The report came in the morning mail. First Sergeant Price detailed two men from the Barracks reserve. They were Privates H. K. Merryfield and Harvey J. Smith. Their orders were simply to proceed at once, in civilian clothes, to Carlisle, where they would meet Private Hallisey and assist him in effecting the arrest of Israel Drake.

Privates Merryfield and Smith, carrying in addition to their service revolvers the 44-caliber Springfield carbine which is the Force's heavy weapon, left by the next train.

On the Carlisle station platform, as the two Troopers debarked, some hundred persons were gathered in pursuance of various and centrifugal designs. But one impulse they appeared unanimously to share—the impulse to give as wide a berth as possible to a peculiarly horrible tramp.

Why should a being like that intrude himself upon a passenger platform in a respectable country town? Not to board a coach, surely, for such as he pay no fares. To spy out the land? To steal luggage? Or simply to make himself hateful to decent folk?

He carried his head with a hangdog lurch—his heavy jaw was rough with stubble beard. His coat and trousers fluttered rags and his toes stuck out of his boots. Women snatched back their skirts as he slouched near, and men muttered and scowled at him for a contaminating beast.

Merryfield and Smith, drifting near this scum of the earth, caught the words "Four-thirty train" and the name of a station.

"Right," murmured Merryfield.

Then he went and bought tickets.

In the shelter of an ancient, grimy day-coach, the scum muttered again, as Smith brushed past him in the aisle.

"Charlie Stover's farm," said he.

"M'm," said Smith.

At a scrap of a station, in the foothills of ascending heights the tramp and the Troopers separately detrained. In the early evening all three strayed together once more in the shadow of the lilacs by Charlie Stover's gate.

Over the supper-table Hallisey gave the news. "Drake is somewhere on the mountain to-night," said he. "His cabin is way up high, on a ridge called Huckleberry Patch. He is practically sure to go home in the course of the evening. Then is our chance. First, of course, you fellows will change your clothes. I've got some old things ready for you."

Farmer Stover, like every other denizen of the rural county, had lived for years in terror and hatred of Israel Drake. Willingly he had aided Hallisey to the full extent of his power. He had told all that he knew of the bandit's habits and mates. He had indicated the mountain trails and he had given the Trooper such little shelter and food as the latter had stopped to take during his rapid work of investigation. But now he was asked to perform a service that he would gladly have refused; he was asked to hitch up a horse and wagon and to drive the three Troopers to the very vicinity of Israel Drake's house.

" Oh, come on, Mr. Stover," they urged. " You're a public-spirited man, as you've shown. Do it for your neighbors' sake if not for your own. You want the county rid of this pest."

Very reluctantly the farmer began the trip. With every turn of the ever-mounting forest road his reluctance grew. Grisly memories, grisly pictures, flooded his mind. It was night, and the trees in the darkness whispered like evil men. The bushes huddled like crouching figures. And what was it, moving stealthily over there, that crackled twigs? At last he could bear it no more.

" Here's where *I* turn 'round," he muttered hoarsely. " If you fellers are going farther you'll go alone. I got a use for *my* life! "

" All right, then," said Hallisey. " You've done well by us already. Good-night."

It was a fine moonlight night and Hallisey now knew those woods as well as did his late host. He led his two comrades up another stiff mile of steady climbing. Then he struck off, by an almost invisible trail, into the dense timber. Silently the three men moved, threading the fragrant, silver-flecked blackness with practised woodsmen's skill. At last their file-leader stopped and beckoned his mates.

Over his shoulder the two studied the scene before them: A clearing chopped out of the dense tall timber. In the midst of the clearing a log cabin, a story and a half high. On two sides of the cabin a straggling orchard of peach and apple trees. In the cabin window a dim light.

It was then about eleven o'clock. The three Troopers, effacing themselves in the shadows, laid final plans.

The cabin had two rooms on the top floor and one below, said Hallisey, beneath his breath. The first-floor room had a door and two windows on the north, and the same on the south, just opposite. Under the west end was a cellar, with an outside door. Before the main door to the north was a little porch. This, by day, commanded the sweep of the mountain-side; and here, when Drake was " hiding out " in some neighboring eyrie, expecting pursuit, his wife was wont to signal him concerning the movements of intruders.

Her code was written in dish-water. A panful thrown to the east meant danger in the west, and *vice versa;* this Hallisey himself had seen and now recalled in case of need.

Up to the present moment each officer had carried his carbine, taken apart and wrapped in a bundle, to avoid the remark of chance observers by the way. Now each put his weapon together, ready for use. They compared their watches, setting them to the second. They discarded their coats and hats.

The moon was flooding the clearing with high, pale light, adding greatly to the difficulty of their task. Accordingly, they plotted carefully. Each Trooper took a door—Hallisey that to the north, Merryfield that to the south, Smith that of the cellar. It was agreed that each should creep to a point opposite the door on which he was to advance, ten minutes being allowed for all to reach their initial positions; that at exactly five minutes to midnight the advance should be started, slowly, through the tall grass of the clearing toward the cabin; that in case of any unusual noise or alarm, each man should lie low exactly five minutes before resuming this advance; and that from a point fifty yards from the cabin a rush should be made upon the doors.

According to the request of the District Attorney, Drake was to be taken " dead or alive," but according to an adamantine principle of the Force, he must be taken not only alive, but unscathed if that were humanly possible. This meant that he must not be given an opportunity to run and so render shooting necessary. If, however, he should break away, his chance of escape would be small, as each Trooper was a dead shot with the weapons he was carrying.

The scheme concerted, the three officers separated, heading apart to their several starting-points. At five minutes before midnight, to the tick of their synchronized watches, each began to glide through the tall grass. But it was late September. The grass was dry. Old briar-veins dragged at brittle stalks. Shimmering whispers of withered leaves echoed to the smallest touch; and when the men were still some two hundred yards from the cabin the sharp ears of a dog caught the rumor of all these tiny sounds,—and the dog barked.

Every man stopped short—moved not a finger again till five minutes had passed. Then once more each began to creep—reached the fifty-yard point—stood up, with a long breath, and dashed for his door.

At one and the same moment, practically, the three stood in the cabin, viewing a scene of domestic peace. A short, square, swarthy woman, black of eye, high of cheek bone, stood by a stove calmly stirring a pot. On the table besides her, on the floor around her, clustered many jars of peaches —jars freshly filled, steaming hot, awaiting their tops. In a corner three little children, huddled together on a low bench, stared at the strangers with sleepy eyes. Three chairs; a cupboard with dishes; bunches of corn hanging from the rafters by their husks; festoons of onions; tassels of dried herbs—all this made visible by the dull light of a small kerosene lamp whose dirty chimney was streaked with smoke. All this and nothing more.

Two of the men, jumping for the stairs, searched the upper half-story thoroughly, but without profit.

"Mrs. Drake," said Hallisey, as they returned, "we are officers of the State Police, come to arrest your husband. Where is he?"

In silence, in utter calm the woman still stirred her pot, not missing the rhythm of a stroke.

"The dog warned them. He's just got away," said each officer to himself. "She's *too* calm."

She scooped up a spoonful of the fruit, peered at it critically, splashed it back into the bubbling pot. From her manner it appeared the most natural thing in the world to be canning peaches at midnight on the top of South Mountain in the presence of officers of the State Police.

"My husband's gone to Baltimore," she vouchsafed at her easy leisure.

"Let's have a look in the cellar," said Merryfield, and dropped down the cellar stairs with Hallisey at his heels. Together they ransacked the little cave to a conclusion. During the process, Merryfield conceived an idea.

"Hallisey," he murmured, "what would you think of my staying down here, while you and Smith go off talking as though we were all together? She might say something to the children, when she believes we're gone, and I could hear every word through that thin floor."

"We'll do it!" Hallisey answered, beneath his voice. Then, shouting:—

"Come on, Smith! Let's get away from this; no use wasting time here!"

And in another moment Smith and Hallisey were crashing up the mountain-side, calling out: "Hi, there! Merryfield—

Oh! Merryfield, wait for us! "—as if their comrade had out-stripped them on the trail.

Merryfield had made use of the noise of their departure to establish himself in a tenable position under the widest crack in the floor. Now he held himself motionless, subduing even his breath.

One—two—three minutes of dead silence. Then came the timorous half-whisper of a frightened child:

" Will them men kill father if they find him? "

" S-sh! "

" Mother! " faintly ventured another little voice, " will them men kill father if they find him? "

" S-sh! S-sh! I tell ye! "

" Ma-ma! Will they kill my father? " This was the wail, insistent, uncontrolled, of the smallest child of all.

The crackling tramp of the officers, mounting the trail, had wholly died away. The woman evidently believed all immediate danger past.

" No! " she exclaimed vehemently, " they ain't goin' to lay eyes on yo' father, hair nor hide of him. Quit yer fret-tin'! "

In a moment she spoke again: " You keep still, now, like good children, while I go out and empty these peach-stones. I'll be back in a minute. See you keep still just where you are! "

Stealing noiselessly to the cellar door as the woman left the house, Merryfield saw her making for the woods, a basket on her arm. He watched her till the shadows engulfed her. Then he drew back to his own place and resumed his silent vigil.

Moments passed, without a sound from the room above. Then came soft little thuds on the floor, a whimper or two, small sighs, and a slither of bare legs on bare boards.

" Poor little kiddies! " thought Merryfield, " they're coiling down to sleep! "

Back in the days when the Force was started, the Major had said to each recruit of them all:—

" I expect you to treat women and children at all times with every consideration."

From that hour forth the principle has been grafted into the lives of the men. It is instinct now—self-acting, deep, and unconscious. No tried Trooper deliberately remembers it. It is an integral part of him, like the drawing of his breath.

" I wish I could manage to spare those babies and their mother in what's to come! " Merryfield pondered as he lurked in the mould-scented dark.

A quarter of an hour went by. Five minutes more. Footsteps nearing the cabin from the direction of the woods. Low voices—very low. Indistinguishable words. Then the back door opened. Two persons entered, and all that they now uttered was clear.

" It was them that the dog heard," said a man's voice. " Get me my rifle and all my ammunition. I'll go to Maryland. I'll get a job on that stone quarry near Westminster. I'll send some money as soon as I'm paid."

" But you won't start *to-night!* " exclaimed the wife.

" Yes, to-night—this minute. Quick! I wouldn't budge an inch for the County folks. But with the State Troopers after me, that's another thing. If I stay around here now they'll get me dead sure—and send me up too. My gun, I say! "

" Oh, daddy, daddy, don't go away! " " *Don't* go away off and leave me, daddy! " " *Don't go, don't go!* " came the children's plaintive wails, hoarse with fatigue and fright.

Merryfield stealthily crept from the cellar's outside door, hugging the wall of the cabin, moving toward the rear. As he reached the corner, and was about to make the turn toward the back, he drew his six-shooter and laid his carbine down in the grass. For the next step, he knew, would bring him into plain sight. If Drake offered any resistance, the ensuing action would be at short range or hand to hand.

He rounded the corner. Drake was standing just outside the door, a rifle in his left hand, his right hand hidden in the pocket of his overcoat. In the doorway stood the wife, with the three little children crowding before her. It was the last moment. They were saying good-bye.

Merryfield covered the bandit with his revolver.

" Put up your hands! You are under arrest," he commanded.

" Who the hell are you! " Drake flung back. As he spoke he thrust his rifle into the grasp of the woman and snatched his right hand from its concealment. In its grip glistened the barrel of a nickel-plated revolver.

Merryfield could have easily shot him then and there— would have been amply warranted in doing so. But he had heard the children's voices. Now he saw their innocent, ter- rified eyes.

" Poor—little—kiddies! " he thought again.

Drake stood six feet two inches high, and weighed some two hundred pounds, all brawn. Furthermore, he was desperate. Merryfield is merely of medium build.

" Nevertheless, I'll take a chance," he said to himself, re- turning his six-shooter to its holster. And just as the outlaw threw up his own weapon to fire, the Trooper, in a running jump, plunged into him with all fours, exactly as, when a boy, he had plunged off a springboard into the old mill-dam of a hot July afternoon.

Too amazed even to pull his trigger, Drake gave backward a step into the doorway. Merryfield's clutch toward his right hand missed the gun, fastening instead on the sleeve of his heavy coat. Swearing wildly while the woman and children screamed behind him, the bandit struggled to break the Troop- er's hold—tore and pulled until the sleeve, where Merryfield held it, worked down over the gun in his own grip. So Merryfield, twisting the sleeve, caught a lock-hold on hand and gun together.

Drake, standing on the doorsill, had now some eight inches advantage of height. The door opened inward, from right to left. With a tremendous effort Drake forced his assailant to his knees, stepped back into the room, seized the door with his left hand and with the whole weight on his shoulder slammed it to, on the Trooper's wrist.

The pain was excruciating—but it did not break that lock-hold on the outlaw's hand and gun. Shooting from his knees like a projectile, Merryfield flung his whole weight at the door. Big as Drake was, he could not hold it. It gave, and once more the two men hung at grips, this time within the room.

Drake's one purpose was to turn the muzzle of his imprisoned revolver upon Merryfield. Merryfield, with his left still clinching that deadly hand caught in its sleeve, now grabbed the revolver in his own right hand, with a twist dragged it free, and flung it out of the door.

But, as he dropped his right defense, taking both hands to the gun, the outlaw's powerful left grip closed on Merryfield's throat with a strangle-hold.

With that great thumb closing his windpipe, with the world turning red and black, " Guess I can't put it over, after all! " the Trooper said to himself.

Reaching for his own revolver, he shoved the muzzle against the bandit's breast.

" Damn you, *shoot!* " cried the other, believing his end was come.

But in that same instant Merryfield once more caught a glimpse of the fear-stricken faces of the babies, huddled together beyond.

" Hallisey and Smith must be here soon," he thought. " I won't shoot yet."

Again he dropped his revolver back into the holster, seizing the wrist of the outlaw to release that terrible clamp on his throat. As he did so, Drake with a lightning twist, reached around to the Trooper's belt and possessed himself of the gun. As he fired Merryfield had barely time and space to throw back his head. The flash blinded him—scorched his face hairless. The bullet grooved his body under the upflung arm still wrenching at the clutch that was shutting off his breath.

Perhaps, with the shot, the outlaw insensibly somewhat relaxed that choking arm. Merryfield tore loose. Half-blinded and gasping though he was, he flung himself again at his adversary and landed a blow in his face. Drake, giving backward, kicked over a row of peach jars, slipped on the slimy stream that poured over the bare floor, and dropped the gun.

Pursuing his advantage, Merryfield delivered blow after blow on the outlaw's face and body, backing him around the room, while both men slipped and slid, fell and recovered, on the jam-coated floor. The table crashed over, carrying with it the solitary lamp, whose flame died harmlessly, smothered in tepid mush. Now only the moonlight illuminated the scene.

Drake was manœuvring always to recover the gun. His hand touched the back of a chair. He picked the chair up, swung it high, and was about to smash it down on his adversary's head when Merryfield seized it in the air.

At this moment the woman, who had been crouching against the wall nursing the rifle that her husband had put into her charge, rushed forward clutching the barrel of the gun, swung it at full arm's length as she would have swung an axe, and brought the stock down on the Trooper's right hand.

That vital hand dropped—fractured, done. But in the same second Drake gave a shriek of pain as a shot rang out and his own right arm fell powerless.

In the door stood Hallisey, smoking revolver in hand, smiling grimly in the moonlight at the neatness of his own aim. What is the use of killing a man, when you can wing him as trigly as that?

Private Smith, who had entered by the other door, was taking the rifle out of the woman's grasp—partly because she had prodded him viciously with the muzzle. He examined the chambers.

" Do you know this thing is loaded? " he asked her in a mild, detached voice.

She returned his gaze with frank despair in her black eyes.

" Drake, do you surrender? " asked Hallisey.

" Oh, I'll give up. You've got me! " groaned the outlaw. Then he turned on his wife with bitter anger. " Didn't I tell ye? " he snarled. " Didn't I tell ye they'd get me if you kept me hangin' around here? These ain't no damn deputies. *These is the State Police!* "

" An' yet, if I'd known that gun was loaded," said she, " there'd been some less of 'em to-night! "

They dressed Israel's arm in first-aid fashion. Then they started with their prisoner down the mountain-trail, at last resuming connection with their farmer friend. Not without misgivings, the latter consented to hitch up his " double team " and hurry the party to the nearest town where a doctor could be found.

As the doctor dressed the bandit's arm, Private Merryfield, whose broken right hand yet awaited care, observed to the groaning patient:—

" Do you know, you can be thankful to your little children that you have your life left."

" To hell with you and the children and my life. I'd a hundred times rather you'd killed me than take what's comin' now."

Then the three Troopers philosophically hunted up a night restaurant and gave their captive a bite of lunch.

" Now," said Hallisey, as he paid the score, " where's the lock-up? "

The three officers, with Drake in tow, proceeded silently

through the sleeping streets. Not a ripple did their passing occasion. Not even a dog aroused to take note of them.

Duly they stood at the door of the custodian of the lockup, ringing the bell—again and again ringing it. Eventually some one upstairs raised a window, looked out for an appreciable moment, quickly lowered the window and locked it. Nothing further occurred. Waiting for a reasonable interval the officers rang once more. No answer. Silence complete.

Then they pounded on the door till the entire block heard.

Here, there, up street and down, bedroom windows gently opened, then closed with finality more gentle yet. Silence. Not a voice. Not a foot on a stair.

The officers looked at each other perplexed. Then, by chance, they looked at Drake. Drake, so lately black with suicidal gloom, was grinning! Grinning as a man does when the citadel of his heart is comforted.

"You don't understand, do ye!" chuckled he. "Well, I'll tell ye: What do them folks see when they open their windows and look down here in the road? They see three hard-lookin' fellers with guns in their hands, here in this bright moonlight. And they see somethin' scarier to them than a hundred strangers with guns—they see *ME!* There ain't a mother's son of 'em that'll budge downstairs while I'm here, not if you pound on their doors till the cows come home." And he slapped his knee with his good hand and laughed in pure ecstasy—a laugh that caught all the little group and rocked it as with one mind.

"We don't begrudge you that, do we boys?" Hallisey conceded. "Smith, you're as respectable-looking as any of us. Hunt around and see if you can find a Constable that isn't onto this thing. We'll wait here for you."

Moving out of the zone of the late demonstration, Private Smith learned the whereabouts of the home of a Constable.

"What's wanted?" asked the Constable, responding like a normal burgher to Smith's knock at his door.

"Officer of State Police," answered Smith. "I have a man under arrest and want to put him in the lock-up. Will you get me the keys?"

"Sure. I'll come right down and go along with you myself. Just give me a jiffy to get on my trousers and boots," cried the Constable, clearly glad of a share in the adventure.

In a moment the borough official was at the Trooper's side, talking eagerly as they moved toward the place where the party waited.

"So, he's a highwayman, is he? Good! and a burglar, too, and a cattle-thief! Good work! And you've got him right up the street, ready to jail! Well, I'll be switched. Now, what might his name be? Israel Drake? *Not Israel Drake!* Oh, my God!"

The Constable had stopped in his tracks like a man struck paralytic.

"No, stranger," he quavered. "I reckon I—I—I won't go no further with you just now. Here, I'll give you the keys. You can use 'em yourself: These here's for the doors. This bunch is for the cells. *Good*-night to you. I'll be getting back home!"

By the first train next morning the Troopers, conveying their prisoner, left the village for the County Town. As they deposited Drake in the safe-keeping of the County Jail and were about to depart, he seemed burdened with an impulse to speak, yet said nothing. Then, as the three officers were leaving the room, he leaned over and touched Merryfield on the shoulder.

"Shake!" he growled, offering his unwounded hand.

Merryfield "shook" cheerfully, with his own remaining sound member.

"I'm plumb sorry to see ye go, and that's a fact," growled the outlaw. "Because—well, because you're the only *man* that ever tried to arrest me."

KATHERINE MAYO

Miss Katherine Mayo comes of Mayflower stock, but her birthplace was Ridgway, Pennsylvania. She was educated in private schools at Boston and Cambridge, Mass. Her earliest literary work to appear in print was a series of articles describing travels in Norway, followed by another series on Colonial American topics, written for the New York *Evening Post*. Later, during a residence in Dutch Guiana, South America, she wrote for the *Atlantic Monthly* some interesting sketches of the natives of Surinam. After this came three years wholly devoted to historic research. The work, however, that first attracted wide attention was a history of the Pennsylvania State Police, published in 1917, under the title of *Justice To All*.

This history gives the complete story of the famous Mounted Police of Pennsylvania, illustrated with a mass of accurate narrative and re-enforced with statistics. The occasion of its writing was a personal experience—the cold-blooded murder of Sam Howell, a fine young American workingman, a carpenter by trade, near Miss Mayo's country home in New York. The circumstances of this murder could not have been more skilfully arranged had they been specially designed to illustrate the weakness and folly of the ancient, out-grown engine to which most states in the Union, even yet, look for the enforcement of their laws in rural parts. Sam Howell, carrying the pay roll on pay-day morning, gave his life for his honor as gallantly as any soldier in any war. He was shot down, at arm's length range, by four highway men, to whom, though himself unarmed, he would not surrender his trust. Sheriff, deputy sheriffs, constables, and some seventy-five fellow laborors available as sheriff's posse spent hours within a few hundred feet of the little wood in which the four murderers were known to be hiding, but no arrest was made and the murderers are today still at large.

" You will have forgotten all this in a month's time," said Howell's fellow-workmen an hour after the tragedy, to Miss Mayo and her friend Miss Newell, owner of the estate, on the scene. " Sam was only a laboring man, like ourselves. We, none of us, have any protection when we work in country parts."

The remark sounded bitter indeed. But investigation proved it, in principle, only too true. Sam Howell had not been the first, by many hundreds, to give his life because the State had no real means to make her law revered. And punishment for such crimes had been rare. Sam Howell, however, was not to be forgotten, neither was his sacrifice to be vain. From his blood, shed unseen, in the obscurity of a quiet country lane, was to spring a great movement, taking effect first in the state in which he died, and spreading through the Union.

At that time Pennsylvania was the only state of all the forty-seven that had met its just obligations to protect all its people under its laws. Pennsylvania's State Police had been for ten years a body of defenders of justice, " without fear and without reproach ". The honest people of the State had recorded its deeds in a long memory of noble service. But, never stooping to advertise itself, never hesitating to incur the enmity of evildoers, it had had many traducers and no historian. There was nothing in print to which the people of other states might turn for knowledge of the accomplishment of the sister commonwealth.

So, in order that the facts might be conveniently available for every American citizen to study from " A " to " Z " and thus to decide intelligently for himself where he wanted his own state to stand, in the matter of fair and full protection to all people, Miss Mayo went to Pennsylvania and embarked on an exhaustive analysis of the workings of the Pennsylvania State

Police Force, viewed from the standpoint of all parts of the community. Ex-President Roosevelt wrote the preface for *Justice To All,* the book in which the fruits of this study were finally embodied, and, in the meantime, Miss Newell devoted all her energies to the development of an active and aggressive state-wide movement for a State Police. *Justice To All,* in this campaign was widely used as a source of authority on which to base the arguments for the case. And in 1917 came Sam Howell's triumph, the passage of the Act creating the Department of New York State Police, now popularly called " the State Troopers ".

In the course of collecting the material for this book, Miss Mayo gathered a mass of facts much greater than one volume could properly contain. From this she later took fifteen adventurous stories of actual service in the Pennsylvania Force, of which some, including " Israel Drake " appeared in the *Saturday Evening Post,* while others came out simultaneously in the *Atlantic Monthly* and in the *Outlook.* All were later collected in a volume called *The Standard Bearers,* which met with a very cordial reception by readers and critics.

During the latter part of the World War, Miss Mayo was in France investigating the war-work of the Y. M. C. A. Her experiences there furnished material for a book from which advance pages appeared in the *Outlook* in the form of separate stories, " Billy's Hut," " The Colonel's Lady " and others. The purpose of this book was to determine, as closely as possible, the real values, whatever those might be, of the work actually accomplished by the Overseas Y, and to lay the plain truth without bias or color, before the American people.

IN THE PHILIPPINES

When the Philippine Islands passed from the possession of Spain to that of the United States, there was a change in more than the flag. Spain had sent soldiers and tax-gatherers to the islands; Uncle Sam sent road-builders and school teachers. One of these school teachers was also a newspaper man; and in a book called CAYBIGAN *he gave a series of vivid pictures of how the coming generation of Filipinos are taking the first step towards Americanization.*

THE STRUGGLES AND TRIUMPH OF
ISIDRO DE LOS MAESTROS

BY

James Hopper

1—Face to Face with the Foe

Returning to his own town after a morning spent in " working up " the attendance of one of his far and recalcitrant barrio-schools, the Maestro of Balangilang was swaying with relaxed muscle and half-closed eyes to the allegretto trot of his little native pony, when he pulled up with a start, wide awake and all his senses on the alert. Through his somnolence, at first in a low hum, but fast rising in a fiendish crescendo, there had come a buzzing sound, much like that of one of the saw-mills of his California forests, and now, as he sat in the saddle, erect and tense, the thing ripped the air in ragged tear, shrieked vibrating into his ear, and finished its course along his spine in delicious irritation.

" Oh, where am I? " murmured the Maestro, blinking; but between blinks he caught the flashing green of the palay fields and knew that he was far from the saw-mills of the Golden State. So he raised his nose to heaven and there, afloat above him in the serene blue, was the explanation. It was a kite, a great locust-shaped kite, darting and swooping in the hot monsoon, and from it, dropping plumb, came the abominable clamor.

" Aha! " exclaimed the Maestro, pointing accusingly at the thin line vaguely visible against the sky-line in a diagonal running from the kite above him ahead to a point in the road. " Aha! there's something at the end of that; there's Attendance at the end of that! "

With which significant remark he leaned forward in the saddle, bringing his switch down with a whizz behind him. The pony gave three rabbit leaps and then settled down to his drumming little trot. As they advanced the line overhead dropped gradually. Finally the Maestro had to swerve the horse aside to save his helmet. He pulled up to a walk, and a few yards further came to the spot where string met earth in the expected Attendance.

The Attendance was sitting on the ground, his legs spread before him in an angle of forty-five degrees, each foot arched in a secure grip of a bunch of cogon grass. These legs were bare as far up as they went, and, in fact, no trace of clothing was reached until the eye met the lower fringe of an indescribable undershirt modestly veiling the upper half of a rotund little paunch; an indescribable undershirt, truly, for observation could not reach the thing itself, but only the dirt incrusting it so that it hung together, rigid as a knight's iron corslet, in spite of monstrous tears and rents. Between the teeth of the Attendance was a long, thick cheroot, wound about with hemp fiber, at which he pulled with rounded mouth. Hitched around his right wrist was the kite string, and between his legs a stick spindled with an extra hundred yards. At intervals he hauled hand-over-hand upon the taut line, and then the landscape vibrated to the buzz-saw song which had so compellingly recalled the Maestro to his eternal pursuit.

As the shadow of the horse fell upon him, the Attendance brought his eyes down from their heavenly contemplation, and fixed them upon the rider. A tremor of dismay, mastered as soon as born, flitted over him; then, silently, with careful suppression of all signs of haste, he reached for a big stone with his little yellow paw, then for a stick lying farther off. Using the stone as a hammer, he drove the stick into the ground with deliberate stroke, wound the string around it with tender solicitude, and then, everything being secure, just as the Maestro was beginning his usual embarrassing question:

" Why are you not at school, eh? "

He drew up his feet beneath him, straightened up like a jack-in-a-box, took a hop-skip-jump, and with a flourish of golden heels, flopped head-first into the roadside ditch's rank luxuriance.

" The little devil! " exclaimed the disconcerted Maestro. He dismounted and, leading his horse, walked up to the side of the ditch. It was full of the water of the last baguio. From the edge of the cane-field on the other side there cascaded down the bank a mad vegetation; it carpeted the sides, arched itself above in a vault, and inside this recess the water was rotting, green-scummed; and a powerful fermentation filled the nostrils with hot fever-smells. In the center of the ditch the broad, flat head of a caribao emerged slightly above the water; the floating lilies made an incongruous wreath about the great horns and the beatifically-shut eyes, and the thick, humid nose exhaled ecstasy in shuddering ripplets over the calm surface.

Filled with a vague sense of the ridiculous, the Maestro peered into the darkness. " The little devil! " he murmured. " He's somewhere in here; but how am I to get him, I'd like to know. Do you see him, eh, Mathusalem? " he asked of the stolid beast soaking there in bliss.

Whether in answer to this challenge or to some other irritant, the animal slowly opened one eye and ponderously let it fall shut again in what, to the heated imagination of the Maestro, seemed a patronizing wink. Its head slid quietly along the water; puffs of ooze rose from below and spread on the surface. Then, in the silence there rose a significant sound —a soft, repeated snapping of the tongue:

" Cluck, cluck."

" Aha! " shouted the Maestro triumphantly to his invisible audience. " I know where you are, you scamp; right behind the caribao; come out of there, *pronto, dale-dale!* "

But his enthusiasm was of short duration. To the commanding tongue-click the caribao had stopped dead-still, and a silence heavy with defiance met the too-soon exultant cries. An insect in the foliage began a creaking call, and then all the creatures of humidity hidden there among this fermenting vegetation joined in mocking chorus.

The Maestro felt a vague blush welling up from the innermost recesses of his being.

"I'm going to get that kid," he muttered darkly, "if I have to wait till—the coming of Common Sense to the Manila office! By gum, he's the Struggle for Attendance personified! "

He sat down on the bank and waited. This did not prove interesting. The animals of the ditch creaked on; the caribao bubbled up the water with his deep content; above, the abandoned kite went through strange acrobatics and wailed as if in pain. The Maestro dipped his hand into the water; it was lukewarm. "No hope of a freeze-out," he murmured pensively.

Behind, the pony began to pull at the reins.

"Yes, little horse, I'm tired, too. Well," he said apologetically, "I hate to get energetic, but there are circumstances which——"

The end of his sentence was lost, for he had whisked out the big Colt's dissuader of ladrones, that hung on his belt, and was firing. The six shots went off like a bunch of fire-crackers, but far from at random, for a regular circle boiled up around the dozing caribao. The disturbed animal snorted, and again a discreet " cluck- cluck " rose in the sudden, astounded silence.

"This," said the Maestro, as he calmly introduced fresh cartridges into the chambers of his smoking weapon, " is what might be called an application of western solutions to eastern difficulties."

Again he brought his revolver down, but he raised it without shooting and replaced it in its holster. From beneath the caribao's rotund belly, below the surface, an indistinct form shot out; cleaving the water like a polliwog it glided for the bank, and then a black, round head emerged at the feet of the Maestro.

" All right, bub; we'll go to school now," said the latter, nodding to the dripping figure as it rose before him.

He lifted the sullen brownie and straddled him forward of the saddle, then proceeded to mount himself, when the Capture began to display marked agitation. He squirmed and twisted, turned his head back and up, and finally a grunt escaped him.

" El volador."

" The kite, to be sure; we mustn't forget the kite," acquiesced the Maestro graciously. He pulled up the anchoring stick and laboriously, beneath the hostilely critical eye of the Capture, he hauled in the line till the screeching, resisting flying-machine was brought to earth. Then he vaulted into the saddle.

The double weight was a little too much for the pony; so it was at a dignified walk that the Maestro, his naked, dripping, muddy and still defiant prisoner a-straddle in front of him, the captured kite passed over his left arm like a knightly shield, made his triumphant entry into the pueblo.

II—Heroism and Reverses

When Maestro Pablo rode down Rizal-y-Washington Street to the schoolhouse with his oozing, dripping prize between his arms, the kite, like a knightly escutcheon against his left side, he found that in spite of his efforts at preserving a modest, self-deprecatory bearing, his spine would stiffen and his nose point upward in the unconscious manifestations of an internal feeling that there was in his attitude something picturesquely heroic. Not since walking down the California campus one morning after the big game won three minutes before blowing of the final whistle, by his fifty-yard run-in of a punt,

had he been in that posture—at once pleasant and difficult—
in which one's vital concern is to wear an humility sufficiently
convincing to obtain from friends forgiveness for the crime
of being great.

A series of incidents immediately following, however, made
the thing quite easy.

Upon bringing the new recruit into the schoolhouse, to the
perfidiously expressed delight of the already incorporated, the
Maestro called his native assistant to obtain the information
necessary to a full matriculation. At the first question the
inquisition came to a dead-lock. The boy did not know his
name.

" In Spanish times," the Assistant suggested modestly, " we
called them " de los Reyes " when the father was of the army,
and " de la Cruz " when the father was of the church; but now,
we can never know *what* it is."

The Maestro dashed to a solution. " All right," he said
cheerily. " I caught him; guess I can give him a name. Call
him—Isidro de los Maestros."

And thus it was that the urchin went down on the school
records, and on the records of life afterward.

Now, well pleased with himself, the Maestro, as is the wont
of men in such state, sought for further enjoyment.

" Ask him," he said teasingly, pointing with his chin at
the newly-baptized but still unregenerate little savage, " why
he came out of the ditch."

" He says he was afraid that you would steal the
kite," answered the Assistant, after some linguistic sparring.

" Eh? " ejaculated the surprised Maestro.

And in his mind there framed a picture of himself riding
along the road with a string between his fingers; and, following in the upper layers of air, a buzzing kite; and, down in
the dust of the highway, an urchin trudging wistfully after
the kite, drawn on irresistibly, in spite of his better judgment,

on and on, horrified but fascinated, up to the yawning school-door.

It would have been the better way. " I ought to go and soak my head," murmured the Maestro pensively.

This was check number one, but others came in quick succession.

For the morning after this incident the Maestro did not find Isidro among the weird, wild crowd gathered into the annex (a transformed sugar storehouse) by the last raid of the Municipal Police.

Neither was Isidro there the next day, nor the next. And it was not till a week had passed that the Maestro discovered, with an inward blush of shame, that his much-longed-for pupil was living in the little hut behind his own house. There would have been nothing shameful in the over-looking—there were seventeen other persons sharing the same abode—were it not that the nipa front of this human hive had been blown away by the last baguio, leaving an unobstructed view of the interior, if it might be called such. As it was, the Municipal Police was mobilized at the urgent behest of the Maestro. Its " cabo," flanked by two privates armed with old German needle-guns, besieged the home, and after an interesting game of hide-and-go-seek, Isidro was finally caught by one arm and one ear, and ceremoniously marched to school. And there the Maestro asked him why he had not been attending.

" No hay pantalones "—there are no pants—Isidro answered, dropping his eyes modestly to the ground.

This was check number two, and unmistakably so, for was it not a fact that a civil commission, overzealous in its civilizing ardor, had passed a law commanding that every one should wear, when in public, " at least one garment, preferably trousers? "

Following this, and an unsuccessful plea upon the town tailor who was on a three weeks' vacation on account of the

death of a fourth cousin, the Maestro shut himself up a whole
day with Isidro in his little nipa house; and behind the closely-
shut shutters engaged in some mysterious toil. When they
emerged again the next morning, Isidro wended his way to the
school at the end of the Maestro's arm, trousered!

The trousers, it must be said, had a certain cachet of distinction. They were made of calico-print, with a design of little
black skulls sprinkled over a yellow background. Some parts
hung flat and limp as if upon a scarecrow; others pulsed, like
a fire-hose in action, with the pressure of flesh compressed beneath, while at other points they bulged pneumatically in
little foot-balls. The right leg dropped to the ankle; the left
stopped discouraged, a few inches below the knee. The seams
looked like the putty mountain chains of the geography class.
As the Maestro strode along he threw rapid glances at his handi-
work, and it was plain that the emotions that moved him were
somewhat mixed in character. His face showed traces of a
puzzled diffidence, as that of a man who has come in sack-
coat to a full-dress function; but after all it was satisfaction
that predominated, for after this heroic effort he had decided
that Victory had at last perched upon his banners.

And it really looked so for a time. Isidro stayed at school
at least during that first day of his trousered life. For when
the Maestro, later in the forenoon paid a visit to the annex,
he found the Assistant in charge standing disconcerted before
the urchin who, with eyes indignant and hair perpendicular
upon the top of his head, was evidently holding to his side of
the argument with his customary energy.

Isidro was trouserless. Sitting rigid upon his bench, holding on with both hands as if in fear of being removed, he dangled naked legs to the sight of who might look.

" Que barbaridad! " murmered the Assistant in limp de-
jection.

But Isidro threw at him a look of black hatred. This
became a tense, silent plea for justice as it moved up for a

moment to the Maestro's face, and then it settled back upon its first object in frigid accusation.

" Where are your trousers, Isidro? " asked the Maestro.

Isidro relaxed his convulsive grasp of the bench with one hand, canted himself slightly to one side just long enough to give an instantaneous view of the trousers, neatly folded and spread between what he was sitting with and what he was sitting on, then swung back with the suddenness of a kodak-shutter, seized his seat with new determination, and looked eloquent justification at the Maestro.

" Why will you not wear them? " asked the latter.

" He says he will not get them dirty," said the Assistant, interpreting the answer.

" Tell him when they are dirty he can go down to the river and wash them," said the Maestro.

Isidro pondered over the suggestion for two silent minutes. The prospect of a day spent splashing in the lukewarm waters of the Ilog he finally put down as not at all detestable, and getting up to his feet:

" I will put them on," he said gravely.

Which he did on the moment, with an absence of hesitation as to which was front and which was back, very flattering to the Maestro.

That Isidro persevered during the next week, the Maestro also came to know. For now regularly every evening as he smoked and lounged upon his long, cane chair, trying to persuade his tired body against all laws of physics to give up a little of its heat to a circumambient atmosphere of temperature equally enthusiastic; as he watched among the rafters of the roof the snakes swallowing the rats, the rats devouring the lizards, the lizards snapping up the spiders, the spiders snaring the flies in eloquent representation of the life struggle, his studied passiveness would be broken by strange sounds from the dilapidated hut at the back of his house. A voice, imitative of that of the Third Assistant who taught the annex, hurled forth questions, which were immediately answered by another voice, curiously like that of Isidro.

Fiercely: " Du yu ssee dde hhett? "

Breathlessly: " Yiss I ssee dde hhett."

Ferociously: " Show me dde hhett."

Eagerly: " Here are dde hhett."

Thunderously: " Gif me dde hhett."

Exultantly: " I gif yu dde hhett."

Then the Maestro would step to the window and look into the hut from which came this Socratic dialogue. And on this wall-less platform which looked much like a primitive stage, a singular action was unrolling itself in the smoky glimmer of a two-cent lamp. The Third Assistant was not there at all; but Isidro was the Third Assistant. And the pupil was not Isidro, but the witless old man who was one of the many sharers of the abode. In the voice of the Third Assistant, Isidro was hurling out the tremendous questions; and, as the old gentleman, who represented Isidro, opened his mouth only to drule betel-juice, it was Isidro who, in Isidro's voice, answered the questions. In his rôle as Third Assistant he stood with legs akimbo before the pupil, a bamboo twig in his hand; as Isidro the pupil, he plumped down quickly upon the bench before responding. The sole function of the senile old man seemed that of representing the pupil while the question was being asked, and receiving, in that capacity, a sharp cut across the nose from Isidro-the-Third-Assistant's switch, at which he chuckled to himself in silent glee and druled ad libitum.

For several nights this performance went on with gradual increase of vocabulary in teacher and pupil. But when it had reached the " Do you see the apple-tree? " stage, it ceased to advance, marked time for a while, and then slowly but steadily began sliding back into primitive beginnings. This engendered in the Maestro a suspicion which became certainty when Isidro entered the schoolhouse one morning just before recess, between two policemen at port arms. A rapid scrutiny of the roll-book showed that he had been absent a whole week.

" I was at the river cleaning my trousers," answered Isidro when put face to face with this curious fact.

The Maestro suggested that the precious pantaloons which, by the way, had been mysteriously embellished by a red stripe down the right leg and a green stripe down the left leg, could be cleaned in less than a week, and that Saturday and Sunday were days specially set aside in the Catechismo of the Americanos for such little family duties.

Isidro understood, and the nightly rehearsals soon reached the stage of:

" How menny hhetts hev yu? "

" I hev *ten* hhetts."

Then came another arrest of development and another decline, at the end of which Isidro again making his appearance flanked by two German needle-guns, caused a blush of remorse to suffuse the Maestro by explaining with frigid gravity that his mother had given birth to a little pickaninny-brother and that, of course, he had had to help.

But significant events in the family did not stop there. After birth, death stepped in for its due. Isidro's relatives began to drop off in rapid sequence—each demise demanding three days of meditation in retirement—till at last the Maestro, who had had the excellent idea of keeping upon paper a record of these unfortunate occurrences, was looking with stupor upon a list showing that Isidro had lost, within three weeks, two aunts, three grandfathers, and five grandmothers—which, considering that an actual count proved the house of bereavement still able to boast of seventeen occupants, was plainly an exaggeration.

Following a long sermon from the Maestro in which he sought to explain to Isidro that he must always tell the truth for sundry philosophical reasons—a statement which the First Assistant tactfully smoothed to something within range of credulity by translating it that one must not lie to *Americanos*, because *Americanos* do not like it—there came a period of serenity.

III—*The Triumph*

There came to the Maestro days of peace and joy. Isidro was coming to school; Isidro was learning English. Isidro was steady, Isidro was docile, Isidro was positively so angelic that there was something uncanny about the situation. And with Isidro, other little savages were being pruned into the school-going stage of civilization. Helped by the police, they were pouring in from barrio and hacienda; the attendance was going up by leaps and bounds, till at last a circulative report showed that Balangilang had passed the odious Cabancalan with its less strenuous school-man, and left it in the ruck by a full hundred. The Maestro was triumphant; his chest had gained two inches in expansion. When he met Isidro at recess, playing cibay, he murmured softly: "You little devil; you were Attendance personified, and I've got you now." At which Isidro, pausing in the act of throwing a shell with the top of his head at another shell on the ground, looked up beneath long lashes in a smile absolutely seraphic.

In the evening, the Maestro, his heart sweet with content, stood at the window. These were moonlight nights; in the grassy lanes the young girls played graceful Spanish games, winding like garlands to a gentle song; from the shadows of the huts came the tinkle-tinkle of serenading guitars and yearning notes of violins wailing despairing love. And Isidro, seated on the bamboo ladder of his house, went through an independent performance. He sang "Good-night, Ladies," the last song given to the school, sang it in soft falsetto, with languorous drawls, and never-ending organ points, over and over again, till it changed character gradually, dropping into a wailing minor, an endless croon full of obscure melancholy of a race that dies.

" Goo-oo-oo nigh-igh-igh loidies-ies-ies; goo-oo-oo nigh-igh-igh loidies-ies-ies; goo-oo-oo-oo nigh-igh-igh loidies-ies-ies-ies," he repeated and repeated, over and over again, till the Maestro's soul tumbled down and down abysses of maudlin tenderness, and Isidro's chin fell upon his chest in a last drawling, sleepy note. At which he shook himself together and began the next exercise, a recitation, all of one piece from first to last syllable, in one high, monotonous note, like a mechanical doll saying " papa-mama."

" Oh-look-et-de-moon-she-ees-shinin-up-theyre-oh-mudder-she look-like-a-lom-in-de-ayre -lost-night-she-was-smalleyre- on-joos like-a-bow-boot-now-she-ees-biggerr-on-rrraon-like-an-O."

Then a big gulp of air and again:

" Oh-look-et-de-moon-she-ees-shinin-up-theyre,——" etc.

An hour of this, and he skipped from the lyric to the patriotic, and then it was:

> " I-loof-dde-name-off-Wash-ing-ton,
>   I-loof-my-coontrrree-tow,
>   I-loof-dde-fleg-dde-dear-owl-fleg,
>   Off-rridd-on-whit-on-bloo-oo-oo ! "

By this time the Maestro was ready to go to bed, and long in the torpor of the tropic night there came to him, above the hum of the mosquitoes fighting at the net, the soft, wailing croon of Isidro, back at his " Goo-oo-oo nigh-igh-igh loidies-ies-ies."

These were days of ease and beauty to the Maestro, and he enjoyed them the more when a new problem came to give action to his resourceful brain.

The thing was this: For three days there had not been one funeral in Balangilang.

In other climes, in other towns, this might have been a source of congratulation, perhaps, but not in Balangilang. There were rumors of cholera in the towns to the north, and the Maestro, as president of the Board of Health, was on the watch for it. Five deaths a day, experience had taught him, was the healthy average for the town; and this sudden cessation of public burials—he could not belive that dying had stopped—was something to make him suspicious.

It was over this puzzling situation that he was pondering at the morning recess, when his attention was taken from it by a singular scene.

The " batas " of the school were flocking and pushing and jolting at the door of the basement which served as stable for the municipal caribao. Elbowing his way to the spot, the Maestro found Isidro at the entrance, gravely taking up an admission of five shells from those who would enter. Business seemed to be brisk; Isidro had already a big bandana handkerchief bulging with the receipts which were now overflowing into a great tao hat, obligingly loaned him by one of his admirers, as one by one, those lucky enough to have the price filed in, feverish curiosity upon their faces.

The Maestro thought that it might be well to go in also, which he did without paying admission. The disappointed gate-keeper followed him. The Maestro found himself before a little pink-and-blue tissue-paper box, frilled with paper rosettes.

" What have you in there? " asked the Maestro.

" My brother," answered Isidro sweetly.

He cast his eyes to the ground and watched his big toe drawing vague figures in the earth, then appealing to the First Assistant who was present by this time, he added in the tone of virtue which *will* be modest:

" Maestro Pablo does not like it when I do not come to school on account of a funeral, so I brought him (pointing to the little box) with me."

" Well, I'll be——" was the only comment the Maestro found adequate at the moment.

" It is my little pickaninny-brother," went on Isidro, becoming alive to the fact that he was a center of interest, " and he died last night of the great sickness."

"The great what?" ejaculated the Maestro who had caught
a few words.

"The great sickness," explained the Assistant. "That is
the name by which these ignorant people call the cholera."

For the next two hours the Maestro was very busy.

Firstly he gathered the "batas" who had been rich enough
to attend Isidro's little show and locked them up—with the
impresario himself—in the little town-jail close by.   Then,
after a vivid exhortation upon the beauties of boiling water
and reporting disease, he dismissed the school for an indefinite
period.   After which, impressing the two town prisoners, now
temporarily out of home, he shouldered Isidro's pretty box,
tramped to the cemetery and directed the digging of a grave
six feet deep.   When the earth had been scraped back upon the
lonely little object, he returned to town and transferred the
awe-stricken playgoers to his own house, where a strenuous
performance took place.

Tolio, his boy, built a most tremendous fire outside and set
upon it all the pots and pans and caldrons and cans of his
kitchen arsenal, filled with water.   When these began to gurgle
and steam, the Maestro set himself to stripping the horrified
bunch in his room; one by one he threw the garments out of the
window to Tolio who, catching them, stuffed them into the re-
ceptacles, poking down their bulging protest with a big stick.
Then the Maestro mixed an awful brew in an old oil-can, and
taking the brush which was commonly used to sleek up his
little pony, he dipped it generously into the pungent stuff and
began an energetic scrubbing of his now absolutely panic-
stricken wards.   When he had done this to his satisfaction
and thoroughly to their discontent, he let them put on their still
steaming garments and they slid out of the house, aseptic
as hospitals.

Isidro he kept longer.   He lingered over him with loving and
strenuous care, and after he had him externally clean, pro-

ceeded to dose him internally from a little red bottle. Isidro took everything—the terrific scrubbing, the exaggerated dosing, the ruinous treatment of his pantaloons—with wonder-eyed serenity.

When all this was finished the Maestro took the urchin into the dining-room and, seating him on his best bamboo chair, he courteously offered him a fine, dark perfecto.

The next instant he was suffused with the light of a new revelation. For, stretching out his hard little claw to receive the gift, the little man had shot at him a glance so mild, so wistful, so brown-eyed, filled with such mixed admiration, trust, and appeal, that a queer softness had risen in the Maestro from somewhere down in the regions of his heel, up and up, quietly, like the mercury in the thermometer, till it had flowed through his whole body and stood still, its high-water mark a little lump in his throat.

" Why, Lord bless us-ones, Isidro," said the Maestro quietly. " We're only a child after all; mere baby, my man. And don't we like to go to school? "

" Señor Pablo," asked the boy, looking up softly into the Maestro's still perspiring visage, " Señor Pablo, is it true that there will be no school because of the great sickness? "

" Yes, it is true," answered the Maestro. " No school for a long, long time."

Then Isidro's mouth began to twitch queerly, and suddenly throwing himself full-length upon the floor, he hurled out from somewhere within him a long, tremulous wail.

JAMES MERLE HOPPER

James Merle Hopper was born in Paris, France. His father was American, his mother French; their son James was born July 23, 1876. In 1887 his parents came to America, and settled in California. James Hopper attended the University of California, graduating in 1898. He is still remembered there as one of the grittiest football players who ever played on the 'Varsity team. Then came a course in the law school of that university, and admission to the California bar in 1900. All this reads like the biography of a lawyer: so did the early life of James Russell Lowell, and of Oliver Wendell Holmes: they were all admitted to the bar, but they did not become lawyers. James Hopper had done some newspaper work for San Francisco papers while he was in law school, and the love of writing had taken hold of him. In the meantime he had married Miss Mattie E. Leonard, and as literature did not yet provide a means of support, he became an instructor in French at the University of California.

With the close of the Spanish-American War came the call for thousands of Americans to go to the Philippines as schoolmasters. This appealed to him, and he spent the years 1902-03 in the work that Kipling thus describes in " The White Man's Burden ":

> To wait in heavy harness
>   On fluttered folk and wild—
> Your new-caught sullen peoples,
>   Half devil and half child.

His experiences here furnished the material for a group of short stories dealing picturesquely with the Filipinos in their first contact with American civilization. These were published in *McClure's,* and afterwards collected in book form under the title *Caybigan.*

In 1903 James Hopper returned to the United States, and for a time was on the editorial staff of *McClure's.* Later in collaboration with Fred R. Bechdolt he wrote a remarkable book, entitled " *9009* ". This is the number of a convict in an American prison, and the book exposes the system of spying, of treachery, of betrayal, that a convict must identify himself with in order to become a " trusty." His next book was a college story, *The Freshman.* This was followed by a volume of short stories, *What Happened in the Night.* These are stories of child life, but intended for older readers; they are very successful in reproducing the imaginative world in which children live. In 1915 and 1916 he acted as a war correspondent for *Collier's,* first with the American troops in Mexico in pursuit of Villa, and later in France. His home is at Carmel, California.

THEY WHO BRING DREAMS
TO AMERICA

" No wonder this America of ours is big. We draw the brave ones from the old lands, the brave ones whose dreams are like the guiding sign that was given to the Israelites of old—a pillar of cloud by day, a pillar of fire by night." " The Citizen " is a story of a brave man who followed his dream over land and sea, until it brought him to America, a fortunate event for him and for us.

THE CITIZEN

BY

JAMES FRANCIS DWYER

THE President of the United States was speaking. His audience comprised two thousand foreign-born men who had just been admitted to citizenship. They listened intently, their faces, aglow with the light of a new-born patriotism, upturned to the calm, intellectual face of the first citizen of the country they now claimed as their own.

Here and there among the newly-made citizens were wives and children. The women were proud of their men. They looked at them from time to time, their faces showing pride and awe.

One little woman, sitting immediately in front of the President, held the hand of a big, muscular man and stroked it softly. The big man was looking at the speaker with great blue eyes that were the eyes of a dreamer.

The President's words came clear and distinct:

You were drawn across the ocean by some beckoning finger of hope, by some belief, by some vision of a new kind of justice, by some expectation of a better kind of life. You dreamed dreams of this country, and I hope you brought the dreams with you. A man enriches the country to which he brings dreams, and you who have brought them have enriched America.

The big man made a curious choking noise and his wife breathed a soft " Hush! " The giant was strangely affected.

The President continued:

No doubt you have been disappointed in some of us, but remember this, if we have grown at all poor in the ideal, you

299

brought some of it with you. A man does not go out to seek the thing that is not in him. A man does not hope for the thing that he does not believe in, and if some of us have forgotten what America believed in, you at any rate imported in your own hearts a renewal of the belief. Each of you, I am sure, brought a dream, a glorious, shining dream, a dream worth more than gold or silver, and that is the reason that I, for one, make you welcome.

The big man's eyes were fixed. His wife shook him gently, but he did not heed her. He was looking through the presidential rostrum, through the big buildings behind it, looking out over leagues of space to a snow-swept village that huddled on an island in the Beresina, the swift-flowing tributary of the mighty Dnieper, an island that looked like a black bone stuck tight in the maw of the stream.

It was in the little village on the Beresina that the Dream came to Ivan Berloff, Big Ivan of the Bridge.

The Dream came in the spring. All great dreams come in the spring, and the Spring Maiden who brought Big Ivan's Dream was more than ordinarily beautiful. She swept up the Beresina, trailing wondrous draperies of vivid green. Her feet touched the snow-hardened ground, and armies of little white and blue flowers sprang up in her footsteps. Soft breezes escorted her, velvety breezes that carried the aromas of the far-off places from which they came, places far to the southward, and more distant towns beyond the Black Sea whose people were not under the sway of the Great Czar.

The father of Big Ivan, who had fought under Prince Menshikov at Alma fifty-five years before, hobbled out to see the sunbeams eat up the snow hummocks that hid in the shady places, and he told his son it was the most wonderful spring he had ever seen.

"The little breezes are hot and sweet," he said, sniffing hungrily with his face turned toward the south. "I know them, Ivan! I know them! They have the spice odor that I sniffed on the winds that came to us when we lay in the trenches at Balaklava. Praise God for the warmth! "

And that day the Dream came to Big Ivan as he plowed. It was a wonder dream. It sprang into his brain as he walked behind the plow, and for a few minutes he quivered as the big bridge quivers when the Beresina sends her ice squadrons to hammer the arches. It made his heart pound mightily, and his lips and throat became very dry.

Big Ivan stopped at the end of the furrow and tried to discover what had brought the Dream. Where had it come from? Why had it clutched him so suddenly? Was he the only man in the village to whom it had come?

Like his father, he sniffed the sweet-smelling breezes. He thrust his great hands into the sunbeams. He reached down and plucked one of a bunch of white flowers that had sprung up overnight. The Dream was born of the breezes and the sunshine and the spring flowers. It came from them and it had sprung into his mind because he was young and strong. He knew! It couldn't come to his father or Donkov, the tailor, or Poborino, the smith. They were old and weak, and Ivan's dream was one that called for youth and strength.

" Ay, for youth and strength," he muttered as he gripped the plow. " And I have it! "

That evening Big Ivan of the Bridge spoke to his wife, Anna, a little woman, who had a sweet face and a wealth of fair hair.

" Wife, we are going away from here," he said.

" Where are we going, Ivan? " she asked.

" Where do you think, Anna? " he said, looking down at her as she stood by his side.

" To Bobruisk," she murmured.

" No."

" Farther? "

" Ay, a long way farther."

Fear sprang into her soft eyes. Bobruisk was eighty-nine versts away, yet Ivan said they were going farther.

"We—we are not going to Minsk?" she cried.

"Aye, and beyond Minsk!"

"Ivan, tell me!" she gasped. "Tell me where we are going!"

"We are going to America."

"*To America?*"

"Yes, to America!"

Big Ivan of the Bridge lifted up his voice when he cried out the words "To America," and then a sudden fear sprang upon him as those words dashed through the little window out into the darkness of the village street. Was he mad? America was 8,000 versts away! It was far across the ocean, a place that was only a name to him, a place where he knew no one. He wondered in the strange little silence that followed his words if the crippled son of Poborino, the smith, had heard him. The cripple would jeer at him if the night wind had carried the words to his ear.

Anna remained staring at her big husband for a few minutes, then she sat down quietly at his side. There was a strange look in his big blue eyes, the look of a man to whom has come a vision, the look which came into the eyes of those shepherds of Judea long, long ago.

"What is it, Ivan?" she murmured softly, patting his big hand. "Tell me."

And Big Ivan of the Bridge, slow of tongue, told of the Dream. To no one else would he have told it. Anna understood. She had a way of patting his hands and saying soft things when his tongue could not find words to express his thoughts.

Ivan told how the Dream had come to him as he plowed. He told her how it had sprung upon him, a wonderful dream born of the soft breezes, of the sunshine, of the sweet smell of the upturned sod and of his own strength. "It wouldn't come to weak men," he said, baring an arm that showed great snaky muscles rippling beneath the clear skin. " It is a dream that comes only to those who are strong and those who want— who want something that they haven't got." Then in a lower voice he said: " What is it that we want, Anna? "

The little wife looked out into the darkness with fear-filled eyes. There were spies even there in that little village on the Beresina, and it was dangerous to say words that might be construed into a reflection on the Government. But she answered Ivan. She stooped and whispered one word into his ear, and he slapped his thigh with his big hand.

" Ay," he cried. " That is what we want! You and I and millions like us want it, and over there, Anna, over there we will get it. It is the country where a muzhik is as good as a prince of the blood! "

Anna stood up, took a small earthenware jar from a side shelf, dusted it carefully and placed it upon the mantel. From a knotted cloth about her neck she took a ruble and dropped the coin into the jar. Big Ivan looked at her curiously.

" It is to make legs for your Dream," she explained. " It is many versts to America, and one rides on rubles."

" You are a good wife," he said. " I was afraid that you might laugh at me."

" It is a great dream," she murmured. " Come, we will go to sleep."

The Dream maddened Ivan during the days that followed. It pounded within his brain as he followed the plow. It bred a discontent that made him hate the little village, the swift-flowing Beresina and the gray stretches that ran toward Mogilev. He wanted to be moving, but Anna had said that one rode on rubles, and rubles were hard to find.

And in some mysterious way the village became aware of the secret. Donkov, the tailor, discovered it. Donkov lived in one-half of the cottage occupied by Ivan and Anna, and Donkov had long ears. The tailor spread the news, and Poborino, the smith, and Yanansk, the baker, would jeer at Ivan as he passed.

" When are you going to America? " they would ask.

" Soon," Ivan would answer.

" Take us with you! " they would cry in chorus.

" It is no place for cowards," Ivan would answer. " It is a long way, and only brave men can make the journey."

" Are you brave? " the baker screamed one day as he went by.

" I am brave enough to want liberty! " cried Ivan angrily. " I am brave enough to want——"

" Be careful! Be careful! " interrupted the smith. " A long tongue has given many a man a train journey that he never expected."

That night Ivan and Anna counted the rubles in the earthenware pot. The giant looked down at his wife with a gloomy face, but she smiled and patted his hand.

" It is slow work," he said.

" We must be patient," she answered. " You have the Dream."

" Ay," he said. " I have the Dream."

Through the hot, languorous summertime the Dream grew within the brain of Big Ivan. He saw visions in the smoky haze that hung above the Beresina. At times he would stand, hoe in hand, and look toward the west, the wonderful west into which the sun slipped down each evening like a coin dropped from the fingers of the dying day.

Autumn came, and the fretful whining winds that came down from the north chilled the Dream. The winds whispered of the coming of the Snow King, and the river grumbled as it listened. Big Ivan kept out of the way of Poborino, the smith, and Yanansk, the baker. The Dream was still with him, but autumn is a bad time for dreams.

Winter came, and the Dream weakened. It was only the earthenware pot that kept it alive, the pot into which the industrious Anna put every coin that could be spared. Often Big Ivan would stare at the pot as he sat beside the stove. The pot was the cord which kept the Dream alive.

" You are a good woman, Anna," Ivan would say again and again. " It was you who thought of saving the rubles."

" But it was you who dreamed," she would answer. " Wait for the spring, husband mine. Wait."

It was strange how the spring came to the Beresina that year. It sprang upon the flanks of winter before the Ice King had given the order to retreat into the fastnesses of the north. It swept up the river escorted by a million little breezes, and housewives opened their windows and peered out with surprise upon their faces. A wonderful guest had come to them and found them unprepared.

Big Ivan of the Bridge was fixing a fence in the meadow on the morning the Spring Maiden reached the village. For a little while he was not aware of her arrival. His mind was upon his work, but suddenly he discovered that he was hot, and he took off his overcoat. He turned to hang the coat upon a bush, then he sniffed the air, and a puzzled look came upon his face. He sniffed again, hurriedly, hungrily. He drew in great breaths of it, and his eyes shone with a strange light. It was wonderful air. It brought life to the Dream. It rose up within him, ten times more lusty than on the day it was born, and his limbs trembled as he drew in the hot, scented breezes that breed the *Wanderlust* and shorten the long trails of the world.

Big Ivan clutched his coat and ran to the little cottage. He burst through the door, startling Anna, who was busy with her housework.

" The Spring! " he cried. *" The Spring! "*

He took her arm and dragged her to the door. Standing together they sniffed the sweet breezes. In silence they listened to the song of the river. The Beresina had changed from a whining, fretful tune into a lilting, sweet song that would set the legs of lovers dancing. Anna pointed to a green bud on a bush beside the door.

"It came this minute," she murmured.

"Yes," said Ivan. "The little fairies brought it there to show us that spring has come to stay."

Together they turned and walked to the mantel. Big Ivan took up the earthenware pot, carried it to the table, and spilled its contents upon the well-scrubbed boards. He counted while Anna stood beside him, her fingers clutching his coarse blouse. It was a slow business, because Ivan's big blunt fingers were not used to such work, but it was over at last. He stacked the coins into neat piles, then he straightened himself and turned to the woman at his side.

"It is enough," he said quietly. "We will go at once. If it was not enough, we would have to go because the Dream is upon me and I hate this place."

"As you say," murmured Anna. "The wife of Littin, the butcher, will buy our chairs and our bed. I spoke to her yesterday."

Poborino, the smith; his crippled son; Yanansk, the baker; Dankov, the tailor, and a score of others were out upon the village street on the morning that Big Ivan and Anna set out. They were inclined to jeer at Ivan, but something upon the face of the giant made them afraid. Hand in hand the big man and his wife walked down the street, their faces turned toward Bobruisk, Ivan balancing upon his head a heavy trunk that no other man in the village could have lifted.

At the end of the street a stripling with bright eyes and yellow curls clutched the hand of Ivan and looked into his face.

"I know what is sending you," he cried.

"Ay, *you* know," said Ivan, looking into the eyes of the other.

"It came to me yesterday," murmured the stripling. "I

got it from the breezes. They are free, so are the birds and
the little clouds and the river. I wish I could go."

"Keep your dream," said Ivan softly. "Nurse it, for it is
the dream of a man."

Anna, who was crying softly, touched the blouse of the boy.
"At the back of our cottage, near the bush that bears the red
berries, a pot is buried," she said. "Dig it up and take it
home with you and when you have a kopeck drop it in. It is
a good pot."

The stripling understood. He stooped and kissed the hand
of Anna, and Big Ivan patted him upon the back. They were
brother dreamers and they understood each other.

Boris Lugan has sung the song of the versts that eat up one's
courage as well as the leather of one's shoes.

> "Versts! Versts! Scores and scores of them!
> Versts! Versts! A million or more of them!
> Dust! Dust! And the devils who play in it,
> Blinding us fools who forever must stay in it."

Big Ivan and Anna faced the long versts to Bobruisk, but
they were not afraid of the dust devils. They had the Dream.
It made their hearts light and took the weary feeling from their
feet. They were on their way. America was a long, long
journey, but they had started, and every verst they covered
lessened the number that lay between them and the Promised
Land.

"I am glad the boy spoke to us," said Anna.

"And I am glad," said Ivan. "Some day he will come and
eat with us in America."

They came to Bobruisk. Holding hands, they walked into
it late one afternoon. They were eighty-nine versts from the
little village on the Beresina, but they were not afraid. The
Dream spoke to Ivan, and his big hand held the hand of
Anna. The railway ran through Bobruisk, and that evening
they stood and looked at the shining rails that went out in

the moonlight like silver tongs reaching out for a low-hanging star.

And they came face to face with the Terror that evening, the Terror that had helped the spring breezes and the sunshine to plant the Dream in the brain of Big Ivan.

They were walking down a dark side street when they saw a score of men and women creep from the door of a squat, unpainted building. The little group remained on the sidewalk for a minute as if uncertain about the way they should go, then from the corner of the street came a cry of " Police! " and the twenty pedestrians ran in different directions.

It was no false alarm. Mounted police charged down the dark thoroughfare swinging their swords as they rode at the scurrying men and women who raced for shelter. Big Ivan dragged Anna into a doorway, and toward their hiding place ran a young boy who, like themselves, had no connection with the group and who merely desired to get out of harm's way till the storm was over.

The boy was not quick enough to escape the charge. A trooper pursued him, overtook him before he reached the sidewalk, and knocked him down with a quick stroke given with the flat of his blade. His horse struck the boy with one of his hoofs as the lad stumbled on his face.

Big Ivan growled like an angry bear, and sprang from his hiding place. The trooper's horse had carried him on to the sidewalk, and Ivan seized the bridle and flung the animal on its haunches. The policeman leaned forward to strike at the giant, but Ivan of the Bridge gripped the left leg of the horseman and tore him from the saddle.

The horse galloped off, leaving its rider lying beside the moaning boy who was unlucky enough to be in a street where a score of students were holding a meeting.

Anna dragged Ivan back into the passageway. More police were charging down the street, and their position was a dangerous one.

" Ivan! " she cried, " Ivan! Remember the Dream! America, Ivan! *America!* Come this way! Quick! "

With strong hands she dragged him down the passage. It opened into a narrow lane, and, holding each other's hands, they hurried toward the place where they had taken lodgings. From far off came screams and hoarse orders, curses and the sound of galloping hoofs. The Terror was abroad.

Big Ivan spoke softly as they entered the little room they had taken. " He had a face like the boy to whom you gave the lucky pot," he said. " Did you notice it in the moonlight when the trooper struck him down? "

" Yes," she answered. " I saw."

They left Bobruisk next morning. They rode away on a great, puffing, snorting train that terrified Anna. The engineer turned a stopcock as they were passing the engine, and Anna screamed while Ivan nearly dropped the big trunk. The engineer grinned, but the giant looked up at him and the grin faded. Ivan of the Bridge was startled by the rush of hot steam, but he was afraid of no man.

The train went roaring by little villages and great pasture stretches. The real journey had begun. They began to love the powerful engine. It was eating up the versts at a tremendous rate. They looked at each other from time to time and smiled like two children.

They came to Minsk, the biggest town they had ever seen. They looked out from the car windows at the miles of wooden buildings, at the big church of St. Catharine, and the woolen mills. Minsk would have frightened them if they hadn't had the Dream. The farther they went from the little village on the Beresina the more courage the Dream gave to them.

On and on went the train, the wheels singing the song of the road. Fellow travelers asked them where they were going. " To America," Ivan would answer.

" To America? " they would cry. " May the little saints guide you. It is a long way, and you will be lonely."

" No, we shall not be lonely," Ivan would say.

" Ha! you are going with friends? "

" No, we have no friends, but we have something that keeps us from being lonely." And when Ivan would make that reply Anna would pat his hand and the questioner would wonder if it was a charm or a holy relic that the bright-eyed couple possessed.

They ran through Vilna, on through flat stretches of Courland to Libau, where they saw the sea. They sat and stared at it for a whole day, talking little but watching it with wide, wondering eyes. And they stared at the great ships that came rocking in from distant ports, their sides gray with the salt from the big combers which they had battled with.

No wonder this America of ours is big. We draw the brave ones from the old lands, the brave ones whose dreams are like the guiding sign that was given to the Israelites of old—a pillar of cloud by day, a pillar of fire by night.

The harbormaster spoke to Ivan and Anna as they watched the restless waters.

" Where are you going, children? "

" To America," answered Ivan.

" A long way. Three ships bound for America went down last month."

" Our ship will not sink," said Ivan.

" Why? "

" Because I know it will not."

The harbor master looked at the strange blue eyes of the giant, and spoke softly. " You have the eyes of a man who sees things," he said. " There was a Norwegian sailor in the *White Queen*, who had eyes like yours, and he could see death."

" I see life! " said Ivan boldly. " A free life——"

" Hush! " said the harbor master. " Do not speak so loud." He walked swiftly away, but he dropped a ruble into Anna's hand as he passed her by. " For luck," he murmured. " May the little saints look after you on the big waters."

They boarded the ship, and the Dream gave them a courage that surprised them. There were others going aboard, and Ivan and Anna felt that those others were also persons who possessed dreams. She saw the dreams in their eyes. There were Slavs, Poles, Letts, Jews, and Livonians, all bound for the land where dreams come true. They were a little afraid— not two per cent of them had ever seen a ship before—yet their dreams gave them courage.

The emigrant ship was dragged from her pier by a grunting tug and went floundering down the Baltic Sea. Night came down, and the devils who, according to the Esthonian fishermen, live in the bottom of the Baltic, got their shoulders under the stern of the ship and tried to stand her on her head. They whipped up white combers that sprang on her flanks and tried to crush her, and the wind played a devil's lament in her rigging. Anna lay sick in the stuffy women's quarters, and Ivan could not get near her. But he sent her messages. He told her not to mind the sea devils, to think of the Dream, the Great Dream that would become real in the land to which they were bound. Ivan of the Bridge grew to full stature on that first night out from Libau. The battered old craft that carried him slouched before the waves that swept over her decks, but he was not afraid. Down among the million and one smells of the steerage he induced a thin-faced Livonian to play upon a mouth organ, and Big Ivan sang Paleer's " Song of Freedom " in a voice that drowned the creaking of the old vessel's timbers, and made the seasick ones forget their sickness. They sat up in their berths and joined in the chorus, their eyes shining brightly in the half gloom:

> " Freedom for serf and for slave,
> Freedom for all men who crave
> Their right to be free
> And who hate to bend knee
> But to Him who this right to them gave."

It was well that these emigrants had dreams. They wanted them. The sea devils chased the lumbering steamer. They hung to her bows and pulled her for'ard deck under emerald-green rollers. They clung to her stern and hoisted her nose till Big Ivan thought that he could touch the door of heaven by standing on her blunt snout. Miserable, cold, ill, and sleepless, the emigrants crouched in their quarters, and to them Ivan and the thin-faced Livonian sang the " Song of Freedom."

The emigrant ship pounded through the Cattegat, swung southward through the Skagerrack and the bleak North Sea. But the storm pursued her. The big waves snarled and bit at her, and the captain and the chief officer consulted with each other. They decided to run into the Thames, and the harried steamer nosed her way in and anchored off Gravesend.

An examination was made, and the agents decided to transship the emigrants. They were taken to London and thence by train to Liverpool, and Ivan and Anna sat again side by side, holding hands and smiling at each other as the third-class emigrant train from Euston raced down through the green Midland counties to grimy Liverpool.

" You are not afraid? " Ivan would say to her each time she looked at him.

" It is a long way, but the Dream has given me much courage," she said.

" To-day I spoke to a Lett whose brother works in New York City," said the giant. " Do you know how much money he earns each day? "

" How much? " she questioned.

" Three rubles, and he calls the policemen by their first names."

" You will earn five rubles, my Ivan," she murmured. " There is no one as strong as you."

Once again they were herded into the bowels of a big ship that steamed away through the fog banks of the Mersey out into the Irish Sea. There were more dreamers now, nine hundred of them, and Anna and Ivan were more comfortable. And these new emigrants, English, Irish, Scotch, French, and

German, knew much concerning America. Ivan was certain that he would earn at least three rubles a day. He was very strong.

On the deck he defeated all comers in a tug of war, and the captain of the ship came up to him and felt his muscles.

"The country that lets men like you get away from it is run badly," he said. "Why did you leave it?"

The interpreter translated what the captain said, and through the interpreter Ivan answered.

"I had a Dream," he said, "a Dream of freedom."

"Good," cried the captain. "Why should a man with muscles like yours have his face ground into the dust?"

The soul of Big Ivan grew during those days. He felt himself a man, a man who was born upright to speak his thoughts without fear.

The ship rolled into Queenstown one bright morning, and Ivan and his nine hundred steerage companions crowded the for'ard deck. A boy in a rowboat threw a line to the deck, and after it had been fastened to a stanchion he came up hand over hand. The emigrants watched him curiously. An old woman sitting in the boat pulled off her shoes, sat in a loop of the rope, and lifted her hand as a signal to her son on deck.

"Hey, fellers," said the boy, "help me pull me muvver up. She wants to sell a few dozen apples, an' they won't let her up the gangway!"

Big Ivan didn't understand the words, but he guessed what the boy wanted. He made one of a half dozen who gripped the rope and started to pull the ancient apple woman to the deck.

They had her halfway up the side when an undersized third officer discovered what they were doing. He called to a steward, and the steward sprang to obey.

"Turn a hose on her!" cried the officer. "Turn a hose on the old woman!"

The steward rushed for the hose. He ran with it to the side

of the ship with the intention of squirting on the old woman, who was swinging in midair and exhorting the six men who were dragging her to the deck.

" Pull! " she cried. " Sure, I'll give every one of ye a rosy red apple an' me blessing with it."

The steward aimed the muzzle of the hose, and Big Ivan of the Bridge let go of the rope and sprang at him. The fist of the great Russian went out like a battering ram; it struck the steward between the eyes, and he dropped upon the deck. He lay like one dead, the muzzle of the hose wriggling from his limp hands.

The third officer and the interpreter rushed at Big Ivan, who stood erect, his hands clenched.

" Ask the big swine why he did it," roared the officer.

" Because he is a coward! " cried Ivan. " They wouldn't do that in America! "

" What does the big brute know about America? " cried the officer.

" Tell him I have dreamed of it," shouted Ivan. " Tell him it is in my Dream. Tell him I will kill him if he turns the water on this old woman."

The apple seller was on deck then, and with the wisdom of the Celt she understood. She put her lean hand upon the great head of the Russian and blessed him in Gaelic. Ivan bowed before her, then as she offered him a rosy apple he led her toward Anna, a great Viking leading a withered old woman who walked with the grace of a duchess.

" Please don't touch him," she cried, turning to the officer. " We have been waiting for your ship for six hours, and we have only five dozen apples to sell. It's a great man he is. Sure he's as big as Finn MacCool."

Some one pulled the steward behind a ventilator and revived him by squirting him with water from the hose which he had tried to turn upon the old woman. The third officer slipped quietly away.

The Atlantic was kind to the ship that carried Ivan and Anna. Through sunny days they sat up on deck and watched the horizon. They wanted to be among those who would get the first glimpse of the wonderland.

They saw it on a morning with sunshine and soft wind. Standing together in the bow, they looked at the smear upon the horizon, and their eyes filled with tears. They forgot the long road to Bobruisk, the rocking journey to Libau, the mad buckjumping boat in whose timbers the sea devils of the Baltic had bored holes. Everything unpleasant was forgotten, because the Dream filled them with a great happiness.

The inspectors at Ellis Island were interested in Ivan. They walked around him and prodded his muscles, and he smiled down upon them good-naturedly.

" A fine animal," said one. " Gee, he's a new white hope! Ask him can he fight? "

An interpreter put the question, and Ivan nodded. " I have fought," he said.

" Gee! " cried the inspector. " Ask him was it for purses or what? "

" For freedom," answered Ivan. " For freedom to stretch my legs and straighten my neck! "

Ivan and Anna left the Government ferryboat at the Battery. They started to walk uptown, making for the East Side, Ivan carrying the big trunk that no other man could lift.

It was a wonderful morning. The city was bathed in warm sunshine, and the well-dressed men and women who crowded the sidewalks made the two immigrants think that it was a festival day. Ivan and Anna stared at each other in amazement. They had never seen such dresses as those worn by the smiling women who passed them by; they had never seen such well-groomed men.

" It is a feast day for certain," said Anna.

" They are dressed like princes and princesses," murmured Ivan. " There are no poor here, Anna. None."

Like two simple children, they walked along the streets of the City of Wonder. What a contrast it was to the gray, stupid towns where the Terror waited to spring upon the cowed people. In Bobruisk, Minsk, Vilna, and Libau the people were sullen and afraid. They walked in dread, but in the City of Wonder beside the glorious Hudson every person seemed happy and contented.

They lost their way, but they walked on, looking at the wonderful shop windows, the roaring elevated trains, and the huge skyscrapers. Hours afterward they found themselves in Fifth Avenue near Thirty-third Street, and there the miracle happened to the two Russian immigrants. It was a big miracle inasmuch as it proved the Dream a truth, a great truth.

Ivan and Anna attempted to cross the avenue, but they became confused in the snarl of traffic. They dodged backward and forward as the stream of automobiles swept by them. Anna screamed, and, in response to her scream, a traffic policeman, resplendent in a new uniform, rushed to her side. He took the arm of Anna and flung up a commanding hand. The charging autos halted. For five blocks north and south they jammed on the brakes when the unexpected interruption occurred, and Big Ivan gasped.

" Don't be flurried, little woman," said the cop. " Sure I can tame 'em by liftin' me hand."

Anna didn't understand what he said, but she knew it was something nice by the manner in which his Irish eyes smiled down upon her. And in front of the waiting automobiles he led her with the same care that he would give to a duchess, while Ivan, carrying the big trunk, followed them, wondering much. Ivan's mind went back to Bobruisk on the night the Terror was abroad.

The policeman led Anna to the sidewalk, patted Ivan good-naturedly upon the shoulder, and then with a sharp whistle unloosed the waiting stream of cars that had been held up so that two Russian immigrants could cross the avenue.

Big Ivan of the Bridge took the trunk from his head and put it on the ground. He reached out his arms and folded Anna in a great embrace. His eyes were wet.

" The Dream is true! " he cried. " Did you see, Anna? We are as good as they! This is the land where a muzhik is as good as a prince of the blood! "

The President was nearing the close of his address. Anna shook Ivan, and Ivan came out of the trance which the President's words had brought upon him. He sat up and listened intently:

We grow great by dreams. All big men are dreamers. They see things in the soft haze of a spring day or in the red fire of a long winter's evening. Some of us let those great dreams die, but others nourish and protect them, nurse them through bad days till they bring them to the sunshine and light which come always to those who sincerely hope that their dreams will come true.

The President finished. For a moment he stood looking down at the faces turned up to him, and Big Ivan of the Bridge thought that the President smiled at him. Ivan seized Anna's hand and held it tight.

" He knew of my Dream! " he cried. " He knew of it. Did you hear what he said about the dreams of a spring day? "

" Of course he knew," said Anna. " He is the wisest man in America, where there are many wise men. Ivan, you are a citizen now."

" And you are a citizen, Anna."

The band started to play " My Country, 'tis of Thee," and Ivan and Anna got to their feet. Standing side by side, holding hands, they joined in with the others who had found after long days of journeying the blessed land where dreams come true.

JAMES FRANCIS DWYER

Mr. Dwyer is an American by adoption, an Australian by birth. He was born in Camden, New South Wales, April 22, 1874; and received his education in the public schools there. He entered newspaper work, and in the capacity of a correspondent for Australian papers traveled extensively in Australia and in the South Seas, from 1898 to 1906. In 1906 he made a tour through South Africa, and at the conclusion of this went to England. He came to America in 1907, and since that time has made his home in New York City. He has been a frequent contributor to *Collier's, Harper's Weekly, The American Magazine, The Ladies' Home Journal,* and other periodicals. He has published five books, nearly all dealing with the strange life of the far East. His first book, *The White Waterfall,* published in 1912, has its scene in the South Sea Islands. A California scientist, interested in ancient Polynesian skulls, goes to the South Seas to investigate his favorite subject, accompanied by his two daughters. The amazing adventures they meet there make a very interesting story. *The Spotted Panther* is a story of adventure in Borneo. Three white men go there in search of a wonderful sword of great antiquity which is in the possession of a tribe of Dyaks, the head-hunters of Borneo. There are some vivid descriptions in the story and plenty of thrills. *The Breath of the Jungle* is a collection of short stories, the scenes laid in the Malay Peninsula and nearby islands. They describe the strange life of these regions, and show how it reacts in various ways upon white men who live there. *The Green Half Moon* is a story of mystery and diplomatic intrigue, the scene partly in the Orient, partly in London.

In his later work Mr. Dwyer has taken up American themes. *The Bust of Lincoln,* really a short story, deals with a young man whose proudest possession is a bust of Lincoln that had belonged to his grandfather; the story shows how it influences his life. The story *The Citizen* had an interesting origin. On May 10, 1915, just after the sinking of the *Lusitania,* President Wilson went to Philadelphia to address a meeting of an unusual kind. Four thousand foreign-born men, who had just become naturalized citizens of our country, were to be welcomed to citizenship by the Mayor of the city, a member of the Cabinet, and the President of the United States. The meeting was held in Convention Hall; more than fifteen thousand people were present, and the event, occurring as it did at a time when every one realized that the loyalty of our people was likely to be soon put to the test, was one of historic importance. Moved by the significance of this event, Mr. Dwyer translated it into literature. His story, " The Citizen," was published in *Collier's* in November, 1915.

LIST OF AMERICAN SHORT STORIES
CLASSIFIED BY LOCALITY

I. THE EAST

NEW ENGLAND

A New England Nun; A Humble Romance, Mary Wilkins-Freeman.
Meadow-Grass; The Country Road, Alice Brown.
A White Heron; The Queen's Twin, Sarah Orne Jewett.
Pratt Portraits; Later Pratt Portraits, Anna Fuller.
The Village Watch Tower, Kate Douglas Wiggin.
The Old Home House, Joseph C. Lincoln.
Hillsboro People, Dorothy Canfield.
Out of Gloucester; The Crested Seas, James B. Connolly.
Under the Crust, Thomas Nelson Page.
Dumb Foxglove, Annie T. Slosson.
Huckleberries Gathered From New England Hills, Rose Terry
Cooke.

NEW YORK CITY

The Four Million; The Voice of the City; The Trimmed Lamp,
O. Henry.
Van Bibber and Others, Richard Harding Davis.
Doctor Rast, James Oppenheim.
Toomey and Others, Robert Shackleton.
Vignettes of Manhattan, Brander Matthews.
The Imported Bridegroom, Abraham Cahan.
Little Citizens; Little Aliens, Myra Kelly.
The Soul of the Street, Norman Duncan.
Wall Street Stories, Edwin Le Fevre.
The Optimist, Susan Faber.
Every Soul Hath Its Song, Fannie Hurst.

NEW JERSEY

Hulgate of Mogador, Sewell Ford.
Edgewater People, Mary Wilkins-Freeman.

PENNSYLVANIA

Old Chester Tales; Doctor Lavender's People, Margaret Deland.
Betrothal of Elypholate, Helen R. Martin.
The Passing of Thomas, Thomas A. Janvier.
The Standard Bearers, Katherine Mayo.
Six Stars, Nelson Lloyd.

II. THE SOUTH

ALABAMA

Alabama Sketches, Samuel Minturn Peck.
Polished Ebony, Octavius R. Cohen.

ARKANSAS

Otto the Knight; Knitters in the Sun, Octave Thanet.

FLORIDA

Rodman the Keeper, Constance F. Woolson.

GEORGIA

Georgia Scenes, A. B. Longstreet.
Free Joe; Tales of the Home-Folks, Joel Chandler Harris.
Stories of the Cherokee Hills, Maurice Thompson.
Northern Georgia Sketches, Will N. Harben.
His Defence, Harry Stilwell Edwards.
Mr. Absalom Billingslea; Mr. Billy Downes, Richard Malcolm
Johnston.

KENTUCKY

Flute and Violin; A Kentucky Cardinal, James Lane Allen.
In Happy Valley, John Fox, Jr.
Back Home; Judge Priest and his People, Irvin S. Cobb.
Land of Long Ago; Aunt Jane of Kentucky, Eliza Calvert Hall.

LOUISIANA

Holly and Pizen; Aunt Amity's Silver Wedding, Ruth McEnery
Stuart.
Balcony Stories; Tales of Time and Place, Grace King.
Old Creole Days; Strange True Stories of Louisiana, George W.
Cable.
Bayou Folks, Kate Chopin.

TENNESSEE

In the Tennessee Mountains; Prophet of the Great Smoky Mountains, Charles Egbert Craddock. (Mary N. Murfree.)

VIRGINIA

In Ole Virginia, Thomas Nelson Page.
Virginia of Virginia, Amelie Rives.
Colonel Carter of Cartersville, F. Hopkinson Smith.

NORTH CAROLINA

North Carolina Sketches, Mary N. Carter.

III. THE MIDDLE WEST

INDIANA

Dialect Sketches, James Whitcomb Riley.

ILLINOIS

The Home Builders, K. E. Harriman.

IOWA

Stories of a Western Town; The Missionary Sheriff, Octave Thanet.
In a Little Town, Rupert Hughes.

KANSAS

In Our Town; Stratagems and Spoils, William Allen White.

MISSOURI

The Man at the Wheel, John Hanton Carter.
Stories of a Country Doctor, Willis King.

MICHIGAN

Blazed Trail Stories, Stewart Edward White.
Mackinac and Lake Stories, Mary Hartwell Catherwood.

OHIO

Folks Back Home, Eugene Wood.

WISCONSIN

Main-Travelled Roads, Hamlin Garland.
Friendship Village; Friendship Village Love Stories, Zona Gale.

IV. THE FAR WEST

ARIZONA

Lost Borders, Mary Austin.
Arizona Nights, Stewart Edward White.

ALASKA

Love of Life; Son of the Wolf, Jack London.

CALIFORNIA

The Cat and the Cherub, Chester B. Fernald.
The Luck of Roaring Camp; Tales of the Argonauts, Bret Harte.
The Splendid Idle Forties, Gertrude Atherton.

NEW MEXICO

The King of the Broncos, Charles F. Lummis.
Santa Fe's Partner, Thomas A. Janvier.

WYOMING

Red Men and White; The Virginian; Members of the Family, Owen Wister.
Teepee Tales, Grace Coolidge.

PHILIPPINE ISLANDS

Caybigan, James N. Hopper.

NOTES AND QUESTIONS FOR STUDY

THE RIGHT PROMETHEAN FIRE

In Greek mythology, the work of creating living things was en-trusted to two of the gods, Epimetheus and Prometheus. Epimetheus gave to the different animals various powers, to the lion strength, to the bird swiftness, to the fox sagacity, and so on until all the good gifts had been bestowed, and there was nothing left for man. Then Prometheus ascended to heaven and brought down fire, as his gift to man. With this, man could protect himself, could forge iron to make weapons, and so in time develop the arts of civilization. In this story the "Promethean Fire" of love is the means of giving little Emmy Lou her first lesson in reading.

1. A test that may be applied to any story is, Does it read as if it were true? Would the persons in the story do the things they are represented as doing? Test the acts of Billy Traver in this way, and see if they are probable.
2. In writing stories about children, a writer must have the power to present life as a child sees it. Point out places in this story where school life is described as it appears to a new pupil.
3. One thing we ought to gain from our reading is a larger vocabulary. In this story there are a number of words worth adding to our stock. Define these exactly: inquisitorial; lachrymose; laconic; surreptitious; contumely.

   Get the habit of looking up new words and writing down their meanings.
4. Can you write a story about a school experience?
5. Other books containing stories of school life are:

   Little Aliens, Myra Kelly; *May Iverson Tackles Life,* Elizabeth Jordan; *Ten to Seventeen,* Josephine Daskam Bacon; *Closed Doors,* Margaret P. Montague. Read a story from one of these books, and compare it with this story.

THE LAND OF HEART'S DESIRE

Central Park, New York, covers an era of more than eight hundred acres, with a zoo and several small lakes. On one of the lakes there are large boats with a huge wooden swan on each side. Richard Harding Davis located one of his stories here: See "Van

Bibber and the Swan Boats," in the volume called *Van Bibber anu Others.*

1. How is this story like the preceding one? What difference in the characters? What difference in their homes?
2. How does Myra Kelly make you feel sympathy for the little folks? In what ways have their lives been less fortunate than the lives of children in your town?
3. What is peculiar about the talk of these children? Do they all speak the same dialect? Many of the children of the East Side never hear English spoken at home.
4. What touches of humor are there in this story?
5. What new words do you find? Define garrulous, pedagogically, cicerone.
6. Where did Miss Kelly get her materials for this story? See the life on page 37.
7. What other stories by this author have you read? This is from *Little Citizens;* other books telling about the same characters are *Little Aliens,* and *Wards of Liberty.*
8. Other books of short stories dealing with children are: *Whilomville Stories,* by Stephen Crane; *The Golden Age,* by Kenneth Grahame; *The Madness of Philip,* by Josephine Daskam Bacon; *The King of Boyville,* by William Allen White; *New Chronicles of Rebecca,* by Kate Douglas Wiggin. Read one of these, and compare it with Myra Kelly's story.

THE TENOR

1. Point out the humorous touches in this story.
2. Is the story probable? To answer this, consider two points: would Louise have undertaken such a thing as answering the advertisement? and would she have had the spirit to act as she did at the close? Note the touches of description and characterization of Louise, and show how they prepare for the events that follow.
3. One of the most effective devices in art is the use of contrast; that is, bringing together two things or persons or ideas that are very different, perhaps the exact opposite of each other. Show that the main effect of this story depends on the use of contrast.
4. Read the paragraph on page 43 beginning, "It happened to be a French tenor." Give in your own words the thought of this paragraph. Is it true? Can you give examples of it?

5. Compare the length of this story with that of others in the book. Which authors get their effects in a small compass? Could any parts of this story be omitted?
6. Other stories by H. C. Bunner that you will enjoy are "The Love Letters of Smith" and "A Sisterly Scheme" in *Short Sixes*.

THE PASSING OF PRISCILLA WINTHROP

1. Does the title fit the story well? Why?
2. Notice the familiar, almost conversational style. Is it suited to the story? Why?
3. Show how the opening paragraph introduces the main idea of the story.
4. To make a story there must be a conflict of some sort. What is the conflict here?
5. How does the account of Julia Neal's career as a teacher (page 64) prepare for the ending of the story?
6. Do you have a clear picture in your mind of Mrs. Winthrop? Of Mrs. Worthington? Why did not the author tell about their personal appearance?
7. Point out humorous touches in the next to the last paragraph.
8. Is this story true to life? Who is the Priscilla Winthrop of your town?
9. What impression do you get of the man behind this story? Do you think he knew the people of his town well? Did he like them even while he laughed at them? What else can you say about him?
10. Other books of short stories dealing with life in a small town are: *Pratt Portraits*, by Anna Fuller; *Old Chester Tales*, by Margaret Deland; *Stories of a Western Town*, by Octave Thanet; *In a Little Town*, by Rupert Hughes; *Folks Back Home*, by Eugene Wood; *Friendship Village*, by Zona Gale; *Bodbank*, by Richard W. Child. Read one of these books, or a story from one, and compare it with this story.
11. In what ways does life in a small town differ from life in a large city?

THE GIFT OF THE MAGI

This story, taken from the volume called *The Four Million*, is a good example of O. Henry's method as a short-story writer. It is notable for its brevity. The average length of the modern short story is about five thousand words; O. Henry uses a little over one thousand words. This conciseness is gained in several ways. In his descriptions, he has the art of selecting significant detail. When Della looks out of the window, instead of describing fully the view that met her eyes, he says: "She looked out dully at a grey cat walking a grey fence in a grey backyard." A paragraph could do no more. Again, the beginning of the story is quick, abrupt. There is no introduction. The style is often elliptical; in the first paragraph half the sentences are not sentences at all. But the main reason for the shortness of the story lies in the fact that the author has included only such incidents and details as are necessary to the unfolding of the plot. There is no superfluous matter.

Another characteristic of O. Henry is found in the unexpected turns of his plots. There is almost always a surprise in his stories, usually at the end. And yet this has been so artfully prepared for that we accept it as probable. Our pleasure in reading his stories is further heightened by the constant flashes of humor that light up his pages. And beyond this, he has the power to touch deeper emotions. When Della heard Jim's step on the stairs, "she turned white just for a moment. She had a habit of saying little silent prayers about the simplest things, and now she whispered, 'Please God, make him think I am still pretty.'" One reads that with a little catch in the throat.

In his plots, O. Henry is romantic; in his settings he is a realist. Della and Jim are romantic lovers, they are not prudent nor calculating, but act upon impulse. In his descriptions, however, he is a realist. The eight-dollar-a-week flat, the frying pan on the back of the stove, the description of Della "flopping down on the couch for a cry," and afterwards "attending to her cheeks with the powder-rag,"—all these are in the manner of realism.

And finally, the tone of his stories is brave and cheerful. He finds the world a most interesting place, and its people, even its commonplace people, its rogues, its adventurers, are drawn with a broad sympathy that makes us more tolerant of the people we meet outside the books.

1. Compare the beginning of this story with the beginning of "Bitter-Sweet." What difference do you note?
2. Select a description of a person that shows the author's power of concise portraiture.
3. What is the turn of surprise in this story? What other stories in this book have a similar twist at the end?
4. What is the central thought of this story?

5. Other stories of O. Henry's that ought not to be missed are " An Unfinished Story " and " The Furnished Room " in *The Four Million;* " A Blackjack Bargainer " in *Whirligigs;* " Best Seller " and " The Rose of Dixie " in *Options;* " A Municipal Report " in *Strictly Business;* " A Retrieved Reformation " in *Roads of Destiny;* and " Hearts and Crosses " in *Hearts of the West.*

THE GOLD BRICK

This story, first published in the *American Magazine*, was reprinted in a volume called *The Gold Brick*, published in 1910. The quotation " chip at crusts like Hindus " is from Robert Browning's poem " Youth and Art." The reference to " Old Walt " at the end of the story is to Walt Whitman, one of the great poets of democracy.

1. To make a story interesting, there must be a conflict. In this the conflict is double: the outer conflict, between the two political factions, and the inner conflict, in the soul of the artist. Note how skilfully this inner struggle is introduced: at the moment when Kittrell is first rejoicing over his new position, he feels a pang at leaving the *Post*, and what it stood for. This feeling is deepened by his wife's tacit disapproval; it grows stronger as the campaign progresses, until the climax is reached in the scene where he resigns his position.

2. If you knew nothing about the author, what could you infer from this story about his political ideals? Did he believe in democracy? Did he have faith in the good sense of the common people? Did he think it was worth while to make sacrifices for them? What is your evidence for this?

3. How far is this story true to life, as you know it? Do any newspapers in your city correspond to the *Post?* To the *Telegraph?* Can you recall a campaign in which the contest was between two such groups as are described here?

4. Does Whitlock have the art of making his characters real? Is this true of the minor characters? The girl in the flower shop, for instance, who appears but for a moment,—is she individualized? How?

5. Is there a lesson in this story? State it in your own words.

6. What experiences in Whitlock's life gave him the background for this story?

7. What new words did you gain from this? Define meritricious; prognathic; banal; vulpine; camaraderie; vilification; ennui; quixotic; naïve; pharisaism. What can you say of Whitlock's vocabulary?

8. Other good stories dealing with politics are found in *Stratagems and Spoils,* by William Allen White.

HIS MOTHER'S SON

1. Note the quick beginning of the story; no introduction, action from the start. Why is this suitable to this story?

2. Why is slang used so frequently?

3. Point out examples of humor in the story.

4. In your writing, do you ever have trouble in finding just the right word? Note on page 123 how Edna Ferber tries one expression after another, and how on page 122 she finally coins a word— "unadjectivable." What does the word mean?

5. Do you have a clear picture of Emma McChesney? Of Ed Meyers? Note that the description of Meyers in the office is not given all at once, but a touch here and then. Point out all these bits of description of this person, and note how complete the portrait is.

6. What have you learned in this story about the life of a traveling salesman?

7. What qualities must a good salesman possess?

8. Was Emma McChesney a lady? Was Ed Meyers a gentleman? Why do you think so?

9. This story is taken from the book called *Roast Beef, Medium.* Other good books of short stories by this author are *Personality Plus,* and *Cheerful—by Request.*

BITTER-SWEET

1. Note the introduction, a characteristic of all of Fannie Hurst's stories. What purpose does it serve here? What trait of Gertie's is brought out? Is this important to the story?

2. From the paragraph on page 139 beginning "It was into the trickle of the last——" select examples that show the author's skill in the use of words. What other instances of this do you note in the story?

3. Read the sketch of the author. What episode in her life gave her material for parts of this story?

4. Notice how skillfully the conversation is handled. The opening situation developes itself entirely through dialogue, yet in a perfectly natural way. It is almost like a play rather than a story. If it were dramatized, how many scenes would it make?
5. What does the title mean? Does the author give us the key to its meaning?
6. What do you think of Gertie as you read the first part of the conversation in the restaurant? Does your opinion of her change at the end of the story? Has her character changed?
7. Is the ending of the story artistic? Why mention the time-clock? What had Gertie said about it?
8. State in three or four words the central idea of the story. Is it true to life?
9. What is the meaning of these words: atavism; penumbra; semaphore; astigmatic; insouciance; mise-en-scene; kinetic?
10. Other books of stories dealing with life in New York City are *The Four Million,* and *The Voice of the City,* by O. Henry; *Van Bibber and Others,* by Richard Harding Davis; *Every Soul Hath Its Song,* by Fannie Hurst; *Doctor Rast,* by James Oppenheim.

THE RIVERMAN

1. In how many scenes is this story told? What is the connection between them?
2. Is there anything in the first description of Dicky Darrell that gives you a slight prejudice against him?
3. Why was the sympathy of the crowd with Jimmy Powers in the birling match?
4. Comment on Jimmy's remark at the end of the story. Did he mean it, or is he just trying to turn away the praise?
5. What are the characteristics of a lumberman, as seen in Jimmy Powers?
6. Read the sketch of Stewart Edward White, and decide which one of his books you would like to read.

FLINT AND FIRE

1. What does the title mean?
2. How does the author strike the keynote of the story in the opening paragraph?
3. Where is the first hint of the real theme of the story?
4. Point out some of the dialect expressions. Why is dialect used?

5. What turn of surprise comes at the end of the story? Is it probable?
6. What characteristics of New England country people are brought out in this story? How does the author contrast them with " city people "?
7. Does this story read as if the author knew the scenes she describes? Read the description of Niram plowing (page 191), and point out touches in it that could not have been written by one who had always lived in the city.
8. Read the account of how this story was written, (page 210). What first suggested the idea? What work remained after the story was first written? How did the author feel while writing it? Compare what William Allen White says about his work, (page 75).
9. Other stories of New England life that you will enjoy reading are found in the following books: *New England Nun,* Mary E. Wilkins; *Cape Cod Folks,* S. P. McLean Greene; *Pratt Portraits,* Anna Fuller; *The Country Road,* Alice Brown; *Tales of New England,* Sarah Orne Jewett.

THE ORDEAL AT MT. HOPE

1. This story contains three characters who are typical of many colored people, and as such are worth study. Howard Dokesbury is the educated colored man of the North. What are the chief traits of this character?
2. Aunt Caroline is the old-fashioned darky who suggests slavery days. What are her chief characteristics?
3. 'Lias is the new generation of the Southern negro of the towns. What are his characteristics?
4. Is the colored American given the same rights as others? Read carefully the opening paragraph of the story.
5. What were the weaknesses of the colored people of Mt. Hope? How far are they true of the race? How were they overcome in this case?
6. There are two theories about the proper solution of what is called " The Negro Problem." One is, that the hope of the race lies in industrial training; the other theory, that they should have higher intellectual training, so as to develope great leaders. Which theory do you think Dunbar held? Why do you think so?

7. Other stories dealing with the life of the colored people are:
Free Joe, and *Tales of the Home Folks,* by Joel Chandler
Harris; *Polished Ebony,* by Octavius R. Cohen; *Aunt Amity's
Silver Wedding,* by Ruth McEnery Stuart; *In Ole Virginia,* by
Thomas Nelson Page.

ISRAEL DRAKE

The Pennsylvania State Police have made a wonderful record for
maintaining law and order in the rural sections of the state. The
history of this organization was told by Katherine Mayo in a book
called *Justice to All.* In a later book, *The Standard Bearers,* she
tells various incidents which show how these men do their work.
The book is not fiction—the story here told happened just as it is
set down, even the names of the troopers are their real names.

1. Do you get a clear picture of Drake from the description? Why
   are several pages given to telling his past career?
2. Where does the real story begin?
3. Who was the tramp at the Carlisle Station? When did you guess
   it?
4. What are the principles of the State Police, as you see them in
   this story?
5. Why was such an organization necessary? Is there one in your
   state?
6. What new words did you find in this story? Define aura,
   primeval, grisly.

THE STRUGGLES AND TRIUMPH OF ISIDRO

In this story the author introduces a number of unfamiliar words,
chiefly of Spanish origin, which are current in the Philippines. The
meanings are given below.

> *baguio,* hurricane.
> *barrio,* ward; district.
> *carabao,* a kind of buffalo, used as a work animal.
> *cabo,* head officer.
> *cibay,* a boys' game.
> *daledale,* hurry up!
> *de los Reyes,* of the King.
> *de la Cruz,* of the cross.
> *hacienda,* a large plantation.

ladrones, robbers.

maestro, teacher.

nipa, a palm tree or the thatch made from it.

palay, rice.

pronto, quickly.

peublo, town.

que barbaridad!—what an atrocious thing!

volador, kite.

1. Why does the story end with Isidro's crying? What did this signify? What is the relation of this to the beginning of the story?

2. Has this story a central idea? What is it?

3. This might be called a story of local color, in that it gives in some detail the atmosphere of an unfamiliar locality. What are the best descriptive passages in the story?

4. Judging from this story, what are some of the difficulties a school teacher meets with in the Philippines? What must he be besides a teacher?

5. What other school stories are there in this book? The pupils in Emmy Lou's school, (in Louisville, Ky.) are those with several generations of American ancestry behind them; in Myra Kelly's story, they are the children of foreign parents; in this story they are still in a foreign land—that is, a land where they are not surrounded by American influences. The public school is the one experience that is common to them all, and therefore the greatest single force in bringing them all to share in a common ideal, to reverence the great men of our country's history, and to comprehend the meaning of democracy. How does it do these things?

THE CITIZEN

1. During the war, President Wilson delivered an address at Philadelphia to an audience of men who had just been made citizens. The quoted passages in this story are taken from this speech. Read these passages, and select the one which probably gave the author the idea for this story.

2. Starting with the idea, that he would write a story about someone who followed a dream to America, why should the author choose Russia as the country of departure?

3. Having chosen Russia, why does he make Ivan a resident of a village far in the interior? Why not at Libau?

4. Two incidents are told as occurring on the journey: the charge of the police at Bobrinsk, and the coming on board of the apple woman at Queenstown. Why was each of these introduced? What is the purpose of telling the incident on Fifth Avenue?

5. What have you learned about the manner in which this story was written? Compare it with the account given by Dorothy Canfield as to how she wrote her story.

6. What is the main idea in this story? Why do you think it was written? Edward Everett Hale wrote a story called "A Man without a Country." Suggest another title for "The Citizen."

7. Has this story in any way changed your opinion of immigrants? Is Big Ivan likely to meet any treatment in America that will change his opinion of the country?

8. The part of this story that deals with Russia affords a good example of the use of local color. This is given partly through the descriptions, partly through the names of the villagers—Poborino, Yanansk, Dankov; partly through the Russian words, such as verst (about three quarters of a mile), ruble (a coin worth fifty cents), kopeck (a half cent), muzhik, (a peasant). How is local color given in the conversations?

9. For a treatment of the theme of this story in poetry, read "Scum o' the Earth," by Robert Haven Schauffler, in Rittenhouse's *Little Book of Modern Verse*. This is the closing stanza:

> "Newcomers all from the eastern seas,
> Help us incarnate dreams like these.
> Forget, and forgive, that we did you wrong.
> Help us to father a nation, strong
> In the comradeship of an equal birth,
> In the wealth of the richest bloods of earth."